I dedicate this book to the wonderful memories of some of the colourful characters I was privileged to meet and work with as a young man in the South West Slopes of the Snowy Mountains. As a teenager, I worked for and alongside returned servicemen on the land, including WW2 Spitfire Pilots and a Tobruk Rat. These gentlemen are all gone now, but they left me with some of my most cherished memories.

CHAPTER ONE

The engine coughed and spluttered. It stopped for just the briefest moment, and so did his heart. The absolute silence was deafening. Then, the engine kicked back to life, and he began breathing again and whispered, 'Thank you,' in tremendous relief.

Opening his eyes as wide as possible, fighting against the urge to just let them close for good, he leaned forward and looked through the foggy glass. There was nothing but white wisps of cloud. Tilting sideways, he could see blue below him, deep dark blue, then flashes of bright white clouds racing by, then blue again. He squeezed his eyes closed tight, then opened them again. He re-focused, and for just a second, there was another flash of the ocean, dark and strangely peaceful. Observed from so high up, it was almost inviting. It seemed to beckon him, to dare him, a soft bed to collapse into and close his eyes for good. And then clouds again, nothing but white. Then he broke out into the blinding sunshine, blue sky and immediately looked for the cover and security of the next cloud. Looking around him, he could see nothing. No sign of Billy. He turned his head from side to side frantically, dipped the wings to the left, looking below, and then to the right. Nothing.

He just wanted to close his eyes. Then the pain set in again, and his senses were sharpened into alertness.

Steeling himself, he looked down at his hand. It took him a second to focus. He lifted the gloved hand up and observed the mess. He thought for a moment about his father. What would he say?

'Quit yer blubbering boy, it's just a couple of fingers. You got plenty more.' He smiled to himself.

He looked down to his right where the spray of bullets had entered the cockpit, leaving neat holes shining with light. One had grazed his thigh. Thankfully, it only opened up a little flesh on its way through and out the other side of the cabin. Another had taken two fingers of his leather glove, and judging by the blood and pain, the fingers were probably gone as well. He didn't know how many were gone. It wasn't possible to tell. The pain engulfed his hand, all of his arm, and even his head throbbed. It was at least two fingers. Anyway, the good news was, it was his left hand. He was right-handed. He put the mutilated hand back down as he felt the warm blood trickling down his wrist and inside his jacket sleeve. He couldn't check it. For now, he had to stay awake and bring his spitfire down to the ground before he died up here in the clouds. At least he'd already be halfway to the Pearly Gates if he died up here, he thought, for one justifiably morbid moment. But then, he also had to land this thing without killing himself in the process. An airstrip was a luxury he just wouldn't have.

Flight Lieutenant Jack Sutherland scanned the horizon again, hoping to see some end to the ocean that met the cloud in the barely visible distance.

He took a long deep breath in through his nostrils. He'd never appreciated the smell of eucalyptus more. He bent forward and rested his hand on the old mare's neck. It was hot under the midday sun. She was true and steady, and he felt safe in the saddle. His two dogs, Jock and Dusty, ran alongside the horse, occasionally looking up at him. He felt happy and at peace. He loved the family property, Sutherland Downs.

His eyes opened, and he was back at the controls of the spitfire. He shook his head, forced his eyes open wider and checked his bearings.

Was he imagining it? In the distance, the slightest dark line? He shut his eyes again and opened them quickly, terrified they would close forever. It was still there, a dark line that was getting thicker, slowly but surely.

His chin almost hit the top of his chest with a jolt, and it woke him up again. He focussed on what must surely be land ahead. The dark line had gotten thicker and more expansive and was starting to get some colour.

He thought of Mary.

Mary held his hand tightly as he ran, and she tried to keep up in her best shoes.

'Slow down Jack, for goodness sake. What's you hurry?'

Jack turned around and looked back at Mary as they ran. He smiled a cheeky smile and winked at her, and enjoyed seeing her blush. Just past the street lamp, he pulled her around the corner of the building and into the shadow.

'I'm in a hurry to tell you I love you, Mary Kelly.' Jack pulled Mary into his arms, and before she could reply, he kissed her.' He loved her more than he'd ever loved anyone or anything in his life.

'About tomorrow Jack . . .'

'Ssshhh. You know I can't talk about it. It's no different to every other time. Just make sure you're waiting for me. I'll be back. I promise.' He kissed her again then pulled her close to him.

His eyes flew open again. The plane's nose had dipped enough that he needed to correct it quickly or risk plunging into the ocean. He levelled it out, checked the gauges and, as satisfied as he could be, he tried to focus ahead again. The horizon was an emerald green line now, and he was beginning to just make out a beach. He had to remain awake and alert and get the old girl down onto the ground. She'd brought him home safely from more than a dozen sorties, and he supposed if he lived through this one, he'd be on the ground for a while, while his injuries came good.

His thoughts turned to Billy, and he knew in

his heart, he was gone. He could only hope it had been quick. There'd be no more long rides mustering or hunting with his cousin Billy, his childhood buddy, up on Sutherland Downs, where they'd grown up together. They had thought this would be an adventure like none other when they joined up. Right now, he couldn't think of anything he wouldn't do in a heartbeat to bring back Billy and all his other mates. All the mates, who'd died in France. The mates who were resting forever in the freezing channel, who'd had a glimpse of England on their return from battle, only to die soon after landing back on friendly soil. All those who never made it back to the warmth of the Australian sun. All those who never made it home.

The shore was closing in rapidly now, and Jack was slowing the plane speed. It was open country, as open as the English countryside could be, with cottages, sheds, lines of stone fences marking paddocks, roads and rows of trees. He was scanning about the area in front of him for a location to land the plane, he needed a good 350 yards for a safe landing, but he wasn't going to get that.

Finally, he crossed the beach, then a small cliff and was over land. He'd gradually slowed the plane from over 200 miles per hour over the ocean back to just under 100 miles an hour over the ground and was dropping altitude quickly. Ahead he could see his only hope, a relatively flat paddock in a valley. There was a stone fence at one end and a row of pine trees at the other. He'd need to slow the plane to below 60 miles an hour, come down as close to the stone fence as possible, get the wheels on the ground and hope like hell he could stop it. The wheels would glide over the wet grass, but he had to commit. He would die if he stayed in the air much longer and lost consciousness. He might die landing if he crashed, but there was no alternative.

He slowed the plane until it almost felt as though it was gliding, and he kept the nose up. He flew over a small stone cottage and barely registered the flurry of movement about the yard as he did. He had the plane low as he approached the stone fence, so low he expected to clip the wheels and go cartwheeling through the air, but he didn't. Some fifty yards on, he touched down with a jolt, and the plane swung from side to side and bounced about. The brakes made little if any difference as he careered through the paddock. The line of pine trees was looming quickly. There was little he could do but hope and pray.

'Mary.' He whispered, squeezing his eyes tight as the plane hit the pines. Then, everything was black. Everything was finally peaceful.

CHAPTER TWO

He became conscious of sounds, of thoughts, of feelings, of touch. Someone stroked his forehead. The hand was soft and warm. He drifted off to sleep again and dreamed of Sutherland Downs, of the hot sun, of his mother and father. He dreamt he was lying in bed, exhausted, needing rest, and his mother stroked his forehead.

He opened his eyes slowly, tentatively. Her smile was broad, her eyes glistened with tears. She let out a huge sigh of relief.

'Oh, thank God. Jack. Welcome back.' Mary leaned down and kissed him, spilling tears on his forehead.

'Ahem!' The matron stood in the doorway. 'Come on then, I've let you sit there all day holding his hand. But I draw the line at this. You have a shift in the morning Sister. You've got five minutes, and you need to be on your way. He's awake now. I'll get the Doctor.'

'Thank you Matron.'

Matron Horsley turned on her heel and headed, ample breast first, into the corridor, no doubt on her officious way to berate some other unsuspecting junior.

'Mary.' Jack's voice was a raspy whisper. 'Thirsty. Thirsty as hell.'

Mary helped Jack lean forward enough to awkwardly take a sip of water from a glass before gently helping him back to the pillow.

'Where am I?'

'Where do you think you are?' Mary smiled at Jack, gesturing around the dull room. 'Hospital.'

'I thought I was in heaven when I opened my eyes and saw your pretty face.' Jack smiled a momentary weak but cheeky smile.

'Jack. You're such a smoocher.' Mary smiled through tears. 'You frightened the heck out of me.'

'I'm ok.' Jack forced another smile. 'My hand hurts like bloody hell though.' Jack held up his heavily bandaged hand. 'What's it look like under there? A mess?'

'I haven't seen it. Not good though. I think the Doctor should tell you, not me. You're so lucky. Barney told me your plane was destroyed. You took both wings off, going through a row of pines. The engine was about 25 yards from the plane, and all you did was bang your thick head on the instrument board. You did more damage to the instruments than yourself.' Mary paused, then kissed his bruised forehead again. 'Your hand's a different story Jack.'

'Yeah, I know. The fingers were gone before I

landed. The funny thing is, I can still feel them all. But I saw it. I remember clearly. A couple of them are gone, aren't they?'

'I am afraid so, my darling.' Tears meandered down Mary's cheeks as she spoke. 'Two of them. Your little pinky and half of your ring finger.' Mary looked forlorn.

'Are you trying to make a run for it?' Jack mustered a smile, and Mary looked confused.

'Did you organise the Red bloody Baron to shoot off my ring finger?'

Mary slapped Jack's arm gently, then realised what she'd done and covered her mouth in shock.

'Ow!' Jack moaned loudly. 'Matron, Matron, help, I'm being attacked.'

'Sshhh.' Mary put her hand over Jack's mouth, and as she did, he wrapped his good arm around her, pulling her close. She leaned in and kissed him on the lips, holding his face in her hands. A voice from behind made them break their embrace.

'That's what I call personal attention.' The Doctor stood in the doorway. 'I suggest you leave him to rest now nurse. I think we can see he's clearly out of the woods. Off you go, you can visit tomorrow.'

Mary squeezed Jack's good hand, smiled at him, stroked his forehead one last time, then left.

'What's the damage Doc? How long am I laid up for?' The euphoria of the last short while with

Mary was quickly wearing off. The horrifying memory of the dogfight in the air and then the plane crash was flashing continually in vivid images and jarring sounds, forcing him to keep his weary eyes open. As much as he tried to shake it off, it threatened to consume him. It wasn't the first time he'd been terrified. In fact, if he was honest, to some degree, he'd been permanently terrified for the last few months. He'd been terrified of being shot, of crashing his plane and of losing yet another good mate. Since he'd met Mary, he'd been terrified of never seeing her again. This sortie had delivered all of his worst nightmares but one. Here he was lying in the hospital, with Mary close by, and nothing more than a couple of missing fingers and a hell of a thumping headache. Someone was looking after him. 'How long will I be in here for. Will I get a bit of R and R for a while?' Jack smiled, his thoughts turning to Mary.

The Doctor looked up from the chart he was reading.

'You'll be getting a little more than a bit of R and R Jack. You've lost a couple of fingers, old chap. You'll be heading home. You've done your bit. You're what we call debilitated now. It's going to be some time before you get used to the change, and learn how to do things that used to be second nature. You certainly won't be flying, and I suspect you'll be discharged unless you fancy a desk job.'

'Desk job, shit. I'm off a bloody half a million-acre

property. The only thing I sat on before the war was a saddle, never an office chair. I only went inside to eat, sleep or shear a bloody sheep. I'd be useless as tits on a bull in an office.' Jack looked down and sat silent for a moment. 'What about Billy?'

'Billy?'

'Yeah, Billy. My cousin. Billy Sutherland. My best mate. We were up there together, but I lost sight of him.' Jack looked at the Doctor who hesitated before he spoke,

'I'm sorry Jack. I'm told you were our only plane that returned. It was bad out there. Really bad. Frankly, you were lucky to make it back and in as good a condition as you did.'

'Lucky you call it.' Jack's tone was bitter. Try as he might, he couldn't stop the tears that fell for his best friend.

'Yes, lucky. I call it very lucky. You've got a family back home, no doubt. You'll get to go home. And I can see you have someone who really cares about you here. Sister Mary. Surely she was worth surviving for Jack.'

'She is.' Jack forced a smile. 'I'd do anything for her. I'd die for Mary. She means the world to me.' Jack wiped his good arm across his face, mopping up the tears.

'Well, don't die for her Jack. Live for her old chap. Now, time you got some shut-eye. I'll see you in the morning.'

* * *

The next morning, Mary came in to see Jack before her shift started. The lights had been turned on early in the hospital ward, but Jack was still fast asleep. Mary approached his bed quietly. She leaned over and kissed him gently on the cheek, and his eyes opened.

'How's the patient this morning?' She whispered.

Jack cleared his throat, then whispered so as not to wake any of the other patients in the beds around him.

'I'm not too bad thanks.' He opened and closed his eyes several times, waking himself up. 'Better than a lot of this mob.' He gestured around the room. 'Some of them were moaning and groaning all bloody night long. That poor bastard over there lost a leg, and the fellow with the bandage around his head, well it sounds like he'll never see again.'

'It doesn't bear thinking about does it?' Mary whispered. 'I'm so relieved you came back almost in one piece. I was terrified when I heard you were in the hospital. And earlier when there was talk of how many planes were missing. You can't believe how terrible it was waiting to find out if you were okay. Don't ever, ever do that to me again, Jack Sutherland.' There were tears in Mary's eyes again as Jack reached out and stroked her arm.

'Yeah, it must have been bloody awful. But I'm here now, and I'm good as gold. In fact, the Doctor reckons they'll probably kick me out by the end of the day. They need the beds, and I can just come in once a day for a check-up. I'll be bunking down in an old hall in town, with a truckload of other buggered misfits.'

Mary laughed. She came from a strict Catholic family in Ireland. There was just she, her sister, her mother and father. Her father ruled the household with an iron fist. There was no excessive drinking, rude jokes, or swearing. Not in his household. Her mother was quiet, devoted to her family, fastidious about her house, and how she and the girls dressed and behaved, particularly in public. Mary couldn't imagine for a moment what her father and mother would think of Jack. She'd only known Jack for a couple of months, but she had fallen madly in love with this larrikin. She had come to London to escape the suppression of her family, her community and culture, and Jack was precisely the spark she was looking for, the spark that lit her fire.

CHAPTER THREE

Two months earlier.

Jack arrived at the hospital mid-morning. He'd been asked by his commanding officer to visit one of the injured pilots. The pilot was an Australian. He was a young man from the country just north of Perth, and his prognosis wasn't good. Command wanted him to have a visit from one of his countrymen, hoping it might ease the young man's pain and suffering, not to mention his fear, if only for a short while.

Jack walked along the hallway, in full uniform, nervously spinning his cap in his hand. He stopped at a nurse's station and asked to be directed to room 14 West. The nurse smiled and pointed down the corridor, indicating to turn left at the end. Jack's stomach tightened as he began to think about the poor young man lying in his bed. He'd lost too many friends. He'd only visited a couple in the hospital because most of his friends, being pilots, either made it back or simply didn't. There was little in between. Although he didn't know this young man, he knew he'd feel an immediate connection, a comradery, not only from being pilots but also Australians.

Room 14 West was a single room, which was unusual. Jack took that as a bad sign which only sought to fray his fragile nerves even further. He stepped quietly into the room. A nurse stood at the bed with her back to him. She was talking quietly to the young man lying in bed.

'Ahem. Excuse me Sister.' Jack tried quietly to attract her attention.

The nurse turned around and smiled at Jack. He caught his breath. She was beautiful, like a ray of sunshine in the dark and gloom. She lit up the room with her smile. His chest tightened, and his stomach flipped. She had dark red hair, pale skin, and bright blue eyes that sparkled. Jack's eyes were fixed, staring at her until the nurse broke the slightly awkward moment.

'Hello.' The nurse said gently. She placed the wounded airman's hand, she'd been holding, back on the bed. 'Can I help you?'

'Ah, yes. I'm Flight Lieutenant Sutherland here to see Flight Lieutenant Reid, Christopher.' Jack whispered so as not to disturb the patient. 'Command sent me in. I'm Jack, actually . . . Jack'

Mary walked toward Jack and beckoned him into the corridor.

'Hello. I'm Sister Kelly. Mary.'

'Hello, I'm Jack.' Jack extended his hand, and Mary took it. She chuckled at how many times he'd awkwardly introduced himself. The warmth from her soft skin travelled from the tips of Jack's fingers along his arm and morphed into a shiver at the back of his neck. The nervous flutter filled his stomach again. He stood, holding her hand and looking into those magical eyes.

'Jack.' Mary blushed. Jack didn't respond, so she tried again more firmly.' Jack.'

'Yes?'

'My hand Jack. You'll have to let go sometime soon, so I can get back to work.'

'Oh, oh, sorry.' Jack turned scarlet. She was just so beautiful. He let go of her hand reluctantly. He was conscious she was also slow to let go of his hand.

'You're here to see Christopher? Please, take a seat.' Mary gestured to a seat in the corridor. He waited for her to sit, then sat down beside her. 'How well do you know Christopher, Jack?'

'To be honest, I don't know him at all. The Command sent me here to sit with him a while.'

'He's not good Jack. He's slipping in and out of consciousness. I don't think it will be long now.'

'Geez, poor bugger. Oh, pardon me, I'm really sorry. Sometimes I forget where I am and who I'm with.'

'Never mind Jack. I've heard far worse, and I think he's a poor bugger as well. You should go sit with him and just talk to him. I'm sure he can hear you, and I'm also sure it will ease his pain and fear.'

‘Ok.’ Jack looked tentative.

‘It’s ok Jack. Just talk about home. Talk about Australia. I believe he’s a country boy. Do you know much about the country?’ Mary looked at Jack.

‘I’ll give it a go.’ Jack smiled as brightly as he could.

‘Would you like a cup of tea?’

‘Yes. If I can’t have a stiff drink, then a cuppa would be good, thanks.’

‘No alcohol here Jack, unless I’m rubbing it on a wound.’ Mary pulled a sad face at him. ‘I have a couple of patients to check quickly, then I’ll be back with a cuppa for you. You should go in now. Remember. Just talk to him.’

Jack sat down next to the dying airman. He looked like he could have been little more than sixteen, although Jack knew he was older. At this moment in time, his last moment in time, he looked at peace and looked his age, no doubt for the first time since he enlisted and left Australian shores. The war put years on the face of every serviceman.

‘How yer going mate.’ Jack spoke gruffly. ‘I’m Jack. Guess you’ve figured out I’m an Aussie by the accent.’ Jack felt self-conscious. He looked about the room and behind him but there was no one there. The airman made a barely audible noise, and Jack turned back to him quickly.

‘Sorry mate, I’m still here.’ Jack leaned in. ‘Can

you hear me?' There was no response. Jack leaned back in his chair and looked at the young man. He must be bloody scared, he thought. Or maybe he wasn't scared anymore, maybe he was the lucky one, maybe he wasn't afraid, afraid like Jack was. Jack leaned back toward the bed and slowly reached out, touching the young man's wrist with his fingertips. His skin was cool. Gradually and self consciously, he lay his hand across Christopher's.

'They tell me you're a country boy. WA ey? Never been there myself, but I will, one day.'

Behind Jack and in the hallway, Mary had arrived back with a cup of tea. She stood silently in the hallway listening to the handsome airman whose touch had unsettled her. He'd held her hand an awkwardly long time, and she'd tried to make a joke and ease the tension. In truth, the momentary spark faded the second he let go of her hand, and she wished he hadn't let go, and she could retake his hand and feel that surge of warmth again. She waited in silence, not wanting to disturb him. She'd seen this scenario so many times, too many times in the last year, and she knew all too well, the dying airman in the bed might last hours, even days, or he might just go any moment. It would be the moment he found his peace. Christopher was as close as he would get to saying goodbye to his family, having the Australian serviceman sitting next to him. So Mary just stood and listened.

'I'm a country boy too, you know. North West New South Wales. Out past Bourke, do you know that country?' Jack paused as though waiting for a reply. 'It's flat, really flat, red as Ayers Rock and hot as hell. It's God's own country. Leastwise, that's what I reckon, but each to his own, I guess.'

'You got a big family? I bet your Ma and Pa are proud of yer mate. Yer a bloody hero.'

Listening carefully, Mary thought she detected a croak in Jack's voice as it faltered.

'I'm going back up again in a couple of days. Back over the channel. Takes ten years off my life every time I get in the cockpit. If you figure that out, I must be dead already.'

Mary drew in a breath, her stomach tightened, and she was surprised by the intensity of her reaction at the thought of Jack flying off into combat.

'To be honest, just between you and me and the bloody fence post, I don't know I would have signed up if I'd had any idea how bloody terrifying this would be.' Jack stopped for a moment and just looked at the young man.

'I'll write to your mum and dad.' As he said this, the airman drew in a sharp breath, and his face tensed. 'Are you ok?' Jack looked anxious, and Mary stepped into the room quickly and put a hand on his shoulder.

'He's okay Jack.' Jack looked up at Mary as she spoke, and it was as though he'd known her forever.

The young man drew in another longer and more laboured breath. He suddenly looked very peaceful again. The corners of his mouth were ever so slightly turned up, making him look strangely happy. Mary walked around to the other side of the bed and took his wrist in her hand, and felt for a pulse. There was nothing. She placed two fingers on his throat. Still no sign of a pulse. She leaned in close to his mouth, listening for breath. There was nothing.

'He's gone Jack.' She looked at Jack, who looked distraught. Tears streamed down his face, but he didn't make a sound. 'He's okay now. He's at peace.'

Mary walked back around the bed and to Jack's side and gently put her arm across his shoulders.

'You know what I believe Jack? I believe he's home now, in Australia, watching over his mum and dad. I believe you gave him peace when you said you'd write to his mum and dad. I believe you gave him the peace he needed to let go. You did a good thing. A good thing Jack.'

Jack stood up and faced Mary. She stepped toward him and put her arms around him to give him a quick and comforting hug, but he wrapped his arms around her and pulled her toward him. For just a moment, she relaxed enough to lean her face against his chest, then, Mary knew she had to break the embrace, and she pushed him gently away.

'Thanks.' His words were choked.

'That's okay Jack. You alright?'

'Yep.' Jack looked at Christopher. 'I didn't even know him.'

'Doesn't make any difference.'

'He could have been any one of my mates, any of them. I've lost so many of them. Bloody good blokes like him.'

'I know. I know Jack. Come on. Come out into the hall. I have to go and let them know at the nurse's station so they can make the arrangements.'

'Ok.' Jack looked shell shocked as he stood, limp, arms hanging at his sides.

Mary squeezed Jack's arm. She pulled the door to the room shut to discourage Jack from going back in, and she strode off quickly to the nurse's station.

Jack made it to the hospital's foyer before he had to sit down and just gather his thoughts. He sat numb, watching staff and patients coming and going. It could have been him, in that room, with some stranger sitting next to him, rabbiting on about home. No family, no friends, no good mates, just a nurse and a stranger to send him off. He shivered. He wished he was home on Sutherland Downs. He missed it so much. He missed his home so much it made his stomach ache. He wasn't aware how long he'd been sitting when he finally stood up and moved toward the front door.

'Jack!'

He turned around, and Mary was walking toward him, dressed for the cold air outside.

'Jack, you're still here. What are you doing? I thought you left an hour ago.'

'I did, but I needed to sit down. I took one look out there, and it looked cold.' He gestured toward the front doors. 'So I just sat here, and then all of a sudden . . . Where are you going?'

'Home. I'm done for the day. That was more than enough.'

They walked together toward the front door, down the stairs and onto the pavement.

'Which way are you?'

'That way.' Mary pointed over Jack's shoulder. 'You?'

'The other.' Jack pointed over Mary's shoulder. 'I could walk you.'

'I'm okay Jack. You need to get home, get some rest and get amongst your mates. You shouldn't be wandering around in the cold and dark after this afternoon.' Mary gave Jack a concerned look.

'Yeah. I guess so. Well, it's been nice . . . no, I guess it hasn't really, but it would have been nice meeting you, under different circumstances, of course.' Jack put his hand out, and Mary took it. He placed his other hand over the top of hers. 'Thanks Mary. Goodbye.'

'Goodbye Jack.' Mary smiled and slowly withdrew her hand before turning away and walking off slowly.

* * *

As Mary walked away, she could still feel the warmth of Jack's touch. What was it about this man, this particular man? She'd met so many servicemen, but none had ever affected her as Jack had. He was handsome, polite, sensitive. Her stomach turned as she walked away, her footsteps slowing. She thought about what he'd said in the room when he didn't know she was listening.

'I'm going back up again in a couple of days. Back over the channel.'

The thought terrified her. She might never see this man ever again, this man that had such an immediate and powerful impact on her. The thought made her heart race and her chest tighten. If she did see him again, would he be lying in a bed like Flight Lieutenant Reid?

She stopped and just stood, people, walking around her. She could picture him, his face as he gathered her into his arms for that brief hug. The feel on her cheek of his warm chest through his shirt.

Mary turned on her heel and looked back in the directions she had come from. There were too many people to see Jack, and the light was too poor. She started walking back in the direction she'd come from. There was no sign of him. She began to walk quickly. Had she lost him already? She grew anxious as she shuffled through the other pedestrians. She began to run. People looked at her as she ran past, one hand on her hat, her other holding her handbag and her coat flying open. She ran past the hospital entrance and along the pavement, scanning around her desperately trying to see Jack. She was some distance past the hospital when she finally surrendered to the realisation she'd lost him. Her heart sank. He could have gone in one of any number of directions. Up streets, into buildings, she had no idea. She stood, her shoulders slumped, disappointed and angry with herself for letting him go. She watched as cars and taxis raced past, their tyres hissing on the wet road. She pulled her coat tight around her against the cold and looked one last time in the direction Jack had walked. Still nothing. She sighed loudly then turned to head home.

'Mary.'

'Jack!'

'What are you doing. I thought you lived back that way?'

'I do.'

'Well, what are you doing back here? I saw a woman run past and I thought it was you. I was just sitting over there on a step. Still getting my head around things before I head home.'

'I wanted . . .' Mary paused.

'You wanted?'

'I wanted to know if you'd like a drink? You've had a rough day, and so have I. I thought you might like a drink and just to talk.'

'Really?' Jack looked surprised.

'It's ok. I know you probably want to get back

to the barracks. It's ok, forget it.' Mary made as though to back away.

'Don't be silly.' Jack broke into a huge smile. 'I can't think of one thing in the whole wide world I'd rather be doing tonight than having a drink with you, Mary Kelly.'

Mary blushed, then smiled.

Jack held out his arm, and Mary threaded hers through the crook of his, and they walked off together.

CHAPTER FOUR

It had been nearly a week since Jack had met Mary and had spent two of the best hours of his life in her company in a cosy little pub, sharing a drink and talking about their lives. They'd both had an emotionally exhausting day which heightened the instant connection they'd felt. That evening was the panacea they both needed.

Jack had told her about his beloved Sutherland Downs. He spoke of his family, his parents, aunts, uncles, cousins. And he spoke of some of the characters who worked on the incredible property in Northern New South Wales, a million miles away in Australia. She'd told Jack about the town where she lived in Ireland, her mother, father, and sister Roisin. He'd discovered her real and very Irish name was Maeve, but most knew her name as Mary. Her father was a staunch catholic and ran a strict household. Jack had remarked he sounded terrifying. Mary had cautioned him that being an Australian and not a churchgoer didn't bode well for a positive relationship with her father. The inference he might one day meet her father had touched Jack.

In the week since he'd seen Mary, Jack had been out on another sortie. It had been incident-free, at least from the Allies' perspective. He'd held on to the thought of seeing Mary right through the horrifying flight. When Mary had asked if he was flying again soon, he'd lied. Not only was he not allowed to discuss the missions, but he didn't want her to worry. They'd only known each other a few hours, but he knew she'd worry, particularly when he'd asked her if he could see her again, and she'd smiled broadly and said, 'Yes please.' He'd laughed, and she'd looked embarrassed. Unbeknown to Jack, she'd heard him tell the dying airman he'd be flying over the channel again soon. He had taken her hand, and they had sat silently lost in each other's eyes. He'd manage to assure her, or so he thought, that he only had a couple of training drills and some other very dull military activities that were of no interest to him, let alone her. Surely it wasn't a lie that would see you in hell, he'd thought. He was already there most of the time anyway.

It was 11:30am, and he stood in the large public gardens not far from the hospital and the nurse's accommodation where Mary lived. It was a perfect day. Not warm by Australian standards, but clear blue skies, and not even a hint of cool breeze. Jack stood nervously waiting. It had been a week. Would Mary still come? Did he have the correct meeting place? He pulled the crinkled piece of paper from his pocket and admired Mary's handwriting and the map she'd sketched. Near the old oak, about one hundred yards inside the main gate, just off the path. If you get to the playground, you've gone too far, she had said. He'd arrived about twenty minutes early, so he'd walked to the oak, counting out the yards in his head. Stupid, he'd thought, there's only one oak tree he could see. He'd walked past it all the way to the playground just to be sure there wasn't another, then he'd doubled back urgently in case Mary was early. She wasn't. He paced back and forward, fidgeting and pulling at his shirt collar that had become uncomfortably tight. He carefully checked his hair that had been oiled and combed with all the precision of an engineer. And then . . . there she was. She walked through the main gate, heading toward him. He could already see her smile. She was like a beacon rendering every other person she walked past dull and colourless. She was beautiful. His heart thumped in his chest.

All morning Mary had fussed about in the nurse's quarters. Her friends couldn't decide if they were concerned or irritated with the activity, but regardless they were excited for her. She had been awake and up and about, long before it was sensible to start getting ready to meet Jack. She had spent more money than she could afford on a new dress and desperately hoped he would like it. One of her good friends had helped with her hair and makeup, and when she was ready to leave, had handed her the picnic basket and kissed her on the cheek, wishing her good luck.

As she walked quickly along the pavement heading toward the park's main entrance, she wondered if Jack would already be there. Her nerves threatened to overwhelm her, and she stood breathing deeply for a moment before turning into the gate. And . . . there he was. Standing by the oak tree as promised, so handsome in his uniform, smiling broadly, a posy of flowers in his hand. Even from a distance, she could tell by the stiff posture that he was as nervous as she was. She strode toward him as confidently as she could, becoming increasingly self-conscious as his gaze fixed on her.

'Hello Jack.' Mary spoke first. She could see just how happy he was to see her. He didn't speak for a moment, just continued to stare at her. 'Jack. Hello there.' She tried again, bemused.

'Wow.' His eyes were wide.

'What?' Mary couldn't contain her delight as she tried to pretend she was unsure what the 'wow' meant.

'You look . . . wow, you look beautiful.'

'You scrub up pretty well yourself, Flight Lieutenant.' Mary watched as Jack remained mostly lost for words. 'Are those for me?' She pointed to the flowers in Jack's hand.

'Yes, yes, sorry.' He offered the flowers to Mary, who struggled to take them with the picnic basket in one hand and a coat in the other. 'Oh, sorry. Here let me take that.' Jack reached for the picnic basket.

'Thanks. That's our lunch. And thank you for the flowers, they're lovely.' Mary held the flowers to her face to smell the sweet scent.

'They're not much, I'm sorry. It's hard to find flowers, not surprisingly. They're hardly essential at the moment.'

'Well, you mightn't think so.' Mary chuckled, and Jack joined her.

'It's good to see you Mary.'

'You too Jack.'

Jack leaned in, and with one hand on her arm, he kissed her cheek lightly. She hoped her make-up would hide the warm flush she felt.

They walked together to a section of the park where there were very few people, and they could secure a bench to sit on away from eyes and ears and just enjoy each others company.

'Are you hungry?' Mary asked Jack.

'Always.'

'Here, I've made us some sandwiches, and I have some biscuits too.'

The next couple of hours passed in a heartbeat. Mary enjoyed the outing every bit as much as the first evening they had sat nestled in the warmth of the little pub enjoying a drink. Once lunch was eaten, they decided to take a walk through the gardens. Mary tucked the flowers carefully and lovingly into the picnic basket before Jack swooped it up and then offered the crook of his arm to Mary.

The week had been stressful for Mary. Jack had insisted he only had training drills and that it would be an easy and safe week. Mary knew better. She'd met many servicemen, and by far and away, they were reluctant to talk about what was going on and when. It was partly because they were under strict instructions to keep all missions and postings confidential and partly because they needed relief from the ever-present anxiety associated with the fear of battle. Discussing upcoming conflicts was anything but a recipe for relaxation.

'So you haven't said much about your week.' Mary carefully inquired as they strolled.

'Not a lot to tell you, to be honest. I have one day R and R for the week, today, and my week was spent looking forward to today and seeing you.' Jack was suddenly serious.

'I'm not silly Jack. We're at war. I know what goes on. I don't know where you are or what you're doing all week. I can't help but worry.'

'Don't worry about me. I'm one of the lucky guys. I get to come home each night after work and have a drink and a good meal. I have a comfortable bed, warm quarters, and I get a day off each week. It's the boys out in the trenches, on the ground, they're the ones we should be worrying about. They're the ones that are doing it hard, real hard.'

‘I know Jack. But every time you take off, your life is in danger and not just a little bit.’

‘It is. But if me and the other fellas don’t go, if we don’t take off, we’ll all be in far more danger and a damn sight sooner than you could ever imagine.’

‘I know. I hate this.’ Mary clutched Jack’s arm, squeezing it and leaning her head against his shoulder, her curls splashing across his arm.

‘You’ve only known me five minutes. You shouldn’t be this worried about me.’ Jack commented with a note of satisfaction.

‘I am. I’m worried about everyone. So you can just get in the queue, Jack Sutherland.’ Mary tried to lighten the mood.

They found themselves pausing to admire what must have been an ancient oak. Its trunk was so thick three men could hide behind it without fear of being seen. The branches formed a vast canopy. They stretched out so far from the tree it seemed impossible that they hadn’t collapsed under their own weight.

‘It’s beautiful, isn’t it Jack.’

‘It is.’

‘You know it’s probably stood here for hundreds of years. Imagine what it’s seen, wars, plagues, fires. I bet it’s seen them all and more, and it’s still standing, thriving. I have to believe we’ll still be standing strong here in another hundred years. I’m sure we’ll be victorious soon. It’s just a matter of time, and we'll all be able to go back to living again. Not just surviving.'

'I think you're right Mary.' Jack sighed. 'You're not just beautiful. You're smart and sensible.'

Mary let go of Jack's arm momentarily as she bent forward to walk under the branches and inside the tree canopy. Jack followed close behind, and once he was back by her side, she took his arm again.

'It's like another world under here.' Mary looked up into the tree, a tangle of branches and leaves.

'It is. I don't think anyone would know we were in here unless they saw us come in. It's very private.' Jack's voice caught a little as he spoke.

Mary felt herself shaking as though she were cold, but she felt warm. She turned to face Jack. He kept hold of her hand as he put the picnic basket down. Her stomach fluttered with nerves. With the basket on the ground, Jack turned back to Mary and took her other hand in his.

'I don't know what it is.' Jack's voice was husky. 'The moment I saw you, I just knew.'

'Knew what Jack?' Mary whispered. Her face tilted back, she held his intense gaze.

'I'm just being silly. I'm sorry. I am getting carried away with the moment. Here in this secluded and peaceful place, with the most beautiful woman in England.'

Mary felt a little disappointed. She was conscious she'd only known Jack a week and only met him a couple of times, but whatever it was he was feeling, she was feeling it too. She had never felt anything like the longing she felt for Jack. Every moment they'd been apart, she'd been thinking about him, worrying about him, daydreaming about him. Even her sleep was laced with dreams of Jack. It was crazy. It was probably the war, the desperate desire for something good, something wonderful to cling onto, but she couldn't dispute it. She wanted him.

'Jack.' Mary was still whispering.

'Yes.'

'I just knew too.'

Mary leaned in toward Jack, still holding his hands and closing the gap between their bodies to just inches.

'I want to kiss you.' Jack whispered.

'I want you to kiss me.' Mary smiled ever so slightly and closed her eyes slowly.

CHAPTER FIVE

Several weeks went by, and the couple settled into as much of a routine as they could forge from their interrupted lives. Whenever Jack had a day away from the base, he'd visit Mary and spend the day and the evening with her. As it was, a day off was usually a reward for another mission, sometimes two. There'd be debriefs, rest, recreation, then the routine would start over.

Jack had arranged to see Mary one evening on the night before a day of R&R. The boys were keen to go out and make a night of it. Jack agreed reluctantly that he and Mary would join them at the Boatman's Arms, a pub they knew well. Mary asked if she could bring one of her nursing friends rather than be the only woman with four rowdy men, and Jack agreed.

'That's Macca, Johnny and Tim.' Jack pointed to each of his mates in turn. 'This is Mary.' He wrapped his arms around Mary's shoulders as if to say, she's mine, so watch your step. Mary nodded at the young men then turned to her friend.

'This is Jean.'

‘G’day.’ The men chorused.

‘So you’re Jacko’s girl.’ Macca spoke to Mary. ‘He wasn’t pulling me bloody leg.’

Mary could tell by the look on his face what he was talking about, and she blushed, turning away.

Jack sat with the girls while the boys went to the bar returning a little while later with drinks for everyone. Paintings of all sorts of watercraft adorned the walls. A fire glowed orange behind a grate and below a timber mantelpiece. High above, two long oars from a scull were fixed celebrating some famous victory. The windows were blacked out by heavy material cocooning the occupants. The bar was crowded and getting busier by the minute. Servicemen and women, and other civilians arrived in the hopes of a quiet night. A night that wasn’t punctuated by the sound of an air raid siren.

The group settled into an enjoyable evening. They were all Australian and competing to impress the women with stories of the terrifying outback of Australia. The women were fascinated with the tales of the unforgiving climate, the endless animals, reptiles and insects that would as happily kill you as look at you. It all seemed to reach a pinnacle when Macca went into a long story about going three rounds in a boxing tent at a travelling show. He was fighting against nothing less than a six-foot kangaroo, or so he said. They all collapsed in fits of laughter when Johnny had outdone Macca, swearing black and blue he’d ridden an emu three miles into town, then tied it up outside the pub while he had a schooner inside.

'Go on bugger off with yer.' Macca shoved Johnny in the chest. 'Come on, who's shout? Reckon yer up Jacko.'

'You girls right for a tick while I get a round?' Jack asked Mary and Jean, and they nodded. 'Be right back.'

The girls sat alone, laughing and discussing the seemingly farfetched stories and how it appeared to make the boys happy telling them so they'd go along with them.

'I like that Johhny.' Jean smiled at Mary.

'I think he likes you too. I think they all do.' Mary laughed. 'He might ask you out.'

'I hope so.' Jean drank the last of her glass of beer. 'If he does, I hope he comes to pick me up on his emu.'

The women burst out laughing. The pub was shoulder to shoulder with people, and they had no sight of Jack and the others when two English sailors squeezed their way up to their table and introduced themselves.

'Good evening ladies. I'm Patrick, and my friend here's Robbie. It's nice to meet you both.'

'Hello.' Jean answered. 'I'm Jean, and this is Mary.' Jean pointed toward Mary. Mary looked uncertain but smiled politely.

'Do you mind if we join you then?' Patrick asked with an overconfident smile and his arm around his mate's shoulder.

'Sorry. We're with some other men already.' Mary was quick to respond.

'Oh, come on. They've gone, and we just need to give the legs a rest for a minute. I promise we're not bad company.' Patrick continued.

'They'll be back any second now. They're just getting a drink.'

'Ok, we won't stay long.' Patrick said, pulling his mate down next to him.

They sat and did their best to engage the two good looking girls in conversation. Mary tried to be polite, all the while getting anxious about the return of the Aussie pilots. Jean, not feeling attached particularly, beyond a yet to be explored interest in Johnny, was far more inclined to engage and encourage the sailors.

It wasn't long before the boys returned, but long enough that the sailors believed they had squatters rights over the table and the ladies as well. The four arrived in single file after snaking their way slowly through the crowd. Macca was the first to arrive, holding a couple of pint glasses filled almost to overflowing above his shoulders. As he pulled up at the table, a look of distaste on his face, Johnny all but crashed into the back of him.

'Who are you?' Macca demanded indignantly.

'Pat and Robbie.' Patrick replied smugly. 'And who are you when you're not chasing a kangaroo.'

'I'm Macca, and you're in my seat. You wanna move on mate?'

'First in best-dressed buddy.' Patrick replied.

'Well, you weren't first in, and yer certainly not best dressed, so bugger off before I get annoyed and have to move yer on.'

'You and who else?' Patrick poked his chin out and then pulled it back slightly as Johnny, then Tim, then Jack squeezed their way out of the crowd and into a line side by side, all looking as displeased as Macca.

'You right?' Jack asked Mary.

'I'm fine Jack, really.' Mary replied, unable to hide her concern at the mounting tension.

'Off you go boys.' Jack tried in a calm tone hoping the two sailors would get up and ease back into the crowd and the night wouldn't be ruined.

'I'm not your boy, buddy.' The sailor spat back at Jack.

'Righto, no worries. We don't want any trouble, that's all.' Jack put his beers down on the table and held his hands in the air in a placatory gesture.

'Yeah, so piss off.' Macca added, which was no help at all.

Patrick stood up and edged closer to Mary.

'Ok, we'll go. We don't want any trouble. We're all on the same side, aren't we?' Just as he finished speaking, he put his arm around Mary's shoulder, and she tried to pull away from him. 'Come on luv, give a lonely sailor a kiss, why don't you.' He leaned down and tried to kiss Mary, but Jack grabbed him by his collar and pulled him up and away from Mary.

'Back off.' Jack said slowly, his eyes fixed on the sailor.

'Or what? What are you going to do about it, Kangaroo?'

The sailor leaned forward and shoved Jack backward. His mate Robbie stood up, looking ready to join in but found himself immediately shoved backward by Macca. The women leapt to their feet and disappeared quickly back into the crowd.

'Haven't got it in you?' Patrick said with a smarmy smile, patting Jack's cheek just hard enough it could be described as a slap, and Jack shoved him backward. He bounced off another patron who spilled their drink and angrily shoved him back toward Jack. He lashed out at Jack with a fist collecting him just below the eye, and then it was on.

Macca reached for Robbie and, grabbing him by the shirt, pulled him forward, upending a chair. Pushed in the back by a spectator, Tim lost his balance, falling forward over the toppled chair legs. He held on to his two pints of beer gallantly until he almost reached the floor, face first, but let them go at the last second. The majority of their contents went down the back of an American soldier's trousers. The American turned angrily and went to throw the last of his beer at Tim, but it missed and went on Johnny, who swung a reflex punch.

Jack stepped forward and drove a fist into Patrick's stomach. Patrick doubled over winded for a second, then charged like a wounded bull smashing into Jack's stomach and sending him careering back into the crowd. Everyone was yelling and swearing, and like cascading dominoes, each bump brought another man into the brawl. Patrick took another attempt at punching Jack, but this time Jack got his arm up to protect his face, taking the blow on his forearm. He drove a straight arm jab into Patrick's jaw and stunned him. He followed that with an uppercut that sent Patrick's head back, then landed the final blow, a hook to the side of the face that left Patrick with no legs to hold himself up. Jack watched as Patrick sunk like the Titanic, slowly into a mass of wrestling servicemen, chairs, tables and beer.

Looking around, Jack spied his mates, Johnny with an American in a headlock, or was it another Aussie? It was hard to tell. An American was kneeling on Tim trying to choke him, and Macca was landing a knockout blow on an Englishman. He somehow managed to wrangle them together, prying them loose from their various positions of combat. There was no sign of the women. He figured they'd made a break for it while they could. At least, that's what he hoped.

In the turmoil, Jack and the boys made their way out into the cold night air without being identified as the ring leaders, leaving the melee in full flight behind them. They found Mary and Jean a couple of hundred yards away, hovering in the doorway of a shop ashen-faced and concerned.

After a quick rundown of the battle, with lots of boasting and embellishment, only tempered by the looks of exasperation from the women, they all parted company. Macca and Tim decided they would head back to the barracks early and hope that no word of the brawl preceded them. Jean accepted an invitation from Johnny to be walked back to the nurses quarters, and Jack and Mary decided to walk a little while before saying goodnight.

Mary took Jack's hand and felt him flinch. She lifted his hand up gently to look at it.

'Are you hurt?' Mary asked quietly.

'Nothing I won't get over, and quickly.'

She gently kissed his swollen and bruised knuckles, and he felt warmth flood through his body.

'You might be able to hide this,' she said, looking at his hand, but I'm not so sure about your face.' Mary ran her fingers along his cheek.

'Does it look bad?' He asked.

'No, you are very handsome.'

'Funny, but seriously, am I bruised?'

'A little, on your cheek, and under your eye.'

'Damn, if we get found out, we are going to be in a truckload of trouble.'

'What will they do?'

'They won't stop us flying. There are not

enough pilots to keep the planes up as it is. But we might lose our R&R and get confined to barracks instead.'

Jack was sorry he had said what he had as he noticed Mary turn her face away. He could only imagine how difficult this was for her if she felt half of what he felt for her.

'I'm sorry about before.' Jack said, breaking the silence that had followed his last comment. 'The fight, I mean. I'm not really a ratbag. I just won't stand by and see my . . .'

Mary threaded her arm through Jack's and pulled him toward her as she leaned against him while they walked. She looked up at him, but he kept his gaze ahead.

'Your what, Jack?'

'My girl, my . . . woman.'

'Am I your woman, am I?' Mary smiled as she nudged him in the ribs gently with her elbow.

'Don't be so silly. You know you are.' Jack's tone was serious, and Mary stopped him, then pulled him around to face her.

'What is it? What's wrong.' Mary looked into Jack's eyes. There was a long moment of silence before Jack spoke. He drew in a long breath.

'I'm scared.' He said finally.

'I'm scared too', she said quickly. 'I'm scared all of the time.'

'What I mean is,' Jack continued, 'I am scared every time I leave you that I will never see you again. When I'm up in the plane, and all hell has broken loose, I'm not scared of dying. I'm scared of never seeing you again. I know that doesn't make sense, but it's how I feel.'

'It makes sense to me Jack.' Mary ran her fingers gently across his face, then reached up on her tiptoes and kissed his chin.

'You see,' he continued, 'I knew the very first moment I saw you.' Jack pulled Mary against him, and he could feel her heart was beating as quickly as his. 'I knew I loved you.'

Mary smiled as tears of happiness tipped just over her eyelids and onto her cheeks.

'I've never felt anything like it before, nothing. I just want you and need you all the time. Nothing else is important.' Jack leaned down and kissed Mary. Her lips parted, and he savoured her taste as he kissed her deeper, pulling her as close as he could without crushing her. She pushed him away for a moment.

'What's wrong?' He whispered.

'Nothing, I just want to make sure you know how much I love you too, Jack Sutherland.' He pulled her against him again and kissed her passionately.

Just as he was completely losing himself in the moment, he felt a sharp tap on his shoulder. He broke the embrace and turned to see a policeman standing behind him.

'Come on, that's enough now.' The policeman said in a stern tone but with a slight smile. 'This is not the place for that sort of shenanigans. It's late, and you should do the right thing and get her home safely.'

'Yes Sir.' Jack replied respectfully and quickly led Mary off by the hand.

Mary and Jack walked in silence back in the direction of the nurse's quarters. They occasionally looked at each other and smiled, feeling happier than either of them could remember having felt before. They were close to the quarters when Jack pulled Mary to the side of the pavement and between two buildings in a slightly shadowed area.

'Mary, I want you.' Jack thought his heart would burst through his chest. He took her waist in his hands and pulled her against him. She wrapped her arms around his neck and met his kiss with passion. He pushed against her, and she moaned with pleasure. He couldn't help himself, and he ran his hands from the small of her back and onto her bottom, pulling her toward him. Her moans only served to excite him even more. He ran a hand slowly over her hip, up and over her rib cage, feeling every individual rib as he did and slid it over her breast, gently squeezing it. He had nothing left, no reserves for restraint. The world around them had disappeared in a haze, and he was lost in this stunning woman.

Their passion continued to heighten, and just when it seemed all sense and reason would be lost, Mary pushed away.

'I'm . . . I'm sorry.' Jack said quickly, catching

his breath and stepping away from Mary. She reached out and took his hand and pulled him back toward her.

'It's ok. I want you too Jack. Just . . . not here and now. I love you Jack. You're the man I want. Forever.'

'Then marry me!' Jack announced abruptly.

'What?' Mary sounded stunned. And her face reflected the tone of her voice.

'I love you, you love me, what else is there. Marry me. Make me the happiest man that ever walked the face of the earth.' Jack was so excited and animated, it looked like he was about to burst into song.

'Jack, you're crazy. I can't marry you.'

'Why not? Why can't you?' He fired the questions back in rapid succession.

'There are a million reasons, that's why.'

'None of them are important. None of them matter. Tell me one reason why we can't get married next week.'

'Jack. Come on. We are in the middle of a war. When this is over, I live in Ireland, and you live in Australia. And besides,' Mary smiled weakly, 'my dad will kill you, and that would spoil everything.'

'You could be my wife, and when this is over, you would come and live with me in Australia, on Sutherland Downs, or we could get our own place and start a family and build our own empire.'

'What about my dad and my mum?'

'Don't tell them. Let's just get married here, in London, and I will go with you, and we'll tell them afterwards.'

'He'll go mad, I'm telling you. He's frightening.'

'Mary. I am going to marry you, whether he likes it or not. I am from a good family. We're good people. He'll eventually realise that although I'm a heathen, I'm not such a bad fella.'

'This is crazy. I must be losing my mind.' Mary looked torn but excited. 'What about my job Jack? I'd have to leave. I can't be married and keep my job. That's the rules.'

'Stupid rules. That's all they are, stupid.'

'Be that as it may, Jack, they're the rules.'

'Then don't tell them either. They don't need to know anything's changed. For god's sake, you are doing an incredible thing, looking after all these poor fellas, working your fingers to the bone. They need you more than you need them. Just don't tell them. They'd have no reason to ask.'

'I'd be lying.'

'Not if they never asked you. Come on, please. I am begging you. I have never been more sure of anything in my life Mary Kelly.' With that, Jack got down on one knee and took Mary's hands in his.

'Jack . . .' Mary didn't know which way to look as the tears streamed down her face.

'Maeve Kelly, would you do me the honour of

becoming my wife?' Jack asked. His eyes lit up like fireworks, and he had a smile from ear to ear. 'Well . . ., will you?' Silence again for a moment, then.

'Yes. Yes, I will, Jack Sutherland.'

Jack leapt to his feet and wrapped Mary in his arms.

CHAPTER SIX

When Jack was discharged from hospital after miraculously surviving crashing his aeroplane, he spent time in the English countryside. He was recovering in an old manor that the government had temporarily requisitioned as a place for convalescing servicemen. Jack had argued black and blue that he didn't need to go, that he was fine to stay where he was. He was desperate not to leave his new wife, his secret wife, but in the end, he'd had no say in the matter, and he'd been sent by train, north out of London and miles away from Mary.

The wedding had taken place in a registry office only ten days before his crash. No one knew what they'd done, except for Jean and Johhny, who had attended them and had been sworn to secrecy on pain of death.

Jack and Mary had been lucky enough to have escaped London together, just once, for two nights to the coast south of London. It had been the one chance Mary had had to be Mrs Jack Sutherland,

and they'd made no attempt to hide their marital status from anyone.

They had their wedding night in an old hotel overlooking the beach and never had either of them been so happy. For just a couple of days, the weight of everything else that was going on in their tormented world had been lifted from their shoulders. They'd eaten dinner both nights at the hotel where they'd stayed and strolled along the beach in the moonlight.

As they walked that first evening, Mary collected shells while Jack told her he'd decided to take up the option to get a new property when they returned to Australia, a soldier settlement block. He wanted something that was entirely theirs. A place from where they could start their own family dynasty. The Jack and Mary Sutherland dynasty. He'd said he wanted to move into the mountain country. He wanted to live in rolling green hills, like the ones in England, and he suspected, more like her home in Ireland.

Mary had listened, trying to imagine what it would be like to live on the vast farm that Jack intended to settle them on. At least one thousand acres Jack had promised. He was going to build them a house, a house big enough for a huge family. She was both excited and afraid. Excited to know she could be with Jack forever and terrified to tell her parents. The only thing that dampened her spirit was the relentless fear of the unknown. The fear of Jack flying. Of Jack going out one day and never returning. The fear of no one having told her he hadn't returned and having to frantically plead for word of him. The fear of no one knowing that she was his wife.

When Jack finally finished laying out their future, they walked in silence along the beach, Jacks arm around Mary, holding her close, sharing their warmth. Mary began to sing quietly.

'That's nice.' He'd commented, resting his chin lightly on her head as she tilted it into his neck.

'Roisin and I used to sing when we were kids, and Ma and Da took us to the beach, and we collected shells. Sweet Molly Malone. I miss her, Roisin. I haven't seen her in ages, you know. She's lovely. She's training to be a nurse like her big sister.' Mary laughed wistfully. 'You'll love her Jack. I know you will.'

'I bet I will. If she's anything like you, how could I help but love her.'

After dinner, Jack took Mary by the hand and led her back to their room. The anticipation of the bedroom filled them both with nervous excitement.

'What a day.' Jack said as he crossed the room to draw the curtains closed. He turned back to Mary, who was standing watching him. 'You ok?'

'Yes, I am.' She replied quietly, and he walked toward her.

He took Mary in his arms, and she wrapped her arms around his neck.

'I love you Mary Sutherland.'

'I love you Jack Sutherland.' Mary smiled then closed her eyes as Jacks lips touched hers.

Jack sat on a seat in the sun, trying to feel warm. The garden was spectacular, and he enjoyed taking a walk in it each day. He felt safe and at peace for the first time in a long time, but his heart ached for Mary. He'd only been in recovery for a week, and he already had cabin fever. Again, he'd tried to persuade the Doctor he didn't need to be there, and to his end, the Doctor had mainly agreed. But, it was a matter of protocol and procedures. The Doctor had to follow orders. As soon as they could get the bulk of the bandages off his hand, and they could properly assess his recovery. After that, they'd give him his marching orders, whatever they might be.

'Attention, Flight Lieutenant.' A woman's voice startled Jack and roused him from his daydreaming. He pushed himself up to his feet and turned away from the lilypond he'd been staring at when he'd begun to drift off, almost to sleep.

'Mary!' Jack almost tripped over the seat in a mad scramble to get to his wife. He took her in his arms, taking care with his bandaged hand, and held her for a long time before speaking.

'What are you doing here?'

'Does a girl need a reason to visit her husband?'

'No, of course not.'

Jack ushered Mary to the seat.

'I've missed you so much.' He said, gazing into her eyes. 'I'm going round the twist sitting here, waiting until I can get out and come back to be with you.'

'I've missed you too Jack. But I'm just so glad you're safe and not up in the air anymore. I don't want you to ever go back up. Promise me you won't Jack. Promise me. You've done your bit. You've given part of you.' She stroked his face, gently looking into his eyes. 'Up here,' she said, stroking his temple, 'and down here,' she continued, touching the wrist of his bandaged hand carefully.

They sat and talked about what they'd each been doing since they'd last seen each other. Mary had been busy. Injuries and casualties were continuing to mount up and overwhelm them. Every day and every night in the hospital was a constant stream of broken and wounded humanity. She was exhausted physically and emotionally.

Eventually, Jack suggested a cup of tea, and she accompanied him back to the manor and into a large and ornately decorated room. It was a complete contrast to the sterile and business-like environment she'd been working in. She was thankful Jack was here and away from all the misery and heartache.

As they stood, talking and looking out the huge windows into the garden, a soldier approached them.

'Flight Lieutenant Sutherland?' He said in an official tone.

'Yes, that's me.'

'The Major would like to see you.'

'I have a guest.' Jack tried not to sound irritated.

'Excuse me.' The young man said to Mary. 'Are you . . .?'

'I'm a relative, Mary cut in quickly. Mary Sutherland.'

'Oh, I see.' The young man looked surprised. 'Just a moment please.' He disappeared out of the room, and Jack and Mary exchanged a glance. He returned just a moment later.

'Please follow me. Both of you. You can come too Ms Sutherland.'

The young man led them into an office where the Major, who was in charge of the facility and a doctor himself, and one other doctor were seated behind a table. The young man fetched a chair for Mary, and she joined Jack at the table opposite the Doctors. After a hastily cobbled together and badly stumbled over story, about how Mary was Jack's cousin, the Doctors briefed Jack and Mary on the next steps. He was heading home to Australia and much sooner than he expected. He'd be on a ship within a week, but it would take many weeks to get Sydney.

Several hours later, Jack was given a short leave of absence to accompany Mary to the train station so that she could travel back to London. As they waited for the train, they made their final and tear-filled plans. Jack couldn't believe the physical ache in his stomach and chest as he looked at Mary sitting next to him on the station platform, tears in her eyes. He felt as though his heart was being torn out of his chest.

'As soon as I get home, I will write to you. Every month I will write and tell you how I am progressing on our farm and our house. It will be amazing by the time you get there.'

'A year Jack. Just twelve months. This war will end soon, it has to. If it ends sooner, then I'll come sooner. I'll come as quickly as I can. The minute the war is over, and it's safe to travel, I will go home and see my parents and tell them about the most amazing man in the world, my husband.'

Jack looked suitably concerned.

'Don't worry. You'll be in Australia, and he'll be in Ireland. He won't be able to get his hands on you, and I won't tell him where you live until he calms down.' Mary tried to laugh.

'Twelve letters, one a month, and then I'll see you again. It will be the longest twelve months of my life.'

'I know, me too.'

The shrill whistle of the approaching train startled them both. They stood up, and Jack took Mary in his arms. He kissed her soft lips, wet with tears, then buried his face against her neck, barely holding back the tears himself.

Her fingertips slid across the palm of his hand and along his fingers until just the tips were touching for just a split second. Then, as the train departed, he was left watching her leaning out the window of the train, waving to him, smiling through tears, then weeping.

CHAPTER SEVEN

Roisin leapt off the bus before it had even stopped in the High St. She ran along the pavement as fast as her legs would carry her. She turned into Church St, running past the cathedral. Two elderly ladies looked at her scornfully as her raincoat flapped behind her, and her hair flew about unkempt. Tears streamed down her face as she panted and struggled to gather enough air into her lungs to keep going. She turned into the street where her parents still lived and where she'd grown up along with Maeve, her elder sister. Maeve had moved back into the little home with her parents only a month earlier when she'd become unwell in London, where she'd been working as a nurse. She'd recovered quickly, with her mother's constant and devoted attention. Even her stern and unaffectionate father had softened as he watched and then accepted how unwell his daughter had been. She was two years older than Roisin, and they had always been close.

A nurse as well, Roisin had been home as often as she could while her sister was unwell, missing work on occasions and bearing the brunt of an unforgiving matron. Maeve understood when Roisin couldn't be with her. She understood the strict rules under which they were governed, the inherent passion for their jobs that nurses held dear, and the impacts of each.

Roisin was exhausted as she slowed to a jog when the road became a little steeper for the last fifty yards. She could see her father now, standing at the front gate to the little cottage. He was tall, strong, very proud and towered over the average man. His physical appearance was quite daunting. But on this day, he appeared to have shrunk in stature, slumped over, and lacked the usual arrogance and self-confidence. The sight of her father in this state terrified Roisin. Her throat tightened, and the tears flowed freely down her cheeks. She could no longer hold back the loud gasping sobs as panic threatened to overcome her. When she finally reached her father, he took her in his arms for the first time in years, and she felt like a small child again. Her tears soaked through his shirt as she listened to his heart beating quickly. He placed a hand on either of her shoulders and pushed her away, holding her at arm's length and looking her in the eyes.

'How is she Da?' Roisin struggled to form the words.

'She's not good baby.' He paused. 'The doctor says . . .' He struggled to speak, and the sight of this big strong man breaking sent the tears flooding down Roisin's cheeks again. 'He says it won't be long now. You best go inside now and see her and your Ma. Your Ma's in a bad way.'

Roisin's father turned away, looking into the garden as she squeezed his arm, then steeled herself for what she would find inside.

Roisin pushed the front door open, placed her handbag down in the hall, hung her coat on a hook. She crept quietly down the hall and stood at the entry to the living room where they had set up a temporary bed not far from the fire for her sick sister. Maeve lay quietly, almost peacefully, with the blankets pulled up to her neck. Her eyes were closed, and Roisin assumed she was asleep. Her mother knelt by the bed, her face buried in the blanket, her hands on Maeve's leg, rosary beads draped over one hand. She was quiet, but Roisin could see the gentle rocking of her shoulders as she wept.

There were footsteps in the hall, and Roisin turned to see the Doctor returning from the kitchen wearing his coat and carrying his bag. He smiled with a sad expression at Roisin, and she walked out into the hallway to speak with him.

'How are you?' The doctor asked.

'As good as can be expected, I guess.' Roisin wiped away her tears with the back of her hand. 'Actually, I'm terrible. And Ma, I don't know what I can do. Da told me you said . . .'

'That's right girl, it's not long now. I'm very sorry. We thought she was through it. We didn't expect it would come back, and with so much force.'

'But how long?'

'I don't know for sure, maybe a day or two, but maybe just hours. You should get in there with Maeve and your mother now. Don't waste a precious moment. She's awake quite a bit, and she's quite lucid, so don't lose any time.' The doctor squeezed her arm. 'I'm sorry Roisin. I'll be back later this evening and again in the morning to make sure she's as comfortable as she can be. There's nothing much else I can do.'

The doctor left, and she watched as he walked down the front path, exchanged a few words with her father and tapped him consolingly on the shoulder before walking on.

There was a cough and some wheezing from the lounge room, and Roisin quickly walked back in. Her mother was sitting on the edge of the bed and wiping Maeve's mouth with a cloth. Maeve's eyes slowly moved from her mother and settled on Roisin, and the curve of her lips shaped a barely perceptible smile. Roisin smiled back, crossed the room, stroked her mother's shoulder as she passed her then knelt on the floor near her sister.

'Oh Marymoo. What are you doing to me?' Roisin choked on the words.

'I'm sorry, baby girl. I don't want to leave you, I promise.' Maeve whispered quietly and slowly.

'Then don't, don't leave me, don't leave Ma and

Da, please.' Roisin knew she shouldn't, but she couldn't help but weep.

With a huge effort, Maeve stroked Roisin's flaming red and curly locks as Roisin lay her head on her sister's chest. She listened to Maeve's heart and breathing, and in contrast to her father, the beat was slow and weak. Her breathing was shallow and laboured.

'I'll get you a cup of tea.' Rosin's mother stood and walked slowly out of the room, passing her father, who was now standing in the doorway watching on helplessly. After a moment, he joined his wife in the kitchen and left his daughters to some final time together.

'Help me sit up.'

Roisin gently pulled Maeve forward and tucked a second pillow behind her sister. The movement made Maeve cough until she looked like she couldn't breathe at all, and Roisin was scared as she held Maeve's hand. When at last, the coughing subsided, Roisin helped her sister sip water from a glass. Maeve spoke quietly.

'I want you to listen to me, okay?' She whispered as she lifted a hand to Rosin's face and her cold fingers stroked her cheek. 'I'm going to be watching over you, you hear me, I am, and I want you to be happy. Be happy for me, for the both of us. You promise me?'

'I will, I promise.'

'I want you to get out of here. I want you to go somewhere warm, sunny, and free. I need to tell you something.' The coughing started again, and Maeve had to stop. Roisin wiped her brow with a damp cloth.

'Ah, Maeve, I'll get out of here, I promise. Can't promise it will be warm and sunny, but I'll go. I'll go for us.'

'Good. Australia.'

'What? What did you say?' Roisin looked a little startled.

'Aus . . . stralia.'

Roisin laughed through her tears.

'That's what I thought you said. You're crazy. I'll go to England, as far south as I can. How's that?'

'No, listen to me.' Maeve looked anxious. 'Australia.'

'Why on earth?'

'I need you to find someone for me.' Maeve coughed again. 'Promise me.'

'Ok, ok I promise.' Roisin didn't mean it, but she wanted to do whatever she could for her poor sister, who was looking distressed.

'In my room, there's a box, a tin box in my, in my cupboard. Don't show Ma and Da, please. Take it. Take it with you.' Tears were streaming down Maeve's face. 'Jack . . .' She whispered.

'Jack?' Who's Jack, my darling.'

'Jack. My man Jack from the Aussie Outback.' Maeve laughed weakly, but another bout of coughing stopped her. 'Oh how I loved him baby, oh how I loved him. I do love him.' Her voice trailed off and her eyes closed. They opened with a start. 'Jack, what must he think of me.' She began coughing again.

'It's ok Marymoo, it's ok. I got you. Ok? Jack, I got that. I promise I'll find him. I promise.' Roisin stroked her sister's cheek and hooked her hair behind her ear. She leaned down and kissed her forehead.

Maeve's eyes were closed again, and her breathing was shallow. She looked somehow peaceful.

Roisin stood up and walked to the door, opened it and quietly called her parents. They came quickly down the hallway. Her mother looked frantic, and her father looked distraught. Her mother went straight to the bedside and dropped to her knees. Her father stood behind her mother. Maeve opened her eyes, and for the briefest moment, Roisin thought she could see her lips turn ever so slightly in a smile as she looked at her mother. And then, Maeve drew a long and eerily loud breath and was still.

Roisin slumped into a chair and let the tears flow freely down her face as she watched her mother's rocking shoulders and heard her gasp then wail. Her father dropped to his knees next to her mother and wrapped his arm around her. The rare and unrestrained show of affection made Roisin's heart shatter.

CHAPTER EIGHT

Neighbours, friends and family milled around the small lounge room. It was drizzling and bitterly cold outside.

Roisin's mother sat in an armchair, a tissue in her hand, dabbing at her eyes. Her father held the same half-drunken glass of beer he'd been holding for nearly half an hour. He smiled at friends, but his smile belied his grief.

Roisin was thanking mourners and showing them to the door, passing umbrellas, helping with coats, kissing tear-streaked cheeks of the women, aunties, cousins and friends. She was shaking the chunky calloused hands of her father's workmates and kissing stubbly cheeks of uncles. The more she did, the more she temporarily kept her own grief at bay. But still, she was both relieved and at the same time stricken when the house finally fell utterly silent.

Roisin helped her mother to bed early, tucking her in and kissing her forehead like a child. She returned to the kitchen and found her father at the table with a bottle of whiskey and a glass tumbler. He took a sip and stared ahead at the cupboard.

'Can I get you something Da, something to eat?'

'Nah, I'm alright Baby.' He sniffed loudly, then took another sip of his whiskey. I just need to sit for a while before I go to bed. It's way too early for me. It's barely dark. Is your Ma ok?'

'She is. I hope she'll sleep now we're through this god awful day. Damn her Da, I could kick her backside for doing this to us. I bet she's watching us now and enjoying our grief.' Roisin did her best to make light of the situation, but it didn't help at all, and the tears flowed again. She stood next to her father as he sat, and he wrapped his arm around her waist.

'I know, I know, baby. I wish I could help you, but I don't know what to say. What to do. I don't know how your mother will ever get over this.'

'Time Da, time. This is all too new. We need time.' She kissed his forehead. 'I am going to my room. I need to lay down. I'll see you in the morning, Ok?'

'Ok baby. Good night then.' He dropped his arm from her waist and grasped at her hand as she moved away slowly. She looked back and smiled as best she could. 'Roisin.' He whispered.

'Yes Da.'

'I love you Baby.'

Roisin covered her face with her hands, drew in a deep breath then sobbed. She moved back to her father, and he hugged her. She couldn't remember a time he'd ever told her he loved her.

'I love you too Da.' She wrapped her arms around his neck, kissed his forehead then rested her chin on the top of his head.

Once Roisin could finally bring herself to let go of her father, she left, walking slowly up the stairs to her bedroom. She crept along the hallway, not wishing to make a sound, not knowing why. Her room was at the end of the hall, just past Maeve's. As she passed Maeve's room, she looked at the door that was slightly ajar. She reached out and grasped the door handle and gently pushed the door open before stepping just inside. The little light coming through the window illuminated the room just enough for her to see the silhouette of shapes, but she knew the room well. She shivered, then nervously walked across to the window and drew the curtains. She wrapped her arms around herself to try and ease the shivering. Standing for a moment, she was sure she could feel Maeve with her. She shook her head, sighed and crossed the room and stepped out into the hall. As she pulled the door shut, she thought about Maeve's words. How she'd made her promise to find the box and take it. She looked back toward the stairs and could see the light coming from downstairs, where she knew her father would still be sitting in the kitchen and would continue to sit for hours into the night.

She pushed the door open, turned on the light and shut the door behind her. The photo of she and Maeve on the bedside table made her throat close, and she forced back the tears. She looked around the room then settled her gaze on the small wardrobe. She crossed and slowly opened the doors. Maeve's clothes hung inside, and she couldn't help but take Maeve's favourite dress and hold it to her face, smelling the fragrance that Maeve loved and that she had given Maeve last Christmas. It was the last Christmas they would ever spend together.

After a moment, and once she had her emotions in check, but only just, Roisin started to look for the box. She pushed the hanging dresses aside and looked to the back of the wardrobe. There was nothing there but shoes. She took the chair from the dressing table and sat it in front of the open wardrobe, and climbed up on it. From this vantage point, she could see what was stored on the shelf above the hanging space. There was a myriad of boxes in all sorts of shapes and colours along with folded clothes. There were so many boxes, she made up her mind to come back another day, perhaps tomorrow when she wasn't so tired. Tomorrow she could take the time required to look through all of them and find she knew not what, although she knew she'd know when she'd found whatever it was.

As she was about to step back off the chair, she noticed a folded jumper she hadn't seen for quite some time. It was hers, and she remembered lending it to Maeve months earlier. She almost felt guilty pulling it off the shelf, but she did. And as she did, something caught her eye. It was a box pushed right to the back of the shelf. A box that had been lovingly covered in cut out pictures of flowers and love hearts. Her heart skipped a beat as she reached for the box and drew it toward her. She lifted it off the shelf and stepped down off the chair. She carried it across the room, placed it on the bed and sat down.

For some time, she sat and just looked at the box, too nervous and still too upset to open it. Several times she put her fingers on it, then took them away again. Finally, she picked up the box, stood up and walked to the door. Closing the door quietly behind her, she crept to her own room, then sat on her bed with the tin box and finally plucked up the courage to open it.

The first thing she found inside the box was a photo of herself, dressed for a party. She knew that Maeve carried that photo with her, and she had a similar one of Maeve that she kept by her bedside when she was living away from home. After looking at the photo, she removed a small bundle wrapped in a silk scarf, tied carefully with a red ribbon. Also in the box was jewellery, some of which Roisin recognised, and another small red box. She placed the silk-covered bundle on her bed and took out the small box. She opened it carefully and was surprised to find a fine plain gold ring which she lifted out and examined. It shone as though brand new, and the box it was in looked as though it might have come straight from a shop very recently. Roisin stared at the ring and wondered where it had come from and why Maeve had it. It posed more questions than answers, and so she put it back, closed the box and returned it to its secret place.

Roisin looked down at the silk-covered bundle. By the feel of it, she was sure it was letters, and she hesitated as she began to feel she was invading her beloved sister's privacy. Then she remembered Maeve's words.

'In my room, there's a box, a tin box in my cupboard. Don't show Ma and Da, please. Take it. Take it with you.'

Roisin picked up the bundle and ran her hands over the smooth silk. She held it to her face and smelt the perfume. Then, slowly and very tentatively, she took one end of the ribbon that was tied in a bow and pulled it until the knot undid and the ribbon fell away. The silk slid off the bundle and revealed 6 white envelopes, all addressed to Maeve care of the Nurses quarters in the Emergency Hospital where she worked during the war. She turned each envelope over and read the sender details. In each case, there was nothing but a simple JS followed by the numbers 1/12, then 2/12 and so on until 6/12. Every envelope was open.

With great trepidation, she lifted the triangular flap on the envelope marked 1/12 and then pulled out the crisp and carefully folded writing paper. The letter, written in an elegant hand, read . . .

My Darling Mary,

I can't begin to describe how much I miss you. It has been three months since I last saw your beautiful face, your sparkling eyes, your smile that melts my heart.

The trip home on the ship was slow and frustrating because I was neither with you nor at home. You cannot believe how I felt when I stepped onto Australian soil, alive! For the first time in so long, I can think ahead more than days or hours. For the first time ever, I am enjoying sweating because I am not sweating from the terror of war but from the Australian sun. Does that sound silly? I bet it does.

I can report, I am home safe on the family property in New South Wales. It is hot and dry, and I love it. It is only missing one thing, you, of course. Soon you will be with me. I have told my brother and sister-inlaw, and they can't wait to meet you. We have already begun discussing where you and I will live until we have a property of our own. All this hot flat country that rolls on as far as the eye can see will be a shock for you. I know it

> will. Does it scare you to know that our property is about a third of the size of Ireland? Unthinkable, isn't it?

The letter continued on with descriptions of a huge family of several generations, all on the one unfathomable size property. There were stories of working with sheep, riding horses and always dogs and more dogs. And there was kangaroos, emus, wild pigs and snakes. Roisin was fascinated, and for a short while, as she read, she became so engrossed in the stories that she forgot that she was reading a love letter.

Finally, she reached the last paragraphs.

> So, I must go now and get some sleep. I wish you could have seen my brother's face when I told him I'd married a beautiful Irish girl. He nearly dropped his beer, and that's unthinkable in Australia. He thinks we are both mad. He's probably right, but we'll show them. I have done as you asked, and there is no return address and just my initials, nothing to alert anyone to our plan, not even a spy (ha ha). For goodness sake, don't forget my address. If your father is as scary as you say, he will undoubtedly follow you to Australia and track me down. I have seen some wild Irish men in my day, and I am not looking forward to the first time I meet him. Maybe we will have our first baby by the time he

gets to Australia, and I can put them in his arms when he comes for me, and he will soften (ha ha).

Twelve letters. One down, eleven to go until you get on a ship. It can't come soon enough. I love you with all of my heart, forever and always.

Your J

Roisin lay back on her bed, clutching the letter to her chest and thinking about the words. Tears streamed down her cheeks. Maeve was married. The ring, was a wedding ring.

'My man Jack from the Aussie Outback.'

Maeve's man Jack from the Aussie outback. JS was Jack. Poor Maeve, poor, poor Maeve. He sounded so wonderful, and Australia sounded amazing. What an adventure she would have had. It was heartbreaking. But Maeve had been married, and no one knew, not even Roisin herself. How could that be? When did it happen? Was she pregnant? Roisin panicked and sat up quickly. No, no, she couldn't have been. There were no signs. She checked the postmark on the envelope, and it had been sent ten months ago. No, she wasn't pregnant. It was some very cold comfort.

She shuffled through the letters and found the last letter marked 6/12. It had been sent more than four months ago. It had probably arrived just before Maeve had first gotten ill and had come home from London. She had been so ill she couldn't possibly have written back to JS. Did he know she, his wife, was sick? Did her brother-in-law, how strange that sounded, know his wife was so terribly ill. Probably not.

Roisin looked at her clock through tear-filled eyes and was shocked to see it was nearly 11pm. She got up from her bed, opened her door, and was relieved to see the lights off throughout the house. She packed up the letters in their box and pushed them under the bed. They would have to wait until tomorrow.

CHAPTER NINE

Jack had been back on Australian soil for two years when he'd finally taken up his soldier settlement block in a valley not far from the town of Granite Gully and moved onto the block permanently.

Granite Gully had begun its life as a small gold mining camp in the South West Slopes of the Snowy Mountains in New South Wales. Gold had been found in rich seams in the local granite, and word had spread quickly. Unfortunately, the gold had run out nearly as quickly, but not before the more enterprising had seen the value of the country and climate for grazing both sheep and cattle. The clearing of the bush started in earnest at the turn of the century. By the time Jack arrived, some fifty years later, there were tens of thousands of acres of good workable land nestled in the hills and valleys in the area.

He'd been on his new property, Snowy Ridge, for a couple of weeks, and there'd been no sign of his neighbour Syd Fredericks. Usually, you'd expect a welcome visit from your neighbour in the country soon after you moved on to a property.

Jack had been told politely in the pub when he'd first arrived in Granite Gully that his neighbour was an unpleasant bloke at best.

Jack woke one morning and decided it was time to meet this gentleman. On the land, neighbours often turned out to be lifelong friends. These were the people that banded together in fire, floods and after storms to mop up and rebuild. These were the people who lent tools and equipment when there was a breakdown in the middle of harvest, shearing and haymaking. These were the people your sons and daughters married. And these were the people who returned your stock, with just a frustrated sigh, when the stock did the wrong thing and broke through a fence onto their best pasture.

Jack mounted his horse, called up one of his kelpies and left the other chained to a steel post near the front door of his house. He trotted off to the Fredericks.

It was a good twenty minutes before Jack arrived at the front gate to Glencoe, the Fredericks's farm. Their drive was about a half-mile long, and the house was set back and low toward the same creek that divided Snowy Ridge in half. He was most of the way along the driveway before the Fredericks's dogs started barking. He rode through an open gate into the house paddock and to the front entrance of the house yard.

A small white weatherboard cottage sat inside a wire fence. Although the Fredericks had been on this farm for nearly twenty years, there was little sign of any established garden in the front yard. Just a few trees and two small beds of flowers that looked more like freshly dug graves with offerings from the mourners. Jack was a little surprised, given Fredericks was married. Actually, when he thought about it, no one had spoken much about his wife, so Jack wasn't sure what to expect.

Jack dismounted and tied his horse to the fence, then pushed the yard gate open. It squeaked loudly. He walked along the short path toward the front door, and as he did, he caught a flash of movement from the corner of his eye. A curtain moved, and Jack saw a face for just a moment before the curtain was left to hang closed again. It was not long enough to tell if it was male or female, but Jack supposed it was Mrs Fredericks.

Jack stepped up onto the small timber front porch and knocked on the door. He hardly had time to step back before the door was cracked open just far enough for the face of a woman to appear and stare at him cautiously.

'Hello.' Jack smiled at the woman. She smiled shyly back at him, still holding the door mostly closed. 'I'm Jack, Jack Sutherland, your new neighbour. I live over on Snowy Ridge.' Jack pointed east over his shoulder with his thumb.

'Snowy Ridge?' The woman looked confused.

'Oh, yeah, well, that's what I've called the

property. I guess you've probably never heard of it. I share your eastern boundary.'

The woman seemed to relax and opened the door. Jack could see she wasn't much older than he was, perhaps a few years, so she wasn't Mrs Fredericks. She was a plain but pleasant looking woman. Her outfit didn't do her justice. She continued to stand, holding the door, just looking at Jack. He wasn't sure if she was just socially awkward or perhaps a little simple. But he was a kind and normally calm and patient person, so he persisted carefully, gaining her confidence as he spoke.

'I thought I would drop in and say hello to your father, Syd. Is he about?' The woman smiled for the first time.

'I'm Bonnie.'

'Pleased to meet you Bonnie.'

'Syd's not my father.' She smiled as she spoke and confidently held eye contact with Jack now.

'Oh, ok, well, I've just come to meet Syd, but if he's not about, I can come back another day. I would have called his telephone, but I don't have one yet. Thought I'd just take a chance on him being home. Will you tell him I called in?'

'Tell him yourself, here he comes now.' Bonnie pointed out into the paddock in the direction of the sheds and stockyards Jack had noticed when he was riding in.

Not dissimilar to what Jack had imagined, an older man walked toward them carrying a tin bucket.

'He's been doing the milking.' Bonnie commented. Jack turned back to her.

'Oh. Okay.'

As the man approached, Jack could see he was in his late fifties, maybe sixty years old. He was tall, with thin limbs and a potbelly. His hair was grey, and he was bald. He had a stubbly face and a snarl. He didn't look pleased to have a visitor, but Jack had expected this, given the descriptions he'd been given. All he needed to do was introduce himself and put a face to the name in case they ever needed to talk to each other, or god forbid, help each other.

'G'day.' Jack waved and smiled at the approaching man, who didn't bother to reply.

Syd continued to walk steadily toward Jack, along the front path and up onto the small porch. He was so brisk in his approach that Jack had to step back out of his way and watch he didn't step back off the porch by mistake.

'Here.' Syd thrust the bucket toward Bonnie, and a little milk slurped over the edge and onto the porch. 'Butter.' He barked at Bonnie again. 'And some cream.'

Bonnie took the bucket and disappeared inside the house. The screen door slammed shut behind her. Jack watched as Syd dragged his hands down the front of his trousers, wiping off milk and cow shit. Jack stood bewildered, watching all this. Syd turned toward him finally and stared at him for a moment.

'Who are you?' He snapped.

'Jack Sutherland. I'm your new neighbour.'

'I know who you are.' Syd barked back at him as he put a still filthy hand out for Jack to shake.

If you knew, why'd you bloody well ask Jack thought.

'Suppose you'll want a cuppa then, will yer?'

That was the last thing Jack wanted. He was ready to mount his horse and gallop home.

'Yeah. Good on yer. That'd be good, thanks.' Jack smiled pleasantly, trying to look keen.

'See you've met the wife then?'

Jack looked stunned, then caught himself.

'Bonnie?' He tried to keep the tone of his voice neutral.

'Mrs Fredericks, yes.' Syd stared at Jack in silence again for a moment before opening the screen door and bellowing into the house.

'Make an extra cup of tea and bring some biscuits, will yer.'

'Yeah.' Bonnie responded from somewhere in the depths of the house.

'Take a seat.' Syd pointed to a small outdoor table with a few rickety odd chairs in the sparse garden. 'We'll sit there if you don't mind, save taking me boots off. I'll just have a wash.'

Syd wandered over to a corrugated iron water tank on an old wooden stand at the corner of the house and picked up a well-used cake of yellow soap, and washed his hands furiously for a moment. Jack looked down at his own hand and the filth from the handshake and wished he could politely do the same, opting to wipe it down his trouser leg in Syd style.

Once he was finished, Syd joined Jack at the table. Again, he sat and just looked at Jack, with a half snarl on his face, like a dangerous dog. By this stage, Jack wasn't particularly inclined to try and make conversation, and he opted to just stare Syd down. Eventually, Syd spoke.

'How yer settlin' in over there?'

'Good. Lotta work to do to start getting things into shape, but I've got plenty of time. Got a lifetime, I guess.'

'Hope you got plenty o' money. Most o' that block's just bloody scrub. Not much good for anything other than pigs and roos. What'cher call it again?'

'Snowy Ridge.'

'Why?'

'Because you can see the Snowies from the front paddock, and I'm on a bit of a ridge, so I figured that made sense.'

'Hah. Well, you gotta call it somethin', I guess.' Syd looked less than impressed.

'You do.' Jack answered.

They sat in silence again for a few minutes until Bonnie appeared with a tray with two cups, a teapot and a bowl with biscuits. She stood by the table and poured their tea. She had a small jug with milk in it.

‘Milk Jack? It’s fresh.’ Bonnie smiled, almost chuckling.

‘Yes, thanks Mrs Fredericks.’ Jack injected just enough tone into his voice to make a point.

‘Mrs Fredericks. Don’t be silly, it’s Bonnie. We’re neighbours, for goodness sake.’ Bonnie smiled warmly at Jack.

‘Quit yer yabbering and pour the tea.’ Syd barked at Bonnie, and the smile left her face.

Jack looked directly at Syd and made no attempt at all to hide his disapproval of the way he spoke to his young wife.

‘I hope you’re joining us Bonnie.’ Jack smiled at Bonnie and enjoyed the palpable irritation he could feel from Syd. Syd shot Bonnie a nasty look, but she sat down defiantly. Jack was pleased, not so much of her company, but to see her resist the treatment from Syd, although it would leave him concerned for the possible backlash from this old bastard.

‘What’s yer background? I ’ere yer from up north. That right?’ Syd stared at Jack, waiting for a response.

‘Yes, out beyond Bourke, on the Darling. The family’s been on the land up there for generations.’

‘Why are you here then?’

Jack looked at Syd and wasn’t particularly inclined to humour the rude old bastard with polite conversation, but looking at Bonnie, seeing her interest and making the assumption she was very likely starved of decent conversation, he decided to continue on.

'When I got back from the war, a couple of years back, I went straight home to the family property. I guess I got itchy feet and wanted something of my own. I wanted a change. It's a bit hard to go back to what was normal before. Nothings normal anymore.' Jack looked up from his teacup where he'd been directing most of his conversation and noticed that Syd looked less than interested. But Bonnie, on the other hand, looked very engaged in the discussion, so Jack continued.

'Anyway, seemed like there was a good opportunity to diversify.'

'Diversify?' Syd grunted. He clearly didn't understand.

'Diversify, it's like when you do two different things so when one turns bad, hopefully, the other one's doing good.' Bonnie answered the question, directing her response to Jack.

'That's right.' Jack smiled.

'I know what it is.' Syd snapped at Bonnie. 'Haven't you got something to do?'

'No. I've done all me chores, and it's my morning tea time.' Bonnie's answer was even more defiant.

'What're you carrying over there?' Syd turned back to Jack.

'First Cross ewes. We're going to breed them up on Sutherland Downs, that's the family property, then truck them down here, and I'll join them to

Dorset rams. Same as most people in the district, I guess, except I can bring in the replacement ewes from the family property.' Jack waited for Syd's next question, but there was nothing. 'Oh, and I've got a few Herefords. Not a lot yet. Not a lot of any stock, really. Got a lot of work to do for the next couple of years getting some pastures established, clearing more land, building dams, building a house.' Again there was an awkward silence, and Jack decided he'd overstayed his welcome. He was about to stand up when Bonnie piped up.

'What'd you do in the war Jack? You go overseas?' Bonnie asked.

'Pilot. Spitfires. Flew out of England.'

Bonnie's eyes widened.

'England. That must have been so exciting. I would love to go to England.'

'England! Why the hell would yer wanna go there? What would a girl like you do in England?' Syd scoffed at Bonnie.

'Buy a new bloody dress, that's for sure.'

'Watch yer tongue.' Syd barked.

'And new shoes. And go to a restaurant.' Bonnie pulled a dreamy face.

'Well, I wish I could say it was like that Bonnie, but it wasn't. Most of the time, it was just bloody terrifying. I have never been happier than the moment I stepped back onto Australian soil.' Jack thought of Mary as he said it and struggled not to show his feelings.

'Dam lucky yer didn't get yerself shot.' Syd commented.

'I did.' Jack held up his hand, exhibiting his missing fingers, and Bonnie covered her face in horror. 'But you're right, I was damn lucky.'

Bonnie looked at Jack with a sympathetic expression, then a little disdainfully at Syd. Noticing her face, Syd had had enough and stood up.

'Well, I got work to do. Bonnie, give him our telephone number. Ah geezus, surely you can remember it. Twenty-two.' Syd looked at Jack. 'You got that?'

'Yeah, I think I can remember that. Twenty three, right?' Jack smiled, and Bonnie laughed.

'Twenty-two, I said. Yer a bit of a bloody joker.' Syd scowled again then mumbled, loud enough for Jack to catch it. 'As well as a bloody hero.'

Jack stood up, and so did Bonnie.

'Well, good to meet you Syd.' Like hell, Jack thought to himself. 'And a pleasure to meet you Bonnie.' He knew the second comment was inappropriate in the context of the situation. It was a little inciteful, but he didn't care. Syd wasn't worth giving the time of day to, and he sure as hell wasn't frightened of him. There wasn't much that really scared him anymore.

'It was a pleasure to meet you too Jack.' Bonnie put out her hand, and Jack shook it before turning and walking to his horse.

Jack untied the mare and stepped up into the

saddle. Bonnie was heading back into the house with Syd right behind her as Jack looked back. She tried to look over her shoulder and wave. Jack watched in disgust as Syd pushed her back firmly, shoving her in through the door. Jack rode off, worrying about what sort of trouble he'd caused for Bonnie. He wouldn't be back anytime soon, he thought, and that would be in Bonnie's best interest.

As he rode home, he thought about Bonnie. She was bright. Not particularly well educated, he supposed, but intelligent. He wondered how she could have possibly ended up with an old pig of a man like Syd, and he felt sorry for her. The sun shone down and warmed him through. For a moment, his thoughts drifted, and he pictured Bonnie. The more he thought about it, she was quite attractive. It was hard to tell under that terrible dress, but he was pretty sure she had a good figure.

'What the hell's wrong with you?' He verbalized his thoughts, and the dog looked up at him. 'It's alright mate.' He answered the dog's enquiry.

What the hell is wrong with me? He thought. What about Mary? His thoughts of Mary became tangled in a primitive and unwelcome desire for Bonnie.

It was now eighteen months since he'd heard from Mary. His wife. No one knew of her, as a friend or a girlfriend, let alone a wife, no one but his closest family and to them, she was little more than a story. He couldn't help but be tormented by the thought he'd made a terrible mistake ever leaving her behind, but he reminded himself he'd had no choice.

CHAPTER TEN

It had been a tough few days. Jack had never come to terms with the silence from Mary and probably never would. For a long time, he'd refused to believe that she wasn't coming. He hadn't had a letter from her in more than a year. She had been so diligent in her replies for the first six months of the twelve-month timeline they had set themselves. Jack was to head home to Australia and establish a home and get himself settled back into life on the family property. Mary was to stay on working for twelve months in London, helping with the terrible toll the war had taken on servicemen and women and the Londoners in that time. Late in the year, she would break the news to her family that she was married and moving to live in Australia. She had refused point-blank to leave when there was so much turmoil. As much as he was bitterly disappointed, he admired her courage and determination. It had only made him love her even more.

Now though, there was nothing. No Mary and no sweet memories, just the bitterness of rejection. Meeting Bonnie and dealing with the feelings that she had roused in him had sent Jack spiralling into one of the periods of depression that seemed to come over him in inexplicable waves. During these times, he could hardly drag himself out of bed to complete his day's chores, let alone take on any of the more significant projects around the property.

It was a warm day, and he struggled to eat the leftover stew from last night's dinner for his lunch. He had no appetite. He was used to this emotional routine now. For a few days, maybe even weeks, he'd be feeling good, able to focus on the future, as alone as it might be. On these days, he felt strong, alive and excited. But inevitably, the darkness would settle upon him again, the anger, the disappointment. He was never angry with Mary, not for one moment. He never thought of her with anything but undying love. But he was angry with himself. How foolish had he been leaving her, his wife, in another country a million miles away? Leaving her by herself in an enormous city, not even with her family. How stupid was he? It wasn't as though he'd a choice. The orders came, and he had been shipped out with hundreds of his fellow servicemen, and he wasn't discharged from service until he reached Sydney. He hadn't even considered mounting a case with the establishment. But what was done was done, and now, he had to accept that she wasn't coming. She'd cut him off. No doubt she'd found some handsome officer and had decided she was better off over there, near her family. And maybe, in reality, she was, Jack thought as he looked around him at what was little better than a hut, in the bush in the mountains in the middle of nowhere. Would she have been happy, arriving and finding this?

Jack tipped the stew out of the saucepan he'd been eating from, onto the dusty floor of the veranda. The dogs growled and fought over the muddy remnants while he watched on, entirely detached.

'Bugger it. I'm the boss here. I answer to no one.' Jack spoke to himself as he pushed the door open and walked into the kitchen, unable to shake a niggling feeling of guilt and disappointment with himself. He pulled open a cupboard door. Bending down and looking inside, he shuffled a couple of bottles around, pulling out a bottle of Scotch whiskey. He held it up to look at the contents. It only had about an inch of whiskey in it, and he hesitated for a moment before grabbing a second and full bottle out of the cupboard. He picked up a tin mug off the kitchen table and then walked back out to the veranda. He needed desperately to wash away this debilitating feeling. He sat down again and went to pour the last of the mostly empty bottle of whiskey into the mug, then thought better of it and upended the bottle and drank it all down in one gulp. Pulling the bottle away from his mouth, he coughed several times as his throat got used to the burning sensation. Then he took the second bottle, opened it and filled the tin mug two thirds full. It was just moments before he felt the all too familiar fuzzy warm sensation of the alcohol. Taking another large mouthful from the tin cup, he sat back in his chair, tipped his head back and closed his eyes.

'Mary.' He whispered. 'Oh, Mary.' He sniffed and wiped his nose on the back of his hand as tears threatened to spill over his eyelids. He'd never get used to these unchecked emotions that plagued him now.

Jack sat on the veranda for quite some time, slowly drinking and thinking about Mary, the war, his friends and even the plane crash. Whenever the plane crash crept into his thoughts, he would do whatever he could to stop it by finding a distraction, something to do or to think about as quickly as he could. But on occasions when he drank, he was powerless to defend himself against the torment of his thoughts, and he would feel the full brunt of that terrifying day in vivid memories.

He took yet another swig from the cup then looked at the bottle. He'd drunk nearly a third of it, and he knew, even in his inebriated state, he was going to be sorry the next day.

'Shit.' He mumbled again, throwing his head back and feeling like sleep. The dogs leapt up suddenly and started barking furiously. 'What?' He sat up and growled at the dogs. 'What the bloody hell are yer barkin' at?'

Looking around for what had unsettled the dogs,

he saw a woman walking across the paddock toward him, smiling broadly. Was he dreaming? He closed his eyes and opened them again, then squinted, trying to focus. There was still a woman walking toward him. He pushed himself to his feet unsteadily.

'Hello Jack.'

'Hello.' He replied.

'Bonnie. I'm Bonnie. Have you forgotten already? Your neighbour.' Bonnie smiled at him.

'No, no, of course not.' Jack did his best to speak clearly through his alcoholic haze.

Even with the effect of the whiskey and the surprise, he was aware she was nicely dressed, and if he wasn't mistaken, she'd done her hair and was wearing a little makeup.

'You look good.' He smiled. 'Where you off to?' He immediately regretted his comment. He knew it would seem overly flirtatious. Regardless Bonnie seemed very happy with the compliment.

'Where am I off to? You're funny Jack. I am off to see you. I brought you some cheese and some jam. I bottled some jam last week, and I thought you might enjoy some.' She slid the strap of a carry bag off her shoulder and handed it to Jack. He stepped forward to take it and stumbled a little as he did. 'Oh my goodness.' Bonnie looked down at the bottle of Scotch sitting next to the empty saucepan on an upturned log next to Jack's chair. 'Bit early for that, isn't it?' She asked, pointing at the bottle.

'It is. It's way too early. I'll be giving myself a bloody good talking to later on when I sober up.' He smiled, and Bonnie laughed.

'Are you okay?' She asked hesitantly.

'Yeah, sure. Never been better. Just had a little spare time today, and it's too far to the pub, so I thought I'd just sit here and have a tipple.'

'Bit more than a tipple, I think. Your tipple nearly made you topple.'

Jack burst out laughing and laughed until it became a little uncomfortable for both of them.

'How about you sit down, and I make you a strong cup of tea. I think you need one.'

'Ok.' Jack gave in quickly. He watched over his shoulder as Bonnie walked inside his home. He heard the kettle being dragged across the top of the old cast iron stove, then the stove's door being opened, and wood being put in the firebox.

'Coffee or tea?' Bonnie yelled from inside.

'Sorry. It's tea or whiskey.'

'Okay, tea it is. Where's the tea?'

'Shelf over the bench. Teapot should be on the table. The good china's on the dresser.'

'Got it.'

It was a few minutes before Bonnie poked her head out of the doorway and called Jack.

'Here you go.'

He pushed himself back out of the chair and joined her in the kitchen, sitting down with a thud at the kitchen table.

'Hope black's okay. I don't have a house

cow yet. Maybe I'll steal Syd's.' Jack winked at Bonnie.

'I think he'd notice if his prized milker went missing. I can imagine the carry-on. So, black tea's fine, thanks Jack.'

'Where's your friendly husband anyway. He's not about to come around the corner, is he?' Jack turned to look toward the door.

'Why?' Bonnie laughed.

'No reason, just don't really feel like looking any further into the eyes of the devil this afternoon.'

'Oh, you're so rude Jack. That's my husband you're talking about. I guess I can forgive you since you're obviously drunk.'

'Drunk?'

'Yes, drunk.'

'I am not.' Jack did his best to sound affronted.

'Here. I made you some cake too.'

'Bloody hell Bonnie. Where's Syd? Does he know your here and bringing me a cake? He'll shoot my arse with a shotgun.' Jack's tone had turned a little anxious.

'Don't worry about Syd. He's gone to Albury for a couple of days to pick up some tractor parts and other stuff he needs. He doesn't know I'm here.' Bonnie held Jack's eyes for a little longer than was comfortable. Her words and her facial expression were having a compromising effect down below the belt, and he was a little annoyed with himself. He tried to change the subject.

'I thought I was dreaming when I saw you before.' Again he immediately regretted his comment, and more particularly when she smiled appreciatively at another unplanned compliment. They sat quietly for a moment. Jack picked up a slice of cake and started eating it, hoping that filling his mouth would stop any more silly comments from escaping.

'What's wrong? Why are you drinking in the middle of the day?'

'Why don't you get to the point?' Jack tried to smile.

'Well, sorry, but I'm worried about you.'

'That's nice, but we hardly know each other. For all you know, I do this every day. You don't need to be worried about me.'

'Well, I am. I like you Jack. You seem nice, and I enjoyed your visit to our place.' Bonne said shyly. 'I'm sorry Syd was so rude. But that's just him.'

They were quiet for a moment before Jack spoke. The whisky made him a little more courageous and less sensitive than he would usually be.

'Can I ask you something?'

'Yes.'

'Isn't he a bit old for you?' He hesitated. 'I'm sorry, that sounds so bloody rude.'

'That's okay.' Bonnie smiled in a resigned fashion, and Jack decided to roll on with little care.

'You know, I actually thought he was your Grandfather. Your father at least.'

Bonnie looked embarrassed and didn't smile.

‘Sorry, that was a stupid thing to say.’ Jack tried to undo the damage.

‘No, it’s ok. You’re not the first person to think that.’ Bonnie sighed. ‘It’s a long and not very interesting story. I’ll tell you one day when I’ve had a whiskey or two.’

Jack sat up eagerly.

‘Do you like whiskey? Do you drink it?’ He asked with enthusiasm.

‘God no. Of course not. Even if I wanted to, Syd would never let me have a sip. He doesn’t let me drink.’

‘What? Not anything?’

‘Nothing. His rules.’

‘Well, bugger Syd. He’s in Albury, and you’re here with me, and it’s my rules in my home. ‘Jack spoke excitedly, and Bonnie chuckled at him. He leapt up and retrieved the whiskey bottle from outside and returned to the table.

‘No, Jack, I can’t.’

‘What do you mean you can’t. You came all the way over here to visit me, here by myself, and I’m betting Syd would think that was far worse than sipping a little whiskey.’

‘What would he think if he found out I did both?’

Bonnie’s smile was almost seductive, and Jack felt another surge of excitement run through him. He did his best again to push his instinctive thoughts away, but they were desperately close to taking complete control of his behaviour.

'Come on.' Jack pressed.

Bonnie looked at Jack with raised eyebrows.

'Maybe just a little sip. Just to see what it tastes like. Just a little. Okay?'

'Okay.'

Jack led Bonnie out to the veranda, and they sat next to each other, looking out across the paddock.

The strong liquor had hardly touched Bonnie's tongue before the fumes made her cough. She looked at Jack, her eyes watering.

'How do yer like that then?' Jack smiled.

'It's strong.' Bonnie said, her face scrunched up.

'You get used to it. Have another sip.'

'Really?'

'Yeah, go on, it'll do yer good.'

'How's that then?'

'Put hairs on yer chest.'

'Jack!'

'Sorry, that's what the boys say.'

Bonnie took another sip, and the whiskey burned her tongue. She clamped her teeth together and suppressed another cough.

'You like it?'

'Not much.'

'Come on, the best thing to do is to skull the lot and get the first one over with. After that, I guarantee you'll love it.' The words poured out, and Jack realised his words were coming out faster than he could review them and keep himself in check.

'Ah, ok.' Bonnie looked nervous, but she was obviously enjoying herself and not wanting to spoil the party.

'Block yer nose while you drink. It'll help.' Jack pinched his nose between his thumb and forefinger to demonstrate and tipped his mug up.

Bonnie followed suit, and it wasn't until she had that it dawned on Jack just how much whiskey he'd put in her mug.

'Ooohhhh. I can feel it already.' Bonnie looked a little shocked as she smiled. She seemed to be enjoying the sensation.

'That's probably enough for you.' Although he was pretty sloshed and his thoughts were jumbled, somehow Jack managed a semblance of sense. It was short-lived. 'I'll be back in a moment, I can hear nature calling me, and she seems pretty keen to see me.' Jack looked at Bonnie, and she laughed. As he walked away, he didn't see her half fill her mug again with whiskey and take another good swig.

Jack was back a few minutes later, and he collapsed back in his chair. It was mid-afternoon, and between the grog and the warm weather, he was feeling sleepy. He kind of wished she'd go now so he could just go and lie down and sleep off the dark mood he'd begun the day with. He looked at Bonnie, and she was staring at him.

'Bonnie.'

'Yes.' She sounded a little drunk.

'What's your story then? You and Syd, how'd that happen?'

Bonnie sighed and slumped back in her chair, and looked toward the roof of the veranda.

'Oh, whoo.' She sat up straight again. 'Thaz better.'

Jack laughed and reached over, placing his hand on her arm. She shivered and turned toward him.

'You ok?' he asked.

'Fine.' She held his gaze, a moment longer than she would have if she'd been sober. 'You want to know about Syd? It's simple Jack. I come from a poor family. Real poor. There were seven of us kids in the house with mum and dad. Mum died giving birth to the eighth. She would have been my baby sister, but she died too. Pretty smart, really. She probably took one look around and decided to give it a miss.' Bonnie took another swig of her drink.

Jack watched her. He didn't feel he could comment. Until the war, he'd had a very privileged upbringing and a happy young adult life. He was different now. Life was different. He knew many things now, more than he should at his age. He knew sacrifice, he knew pain, physical and emotional, he'd fought for survival, he'd loved and lost, and he was still only very young. Even still, he'd never gone without the most simple things with everything he'd been through. He'd never wanted for food, clothes, or shelter. Even in his worst moments, he'd had the confidence he would be ok. He just would because he was a Sutherland, and he grew up with that understanding and rock-solid belief. Bonnie continued.

'I had one sister and five brothers. I'm number two. My sister comes after me, then four brothers.'

'Strewth.'

'Strewth's right.' Bonnie chuckled.' As soon as my brothers could help on the farm, Dad put them to work. My sister and I kept the house. We struggled, the family that is. The farm was too small for such a big tribe.' Bonnie took another sip of her whiskey and seemed to be becoming quite accustomed to the taste. Her story continued.

'Syd has a younger brother, Neil, in Cootamundra, where I came from. Anyway, he and Dad got to talking over a beer at the pub one day. We were stony-broke, but of course, we had just enough for Dad to get a skin full at the local once a week.' Bonnie sounded bitter. 'Neil was a nice bloke. I'd met him once or twice. He had a small block and did a bit of shearing. A hard worker. So he gets to telling Dad about his brother Syd and the big property he has down at Granite Gully. He makes a point of telling Dad that Syd could do with a wife. And that was all well and good, but he didn't tell Dad that Syd was near on twenty years older than him. This part you won't believe. Here we are in the nineteen forties, in Australia, and my Dad promises me to Syd.'

Jack sat in silence, stunned and fascinated all at once.

'Dad made a pretty bloody good argument.'

Bonnie went on. 'There wasn't enough money, and I had to leave. He was going to kick me out, or so he said. But, if I was good, and behaved myself, then I could marry this fella Syd. Of course, I panicked. Where the hell was I going to go if he kicked me out. I didn't doubt he'd do it. There wasn't enough money to buy food where I was, let alone on the street, so the thought of being thrown out terrified me. In my mind, I'm seeing Neil, and I'm thinking, that's gotta be better than where I am now, half-starved and miserable all the time. So, foolishly I agreed. Two weeks later, I was married.'

'Geezuz, I've never heard anything like it before. What happened? What did you say? What'd yer do when you saw Syd, and how old he was?'

'What could I do? He was standing at the altar, in the church, his back to me, when I walked in on Dad's arm. He never even looked at me until I was standing right next to him, and the minister had started to talk. Dearly beloved and so on. I was terrified. I just stood there. Speechless.'

Bonnie leant forward, her hands clasped and looked at the dusty floor. Jack watched her and wondered if she was crying. He placed his hand gently on her back to console her, and she shivered as he rubbed his thumb tentatively back and forward.

'Are you ok?' He asked again, slowly taking his hand away.

'Don't stop.' Bonnie hesitated. 'Keep doing that,

please, it's nice. Nobody's ever touched me like that.'

Jack knew he shouldn't, but he put his hand back where it had been.

'Syd never touches me, you know.'

Jack wasn't sure what to say, and he hesitated.

'Well, not like that.' Bonnie sniffed and rubbed her eyes. 'He never talks to me. He just gives me my chores and complains if his dinner's cold or his beer's warm. Treats me like a servant. I guess that's all I really am.'

'I'm sorry Bonnie. That must be god damned awful. I guess you're lucky he doesn't touch you then.' Jack immediately regretted his comment. He was usually a sensitive person who cared about other people's feelings, and he was frustrated with himself and his lack of tact. They sat quietly for a moment.

'He touches me Jack. It's not love, that's for sure, but he touches me every now and again when he feels the urge. When we first got married . . .' Bonnie took another long gulp on her whiskey, and Jack did likewise. His stomach tightened in anticipation of whatever was coming next. 'When we first got married, he had a routine. Every Saturday night. You could set your clock by him. At first, I thought he wanted me. But I soon wised up to that. Thank goodness he's quickly getting old and slowing down.'

'What about kids? You don't have any kids, do you? Hope you don't mind me asking?'

Bonnie raised her hands to her face. He could see this upset her even more than the other awful things she'd been telling him.

'No. No kids. I'd have liked to have had a couple of kids. Just a couple. But not with Syd. He wouldn't make much of a Dad. He thought we would have them quickly when we first got married. That was the reason for his routine. He wanted a son. But there was nothing. He told me I was barren. He got really angry when nothing happened. He yelled at me. Yer no good, yer a bloody barren bitch, he said.'

Jack knew she was crying now, although her face was covered. He couldn't believe his ears. He hadn't liked Syd one bit when he'd met him, and this put the very bitter icing on the cake as far as he was concerned. He really needed to change the subject and try and make Bonnie feel better. She'd come all this way to see him and escape that misery for a while, but he'd somehow managed to drag her down into the darkness he'd been wallowing in when she arrived. The drink had been a terrible idea. In his half-cut state, he thought it might be fun. He thought it might be a laugh and that it might lighten his own mood, but it had become even darker and far too intimate. All of a sudden, Jack became very conscious of his hand resting lightly on her back as she turned and smiled at him through tears.

'Why don't we talk about something that'll make you happy again. What would bring back that lovely smile of yours?' Jack tried to lighten the mood, but realised he'd sabotaged himself even further. Lovely smile, he thought, what am I saying. His stomach tensed as Bonnie leant toward him, smiling and then slowly putting her hand on his thigh.

'You're making me smile Jack.' Bonnie ran her fingers in circles on Jack's thigh as she gazed intensely into his eyes. He couldn't help but respond, running his hand up and down her back as her hand began to explore more of his leg. Bonnie leaned in close to Jack, her face just inches from his. 'You make me smile Jack.' She whispered in a husky voice. Jack had nothing left, no reserves of strength from which to protect himself or Bonnie, and he leaned in and kissed her.

Bonnie stood up, reached for Jack's hand and pulled him to his feet next to her. She tilted her head back, wrapped her arms around him and closed her eyes. Jack kissed her passionately and with an instinctive urgency. After a moment, she pulled away then led him by the hand into his house.

Standing near his bed, Bonnie looked up at Jack and smiled. She began to unbutton her blouse.

'Bonnie.' Jack whispered.

'Yes Jack?' Bonnie's blouse fell open.

'I'm married.' If Bonnie was surprised, she didn't show it.

'So am I Jack.' Her skirt fell to the floor.

CHAPTER ELEVEN

Jack woke. He lay still with his eyes closed. Had he dreamed that? Memories of skin, lots of warm, soft perfumed skin. God, it had felt good. Surely he hadn't. He felt suddenly terrified by his actions. What had he done? He continued to lie on his bed, eyes closed, trying not to make a sound, his breathing shallow. He hoped that if he just lay still long enough, he'd wake from the nightmare he found himself in. But eventually, he had to open his eyes, and he did, slowly. He stared at the ceiling for a long moment before he summoned the courage to turn his head and look at Bonnie. When he finally did, there was no one in the bed with him. He'd imagined it. It was just a dream. Even the blankets were pulled up neatly as though no one had slept there.

Jack sat up, and his head thumped. How long had he been asleep? Maybe a couple of hours. He spun around and put his feet on the floor. 'Ahhh.' He tried to cool his forehead by pressing the soft pads of his hands against his eyelids. He pushed himself slowly to his feet. He realised he was totally naked, and his hopes of an incredible dream were dashed. He glanced toward the kitchen table where the cake sat that Bonnie had brought him. The knife lay next to it, still covered in crumbs.

He moved toward the window and pushed the old hessian sack away and was surprised to see that the light was fading outside. Where was she, he thought. He pulled on his trousers and slipped on his shirt, then walked to the door. He assumed she'd be sitting in one of the chairs on the veranda waiting for him to wake up. He was surprised to find she wasn't.

'Bonnie.' He spoke quietly at first. 'Bonnie, you there?' Nothing, everything still and quiet. The only movement was two dogs wagging tails waiting for dinner. Just the lowing of cattle in the distance as they gathered their calves and walked to their evening camp. Only the last birdsong of a Magpie. Nothing else.

Looking around, he could see she had put the two tin mugs together neatly with the empty bottle and a nearly finished second bottle of Scotch. He thought of her with affection. He'd enjoyed her company. He'd felt close to her as he held her. She was a good person. But what of himself? He'd just cheated on Mary, on his wife. He hadn't heard from her for so many months. There were moments when he accepted he'd never see Mary again and that she no longer wanted him. And then, there were moments when he was sure he would see Mary again, and something had gone wrong, and she'd just been delayed. And finally, there were moments when he was frantic, wondering where she was, what had happened, who she was with, if she thought about him, and if she ached for him as much as he ached for her. Right now, there was just remorse. How could he have done that? There'd been times, plenty of times since he'd returned to Australia when he could have broken his vows, broken his promises to Mary, but he didn't. He'd never desired anyone but Mary from the moment he'd laid eyes on her. And now, everything had been undone, everything, in just a couple of hours of desperate need.

Jack returned inside with the mugs and the plates that Bonnie had served the cake on. He put on his socks and boots and walked back outside into the quickly cooling evening air. He wondered if Bonnie was ok, walking home in the dark. He reassured himself with the fact she'd probably left for home a couple of hours ago while he slept. It was better that she'd gone. It was good that she'd gone. Maybe she felt as guilty as he did. Maybe.

Jack walked to the meat safe, followed enthusiastically by the dogs. He stepped inside the small shed. The cool breeze blew through the gauze as he unhooked a kangaroo leg and dropped it onto the chopping block. He took a sharp knife and cut two large slices of meat. Then he hung the leg up again. Outside the meat safe, he gave one dog a piece of meat, and it scurried off. He gave the second piece to the other dog, and it did the same. Then he wandered over to the horse yard. His horse had come in from the paddock into the yard and was waiting for a feed. Jack took a couple of biscuits of hay from a shed near the yards and walked over to the fence.

'Here you go girl.' He made the mare put her head between the rails and crane for the food so he could pat her for a moment before dropping the hay between the rails and letting her eat in peace. He checked her water and, confirming she had plenty to drink, headed for the woodpile.

After Jack had lit the fire and warmed up the small shack, he cut himself a large slice of Bonnie's cake and ate it along with a cup of black tea. Soon after, he collapsed into bed. He could smell her fragrance on the pillow as he drifted off into a guilt-ridden sleep.

Jack woke early the following day, and once his thoughts cleared, the memory of yesterday came back to him with a thud. He got out of bed and headed outside to perform the morning's ablutions. It was early, and he'd had less than a refreshing sleep. The hangover had receded, although it had been a long time since he'd drunk as much as he did yesterday. Again, his thoughts turned to Bonnie, and as much as he had no real concern that she'd made it home, he felt he needed to be sure. What had she said? Syd was gone to Albury for a couple of days. He could saddle up

Bella and quickly ride over to Glencoe, check on her, then leave. No repeat of what had gone on the day before. Just check on her quickly, and leave.

Ten minutes later, Jack had eaten yet another piece of Bonnie's cake, fed the remains to the excited dogs before tying them up, saddled up Bella and headed off. As he rode, he replayed what he could piece together from the alcohol-soaked afternoon that had ended up in his bed. Had he manipulated Bonnie? Why was she even at his house and without Syd? What would she think when he turned up this morning? Surely she would feel the same as he did. It had all been a big mistake.

Jack rode on. The morning was overcast and chilly. The air was damp. The bush was quiet but for an occasional bird song. He entered Syd's property through a boundary gate and cantered through the last couple of paddocks until he could see Syd's sheds and then the house. At the entrance to the house paddock, he got down from Bella, unhitched the gate chain, led her through and closed the gate after himself. He walked tentatively toward the house yard, still hoping they could put this down to a moment of very poor judgment on both of their behalf's and quickly move on. He was relieved when he noticed the smoke billowing out of the chimney. She was home and safe.

Syd's dogs were slow off the mark, but they furiously barked when they became aware of Jack and Bella. They'd been caught out asleep on the job and were doubling down on their show of ferocious security. Jack tied Bella to the wire garden fence, just as he had done the first time he had visited. And again, like the first time, when he'd seen the curtains move, they were pulled aside carefully. This time he was watching for them. Bonnie's face appeared at the window, but she wasn't smiling. Ok, Jack thought to himself, she is as uncomfortable as I am about this, that's good. He mustered a sheepish smile and waved half-heartedly. Her expression changed, and she began to look very concerned. Jack was worried she felt threatened. He put two hands up, palms facing her in a gesture of peace and to indicate it was ok. He needed to let her know that he was just here to make sure she was ok, not for any repeat of yesterday's very intimate visit. That was a one-off, a very pleasant but very bad mistake. His mind was wandering again, and his resolve was weakening. No, never again. Suddenly the curtains dropped, and Bonnie was gone. Jack turned to walk toward the garden gate.

'Good morning.' Syd's voice boomed out from behind Jack.

'Shit.' Jack mouthed quietly to himself. He turned around and forced a smile.

'You're here bloody early. We don't serve breakfast you know.' It was hard to tell if Syd was trying to make a joke because he only had one facial expression, a snarl. Jack hoped it was a joke.

'Really, I heard you did a morning banquet, I'm disappointed.' Jack mustered the most cheerful smile he could as his mind raced madly.

'Hmm.' Syd didn't look impressed. 'Do you need a feed or something? I can tell her in there to cook a bit extra.' Syd sounded like he clearly resented the intrusion as he motioned toward the house with a tilt of his head. 'I haven't had my breakfast yet.' Syd squinted as he looked at Jack, obviously summing him up.

'No, no. I'm not here for breakfast. I was just joking.'

'Well then, what?'

Syd was one of the most abrupt and unpleasant men Jack had ever had the displeasure to meet.

'I'm . . . I'm looking for some ewes.'

'What do yer mean?'

'I've got a dozen ewes missing.'

'What, and yer reckon I've got em do yer?' Syd looked affronted.

'No, no. Well, not on purpose. I just wondered whether they'd gotten through the fence. Just thought I'd check with you before I went up the hill out the back into the scrub and took a look around there. They probably just got through up there somewhere. I'll head up there and check around.'

'I wasn't aware the fence between us was shot. Where's it buggered. I can meet you up there, and I'll help you fix it up.'

Jack was getting into a real mess now and was madly trying to untangle himself. He just wanted to get on Bella and get out of there.

'I'll check the fence and make sure it's ok. I'll give you a yell if there's a problem.'

'So, if you haven't checked the fence, why do you think they're in here.'

'Yeah, yer right. I leapt out of the gate a bit fast. Look, chances are they're in my place and just got mixed into another mob. There are two mobs side by side, and I didn't count the other mob. Too bloody big to count in the paddock.'

Syd, looking confused, eyed Jack as though he was plain stupid, and Jack felt like he was. Jack made the mistake of looking up at the house for just a moment after catching movement at the window out of his peripheral vision again. Syd turned around to see what Jack was looking at and caught Bonnie at the window. He turned back to Jack, and whether he was or wasn't, Jack couldn't help but think Syd looked suspicious.

'Well, I better get going and find these ewes. Thanks Syd. Sorry, I wasted your time. Heads a bit thick this morning. Might be coming down with something. Not thinking things through properly.'

'Seems not.' Syd huffed. 'Must be catching.' Syd inclined his head back toward the house. 'She said she had a headache this morning too.'

She's got a bloody name, you rude bastard, Jack thought to himself without allowing the expression on his face to change at all.

‘Hah, well you better look out then. Ok, I’m off. I’ll let you know if the fence is down anywhere. If I need a hand, that is. Otherwise, I’ll fix it myself. Thanks.’ Jack went to turn toward Bella. He’d made a mess of this, and it wasn’t going to get any better. The best bet was to leave as soon as possible and hope Syd just thought he’d been out in the bush by himself too long.

‘Hello Jack. ‘A soft voice called out from behind him, and his stomach lurched. He turned back to see Bonnie standing on the doorstep smiling. She waved to him. He waved tentatively back. She looked really nice. He metaphorically shook himself.

‘Morning Bonnie.’ He called out without smiling, doing his best to look disinterested.

‘You going already?’

‘Yep, just a quick visit to see Syd. All sorted, so off to get some work done. I’ll see you next time.’ He went to turn away.

‘You had brekkie? It’s early.’

‘Early, you’re joking. The sun’s been up for ages. I’ve been up so long I’ve had a cup of tea and a slice of cake already.’ As Jack said it, he immediately regretted it as he noticed the colour in Bonnie’s face. Just get out of here, he chastised himself.

‘Cake.’ Syd grumbled. ‘Half yer bloody luck. I wouldn’t mind getting me some cake.’ He turned toward Bonnie. ‘When are you going to make me some cake, or do I have to bake me own like him.’

He pointed over his shoulder toward Jack with his thumb.

'Your breakfast's on the table.' The smile left Bonnie's face as she spoke to Syd. 'Hurry up, or it'll be cold.'

'I really should go.' Jack nodded at Syd then looked toward Bonnie.

'See yer later Jack.' Bonnie waved, turned on her heel and was gone.

'Let me know about the fence.'

'Will do, thanks.' Jack turned and stepped toward Bella. By the time he'd put a foot in the stirrup and swung up into the saddle, Syd was walking through his front door. He sat for a moment and looked at the house before turning Bella and cantering off toward the gate. He didn't notice Bonnie watching him again, from behind the sheer curtain as always.

CHAPTER TWELVE

Lenny Henderson hopped down from his horse and bent down to pat the dog sniffing at his shin.

'G'day mate.' He ruffled the dog's fur behind its ears. He opened the gate to the yard and walked his horse in. He undid the straps, slid the saddle off the horse, and swung it up over the yard's top rail. He picked up the sweat-soaked saddle blanket from where it had dropped on the ground and laid it over the railing to dry. He took a leather halter from off the railing where Jack had put it for him earlier and put it onto the horse as soon as he'd slipped the bridle off. The horse pulled away, looking for the hay that Jack had thrown in the corner of the yard for it.

'How yer going Lenny?'

'Good thanks Mr Sutherland. How are you?'

'Not bad boy. Hope you got a good night's sleep did yer? We got a lot to get through today.'

'What's on?'

'Well, we're moving a small mob of cows into a fresh paddock, then we're going to blow the buggery out of a few stumps out the back.'

Jack could see the excitement in Lenny's eyes, although Lenny was clearly trying to look nonchalant.

'Righto Mr Sutherland. Sound's good.'

'Take a look at yer.' Jack stared at Lenny. He hadn't seen him for a few weeks. 'You must be on a bloody good paddock at home. I reckon you've grown a foot since I last laid eyes on you.'

'Nah, I don't think so Mr Sutherland.' Lenny looked embarrassed. He clearly thought Jack was serious. 'Maybe an inch or two.' He smiled self-consciously.

'Bout time you put on a bit o' beef though. Reckon you'd blow away in a stiff breeze.'

Lenny laughed politely.

'How's school?'

'Good now. I'm done. Finished a few weeks back. Dad finally said I could finish up. He and mum had a terrible blue, but he won. I reckon if she'd got her way, she'd have made me stay until I was sixteen.'

'Sixteen?' Jack raised his eyebrows.

'Yeah. She's got no idea. Wasting me time in that place. Now I can get on with me life and help Dad out.'

'How old are you?'

'I turned fifteen a few months back.'

'Hah, fifteen. Well, you need a bit of education Lenny. You haven't wasted your time, I can tell you.'

'How old were you when you left Mr Sutherland?'

'Twenty one mate. I went to university before the war. I studied agriculture. I went to boarding school in Sydney, then to university.'

'One of them flash schools was it?'

'Yeah, I guess you'd say that. Anyway, that's enough gas bagging. I'm not paying you to stand here and talk, am I?'

'No, yer not Mr Sutherland.' Lenny looked suddenly serious, and Jack felt sorry for him.

'I'm just ribbin' yer mate. I reckon now you've left school and you're a serious worker you can stop calling me Mr Sutherland ey? You can call me Jack or just plain Sir.'

Lenny looked very excited and smiled broadly.

'Yes Sir.'

'Righto boy, go get in the Land Rover.' Jack turned away and laughed quietly to himself.

'That them?' Lenny pointed ahead as they bumped along a rough track through the paddock. He'd spotted a small mob of Herefords standing peacefully in the shade of a small clump of eucalyptus trees that sprouted up through and around a rocky outcrop. The large granite boulders, bluey grey and covered in pale green lichen, looked like an assortment of roasted vegetables that had sat too long on a plate.

'Yep.'

'Where they gotta go?'

'Not far, just down there to the gate in the corner and into the next paddock. We just have to poke them through the gate and let 'em go. We'll run around the fences before we leave them and make sure the fences are all sound, then we'll head over to Fredericks.'

'Fredericks? What are we going there for?'

'Just going to let Syd know what we're up to. Once before, I blew a couple of things up out back, and he came roaring over the bloody hill carrying on like a prize turkey.'

Lenny laughed.

'He must have thought the bloody Krauts had arrived.'

Jack looked sideways at Lenny without smiling, and Lenny stopped laughing and sat quietly.

'Here, take the Land Rover down and open that gate, then park back there.' Jack pointed out to the left of the gate. 'I'll walk them down with the dogs.'

The mob bunched up quietly and calmly and wandered over toward the fence that led to the gate. Jack walked along a little behind them with the dogs hard on his heel. The cattle were quiet. He looked around him. This was one of the paddocks he'd been able to sow pasture into, and it was quite lush. He wanted to move the cows into another paddock before they chewed the grass too low. That way, it would recover more quickly. If he didn't look up into the gum trees, he could imagine he was in England. The undulating paddocks, the rocky outcrops, a sunny day that was still quite cool. This would have been the right time of year for Mary to have arrived. It would have felt like home for a little while, at least. At least, that was until the weather started to quickly warm up and the grass started to dry off. Then, it was a different story. Relentless heat, long dry spells, droughts and bushfires were all part of life in the bush. The concept of the bush exploding in a storm of flames in the heat of a dry lightning storm would be so foreign and terrifying for Mary. But she was strong, she was smart, she was practical and determined. She'd survive, she'd thrive. He thought about the ancient oak where he'd first kissed her and smiled sadly to himself.

'That was easy!'

Lenny's voice broke through the daydream. Jack was conscious his eyes were filled with tears, dangerously close to spilling over and running down his cheeks. He would never understand why she didn't come. He'd thought about going back to England and finding her and asking her why, but in his heart, he knew it was hopeless and would be nothing more than a fool's errand. She'd moved on without him. She may have had a new man, and she may not. Still, she'd spoken of her family, particularly her sister, with so much love in her heart. He knew she couldn't leave them and move across the other side of the world and risk never seeing them again. He now realised he couldn't ask her or anyone else to do that. He wouldn't be able to do it himself, so how could he have expected Mary to. He had been desperate to get home to Sutherland Downs and his family. He understood why she couldn't leave, if that was why she didn't leave.

'You right Jack?' Lenny's tone was cautious, and Jack wasn't sure if it was because it was the first time he'd called him Jack or because he was concerned about Jack's wistful mood.

'I'm good mate. Just off thinking about the past. That's all.'

'Really? The war?' Lenny sounded eager.

Jack turned and looked at him.

'No.'

Lenny turned away, looking uneasy.

'You know the Fredericks do you?'

'I've met Syd.'

'Righto. We won't stay long, okay? In and out, then get up the back to the scrub and get some work done. Grab the gate mate.'

Lenny leapt out of the Land Rover and opened the gate to the Fredericks house paddock. He shut it after Jack drove through and got back into the vehicle. They bumped along the track and parked near a machinery shed just off to the side of the house yard. Syd was standing at a workbench hammering something he had fastened in a vice and making enough noise that he hadn't noticed the Land Rover until it was nearly parked, and his lazy dogs had finally stood up to greet the visitor.

Syd emerged from the dark interior of the shed with a hammer in one hand and a small shaft from a shearing handpiece in another. As always, he had a scowl on his face. Jack looked at him and couldn't remember having ever seen him without that unpleasant expression.

'Problem?' Jack inquired.

'Sheared a pin. Trying to punch it out so I can put a new one in. Want to clean up a few ewes. Green grass is making em bloody daggy. Gotta get on to the worst of it now, before the weather warms up and the flies get started. Won't be long now.'

'No, just round the corner, I reckon. Won't be sorry to see a bit more sun, but not looking forward to the flies.' Jack replied, trying to sound neighbourly.

'No.' Syd grumbled. 'Who's that?' He pointed the hammer at Lenny. 'Is that Bob Henderson's boy?'

'It is.' Jack patted Lenny on the shoulder, and Lenny smiled.

'Yeah. Thought so. You got your father's bloody ears, you poor bastard.' The corners of Syd's mouth turned up in a rare show of a smile.

Jack looked at Lenny, and Lenny had stopped smiling.

'What're you after?' Syd directed his question at Jack.

'Nothing. Just dropped in to let you know Lenny and I will be blowing out a few stumps today.

Want to get some piles ready to light up as soon as I can get 'em dry. Early spring, I hope.'

'Righto.'

'You got any stock up the back.'

'No, just moved a mob of cattle out of that boundary paddock last week. They should be alright. There's a bit o' distance between you and them. Bloody near stampeded through a fence last time, you know.' Syd directed his angry comment toward Lenny, who just looked even more awkward, as though he was somehow to blame.

There was a flash of movement to Syd's left, at the side of the machinery shed, and Jack thought he caught a glimpse of Bonnie, but when he turned to look, she'd backed away and disappeared. He looked down at Lenny and could see he'd seen her. Syd looked to see what they were looking at.

'I just thought I'd seen Bonnie.' Jack looked back at Syd.

'You can't bloody miss her. Size of a bloody house.'

Jack was angry at how rude Syd was, but it wasn't his place to defend her. It had been months since he'd seen her. After she'd visited him, and he'd been over the next day to check she was ok, he'd managed to avoid both she and Syd as much as he possibly could. He'd seen her in the distance a couple of months later in town. He'd quickly ducked into a store, and when he had come back out onto the pavement, she'd gone. He planned to stay well clear of her for fear of another misunderstanding. They'd both been very fortunate that her visit had never been discovered.

'There she is.' Lenny was pointing toward the house yard.

Syd and Jack turned to see Bonnie hurrying as quickly as she could through the garden, carrying a bucket and heading for the door.

'Ey. Bonnie.' Syd yelled out, and she stopped, her back to the trio.

'Don't worry about it Syd, she's right.' Jack looked at Syd, then back at Bonnie, her back still turned toward them. 'We got to get going. This young fella's on the payroll. Hasn't even broken a sweat yet. Come on Lenny. Let's get going.'

'No wait.' Syd broke in, looking at Jack. 'Get a look at this.' He turned back toward Bonnie. 'Bonnie, come 'ere. What are you doin? Sutherland's 'ere. Come and say hello.'

Jack felt terrible for Bonnie. Like him, she clearly wanted to put it all behind her and move on, avoiding each other at any cost. He watched as she put the bucket down and very slowly turned around. Jack caught himself as he gasped, and his eyes widened. Bloody Syd was right, she was big. She was a very different shape from what he remembered. She was . . . she was heavily pregnant. He didn't need Syd to confirm anything.

'Yer having a baby?' Lenny spoke in a bright and innocent tone. 'Congratulations Mr Fredericks.'

'We are. At last. Gotta say I thought she was barren.' Syd tried to direct his comment quietly to Jack.

Jack's fists were clenched, and he was close to slamming one of them into the side of Syd's head.

'Turns out I'm pretty bloody potent after all.' Syd laughed as he looked at his heavily pregnant wife.

She must be close, Jack thought as he madly tried to compute dates. Surely it couldn't be. Surely he couldn't be.

Bonnie stood in the garden looking forlorn. She raised a hand and waved shyly at Jack, and he could just hear her say 'Hello'. He waved back and mouthed hello.

'You can go now.' Syd yelled back at Bonnie before turning to Jack and mumbling. 'Show's over.'

Jack and Lenny returned to the Land Rover and sat in silence as they made their way out to the paddock that Jack had been clearing through summer and into autumn.

CHAPTER THIRTEEN

Rosie opened the door and stepped into the warm waiting room. She smiled at Betty Clark, perched behind the reception desk. There were already a couple of patients sitting in the room waiting to see the Doctor. There was a friendly looking old lady, who smiled at Rosie, and a young woman with a boy with a bloodied bandage over one knee. No doubt a stitch, Rosie thought.

'How are you Betty?'

'I'm good thanks Dear, but I can't say the same for the Doctor.'

Betty was in her late sixties and looked like she should have retired years ago. Rosie always wondered whether Betty was eating properly, she was such a slight little thing. She couldn't help but think she wasn't the picture of health you'd hope to see behind the desk in the Doctor's surgery. Regardless, she was organised, efficient and devoted to Doctor Hadley

'Really? What's wrong with the Doctor?'

'He took a fall out the back in some mud near the woodpile, and he's twisted his ankle. It's blown up like a balloon. He won't be getting out and about for a few days. He asked me to tell you to go in when you arrived.'

'Ah, that's no good.' Rosie was disappointed. She'd been looking forward to travelling with the Doctor out to a couple of the local farms to deliver some medication, check on some patients and meet more of the locals. She walked across the waiting room, smiled at the young mother, then knocked on the Doctor's door.

Doctor Hadley sat behind his desk, with one leg up on a pillow on a stool. Hadley was nearly sixty, and although he was relatively tall, he was stout in stature. He had grey curly hair that, by nature, always looked untidy. He had glasses that he looked over the top of, for the majority of the time, except when performing surgery or stitching a wound. He had a frustrating tendency to validate every diagnosis with a story or two from his many years of practice, and Rosie was quickly developing a set of escape routines she'd activate at the slightest hint of a tale. But Hadley was a practical man, well respected in the community, and most importantly, he genuinely cared about everyone.

'You look sore.'

'I am, and unfortunately, I won't be getting out tomorrow.'

'Obviously.'

'Yes, well, we still need to get out there, so . . . I am wondering if you're up to it. The trouble is,

I don't have anyone who can go with you at such short notice. You can't take the ute. After the storm last night, the track will be as slippery as hell, and if there's a tree down, and there's bound to be, you won't get through. You'll have to take your horse. She looks like a good strong and steady mare, is she?'

'She is.' Rosie was excited. This would be far more fun than sitting in the ute and listening to Doctor Hadley's dry old stories all day.

Hadley spent the next ten minutes showing Rosie a map of where she needed to go, which farms to visit, which people would be expecting her and what to expect when she got to each of the properties.

'You need to see Bonnie Fredericks when you get to their property. Syd, her husband, will be there, and he will no doubt dominate the conversation. You need to get some time with her by herself. She's very shy and quiet, and she can't get a word in edgeways when her husband Syd's there. I want to know if the babies are ok. They're only a couple of months old. I want to know if Bonnie's ok. She seemed pretty down the last time I saw her. More than usual. More than she should. She's working hard with those two and no doubt, no support at all.'

'Ok, I will.'

'And if you happen to get time, I doubt you will, you might just ride over and see Jack Sutherland. He's by himself on Snowy Ridge, next door to Fredericks. Syd will give you directions. Probably only a twenty-minute ride. He's a patient, and he's a good bloke but a bit of a loner.'

'Oh, ok. Is he well?'

'Yes, he's well. Physically well, mostly.' Hadley seemed hesitant.

'So why do I need to see him then? It's not that I mind at all. It's just good to know a little bit about him first. Especially since I'm a midwife. Problems of the mind aren't really my expertise. Except my own, of course.' Rosie snickered.

'He's a veteran. Just one of many we have here. He's just a young bloke, but his wild and woolly appearance makes him look older and a little odd. Don't let that put you off. As I said, he's a good bloke. He's bright, and he comes from good stock. I just think it's not good for him, or any of the returned boys for that matter, to be off by themselves too much. A bit of conversation's good medicine. That's all.'

'Ok. He sounds interesting. Maybe a little scary, but if you say he's safe, I'll trust you.'

'He's a gentleman, a true gentleman, and you have no need to fear him. Just be patient with him. He can be a bit cranky if you get him on a bad day.'

The conversation went on a short while longer whilst Hadley packed a box with supplies, medicine, bandages, some notes etc.

'You better get going bright and early tomorrow. It'll be a long day. If you have any problems, get someone to telephone me. Ok?'

‘Ok.’ Rosie smiled and left the office. The rest of her day involved visiting locals in the town, some of whom Hadley would have visited if he’d been able, and some with young children and babies who simply needed a check-up.

CHAPTER FOURTEEN

It had been quite a storm the night before. Jack could generally sleep through anything. There was little that made him nervous other than the crash of thunder. At times, it sounded too much like explosions. During the storm, he'd be startled to look down and see his hands were shaking. But Jack was a practical bloke, and he wasn't surprised the war had had this impact on him. He didn't like it, but he acknowledged it. 'Shit, you've only gotta kick a dog in the guts a few times, and it shies every time it sees a boot. Yer reckon a bloke's gonna be any different?' The Doctor had smiled at Jack and acknowledged his coarse yet logical theory.

A stringybark tree had uprooted in the storm after several days of heavy rain and strong winds. Jack stood looking at the damage, his horse tied loosely to the fence. It wasn't much, just a few branches, not much thicker than his arms and legs, laying over the barbed wire. If he cut them off, the wire would hopefully spring back enough to stop a cow, and he could come back the next day with the wire strainers.

The sky was clear, and except for the smell of

damp soil and the puddles still full to the brim, you'd never know that the weather last night had been so rough.

Sweating already, in the unusually humid conditions, Jack took off his shirt and went to work with the axe. The dogs lay in the shade of a tree. They watched as he swung, blow after blow, swiftly and deftly, quickly severing the branches, dragging them off the fence. Cut free, he threw them against the trunk to be burnt in a year when they were thoroughly dried out.

A good hour later, he was mostly through the task when one of the dogs stood up and began to growl, followed soon after by the second dog. Jack turned to see a horse approaching, a couple of hundred yards away, coming up the track. He swung the axe down in line with the grain of the trunk. It bit hard, and he left it there as he picked up his shirt and wiped the sweat from his face. Squinting into the bright light, he focused on the horse and its rider. If he wasn't mistaken, it was a woman. He rubbed his face again and watched as the rider kicked the horse into a trot and approached quickly. Geez, it is a woman, he thought, and he quickly threw his shirt on and began buttoning it up. The dogs barked furiously, and he yelled at them.

'Siddown yer bloody mongrels, siddown.' They slinked off back under the tree.

Jack turned back to the rider, who was quite close now. His heart stopped. It was like time had stood still for a moment. He was hit with a tidal wave of emotion, and his heart thumped. 'Mary.' He whispered, just to himself. 'Mary.' His throat tightened, and his eyes widened.

'Hello.' The rider smiled as she pulled up the horse just a few yards away.

'Mary.' Jack whispered again, dumbfounded.

'I beg your Pardon?' the young woman answered with an Irish lilt that only served to unsettle Jack even further, as if that were possible.

'Ah, nothing, sorry.' Jack hesitated whilst he composed himself. 'You just reminded me of someone. You're the spitting image of a woman I used to know. A long time ago.' Jack couldn't help but look sad, as hard as he tried to smile. 'She was Irish too, like you, if I'm not mistaken.'

'You're not mistaken. I am Irish, although I've been here for a couple of years, and I am trying to pass myself off as an Aussie. I hope she was nice, was she? A nice Irish girl.' The young woman's smile was warm and friendly.

'You gotta believe it.' Jack said, recovering quickly. 'She was a top sort. She was the most beautiful person in the world, inside and out.'

'Beautiful, well I am pleased to hear that. Especially if I'm her spitting image.' The stranger laughed, and Jack blushed. Regardless of being embarrassed, he was taken aback by this beautiful stranger on the horse.

'My name's Jack, by the way.' Jack took off his hat and wiped his sweaty brow with his arm.

'Hello Jack. I'm Rosie.'

'Rosie? Rosie, you say.'

'Yes, Rosie. I'm a new nurse in town, and I've been out to see the Fredericks and a couple of other families.

'Rosie, who?' Jack asked quietly and slowly, trying to disguise the nervousness in his voice.

'Rosie O'Reilly.'

'Oh.' Was all Jack could say.

'Doctor Hadley said if I had time, I should drop in and see you. Syd Fredericks gave me directions to your house, so I thought I would say hello and see if there was anything I could do while I'm all the way out here today.'

'Hadley sent you all the way out here by yourself? A bit bloody silly, isn't it?'

'Why?' Rosie sounded defensive.

'You're out here by yourself. That's the point. I'm not the only bloke around here living by himself. Blokes who rarely see a woman, let alone one that looks like you do.' Jack noticed as Rosie blushed again. 'And what if you come off your bloody horse. No one would find you out here for days, other than wild dogs and bloody crows.'

'Well, I'm not going to fall off my BLOODY horse, am I. And, while we're on it, am I safe here with you? You're a bloke living by yourself.'

This new nurse Rosie had plenty of fire. Jack was surprised but realised he'd been a bit abrupt. He was protective by nature and by upbringing, and he felt an immediate and inexplicable urge to protect this woman, this Rosie O'Reilly. Perhaps it was just that she'd reminded him so much of his Mary. There was an uncanny likeness.

Finally, Rosie broke into a huge smile and laughed at Jack.

'What are you laughing at. The world's changing, and it takes a bit of getting used to, that's all. Women riding around the bush by themselves, talking to strangers, hell, even wearing pants.'

Rosie laughed again and was clearly enjoying herself.

'Pants. Oh, that's so funny. You're so old fashioned. Did you expect me to come up here on a horse in a dress, riding side-saddle, with a chaperone?'

'Ok, ok. I get it. I'm a bit silly.'

'No, not at all. You're just old Jack. That's all. Look at you, you must be forty-five if you're a day.' Jack was sure she was trying to get a rise out of him.

'Forty-Five, I'll give you bloody forty-five. I'm twenty-six and not a day older, and you're bloody cheeky. That's what you are.'

It was odd, but Jack felt completely comfortable with Rosie almost immediately. It was like he was greeting an old friend. A very attractive old friend.

'I'm sorry Jack. Your bushranger beard puts a good ten years on you.' Rosie laughed at Jack again.

Finally, Jack smiled, albeit self-consciously.

'How long'd it take you to ride out here?'

'Bit hard to say. The Fredericks property was my third stop. The other two were pretty quick. A cup of tea with Mrs Johnson at Meadowvale, dropped off a parcel with Jean Wright at Ballina and then the Fredericks's for lunch.

'What are you, the bloody postman? I mean postwoman.'

'No, I'm not. I dropped off some medical supplies for Doctor Hadley, but that's none of your business and for goodness sake, stop swearing so much if you're so old fashioned. Doctor Hadley said you were a gentleman. Pfft.'

Jack blushed this time. Rosie was feisty, a typical redhead just like Mary. She was damn attractive, and she was the first woman that had given him butterflies since Mary.

'I'm sorry, sorry again. I spend too much time alone with the dogs.' He paused and looked off into the distance. 'I think you've got a two-hour ride to get back to town. It's easier coming out cause there's a lot of downhill, but much slower going on the way back.

'That's okay.'

'No, it's not.' It'll be dark in about an hour and a bit, and look over there.' Jack pointed to the west. In the distance, the sky was turning purple and black, like a bruised eye. 'There's another storm coming in, and you'll get caught in the thick of it.'

For the first time, Rosie's demeanour changed, and she looked anxious.

‘What do you suggest I do then? I don’t see any sign of a hotel around here.’ She was doing her best to make light of the situation.

‘I don’t see as you have many choices. I think you might have to stay the night at my house.’

Rosie looked shocked.

‘You’ve got to be kidding?’

‘I’m not kidding one bit.’ Jack was perfectly serious. ‘There is no way you’ll make it back before the storm starts, and it is way too dangerous to be riding around in the bush during the storm.’

‘But it’s a road all the way back to town.’ Rosie argued. ‘If I get going right now, I can beat the storm into town.’

‘It’s hardly a road. It’s a track at best. And speaking from experience, I know how slippery and dangerous it can get when it rains. Even I wouldn’t attempt to beat that storm into town, and I live here and know the country well. Believe me, you’ll be safer staying here with me.’

Rosie looked Jack up and down as if weighing up her options and remembering that Dr Hadley had vouched for him.

‘I guess if I ring Doctor Hadley, and let him know where I am and why I’ve stayed, then that’ll be OK. I can’t imagine what this will do to my reputation. It’ll set the tongues wagging in town.’

‘I hate to break it to you, but I don’t have a phone. The nearest phone is back at Glencoe. Let’s get back to the house, and I’ll get you settled in.

Then I'll ride over to the Fredericks's and ring town and let them know that you're safe.'

'I'll come with you.' Rosie looked nervous. 'In fact, why wouldn't I just stay at the Fredericks's? Surely it would be more appropriate if I was there at their home with Bonnie, than out here alone with you. I mean no offence to you, of course.'

'None taken, but regardless, I wouldn't let you spend the night in the house with Syd, even with Bonnie there.'

'Why on earth not?'

'We don't need to go into that right now. You're just going to have to trust me.' Jack's tone was firm and gave every indication that the conversation was over, at least for now. Rosie looked back to the West and could see the speed at which the storm was approaching.

'Well, okay.' Rosie gave in but not without hesitation. 'I have to say, I'm not very happy about this, but I can see the storm will be here even sooner than you suggested, and you're right, I don't want to be stuck out there in the middle of all that.'

'Right, well, let me gather up my tools and fetch my horse, and we'll be on our way. We best move quickly so that I can get you settled in and get over to Glencoe and call town. Otherwise, I'll get caught in the storm.'

Jack retrieved his axe from where he had speared it into the fallen stringybark. He wrapped the axe head in a hessian bag, tied it off, and then attached it to the saddle. He untied his horse from where he hitched it to the fence and climbed quickly into the saddle. As he did, the breeze began to pick up, and the air temperature dropped almost instantly. The leaves in the trees began to rustle loudly. Jack looked at Rosie, and with a tilt of his head, and a nod of reply from her, he kicked his horse into a canter, and she followed soon after.

Rosie raced along behind Jack, trying to look about her and take in her surroundings, but the pace was relentless, and the path they took was littered with hazards. She'd only learned to ride properly since arriving in Australia and although she was a natural, keeping up with Jack was a huge challenge. He may as well have been walking on his own two feet he was so comfortable in the saddle. They ducked about the paddocks, between granite outcrops, around fallen trees, and past rabbit warrens. She had to really concentrate and began to wonder, in the end, whether the ride back to Jack's house was equally as dangerous as the ride into town would have been during the storm. Finally, they arrived at a gate, and Rosie could see numerous sheds a couple of hundred yards away on the other side of the fence.

'Sorry about that. It's much faster just to cut across the paddock when you're in a hurry.' Jack leaned forward and unchained the gate. Rosie didn't answer.

Once they were through the gates along with the dogs, Jack led the way toward the sheds. Rosie looked around the paddock. There was no sign of the house.

'Oh, I thought we were here.' Rosie looked a little frustrated. 'Where's your house?'

'We are here. I'm not sure what you were expecting, but this is my home.' Jack sat on his horse facing what seemed to be just an old corrugated iron shed. At least that's what it was by Rosie's standards. She stared in surprise. 'That's my house.' Jack pointed at the shed. 'That's my bathroom.' Jack pointed to an old bath sitting under a lean-to at one end of the shed. 'And that's the toilet.' Finally, Jack pointed to a small shed, with a wooden door some fifty yards from the house.

All the sheds were made from corrugated iron and looked like different sized versions of each other.

'Come on, we'll put the horses in the yard over there and give them some hay. I'll leave mine saddled so I can get over to Glencoe as soon as you're safe inside.'

'I'm still not sure why I can't come with you.' Feeling agitated, Rosie looked around at the buildings, the trees and the scrub just beyond. The bush didn't seem very far away, and she wondered what it hid within its cover, particularly at night. She wasn't sure she'd feel comfortable by herself in the shed, waiting for Jack as a storm closed in.

'Because I am going to have to move really fast to beat the storm. It's dangerous enough in daylight. Surely you noticed that just then on the ride back home. Well, imagine if it's dark as well, and you don't know your way around. No, it's too dangerous, and I am not going to risk you getting hurt.'

They dismounted and led the horses into a yard made of roughly cut timber. A three-sided shed with one face open to the yard provided shelter for the horses. They unsaddled Rosie's horse.

'Give me your saddle and bridle, and I'll bring them over to the house with us. They'll be better off inside the house and out of the weather.'

The tin shed, or house as Jack called it, was a small building surrounded by a veranda. The veranda had no floor, just dirt. Rosie looked nervously about her. It was clear the veranda's main purpose was to store farm equipment and supplies that needed to be kept dry.

Jack swung a wooden door open, and Rosie was relieved to see the floor inside was up off the dirt. It took a moment for her eyes to adjust to the dark when she got inside. There were two windows on each side of the building, but they were entirely covered by hessian sacks acting as curtains. Inside the doorway and to her left, Rosie could see a fireplace. To her right, Rosie assumed, was the kitchen. Saucepans, tin mugs, plates and cutlery sat on a bench over cupboards next to a slow combustion stove. Dividing the one large room in half was the frame of a wall that had never been completed. Rosie stood and stared at the framed wall.

'That's the bedroom through there.' Jack pointed at the bed on the other side of the framed wall. 'I'm afraid I haven't gotten around to finishing the wall. Didn't seem to be much point since I'm the only one here. One day I'll finish it off. No rush now.' The 'now' comment left Rosie assuming something must have changed to make him stop building his home.

This is going to be a long night, Rosie thought to herself. Nowhere to sleep, and the sound of rain on the roof was already getting loud.

CHAPTER FIFTEEN

Jack left Rosie soon after, taking off in a hurry for the Fredericks's farm. She stood for a moment in the little shack, warming by the fire, and more than a little stunned. What on earth had she gotten herself into? She was suddenly terrified she'd made a dreadful mistake and wondered whether she might make an escape on her horse whilst he was away. She felt like a prisoner.

'He's a gentleman. A true gentleman, and you have no need to fear him. Just be patient.'

Doctor Hadley's words came back to her. But what if he'd fooled Hadley. What if he was some crazy lunatic killer with half a dozen bodies buried in the bush. The war could understandably have some terrible impacts on a person. All that death and horror. No, that was just crazy. Hadley had known Jack for some time. Well, at least she thought he had, but now, when she really thought about it, she had no idea.

Rosie wondered how long Jack would be gone. It was dark in his house, hut, shack, however you might describe it. She looked around the room, put another piece of timber on the fire and then wondered what she'd do next to keep herself distracted and her nerves at bay. Jack had only been gone about ten minutes, so she figured she had time to poke around undetected and try and better understand this odd man, this strange and unusual man.

Rosie walked into his bedroom. She felt as though she was invading his private space, then mused at the fact the wall was just a frame, and there really wasn't any physical separation of the rooms. So was it really anything other than just part of the living space?

By his bed, he had a small table with nothing other than a candle and a book. She picked up the book. *The Power and the Glory*, she knew it. She opened the cover and flipped through the first few pages reading a few lines. He was a reader and interested in literature as well. Perhaps he was educated. There was very little else in his bedroom other than a chair with clothes strewn across it and a chest of drawers. A leather box on top of the chest of drawers caught her attention. An intricate and colourful pattern was embossed on its lid. It looked precious and surprisingly valuable and very out of place in this bare room. She found herself creeping over to look at it almost as though her betrayal of his private space might be discovered if she made the slightest sound. She ran her fingertips across the lid, feeling the texture of the carefully painted design and then chastised herself for touching and examining his private belongings.

Stepping back and looking again at the box, she was reminded of Maeve and the box she'd left behind. She thought about all it contained and the commitment she'd made to her sister. She remembered how Maeve had begged her to promise she would travel to Australia and how she had humoured her poor sister. Distressed, Maeve had begged her, the light fading in her eyes. Rosie would have done anything for her. Then there were the letters, the man that loved Maeve more than life, her brother in law. Would he have known her as Maeve or Mary. She hadn't thought to ask her sister. The poor man, seemingly with no idea about what had happened to his wife. To lessen her guilt, Rosie tried to reason with herself that Maeve hadn't actually asked her to find her husband, but she knew of course, that her sister had wanted her too. She had searched, but she had nothing to go on other than he and his large family lived in the outback of North Western NSW. She was surprised to find that there were a lot of huge properties in Australia. She hadn't given up, but she couldn't devote all of her time to the search. She had to live. She had to establish her own life. Maeve hadn't even confided in her that she had a husband until there was no time left. Somewhere deep down, that had hurt a little, but at the time, the war, and the environment, all led to strange reactions and decisions, and no one could be judged. Try as she might, Rosie often found herself wondering what could have been. 'Ah, Maeve.' She whispered as she wiped a tear from her eye. 'Okay Rosie, dinner. Perhaps if I fill him up with food, he'll fall asleep, and I'll be safe.' She spoke quietly to herself, then laughed at the image of Jack comatose on the bed, his belly distended from overeating.

Jack was gone for no longer than an hour. The wind and rain had set in. After unsaddling Bella, he strode from the yards to the house. He was relieved to make out the smoke coming from the chimney and the light around the edges of the windows. Jack was conscious of being excited to see Rosie again, although he knew he shouldn't be. Particularly since he'd nearly gotten himself in enormous trouble once already. His thoughts had wandered through what it would be like to hold her close and feel her soft and curvy body against his.

Jack pulled the door open and saw Rosie visibly jump on the seat where she sat at the table reading a book.

'Jack. You frightened the life out of me. How'd you go? Did you get a hold of Doctor Hadley?'

'I did.' Jack stood in the doorway, his oilskin shiny and dripping water onto the dust, his Akubra wet through, rivulets of water running down his face.

'You look like a drowned rat.'

‘Thanks.’

‘Come on, get inside. You’re letting the cold air in.’

Jack looked at the beautiful woman standing in this dump of a shack, bossing him around. It was like coming home to a wife, he thought and smiled. It would be like coming home to Mary, and his expression shifted.

‘What? What are you smiling at? Hurry up.’ Rosie moved forward and looked like she was going to shut the door on him.

‘Ok. I’m just going to feed the dogs and get some meat for our dinner. I’ll be back in a moment, and I’ll organise some vegetables.’

‘Done.’

Jack looked across at the stove and could see saucepans sitting on it, then looked back at Rosie.

Really?

‘Yes.’ Rosie answered. ‘I peeled some potatoes, and I’ve opened a couple of cans, so we have peas and carrots as well.

‘A feast.’ Jack smiled.

‘Quick, off you go. I’ll keep this place warm.’ Rosie pushed the door shut, and Jack wandered dutifully back out into the rain.

A short while later, Jack was back. Rosie looked up at him from the table where she sat.

‘Grab these will yer, while I strip all this off?’ Jack held out a handful of chops, also dripping wet. Rosie pulled a concerned face. ‘Don’t worry, they’ll soon dry out in the pan.’

Rosie stood up and took the chops from Jack. She turned around and found a well-used skillet hanging from a hook above the stove. She unhooked it and began to inspect it. It was burned black on the underside and scratched clean on the cooking surface. She lifted the skillet and made to smell it. She didn't realise that Jack was watching her.

'Does it pass inspection?'

'Oh, yes, yes, I was just checking.'

'It was clean?'

'Well, yes.'

'I'm not a pig, you know.'

Rosie had looked around the small shack as if to consider his comment and to judge him before she realised. She blushed. Jack followed her gaze around the room and was conscious of how this would look to a woman. It wouldn't have been like this when Mary arrived. If she'd arrived. He'd had plans, big plans. The place would have been five times the size, with a bedroom for them and one for their children. There would have been a separate kitchen and dining room and even a lounge room. He'd begun by building the absolute essentials, just enough to cater for his needs whilst he lived as a bachelor waiting for her. Just enough so that he could focus on the farm, the pastures, the fences and the animals. He needed to clear as much land as he could and, as quickly as he could, but not so much that he couldn't keep up. And he had sheds and yards to build, one of the most important being the shearing shed that he'd recently started. All of that had left little time for fussing about a house.

When Mary's letters had suddenly stopped, he had tried to distract himself by burying himself in work in the paddocks. The shack and his plans for the house just made him think of Mary and fret. The third letter returned to sender had plunged him into a depression that had taken months to emerge from. Living by himself hadn't helped one bit, but regardless, he hadn't wanted anything to do with anyone. Dr Hadley had been one of the few people he had opened up to, but he'd even been reserved with him and dismissive of his own feelings in a typically masculine way. He had it good, he would always say. He came home. He made it back to Australia. He had no right to complain, and he wouldn't.

'I know.' Rosie replied.

Jack was brought back to the present.

'What?'

'I know you're not a pig. I wasn't suggesting that for a moment. I'm sorry you got the wrong impression. I'm just fussy, is all.'

'No, it's ok. I don't blame you. Look at this place. It's ok for a fella, but not suitable for a lady, that's for sure.'

Rosie smiled, and Jack smiled back. They held each other's gaze just long enough for it to feel a little awkward.

'I am just going to put a dry shirt on. Do you

mind turning your back for a minute, please? It's not very private here. If you look carefully, you can see right through into the bedroom.'

Rosie laughed and turned to busy herself at the stove.

The skillet was hot, and as soon as she threw the chops in, they began to sputter and spit.

'Oh.' She shrieked in response to a crackle like a firecracker and leapt back from the stove.

'You ok?'

Rosie turned to look at Jack, who was still buttoning up his clean and dry shirt. She blushed and looked away. She wondered what he would like if he had a shave and a haircut, but it was almost impossible to speculate whether a handsome man was hidden under all that hair and beard.

'Yes. Do you have an apron?' She asked, looking back toward the stove.

Jack burst out laughing.

'Really?'

'I guess that's a no then.'

'You guessed right, I'm afraid. Here.' Jack picked up a shirt off the chair near his bed and threw it to her. She caught it but looked hesitant. 'It's ok, it's clean. Put it on. Even pigs wash their clothes.'

Rosie put the shirt on and buttoned it up to protect her clothes. She rolled the sleeves up over her hands and turned to face Jack, who'd returned to the table. The shirt hung halfway down her thighs. She smiled at Jack and curtsied. He just stared at her without smiling, and she was immediately uncomfortable. He had a serious longing look in his dark and troubled eyes, his eyes that she realised all of a sudden, she found very attractive. Thank goodness the rest of him was so unkempt and unappealing. Finally, he smiled and broke the stalemate. She turned back to the chops, and an odd shiver ran down her spine. She hoped he wasn't watching her, although she could almost feel the warmth of his eyes on her back.

A half-hour later, Jack was sitting at the table as Rosie served the dinner.

'You didn't have to make the dinner by yourself, you know.'

'I know. But it's the least I could do since you rescued me from the storm and provided the food.'

'Wine?'

'You have wine?'

'I have a couple of bottles put away for a special occasion.'

'Is this a special occasion?' Rosie asked, not smiling and starting to feel nervous and uncertain.

'Any visitor for dinner in my house is a special occasion. Especially a . . . especially a lady.'

Rosie was sure he was about to pay her a compliment when he hesitated, and she was relieved when he didn't.

'Ok, a wine, just one glass, would be very nice, thank you.'

Jack leapt out of his chair enthusiastically and walked quickly into his bedroom. Rosie smiled at how silly it was that she could see exactly what he was doing, although he was supposedly in another room. She watched, intrigued, as he crossed the room and went to the chest of drawers. He opened the bottom drawer and lifted out a bottle, and put it down on the chest of drawers. Then he slowly opened the lid on the precious leather box. She watched as he moved some papers aside, then some envelopes that he seemed to handle with great care, and then he lifted out a fine crystal wine glass, first one then another. He placed them on the top of the drawers near the bottle of wine. Then he picked each one up by the stem between the thumb and forefinger of each hand and just stood as though contemplating something. She thought he looked a little like he was praying at an altar. Finally, he picked up the bottle and glasses and returned to the table.

'Jack.'

'Yes?'

'Are you sure?' Rosie watched his eyes. The rest of his face was hidden by the woolly beard.

'What do you mean?'

'They are quite lovely.' Rosie looked at the glasses. 'They look precious. Like they really are for a special occasion.'

'They are precious,' he answered wistfully. 'And they were for a special occasion, but . . . anyway.'

‘Where are they from?’

‘They were my mum and dad’s. From their wedding, believe it or not. I brought them with me from the family home. As I said, they were for a very special occasion.’

She thought he looked sad, watching him closely, as his eyes seemed to moisten.

‘Who was she.’ Rosie asked gently and intuitively.

‘Someone very special.’ He whispered hoarsely.

‘You want to talk about it.’ She watched him carefully, waiting for his reply. He seemed to have drifted off to another faraway place. It was a few moments before he answered.

‘Nope. She’s gone. I just want to enjoy my dinner.’ She could see he was forcing a smile as he went about removing the cork from the bottle and pouring them each a glass of wine. Watching him, she felt safe. Any concerns of being locked up for the night with this odd recluse had faded. He was simply a man. A man who had lost someone he loved.

Jack and Rosie sat at the table for a couple of hours talking about the local people, how Rosie had nursed in Goulburn and Sydney, and all Jack’s plans for the farm. She thoroughly enjoyed the conversation, and the time passed quickly. There’d hardly been a gap in the discussion, and at times they’d competed with each other to tell a story first, laughing and firing questions at each other.

Finally, during the briefest pause in the conversation, Jack stood up.

'Well Rosie, I've had a really good night, thanks. It's actually been really good to have some company, but I'm beat. I've been up since really early this morning, and I need to get some beauty sleep.' Jack knew he had to end the conversation with this charming woman. Her presence was unsettling. It was all too easy and far too enjoyable. It had left him feeling a little like he was betraying Mary. Again.

Jack walked into his room, and going to the chest of drawers, he pulled out a pair of clean sheets and a pillowcase.

'What are you doing?' Rosie looked concerned.

'I'm putting some fresh sheets on the bed for you. You can't sleep in them.' He pointed to the bed.

'Where are you sleeping? Rosie looked very anxious.

'Relax, relax. I'm going to throw my swag down there by the fire. You can have the bed, and I'll get the nice warm fire. It's too bloody cold in the bedroom anyway. There's no heating in here.'

Rosie laughed, relieved and got up to help Jack. They made the bed, and within 20 minutes, she was tucked up in his actually very comfortable bed, and he was flat out in his swag, his face glowing orange from the fire.

'Night Jack.'

'Night Rosie.'

Rosie stared at the ceiling and smiled.

Jack closed his eyes, felt the warmth of the fire on his face, a spark in his heart, and he smiled.

The following day Rosie woke, unsure of where she was for a moment. There was a noise from outside, and the door opened. Jack walked in. His hair was wet and slicked back. His beard still had droplets of water from where he'd washed his face. He held up his hands, two brown eggs in each.

'Eggs for Brekkie? The storm's cleared again. It'll be a good day. I've given your horse a little hay. A bit of a feed now will do her good before you ride her back into town.'

Rosie sat up in bed, keeping the blankets pulled up to her neck. She was still wearing her clothes from the day before, and she felt like a wreck.

'Eggs are good, thanks.'

'You know, I love your accent, Rosie.'

'Do you Jack? That's nice.'

He turned away from her and focused on making their breakfast.

An hour later, Rosie was on her horse and ready to head back into town. Jack had insisted on riding back some of the way with her until he was sure she was well on the road, and there was no way she could get lost. She protested but was secretly pleased. She'd enjoyed his company, and there was no suggestion she would see him again any time soon, if at all.

At a fork in the road, Jack reined in Bella.

‘Ok. This is where I leave you. As long as you stay on this road for the next three-quarters of an hour, you can’t miss the town. If you wander off the road, I can’t be held responsible.’ Jack laughed.

‘Thanks Jack. Thanks for looking after me last night. It was good. Strange at first. I must say you had me very anxious when you insisted I stay the night, but Dr Hadley was right.’

‘Right about what?’

‘He told me you were a gentleman. A bit wild and woolly, but a gentleman underneath that fleece. I’ll see you sometime.’

‘Hope so.’

‘Me too.’

CHAPTER SIXTEEN

Jack rode into town, leaving his horse in a paddock at the rear of the Snowy Hotel. He checked himself in with the publican, took his gear up into a room upstairs, then headed back down to the bar.

'What'll it be Jack, other than a haircut and good shave?' Behind the bar, Archie laughed as he looked at Jack. 'Mate, I could turn you upside down and mop the bloody floor with that head of hair. I hope you didn't bring any friends in from the farm with yer. A bloody brown snake could hide in there a week before you'd even notice.'

'Righto Archie, give it a break and get me a beer. I need some Dutch courage to get me through the barber. I'm going over straight after this and getting tidied up.'

'I better pour a whiskey for the barber too.' Archie laughed away, enjoying his own joke. He placed a beer in front of Jack and picked up the coins Jack had thrown onto the bar. Jack downed the beer quickly. After the barber, he had a few chores to get through, including going to the hardware and general store. He left soon after.

An hour and a half later, Jack walked back through the bar, carrying a couple of bags. He nodded at Archie, who stopped what he was doing then gave a loud wolf whistle. Jack smiled and walked on without looking back.

Mrs Bourke placed the teacup on the table, along with a plate of biscuits.

'Come on Rosie. Come and get your tea while it's hot dear.' She called out.

Rosie bounced through the doorway and into the dining room and sat down with a crash at the table. Mrs Bourke raised her eyebrows but couldn't help but smile.

'How are you dear?'

'I'm good, thanks. I'm enjoying my day off. I think I'll get out into the garden and read a book while it's still warm enough.'

'That sounds like a good idea.'

There was a knock at the door, and Rosie went to stand up. Mrs Bourke raised her hand to stop her.

'You stay there and finish your tea dear, or it will get cold. I'll get that.'

Rosie sat eating her biscuit and drinking her tea until Mrs Bourke returned a few moments later.

'There's a young gentleman at the door for you dear.' Mrs Bourke raised her eyebrows again.

Mrs Bourke's husband had been the local primary school principal for eleven years before he retired and died just a few years later. She lived by herself and was very happy to let a room to Rosie when Doctor Hadley had suggested it. She enjoyed the company and having something or someone to focus on.

'Oh, a young gentleman. Is he handsome?' Rosie smiled at Mrs Bourke and knew the sparkle in her eyes would frustrate the old lady. Rosie couldn't help but enjoy being a tease.

'You're a flirt Rosie O'Reilly, and you'll get yourself in trouble if you're not careful.' Mrs Bourke pulled a stern face at Rosie.

'I won't, I promise. Who is it?'

'Some man called Jack. I don't know him. I've never met him before, and yes, he is very handsome.' Finally, Mrs Bourke smiled and joined in the fun as Rosie strode off to the door.

Rosie pushed the screen door open and stepped onto the veranda. Mrs Bourke was right, a very handsome young man stood on the veranda. He smiled, and Rosie caught her breath. He looked a little familiar, but she didn't know him. She cleared her throat.

'Hello. I'm Rosie. Mrs Bourke said you were looking for me.'

'I am.' He answered, then said nothing more. He just stood there, looking at her with a slight and very odd smile, as though he was waiting for her to say something. It left Rosie more than a little uncomfortable.

* * *

When Rosie had opened the screen door and stepped out onto the veranda, Jack had realised he'd forgotten just how beautiful she was. Her eyes sparkled, and she smiled broadly. She looked at him quizzically, and it quickly dawned on him she didn't know who he was. This could be fun, he thought to himself. It had been nearly six weeks since she stayed at his home and they hadn't spoken or seen each other, so why would it be a surprise that she didn't recognise him. He'd thought of her every day since she visited, but when he had seen himself in the barber's mirror earlier that day, he realised she probably hadn't given him a second thought. Well, certainly not in a romantic sense.

'Hello. I'm Rosie. Mrs Bourke said you were looking for me.'

'I am.'

He waited enough time to make her uncomfortable.

'And you're Jack?'

'No. I'm John. I'm Jack's mate. I'm a close friend. He asked me to come and see you.'

'Okay.' Rosie tilted her head slightly to one side. 'Sorry, who's Jack?'

'Jack. You know, Jack. He tells me you spent the night with him a while back, and you disappeared, and he's never seen you since.'

'I beg your pardon.' Rosie looked taken aback.

'Woolly Jack. You know the old recluse out at Snowy Ridge. Surely you remember Woolly Jack.'

'Yes, of course I remember Jack Sutherland.' Rosie looked a little annoyed. 'And I only stayed the night there because I got caught in a storm, thank you very much. Now what can I do for you Mr . . . err, John.'

'I have a message for you from Jack.'

'Well?' Rosie answered abruptly.

Just then, Mrs Bourke appeared behind Rosie.

'Excuse me, Mr . . . err.'

'John.' Rosie finished Mrs Bourke's sentence in a frustrated tone.

'Mr John, yes, would you like a cup of tea? I've just made a fresh pot, and I have some freshly baked biscuits as well.'

Rosie rolled her eyes, making no attempt to disguise it from Jack, who couldn't help but smile.

'I am sure Mr John is very busy Mrs Bourke but thank you.'

Jack cut in quickly.

'I'd love a cuppa, thanks Mrs Bourke. That's very kind of you. And I haven't had a good home-baked biscuit since I left home. My mother was a wonderful cook.'

Mrs Bourke's smile beamed, and her face lit up.

'Please take a seat, and I'll be right back.' Mrs Bourke pointed to two chairs and a small table further along the veranda. 'For goodness sake Rosie, let the poor man sit down.'

Rosie's shoulders slumped as she let go of the screen door, and it closed with a bang.

'Please. Take a seat Mr John.' Rosie gestured to the seats. She and Jack sat down. 'Now, you have a message for me from Woolly Jack as you call him.'

'I do.'

'Well?'

Mrs Bourke arrived with the tea and biscuits and smiled at them both in a knowing fashion as she poured their tea.

'Thank you Mrs Bourke. These biscuits would certainly rival mum's, and that's saying something.' Jack announced in an almost theatrical tone designed to take Mrs Bourke to happy places.

'Oh, thank you, Mr John, but I am sure you're just kidding me.'

Rosie rolled her eyes again and looked at Jack expectantly as Mrs Bourke walked back inside.

'So, Rosie.' Jack drew out her name. 'My friend, Woolly Jack, sent me to ask you out to dinner on his behalf.'

Rosie looked shocked and snorted.

'You're kidding?'

'Not at all. Why would I be? Is there something wrong with Woolly Jack?'

'No, not at all. And stop calling him Woolly. It's disrespectful.' Rosie was unsure why she had the urge to defend Jack.

'I'm sorry. Anyway, like I said. Jack is in town, and he'd like to know if you would care to have dinner with him.'

'Oh, then why didn't he come himself?' Rosie looked suspicious.

'He was busy with a couple of very important errands. But secretly, I think he thought if I came on his behalf, you could say no without it being too uncomfortable.'

Rosie watched Jack cautiously for a moment, assessing him as best she could.

'I'm really not sure. I don't want Jack getting the wrong idea. He is very nice, of course. I really quite liked him. But he is a bit gruff, and his appearance is hardly conducive to attracting a young lady's attention.'

Jack laughed.

'Yes, he is a cranky old bugger. Well, not so old, actually. But he was taken by you. Perhaps you should give him a chance and just have dinner with him. He's staying at the pub, and he said he'd like to meet you in the lounge, say 6:30?'

Rosie was struggling to think of an excuse.

'I can certainly see what he sees in you.' Jack smiled and Rosie's face filled with colour. 'Would it make it more acceptable if I came along to make sure you're ok? A chaperone, so to speak.'

Rosie looked at Jack as if weighing him up. He could see he almost had her.

'Well, I don't know you either. What's to say you're not some crazy nut case.' Rosie looked at Jack defiantly before her expression softened. 'Okay. I'm not busy, and I don't want to be impolite. But please tell your friend that it's not a date. It's just dinner, okay? And yes, I would prefer if you came along, just to begin with, at least, unless you can stay. I want to make sure Jack understands this is not a romantic dinner or some such.' She waved her hand about in the air to indicate all manner of possibilities.

'I'll be there. For sure. I wouldn't miss it for quids.' Jack smiled, then stood up.

'I really have to go, but it has been a great pleasure meeting you Rosie. I will look forward to seeing you tonight at 6:30.'

'Yes. Me too.' Rosie answered, albeit reluctantly.

Jack turned to leave.

'Mr John.'

'Yes?'

'Have we met before? It's just you look awfully familiar.'

'I'm not sure. Perhaps. I doubt it, though. I don't believe I'd ever forget a face like yours.'

Rosie blushed again as she watched Jack walk down the steps, cross the garden, and then disappear down the road in the main street direction.

At 6:30, Rosie pushed the door to the pub open. It opened to a hall that led to a lounge at the rear of the building. She could hear the raucous behaviour of the men in the bar still working their way through the final drinks that might go on for some time. She sped up a little as she passed the door to the bar.

Rosie was anxious and wished she'd never been so weak as to say yes to Mr John. Jack, or Woolly Jack, was a nice person, and Doctor Hadley had vouched for him being a gentleman. And, when she thought back, it had been a pleasant evening and good conversation, but that was many weeks ago and, being as busy as she was, she'd not given him that much thought since. Regardless, feeling a little snooty thinking it, Rosie didn't really want to be seen at dinner with such a rough-looking bushy as they called these men. But, she'd been brought up to be a good charitable Christian, be kind to all people and treat everyone equally, as best as she could. Hopefully, it was just an hour or so of being polite, and he'd go bush again and not come back for months.

Entering the lounge area and feeling a little sick with nerves, Rosie looked about the room, and to her dismay, it was packed. It was Friday night, after all. She recognised several people, you couldn't help it in a small town. By tomorrow the whole town would be talking about Rosie and the bushy. Bushy hair, bushy beard and bushy habits. Her cheeks coloured as she walked toward the bar. She recognised Archie serving. He seemed to live behind the bar.

'What'll it be, Miss Rosie? Nice to see you in here tonight.'

'I'd like a sherry, thanks Archie.'

'Certainly. By yourself?'

'No, I am meeting someone for dinner.'

'Oh, that's good. Who's the lucky fella then?' Archie winked at Rosie, and she blushed again.

'Ah, well, it's private Archie.' A soon as she said

it and Archie laughed out loud, she realised what a silly thing it was to say. 'Okay, okay. It's just a neighbourly catchup, that's all. It's with Jack Sutherland. Woolly Jack . . . they call him. That's not what I call him, of course' sounding almost apologetic, 'although he is . . . woolly.' Rosie paused, then added quickly. 'But it's not a date, okay?'

'Okay. So, who are you trying to persuade then? Me or yerself.' Archie handed her a glass of sherry.

'Thank you. It's just that . . . the man, Jack, is a bit . . . a bit odd. You know? No, that's not right, he's not odd, he's unusual, well he's a bit of a loner.' Rosie just couldn't find the words to describe Jack. 'He's a bushy. He's . . .'

'He's here now, I think.' Archie smiled at someone behind Rosie approaching the bar. Rosie turned around anxiously, then turned back immediately with a relieved smile. The very handsome and dapper Mr John was approaching, and she was thankful he'd arrived before Jack. In fact, she felt a little guilty about having wished she had a date with the mysterious Mr John instead of Woolly Jack. His appearance now didn't change her mind.

'No, that's his friend, Mr John.'

Rosie was surprised when Archie burst out laughing again.

'Mr John.' Archie laughed out loud. 'That's a good one.'

'What do you mean?' Rosie asked defensively.

'Mr John, I'm afraid not. That's Jack Sutherland. That's Woolly Jack.'

Rosie turned around, speechless. No wonder he was so familiar. It was. It was Jack Sutherland, bloody Woolly Jack fresh off the shears. She was angry.

'You . . .'

Realising his cover was broken as he approached Rosie and Archie, Jack prepared for the sting of the fiery Irish redhead's tongue, and he wasn't disappointed, boy did he get it.

'You . . . you deceitful, deceptive, rude . . .'

'Hang on, hang on, please.' Jack placed his hands on Rosie's bare arms, and she drew in a deep and quick breath.

'I . . . I thought I was . . .' Rosie stuttered.

'Yes? Go on, you thought?' Jack couldn't contain his smile.

'I thought I was . . ., in fact I was looking forward to dinner with Woolly Jack, not you.' Again Rosie looked like she'd been made a fool of. She shuddered and looked down at his hands. He realised his touch was affecting her, and he slowly released her.

'I am, I'm Woolly Jack. I've just been to the barber, that's all. It is me, I promise.'

'Why did you lie to me?' Rosie was calming down but still looked affronted.

'I couldn't help it. I am truly sorry. I could see you didn't recognise me and I thought I would have some fun with that. And then I quickly got in too deep to undo the story, so I figured I'd just beg your forgiveness tonight.'

Archie, who'd been listening to all of this, chimed in with an unwanted comment.

'You're right Rosie, he is a bit odd.'

Rosie coloured up even more. And Jack looked at her questioningly.

'I'm sorry.' Rosie directed to Jack. 'Anyway, you deserve that. Now, are you going to feed me or just keep me here by the bar, making me feel ridiculous?'

'This way please.' Jack led Rosie to a table.

As quickly as Rosie could do her block, she could regain her sense of humour, which it turned out was equally as wicked as Jack's. In the end, she admitted that if she'd been him, she would have done the same and enjoyed it just as much. And anyway, why spoil a dinner date with a man who was clearly the most handsome in town. His property and house mightn't be much, not much at all, but he was sure easy on the eye, and she would feel proud to walk down the main street on his arm.

'What have you been up to Jack? I haven't seen you since I was at Snowy Ridge. It must be six weeks.'

'It is.'

'Why've you come to town all of a sudden.'

'I thought that was obvious.' Jack looked deep

into Rosie's blue eyes, and heat rose in her cheeks.

'Well, I'm glad you did Jack.'

'Really?'

'Really.'

'So I'm forgiven.'

'You are. I've had a fun night thank you. But you could have told me.'

'Told you what?'

Rosie looked shy but continued, her words like dipping toes in cold water, testing the temperature. 'You could have told me you were such a dasher.'

'A dasher ey?' Jack smiled broadly. 'Well, I've never been called that before.'

'Oh, I bet you have.' Rosie gave him a cheeky and slightly flirtatious smile.

'Maybe now's a good time to ask you if I can take you on a picnic next weekend. Next Saturday, down on the river flats just out of town. We can ride there in half an hour. You'll like it down there amongst the willows and poplars. It's a bit greener, more like your home.'

'I'd like that very much, thanks. I do miss the green of home. But I don't think I could ever go back now. I feel attached to this country now. Too attached to ever leave. It's definitely my home now.'

'I'm glad to hear that.'

The rest of the dinner went on peacefully and happily. Rosie told Jack about her first couple of years in Australia working as a midwife in Sydney. After a year, she moved to take a job in a hospital in Goulburn before finally, in a moment of madness and looking for adventure, she accepted a position assisting Dr Hadley. The town population was growing rapidly, which meant work for a good nurse and, more particularly, a midwife. Jack told her about returning home from the war, spending time with his family and finally taking possession of his one thousand acre soldier settlement block in Granite Gully.

It was nearly 9:00pm when Rosie finally declared that Jack had better take her home.

'Poor Mrs Bourke will be having a pink fit wondering where I am. She called me a flirt earlier. Would you believe that?'

'Well, it's not for me to say, but I hope not.' Jack smiled.

Jack paid up their tab at the bar, and they bid Archie farewell.

They walked swiftly, Rosie's arm threaded through Jack's. It was only a short distance to Mrs Bourke's.

'Thank you for coming out Rosie. My good opinion of you only grew stronger when I realised what you thought of me when you knew me as Woolly Jack.' Jack smiled teasingly.

'Oh, please, don't say that. You make me feel terrible.'

'So it's a picnic next weekend?'

'It is, thank you.'

No one spoke for a moment. They just stood, smiling and looking at each other. Eventually, Jack leaned down toward Rosie and kissed her cheek, and her face lit up in a broad smile.

'I'm going to miss you this time, Woolly Jack.' The words came out before Rosie realised, and she blushed again.

'I have an idea.' Jack announced.

'What?' Rosie couldn't help but look a little concerned. What would this trickster come up with next?

'I have a mob of sheep arriving in town tomorrow, by truck, from my brother's place up North. They'll drop them off at the yards in town here, and I am going to drive them home early Sunday morning. It will take most of the day, but would you like to come along?'

'You know I'd love to Jack, but if it takes all day, I won't have time to get home. I can't stay the night again. Especially not now that everyone's seen us out together.'

'Well, assuming the weather is ok, then I'll drive you back in the afternoon. If we get started by 7:30 in the morning, we will have them home by mid arvo, definitely before dark. Then I'll drive you home.'

'What about my horse?'

'I'll bring her back in for the picnic. Do you need her next week?'

'No, I guess I can borrow one of Doctor Hadley's if I'm desperate. Tell you what, let me see what I can work out, and I'll meet you tomorrow to let you know. When do your sheep arrive?'

'All going according to plan, about two in the afternoon. Why don't you come up to the yards and see them there.'

'Ok. Now I must go. Mrs Bourke has turned the light on in the lounge, and I am sure she knows we're out here.'

Rosie stretched up on her toes and kissed Jack's cheek, and this time he smiled broadly.

'Goodnight Rosie.'

'Goodnight Woolly.'

CHAPTER SEVENTEEN

The local stockyards were located on top of the last hill before the main road from the south led down into the valley where Granite Gully was situated. As was very common, the town was established alongside a creek, named simply after it, Granite Gully Creek. It was a reliable water source for people and stock. This town began, as many did, when men rushed into the valley in search of gold. If you knew where to look and what to look for, you could still see the remnants of the rush that left the landscape scarred. Channels dug, creating watercourses to drive water wheels and sluices for gold. Piles of scalpings.

As Rosie trotted along the edge of the road, approaching the stockyards just out of town, she could see the first of three trucks had just arrived and was reversing into the loading ramp. Jack was waving and calling directions to the driver as he maneuvered the truck into position. Then there was a sharp whistle. It was Jack, and the breaks squealed as the truck stopped abruptly. The driver cut the engine as Rosie arrived, and she could hear the sheep bleating. She scrunched up her nose at the strong smell of the sheep on board.

'Hello there.' Rosie smiled and waved to Jack.

'Hello, how are you? Put your horse in the yard over there and come over while we start unloading.' Jack pointed to a yard where his horse was tied up. Rosie dismounted and led her horse to the yard, then walked back over to Jack standing at the back of the truck.

'We've got about one hundred ewes on this truck and two more loads coming. This is Gus.' Jack pointed to the driver. He was a big barrel-chested older man with jet black oily hair. His first task was to roll a smoke before they unloaded anything.

'How yer goin?'. He addressed Rosie, then looked at Jack.

'Rosie's the local midwife Gus. She's new in town, and she's come up to see what sheep farming's all about.'

'Yer a midwife then?' Gus asked, licking his rolled cigarette and adhering to his bottom lip while he lit it.

'Yes.'

Gus patted his stomach proudly and smiled.

'Not much use here, I'm afraid. It's all grog. Good beer.' He laughed at his own joke.

'Well, I don't deliver beer babies Gus, so you're on you're own with that one.' Rosie looked disgusted but laughed along with Gus. Jack enjoyed the exchange and was impressed with Rosie's ability to engage with Gus and quickly win him over. He was a rough-looking old bloke, and many women might have been frightened away.

Rosie watched as Gus unlocked a couple of steel boxes with mesh doors on the side of the truck. A dog leapt out of each, muzzled and ready to work.

'Git ere.' Gus yelled as he directed the dogs between the rails of the race, and Jack slid the truck gate open. 'Get up.' He shouted again.

The dogs bounded up the ramp, nipping at the noses of the first sheep before jumping up and onto their backs and disappearing into the darkness of the truck. A moment later, the dogs were barking furiously, and the first sheep were being pushed toward the gate by the mob behind. They burst out of the truck and down the race.

Rosie watched on excitedly as Jack counted the sheep off the truck. She looked up as the rumbling of the second truck added to the noise of the bleating sheep. Swinging around in a wide arc, the second truck sent dust billowing into the air, before the driver positioned it to back in once Gus's truck was empty. The driver got out and strolled over to Jack and Rosie. He nodded at Rosie but didn't disturb Jack, who was still counting. He seemed to grunt at Gus, who grunted back.

'That's Bruce.' Gus pointed at the other driver. He nodded at Rosie again.

'I'm Rosie.' Rosie added when Gus made no further introduction.

When the last of the sheep were out of the truck and in the yards, and the dogs had been called off, Jack greeted Bruce like a long lost friend, then turned to Gus.

'Well?' Gus punctuated the question with an upward nod of his head.

'Spot on.' Jack replied. 'One hundred. They look pretty good.'

'Yeah.' The word was drawn out. 'They're a good drop this lot. Last year was good for lambs. You'll do alright out of them lot.' Bruce smiled, and Rosie grinned to herself at the friendly face with its several missing teeth, including one right in front.

Gus climbed into his truck and pulled it away from the ramp, making room for Bruce as he maneuvered his truck deftly into position. No sooner than he had cut the engine to his truck, there was the sound of another truck. Rosie looked up to see the third and final truck pulling into the large area in front of the stockyards.

Jack glanced at the third truck but was busy at the rear of Bruce's truck, unlocking the sliding gate and watching as Gus sent his dogs in again to push the next lot of sheep out.

Rosie watched as the next truck pulled in closer and wondered what sort of character would get out of the vehicle. She was a little startled when a good looking tall gentleman, not much older than Jack, got out of the driver's side. She could see there was a passenger as well and she was equally surprised when an attractive young woman got out, followed just a moment later by a young boy, just a few years old at most. The little boy squealed, and Jack turned around immediately. She could see Jack's face light up as he burst into an enormous smile.

'What the hell?' He yelled out his hands in the air. Clearly, Jack was surprised. The two drivers were smiling. Gus turned to Rosie and winked. Rosie screwed her face up in question.

'That's his brother.' Gus told Rosie. She watched as Jack strode over to his brother and shook his hand furiously. He then turned to the woman, took her in his arms and hugged her tight. When he broke that embrace, he dropped to his knees and held his arms out to the little boy who ducked behind his mother's legs.

'Oh, come on. Give Uncle Jack a hug.' The little boy's mum encouraged him forward, and finally, he smiled and embraced Jack. Jack stood up, lifting the little boy and hugging him, kissing his cheek. He turned to Rosie and smiled. She was a little overwhelmed by the situation, feeling like an intruder, but she walked forward as Jack carried the little boy over to meet her.

'This is Tommy Sutherland. My nephew.' Jack beamed with pride. Rosie put her hand out, and the little boy shyly took her hand and smiled as she shook it.

'Hello Tommy. I'm Rosie. I am very pleased to meet you.' He smiled then buried his face in his uncle's shirt.

'Come on, come meet my brother.' Jack gestured toward Tommy's parents, and Rosie followed as he walked toward them.

'Rosie, this is my brother Edward and his lovely wife, Elise. Ed, Elise, this is Rosie.'

Elise stepped forward and took Rosie's hand.

'I'm very pleased to meet you Rosie.' Elise smiled.

'I know, I know, don't say it.' Rosie laughed nervously. 'Jack's told you all about me.'

'Well, no, not really.' Ed replied seriously and offered his hand to shake as well. 'But he is a man of few words.'

'Ah yes. That I can attest to.' Rosie replied and laughed.

'Rosie is a very new friend of mine. In fact, we had our first date just last night. Is it ok to call it a date?' Jack smiled at Rosie, who simply blushed. 'Although,' Jack continued, 'Rosie did spend the night with me out at Snowy Ridge a few weeks back.' Jack winked at Rosie.

'Oh really!' Elise exclaimed.

'No, O'Reilly.' Rosie countered. 'It's Rosie O'Reilly.' Rosie laughed, and the others followed suit. 'Jack is a man of few words and gross exaggeration.' She continued. 'I got caught at Jack's house.' Rosie turned to Jack. 'Can you call it a house?' Jack looked slightly embarrassed by his friend, who was well and truly capable of holding court. Rosie turned back to Elise. 'Well, anyway, as I was saying. I was out doing visits for Doctor

Hadley because I'm a midwife, you see, the local midwife, and a terrible storm blew up, and I got caught at Woolly Jack's.'

'Woolly Jack?' Ed raised his eyebrows.

'Yes, Woolly Jack. Your brother. And last night, he took me out to dinner at the pub. He surprised me with a whole new look. I had no idea at all he was actually quite handsome. But now I am wondering if he cleaned himself up for his brother and lovely sister-in-law, or perhaps so he wouldn't frighten Tommy out of his wits.' Rosie was rambling on both excitedly and nervously.

'He had no idea we were coming.' Elise chimed in. 'So I believe the honour was all yours, Rosie.'

'I'm not surprised he had a wash and a shave for you Rosie.' Ed smiled broadly, and Elise elbowed him in the ribs.

'Righto you lot. This is all good fun and at my expense, but the sooner we get the sheep unloaded and out in the stock reserve for a feed, the sooner we can get to the pub for a beer and catch-up. I want to hear all about home and everyone up there.'

'And I want to hear all about Snowy Ridge.' Ed added enthusiastically.

Once the sheep were all unloaded and safely in the reserve, with feed and water, the group all headed off to town. Ed and Elise were staying at the pub with Jack. Gus and Bruce were keen to get a belly full of grog before heading back to sleep near the trucks and the sheep. Rosie headed home with an invitation to join the others for dinner again and an opportunity to get to know everyone.

The next morning, Jack was mounted on his horse and waiting outside Mrs Bourke's when Rosie led her horse down the laneway next to the house and joined him. The sun was just appearing above the horizon to the east, and they'd be shielding their eyes against the bright light for the first hour while they pushed the sheep along. Jack had been able to borrow a mate's Land Rover for the day, so Ed, Elise and Tommy were coming along on the ride. Later in the afternoon, they would be able to return Rosie to town.

At the stock reserve, Jack and Rosie said their goodbyes to Gus and Bruce. They were heading off in their trucks ahead of the mob. The road they were taking the sheep along headed north-west out of town for the first few miles. At a fork in the road, the mob would be guided left. After that, the road deteriorated quickly to a bush track. Ed and Elise would travel ahead of the sheep to the fork in the road and set themselves up to direct the mob, then they'd join Jack and Rosie at the rear of the mob and help push them along.

'Can you just stay here and guide the girls onto the road.' Jack spoke to Rosie. She looked excited and eager to help. There was little if any trepidation, given she had no experience at all. Jack couldn't help but get caught up in her excitement and smiled broadly once he turned away from Rosie.

'I can.'

Jack took his two kelpies into the paddock.

'G'way out.' He yelled and gestured with his arm. The dogs took off at a race, out wide around the sheep. The sheep were rested, and with the cool of the morning, responded quickly, bunching up into a mob. The dogs had them quickly moving toward the gate, and in no time, they were funnelling through the opening and out onto the flat pan area where Rosie waited with her horse. She called out and waved her hands, mimicking what she'd seen from Jack and the drivers the day before.

'Go on. Get up girls. Up you go. Go on.'

The sheep turned and headed precisely in the direction required, and Rosie beamed with pride. Jack joined Rosie as soon as the mob were all out of the reserve and the gate was closed. They walked the horses side by side and let the dogs do the work.

'Well done. You'd make quite a farmer.' Jack smiled at Rosie.

'Hah, doesn't seem that hard to me.' Rosie smiled back.

CHAPTER EIGHTEEN

Jack and Rosie rode side by side, ambling along slowly through the scrub on the edge of the road. There was very little green grass for the sheep to pick at, so they kept up a good pace between watering spots.

'Are you happy with the sheep Jack?'

'Very. They're a good strong looking mob. They've got a good big frame, and I took a look at the wool on a few of them back at the yards with Ed. It's a good medium crossbred staple and looks pretty even across the mob, which is important. I reckon they'll do alright.'

Rosie watched the sheep as they weaved their way between the trees and rocks in a determined fashion. For the most part, she and Jack simply rode along the roadway, which in reality wasn't much more than a track. Occasionally as the sheep slowed down too much, Jack would send his dogs out behind the mob and get them moving again. Then he'd call the dogs back in behind the horses. Along the way, they slowed down to cross a creek. Some of the mob crossed the rickety wooden bridge, and some went straight for the water to drink before crossing. The dogs leapt into the shallow creek and lay down, panting and lapping up the cold and now very muddy water.

'Let's water the horses here. We've only got about forty minutes to go, and we'll be at the front gate. We've made good time.' Jack looked pleased. It was only two in the afternoon. 'Are you hungry?'

'Yep, but I can wait. Getting a sore backside though. I ride quite often, but this is the longest I have sat in the saddle nonstop for a few weeks.'

'Oh, sorry. Didn't even think about that. I do that much riding that I never really get sore.'

They both turned as they heard the sound of the Land Rover approaching. It pulled up near them. Ed, Elise and Tommy got out of the vehicle and strolled over to the horses.

'Going well.' Ed commented. His hand, shading the sun from his eyes as he looked up to the riders still mounted.

'It is.' Jack replied with a smile.

'It's not too far now, is it?' Ed asked.

'It isn't.' Jack looked at Rosie, then at her horse, and then at Ed. 'You fancy a ride Ed?' Jack knew his brother loved horses and was happiest out in the paddock working the stock. Ed looked at Rosie's horse.

'Might be a bit big for her.' He eyed the horse critically. 'She's a fair size though.'

'Excuse you two, what about Rosie?' Elise piped

in. 'It's her horse, and she might be enjoying the quiet ride along with Jack.'

'I'd be happy if you wanted to take her the rest of the way. It's not far now, and I think I've had the best of the ride on horseback. Besides, maybe I should take a ride in the Land Rover with Elise and hear the truth about Woolly Jack. Is he really the gentleman I'm told he is?'

'I doubt that.' Ed laughed.

Rosie slipped down from her horse and held the reins while Ed adjusted the stirrup leathers to his longer legs. He swung each stirrup up under his arm, then adjusted the buckles until the stirrup would sit in his armpit, a full arm's length from the saddle. He swung up into the saddle, and Tom whistled the resting dogs out of the water and sent them around the sheep. They barked furiously, turning the last of the mob away from the edge of the water and toward the bridge. Elise and Rosie walked around the sheep and formed a human fence line as the sheep walked across the bridge.

'Ha, ha, hut, hut.' Tommy yelled and clapped his hands, mimicking his father's actions, and Rosie smiled at him. There was quite a strong family resemblance, and she could imagine what Jack would have looked like as a little boy.

The mob were out and moving again steadily. The country had opened up and flattened out into gentle undulations, now that they had come down out of the hills that led into town. The Land Rover motored along slowly in first gear, and with little attention required, there was plenty of time to talk.

'Are you from the country, Elise?'

'Me, no, not originally. I met Ed at University in Sydney. All the boys in the family get shipped off to boarding school and then university before they're allowed back on the farm.'

'Tommy?'

'Well,' Elise laughed, 'he's a bit little yet, I think.'

'I know.' Rosie smiled. 'I mean when he gets older.'

'Yes. I'm not sure how I am going to cope with letting him go when the time comes. At least my parents are in Sydney, so he will have Grandparents not too far away, but I know I'll miss him, and so will Ed.'

'I guess it will be good for him to be around other kids, but it must be hard being taken off the farm when you grow up on it.'

'Yes, they all suffer for a while when they first go. You just have to be brave. The last thing you can afford to do is show them how sad you are as you say goodbye. And, he has some little friends where we are, so no doubt he'll miss them when the time comes. He even has a little girlfriend called Millie, who lives on a neighbouring property. She's the daughter of our best friends, Len and Irene Patterson. There are also a few families on our property, our family that is, his aunts and uncles. And then there are the workers, and some of them have children. Most don't. Mostly they are single men, living in the stockman's quarters.'

'There's a lot of people there. It must be a huge property, is it?'

'It is. It's over half a million acres.'

Although Rosie was focused on the conversation, the sheep work and new friends, something niggled inside as Elise described the big family. The family lived on a huge property up north in the outback. But there'd be time to think about the conversation later.

'Wow. You left Sydney to go live in the outback on half a million acres. Was that tough?'

'Sometimes, but on the whole, no. I was a little worried leaving Sydney, but it's pretty hard to say no to a handsome and soon to be very wealthy pastoralist.'

Both the women laughed and then shrieked as they hit a deep pothole and bounced in their seats. Rosie turned around to check on Tommy.

'You right buddy?'

'Yes Miss.'

Rosie smiled at Elise.

'He's gorgeous and so polite and a very serious young man too.'

'He's just a little shy. I can guarantee when he gets to know you he's not so polite.'

'What do you do for a social life up there? Big

family dinners, I guess, neighbours, Church?' After living in Granite Gully for a while, Rosie was beginning to really understand the social structure of country communities. Yet, this was a community on one property.

'Yes, all of those, and local dances. We're lucky, we have great neighbours, unlike Jack, so I hear.' Elise turned to Rosie and raised her eyebrows before continuing. 'As I said, our next-door neighbours are our best friends, Len and Irene. We are lucky they are about our age. And they have their beautiful little daughter, Millie. Don't they Tommy?' Rosie turned and looked at Tommy, who smiled shyly. 'She's your girlfriend, isn't she mate?' Elise looked at him in the crackled mirror over the top of the windscreen, and he pulled a face.

'Is she?' Rosie teased Tommy with an exaggerated smile and with her eyes open wide like saucers.

Elise continued.

'We have a small chapel on the property, so there is a service usually about once a month, but we are not very strict about that. A bit naughty, I guess. We're Anglican. What are you?'

'Catholic.'

'Oh no. It's over between you and Jack before it even starts. A bloody Tyke, Ed will say.' Elise laughed.

'That's nothing. My dad's a staunch Irish Catholic, and I hate to imagine what he'd do to any bloke I brought home if he found out he was a protestant. But I couldn't care less. I lost a bit of faith during the war, to be honest. I think there's more to life.' Rosie looked out the windscreen. Her mood had suddenly changed.

'You'll get your faith back.' Elise put a hand on Rosie's leg and rubbed it gently. 'It's hard not to, out here, in all of this beauty.'

'It is beautiful, isn't it?' Rosie looked out into the pastures, green and long. 'Late spring has to be the most beautiful time of the year, doesn't it?'

'It is.' Elise agreed.

Rosie looked across at Elise. She was beautiful. She had the same graceful and calming aura Mary had had. For the briefest moment, she felt strangely homesick. She missed her mother and father, and she'd never stopped missing Mary. She never would. The thought of her sister could make her throat ache and tears well in her eyes at a moment's notice.

'So what brought you to Australia, Miss Rosie O'Reilly?' Elise broke the silence and waited patiently for Rosie as though she intuitively understood this was a sensitive and personal subject. After a long moment, Rosie spoke quietly.

'My sister.'

'You have a sister here too?' Elise smiled. 'That's nice for you. I wish I had a sister, but just a brother.'

'No . . . I don't.'

'Pardon?'

‘I don’t have a sister here. She passed away quite some time ago.’

‘Oh Rosie, I’m so sorry. That’s awful. That must have been hard.’

‘It was. She died of Tuberculosis. She made it through the war, the bombings in London, devoting her life to everyone else’s welfare, only to be struck down just months before the war ended. Is it any wonder I question my faith?’

‘I understand, and I don’t blame you.’ Elise paused, giving Rosie time. Rosie appreciated the empathy.

‘So she wasn’t in Australia when she passed away?’ Elise looked confused.

‘No, she was home in Ireland with Mum and Dad.’ Rosie looked at Elise, and understanding she had confused her, she continued on. ‘I was called home in a hurry when Maeve was finally losing her battle, and we knew it wouldn’t be long before we lost her. I was nursing and had to travel from the city to our village by bus. It was a horrible night, cold, raining and miserable, fitting really, given what was happening. Anyway, I made it home just in time to sit with her and talk with her for a little while. It was the last conversation we ever had. We talked about a few things, including lost love . . . heartbreaking stuff, I realised much later. She told me to go somewhere warm and safe and to be happy. She made me promise I would come to Australia. I thought it was crazy, if I’m honest, but in the end, I just needed to leave, to get away from it all. All the memories. It was hard leaving Mum and Dad, but I think they'll come out here eventually. I hope they will.'

'Look out Jack.' Elise did her best to lighten the mood.

'Elise, stop it. Come on, I actually hardly know Jack. We got thrown together when I made what was really just an official visit to Snowy Ridge. There he was, this wild and woolly bushman who quite frankly looked terrifying. Fortunately, he was very polite and obviously a gentleman, even if it was well disguised. Then . . . next minute, well six weeks later, he turns up on my doorstep, handsome as Errol Flynn, pretending to be someone else and tricks me into dinner. I don't know that much about him yet, but . . .'

'What do you want to know? We are all very close. I can tell you all you need to know. He's a good man, just like Ed, and, easy on the eye, just like Ed.' They smiled at each other.

'Ok, well, believe it or not, we are almost at Snowy Ridge,' Rosie commented, looking ahead, 'the time has flown, but I would like to know a little more about him.'

'We missed him when he went away to war. Two long years he was gone. I have never hated the mail deliveries more. Every delivery might be the letter we dreaded. One day, much to our horror, there was an official letter from the department. It sat unopened on the table all afternoon. I think Ed had three beers, and I had a couple of sherries before we opened it. His parents couldn't. We had never been so relieved in our lives. Seems crazy. He'd been injured. Badly enough that he was coming home, but we were so pleased he was injured. You can imagine the alternative. It was some time before he actually got home to Sutherland Downs, in fact, months. He'd changed. He had grown up ten years in two. We were just happy to have him home and safe. He was worn out, but he was also happy. Like so many other servicemen, he'd met a lovely lady in London.'

'Really?' Rosie felt a pang of jealousy, although it was obviously unfounded. He was here, wasn't he? Out here in the middle of nowhere and very much by himself. 'Yes, so many girls ended up with soldiers. Though I have to say, so many hearts were broken too.'

'Well, in the end, Jack's heart did get broken. She wrote to him for a while, in fact for several months, and he wrote back. I know there was a lot of that with soldiers and their belles straight after the war. During that time, he moved down here to Snowy Ridge. I think he had some grand ideas she would come to Australia and be with him on his little property in the mountains. He wanted something that was completely his own. The poor girl probably got terrified at the thought of being stuck out in the middle of nowhere ten thousand miles from home with no family. And I don't know how well they really knew each other. No doubt it all sounded very romantic against the backdrop of war, and London being bombed and all that terror. I guess it lost its sheen when things began slowly returning to normal over there. In the end, she just stopped writing, and of course, she never came out here.

'That's so sad. And all too familiar.' Rosie was thinking about Mary.

'Yes, terribly sad. He hasn't been the same since. I think if she'd made it to Australia, we would have had our Jack back. I am not saying he's not still a wonderful man because he is. He's just different now. He's quieter, more withdrawn, sort of sad, always sad. Ed worries about him all the time, down here by himself. Got to say, we were very relieved to find him looking so happy when we got here yesterday. Nice to see him clean-shaven, neatly dressed, full of energy and enthusiasm again.

'Really?' Rosie did her best to look surprised. 'That's good. I wonder what's changed.'

'Oh, you come on now Rosie. We both know what's changed.'

Rosie blushed, and they sat in silence for some time.

Rosie watched as the two horsemen disappeared over a ridge in the paddock with the new sheep as she and Elise continued on toward the house without them. The Land Rover rattled to a stop at the gate to Jack's house paddock. Turning back to look at the sheds in front of her, she spoke.

‘Have you been here before Elise?’

‘No, I haven’t. Ed has, a few times, actually. So I know what to expect.’

‘It’s not much, is it?’ Rosie stared at the house, or the shed, whatever it was. She wasn’t sure how to describe it.

‘Well, there was absolutely nothing here at all when Jack arrived. I think he’s done ok living by himself. He’s a Sutherland. The land and the animals come first. Once he gets all that under control, good pastures, good yards and sheds, then he’ll no doubt focus on the house.’ Elise was obviously aware of the subject of Rosie’s gaze and her corresponding thoughts.

‘It must be overwhelming for those girls from back home who followed a serviceman out here. The weather’s so different. It takes a long time to get used to the heat. And imagine turning up to keep house out here, all by yourself, in that shed . . . house. I’m sorry. I don’t mean to be critical, and I’m not. I’m not critical of Jack. He is doing a wonderful job and with everything he’s been through.’ Rosie’s thoughts turned to Maeve again and wondered how she would have managed, although she would have been up in Northern New South Wales with a big family and probably a far more substantial and sophisticated home. The county would have been so foreign to her. Would she have learned to love it as quickly as Rosie was falling in love with this mountain country?

'If it says anything Rosie, the one thing these Sutherland men do put before their sheep and pastures, is their girls. They're good men. The best.' Elise looked at Rosie and smiled.

Rosie climbed out of the Land Rover, and Tommy insisted on joining her. She unlocked the gate and swung it open. Tommy ran beside her to keep up, and he took her hand as she waited for Elise to drive through. She smiled down at the little boy, and his bright smile warmed her heart. She remembered watching Jack hug Tommy at the yards the day before and thought what a wonderful father he would make. She was shaken out of her very brief daydream when she heard the sound of horses cantering. She looked up to see Jack and Ed approaching. She picked up Tommy to keep him safe, and he looped his arms around her neck.

The men slowed their horses to a walk as they passed through the gate, and Jack smiled at Rosie with the little boy holding her tight.

While the men were unsaddling the horses, Rosie and Elise walked toward the house. They let Tommy run over to the yard to join his father, and Ed had sat him on a hay bale at a safe distance from the horses.

'This way.' Rosie led Elise to the veranda that sheltered the front entrance.

'You know your way around.' Elise's poked at Rosie.

'I do not.' Rosie laughed, sounding indignant.

'I've only been here once.' She stopped in her tracks. 'Wow, look at this!'

'What?'

'Jack's done quite a bit of work since I was last here. See this veranda floor, it's all brand new. It was just dirt last time. And he's really tidied up as well. Last time, there were machinery parts, drums, and all sorts of farm stuff stored around the house. It looks so much better.'

Rosie didn't see Elise's knowing smile as she pushed the door open.

'Look.' Rosie couldn't contain her excitement.

'What now?' Elise joined in with the infectious enthusiasm.

'Look what he's done in here. There are curtains . . . well, sort of . . . not what I'd choose, but pretty good for a man. And he's filled in the wall.' She was facing the newly clad and painted bedroom wall. 'He has a wall and a door.' She stepped forward and looked through the open door. The bed was made, his clothes were put away, or hidden at least. He'd really made an effort. The cement sheeting walls were all recently painted. It was quite a transformation. There was a long way to go, but Rosie couldn't help but be amazed by how much work he'd done on the house since she'd last been there. She didn't dare look at Elise. She knew what she'd be thinking and would no doubt say.

'You're impressed?' Elise baited Rosie.

'I'm just very happy for him. It is much brighter and much better for him.'

'What is?' Jack's voice boomed through the door as Tommy ran into the kitchen.

'Rosie was just saying how impressed she is with everything you've done here lately.'

'And he's made a solid start on the shearing shed too. You should see it.' Ed directed his comment to Elise. 'You must have been working your fingers to the bone mate.'

'I have.' Jack was looking straight at Rosie, and she could tell he was looking for her approval.

'It's amazing Jack. You've done a wonderful job.' She smiled shyly and tentatively, and he looked pleased.

'Let me put the kettle on.' Rosie broke the moment and felt more comfortable as she busied herself with the teapot and the stove. Behind Rosie's back, Elise and Ed smiled at each other. She looked perfectly at home in the kitchen with Jack.

They spent what was left of the afternoon on the veranda, drinking tea and eating biscuits and the cake Elise had brought with her. When it was finally time to leave, Rosie had no desire to go, but it was starting to get dark, and Tommy was exhausted and getting cranky. Elise wanted to get him back to the hotel where she could feed him at a reasonable time and get him to bed. Rosie had work the next day, and Ed and Elise had a long trip ahead of them.

Ed and Elise said their goodbyes to Jack. Tommy clung to his uncle until his dad pulled him away in tears and took him to the Land Rover. Rosie had a moment alone with Jack.

'Well, bye Jack.'

'Bye Rosie. Thanks for helping out today.'

'Helping out.' Rosie smiled. 'I think we both know you didn't need me, but I did have a good time.'

There was a moment of silence as they stood looking into each other's eyes.

'So, I'll see you next Saturday for the picnic?'

'You will.'

'I'll be there at 10:30am sharp.'

'I'll make the food.'

'I'll sneak a bottle of wine into the saddlebag. Don't tell Mrs Bourke.'

'I won't.'

Rosie stepped forward and, rising on her toes, and grasping his arm, she brushed her lips across his cheek, holding the kiss just long enough to give it intimacy.

Jack watched as Rosie turned and walked back toward the vehicle where Elise had undoubtedly watched the kiss with an eagle eye.

It was a slow and bumpy ride back to town. Everyone was exhausted, and it was a trip made almost entirely in silence.

'I hope we will see you again sometime and not too far away.' Elise spoke to Rosie as they approached Mrs Bourke's house.

'I hope so too. Thanks for today. I had a great time.' Rosie replied.

'Look after my baby brother, will you? He needs some good in his life.'

'Ed, you can't say that. Jack's not Rosie's responsibility.' Elise chided.

'That's okay. I'll look out for him as best as I can. He's . . .,' Rosie hesitated, 'a good friend. Actually, you'll be pleased to know we are going on a picnic next Saturday.' Rosie replied in a happy tone.

Ed pulled the Land Rover up outside Mrs Bourke's house, and Rosie stepped out along with Ed and Elise. They made their goodbyes, with hugs and kisses on the cheek like old friends. In fact, that's how it felt to Rosie, like she'd known them forever, and yet it had only been a couple of days.

Ed made his way back to the vehicle. The screen door slammed shut as Mrs Bourke appeared on the veranda and smiled and waved to all the Sutherlands who had dropped her boarder off.

'Rosie.' Elise took Rosie by the shoulders. 'Just one more thing.'

'Sure, what is it?' Rosie smiled, but Elise looked serious.

'If you don't mind, please don't tell Jack I told you about Mary.'

'Mary?' Rosie looked confused.

'Yes, Mary. She was the girl that he was writing to in London. He was very hurt, very hurt when she just stopped writing and when she didn't come out to Australia. They had obviously planned it all together. She was a nurse in London. A nurse like you and also Irish. I hope that doesn't seem a bit odd to you. I can assure you it isn't.'

'Mary.' Rosie whispered.

'Are you ok?' Elise looked concerned. It was a moment before Rosie replied.

'Mary.' Rosie whispered again.

'Yes, Mary.'

'I think he called me Mary the first day I met him.'

'Really?' Elise looked surprised. 'You sure you're ok. You look pale all of a sudden.

'Yes. Yes I am just very tired all of a sudden. It's been a big day, and it's just caught up with me.'

'Ok. Well, poor old Jack. I think Snowy Ridge was going to be his big surprise for this Mary. That's why all the work on the home had stopped. I believe she thought she was coming to live on Sutherland Downs with us. He was going to tell her when she arrived, surprise her with a home of their own.'

'Northern New South Wales. Flat, red and hot.' Rosie was almost whispering again. Elise frowned.

'Are you sure you're ok?'

'I'm tired, that's all. You should get that little man some dinner and bed. I know how he feels, he slept most of the way into town. You're secret is safe with me Elise.'

'Thanks. Ok, you get inside.' Elise hugged Rosie again.

'Bye Rosie. See you soon.'

'Bye.'

Rosie turned on her heel and didn't look back. Tears filled her eyes, her throat ached, and her head was suddenly pounding. She pushed past the startled Mrs Bourke and headed straight to her bedroom.

CHAPTER NINETEEN

Jack bounced out of bed with a whole new lease on life. What a day yesterday had been. The new sheep had been even better than what he'd hoped for. He and Ed had done a wonderful job choosing some of the best of the Merino ewes on Sutherland Downs to join with the Border Leicester rams they'd purchased from a breeder way down south in Deniliquin. There'd been the ride with Rosie through the foothills that led out of town, pushing the new sheep back to Snowy Ridge. There'd been afternoon tea where Rosie had fit in with his family like she was already a part of it. She had obviously enjoyed Elise's company, and Tommy had taken to her like she was actually his aunt. The day couldn't have gotten much better.

Jack dressed and ate a quick breakfast. He couldn't relax. He strode across to the horse paddock and whistled Bella up to the yards. She came quickly to the promise of a handful of oats. He saddled her and headed out to check on the new ewes. All three hundred were in one large paddock, but he would split them in three once they were close to lambing to make them more manageable. He was expecting a dozen Dorset rams to be delivered this week. They'd be on a small truck that could make it along the track and all the way out to Snowy Ridge and drop them off at his yards. They would be put out with the ewes almost immediately. The good strong Spring had meant plenty of grass, and Jack wanted to get the rams out and to join the ewes while they were in prime condition. He had little doubt that would lead to a good lambing percentage in Autumn when the lambs started to drop. It was bloody exciting, and he smiled as he rode along.

Hardly a moment went by when he wasn't thinking about Rosie. He remembered what it was like when he spent those wonderful months in London with Mary. This was exactly what that feeling was like, although the realisation made him feel a little guilty. He wasn't sure he could wait another week to see her, and he was tempted to find some poorly thought out excuse to make a visit into town. He remembered how her smile beamed as she looked about his house and admired the work he'd done since she'd last visited. He knew the house still wasn't much. It wasn't much at all. But he also knew that being a woman, she would be able to see the potential, and her face had confirmed that. He was sure she approved. He was inspired.

On the previous day, when he'd finished droving the sheep, riding alongside Ed, they'd been planning and scheming. It was like old times. Like the happy days before the war. He and Ed had always had grandiose ideas. In their teens, they talked about their plans for Sutherland Downs, and its expansion and development. It had been the same for the generations of Sutherlands that had come before them. Jack was always comfortable with the fact that Ed would one day be head of the family. He was the oldest, after all, and that's just how it had always been. Ed had always been conscious of ensuring that Jack didn't feel any less part of the family dynasty than he did. Inclusion was a valuable lesson passed down from their father. It was how the family had flourished for generations in relative harmony.

Jack was aware that Syd Fredericks was doing it tough next door. It was a big property for this area at three thousand acres and a lot for him to handle as he got older. However, it wasn't big in Sutherland Downs terms. Jack and Ed had discussed how Syd's property and Snowy Ridge combined could be a highly profitable enterprise for the Sutherland family at four thousand acres. It was agreed that if the local rumours were true, Jack should be the first to make an offer and secure the property. They were prepared to pay a little above the market rate to expedite the deal.

Syd Fredericks wasn't old enough to retire completely in Jack's mind. The thought of what that might mean for Bonnie made Jack feel concerned for her, but he reminded himself, she wasn't his responsibility. If Syd wanted to retire and live in town, or back in Cootamundra for that matter, it might well be better for Bonnie in the long run. And for the children, Jack thought. Bonnie could make friends with women her age, and the kids could go to the local school when they were old enough. By the time Jack had arrived at Glencoe, he'd persuaded himself he was doing Bonnie a service, and he felt good about it. But something, and he didn't know what, still nagged at his subconscious.

'What'er you after now, Sutherland? You got a habit of turning up early, haven't yer?'

Jack looked at Syd and thought what a miserable old bastard he was. He could count on his fingers the number of times he'd ever visited. He could hardly be accused of forming a habit.

'I wanted to chat to you about something.'

'Oh yeah, what's that then?' Syd replied in a wary tone.

He turned back to his workbench and dipped a rusty bolt into a small tin of fuel before attacking it with a wire brush as though Jack wasn't there.

'It'd be good if we could sit down for a bit. I have a proposition for you.'

'Proposition ey? What kind 'er proposition. The only kind of proposition I'm interested in is one that's gonna make me a quid, and the sooner, the better.'

Good, Jack thought. This is a good start. Then Syd continued on.

'Unless o' course you want a kid. Sick to bloody death of their squawkin'. Mornin' till night. Second I nod off, one starts up. Then when she sorts that one out, the other one starts. You want a kid?'

'Ah, no, not really, thanks Syd.' Jack tried to smile.

'Yeah, well, I'm just jokin', of course. I wouldn't give young Charlie to no one. He's a strappin' young fella that one. He'll make a bloody good farmer one day.'

'Hah, that's good Syd, but . . .' Syd cut in again.

'You can have the sheila. Couple of quid and she's all yours mate. I don't need two, never wanted two. It's enough to feed one, and he hasn't really started eating yet.'

'Yeah, I don't think so Syd. I don't think Bonnie'd be too keen on letting go of her baby mate.' Again Jack tried to make light of Syd's humour, although it actually disgusted him. Frankly, if he could, he might just have taken them away and found a good home for both of them. But that wasn't fair. Bonnie was a good person, and he knew she'd be a devoted mother. He had to refocus on the task at hand.

'So what is it you want then, mate?'

'Twenty minutes, that's all Syd.'

'Righto then. Tea? Let's get a tea and sit in the garden.'

'Ok.' Jack would have preferred to stay clear of the house, but he had to stay the course on his and Ed's plan. He had to get Syd sitting and concentrating on him and the offer.

Syd led Jack to the garden and told him to sit down while he washed up at the tank stand. Once he'd washed his hands and wiped them partly dry on his shirt that stretched over his growing potbelly, he stepped up and opened the screen door. The main door was already open.

'Morning Tea Time.' He yelled through the doorway. 'Sutherland's here. Get him a tea and bring us a biscuit.'

'Syd returned to the table and sat down next to Jack.'

'So?' Syd questioned with a nod of his head and raised eyebrows.

'So. I've heard, and maybe it's just gossip, but I've heard around town you're thinking about selling up.'

'What!' Syd looked annoyed. 'Horseshit. Who told you that?'

'I've heard a couple of people say it. Just second hand, of course.'

'So what if I was? You interested or something?'

'I might be.'

'It's worth top dollar this land. Some of the best land in the district. We run right down to the river to the north and a bloody good creek running through the Eastern side. It's a bloody good property. You won't be getting this place for a bargain.'

‘So, can I ask? Is there any truth in it?’

The door squeaked open behind them. Bonnie pushed the door open with her bottom as she backed out, a tray in one hand and a baby in the other. She turned and smiled.

‘Hello Jack.’

She looked exhausted. Jack leapt to his feet and took the tray from her.

‘Hi Bonnie. How are you?’

‘Tired.’

‘I bet.’ Jack returned to the table with the tray, and Bonnie followed. ‘Here.’ Jack pulled a seat out for Bonnie, and Syd just sat with a scowl on his face, poking around in the bowl of biscuits.

Bonnie went to sit, and just as she did, there was a squawk from inside.

‘God strewth, do they never shut up!’ Syd’s face scrunched up in a frown as he looked at the baby in Bonnie’s arms.

‘Oh.’ She sighed and went to stand.

‘Here, give me her.’ Jack held his hands out, and Bonnie looked so grateful that it made Jack’s throat tighten a little. She disappeared inside and returned with baby Charlie. Fortunately, he bore no resemblance at all to his father. Jack smiled at Bonnie.

‘He’s a handsome young man Bonnie.’ He looked down at the baby in his arms. ‘And she’s a very pretty little lady.’ Jack looked at the little baby girl who was sitting peacefully in his arms. He realised he had no idea what her name was. How silly was that?

'I'm afraid I don't know your name, young lady.' He said, smiling at the tiny blue eyes staring back at him.

'It's Mary.' Bonnie replied proudly. 'We were a bit slow naming her. Charlie was an obvious choice for this little fella, Syd's father's name.' She looked down at the baby on her lap. But we were stuck on a girl's name. The whole twins thing was a surprise, of course. A big surprise.'

'Bloody huge surprise.' Syd interjected. 'You saw her Jack, she was bloody huge.'

Bonnie blushed and looked uneasy.

'Well, like I was saying. We didn't have a name for her until that nice nurse helped me. You know the midwife. Her name's Rosie. I'd just been calling her baby until Rosie suggested Mary. I think she might have had a sister called Mary who died, so she was so pleased when I said yes.'

'Midwife!' Syd butted in again. 'Why would he know the bloody midwife? He lives by himself, for god's sake. Unless you get the midwife out for yer ewes, do yer? By the way, I heard you got some new ewes this week. Where'd they come from then?'

Jack was completely distracted and hardly heard Syd.

'Ah, um, the ewes, yes, they came from my brother's property up north. And the midwife, yes, I've met Rosie, a couple of times actually.'

'Have you now?' Syd replied. 'You could do a lot worse than her, couldn't yer? She's a good looking young filly. But there's no need to rush yerself, you're still just a whippersnapper. Yer still bloody wet behind the ears. Take a look at me, I took me time, and I got her.' Syd pointed at Bonnie. 'And plenty of lead in the pencil. Them two's the proof.' He pointed at the babies. He smiled broadly, but it wasn't with pride for his offspring but rather for himself.

Jack looked across at Bonnie and could tell her mood had shifted. The motherly love and pride she'd had written all over her momentarily happy face when introducing Mary had gone. He couldn't be sure whether it was Syd's constant self-centred and thoughtless banter or whether it had been his announcement he knew Rosie and Syd's subsequent comments. Still, he reminded himself, she wasn't his responsibility, no matter how his conscious nagged at him.

'Well, you better get on with it then.' Syd's scowl had returned, and he eyeballed Jack.

'Sorry?' Jack replied.

'Get yer offer on the table, and I'll consider it.'

'What offer?' Bonnie chimed in.

'Do you mind?' Syd looked at her dismissively.

'It's ok. Some other time.' Jack decided it was best to drop it for now.

'Come on. If I've been talking to others about it, then you'd be smart if you got your offer in before you lose your chance.'

'But you said . . .' Jack started.

'Don't worry about what I said. Just do yer

talkin' while I'm prepared to listen and hurry up before I change me mind.'

'About what? What offer?' Bonnie tried again, starting to sound anxious.

'It's nothing Bonnie, really. It's time I got on my way.' Jack tried anxiously to back out.

'Make your offer Boy. It's now or never.'

Bonnie watched the exchange, her expression not hiding her concern.

'Well.' Jack looked at Bonnie and really didn't want to continue. Regardless, he didn't want to hear on the bush telegraph that Syd had sold out to another person in three weeks' time.

'Thirty-two pounds an acre.' Jack had turned back to Syd and was observing his eyes, looking for his reaction. He wasn't sure, but he thought it was favourable. Well hidden, but favourable. 'It's a good fair price. I'd buy all your stock separately, or you could sell them yourself.'

Jack was startled when Syd broke into peels of laughter. It wasn't genuine, and he wasn't much of an actor, but it did suffice to convey his message. He followed up in words.

'Don't insult me Boy. I told you I'm not selling. I just wanted to know what you were prepared to pay. I'll be on this property until the day I die, and then, it will be young Charlie's property. So pack up your pipe dreams in yer saddlebag and take 'em back home to your Snowy Ridge.'

Jack stood up as anger bubbled up within him, he'd had enough. He'd go home and rethink his plans. There were other equally as good and better properties in the district. He'd show this old bastard what a Sutherland was made of. He thought about Sutherland Downs and all that his family had achieved over generations. He instantly recovered from the disappointment and insult of this failed transaction. In fact, this failure would be the impetus for his family's future success and dominance in this district. The success that would come a damn sight sooner than Sydney bloody Fredericks could ever imagine.

'You've made your point, Fredericks. Good luck with the sale.' Jack stood up and made to leave when he realised he was still holding baby Mary. He felt a terrible pang of guilt and looked at Bonnie for the first time since the discussion had become heated. She looked distressed.

Syd stood up and eyed Jack through squinted eyes. His mouth was set hard in a straight line, and he was almost grinding his teeth in agitation. Jack looked down at Mary, who was still watching him through knowing little eyes. He held her out to Syd. Syd looked down at her, then back at Jack and turned on his heels and walked off to the machinery shed where he'd been working when Jack arrived.

Looking down, Jack could see Mary was about to start crying, and he pulled her in close to his chest and made a soft cooing sound. It was damn hard to stay so angry and bitter with such a beautiful little face looking at him.

'What are you doing Jack?' Bonnie's voice was quiet and steady.

'What do you mean?' Jack tried to look like he didn't understand the question, but he did.

'You know what I'm asking. Why are you trying to buy the farm out from under us, under me, the babies?' Bonnie's tone was growing bitter. He could sense she felt betrayed.

'It would set you up Bonnie. And your babies as well. You could live in town, or somewhere else. It would be good for you. You'd have friends. Your husband could retire.'

'And sit in the pub, like my dad did and spend all our money until it runs out and then ship Mary off to marry some horrible old man that no other woman ever wanted.' Bonnie was getting angry and raising her voice.

'Sssshhh. Bonnie, keep it down. For god's sake, he'll hear you.'

'I don't care if he does. I don't know anything about this talk of selling. Not that he'd ever tell me anyway. But this is my home now Jack. I haven't lived with him,' she pointed aggressively in the direction of the shed where the sound of hammering had started, 'and put up with his mean hearted treatment for the last seven years, just to have some rich smart aleck come in and pull the rug out from under me again. I don't deserve this. I deserve to be treated with decency. This is my farm too, you know, by law. And this is Charlie's farm and Mary's farm, and this is their future. I thought you cared about family. I thought you were different Jack. Here . . .' She reached toward Mary, 'give me her.'

Jack handed Mary over and watched as Bonnie settled her on her spare hip. It was obvious she was adept at handling both babies at once. No doubt she did all the work herself, and Syd contributed little if anything to their care. He was struck dumb by her outburst. He hadn't expected it. He figured she might question the motivations, but her reaction floored him. In truth, he hadn't wanted to discuss the issue in front of her at all. Perhaps subconsciously, he did know how she would react and why she would feel the way she did. He'd gone ahead with the proposal regardless, and he was angry and disappointed with himself.

'I should go.'

'You should.'

'I'm sorry Bonnie. I didn't mean to make you so upset.'

'Then just how upset did you mean to make me Jack? Would just a little have been OK?'

'You know what I mean. I'm sorry, what else can I say.'

'You've hurt me and disappointed me.'

'I know, I know that now. I won't bring this up again. You have my word.'

'Will you promise me you'll put our children first?' Bonnie's anger had subsided, and she looked sad.

'What?' Jack couldn't hide his confusion and uncertainty at her turn of phrase.

'My children. Will you promise me you'll put my children first . . . For me?'

'I will.' Jack responded quietly, searching her eyes for an answer to a question he would never dare to ask. He looked back down at Baby Charlie and then Mary. He could have sworn Mary smiled at him, but she couldn't have, she was too little. He looked back at Bonnie, her eyes wet with tears.

'Goodbye Bonnie.'

She was silent as he walked back to his horse, mounted it and rode off. As he shut the house paddock gate behind him, he looked back. Bonnie was still standing in the garden, watching him.

CHAPTER TWENTY

It was a long week, but perhaps not long enough for Jack. There were things, silent and hidden from his consciousness, that were eating at him. He hadn't had a moment all week where he hadn't felt slightly anxious, where his stomach hadn't fluttered. He hadn't felt much like eating. He'd opened a bottle of whiskey but had only drained it to just below the neck. He hadn't been able to concentrate on any of the tasks he'd planned, knocking off early each day and just sitting on the veranda staring out into the paddocks. He'd spent a lot of time thinking about Mary. Far more than he had since he'd met Rosie, and it was almost a relief for his guilty conscience to put her back where she belonged, as number one. Whether he deserved to feel guilty or not, it didn't help how he felt. The trouble was, he had strong feelings for Rosie now, very strong. And then there was Bonnie and her children. 'Our children,' she had said before correcting herself. Surely not. He couldn't even form the words in his thoughts. And Mary, baby Mary named after Rosie's sister Mary who'd passed away. There must have been a million Marys in Ireland. He was finally going around the bend and was probably facing a breakdown. He'd been as strong as he could for as long as he could, but he knew of plenty of servicemen who'd never been right again after returning from the war. Who'd he been kidding? He thought he was tough, sensible, pragmatic. But now, everything, absolutely everything, was getting on top of him. His head ached. He had no choice but to shake himself out of this and get going. Rosie was expecting him at 10:30, and there'd been no word to say anything had changed, although part of him wished the picnic had been cancelled just while he got his head together.

'Look at you, Mr Sutherland. You look very handsome, don't you?'

'Thank you Mrs Bourke, but please call me Jack.'

'Jack it is then. Young Rosie will be with you in just a minute. She is wrapping up the last of the sandwiches. She was a bit slow getting out of bed this morning. Unusual, actually, but she's almost ready.'

'Oh, that's fine, there's no hurry.' Jack turned around to make sure Bella was settled where he'd tied her and Rosie's horse to the top wire on Mrs Bourke's garden fence. The last thing he wanted was for her to shy and break a rein.

'I'll go and see how she's going.' Mrs Bourke retreated behind the screen door and left Jack waiting on the veranda, nervously fidgeting with the rim of his hat.

'Good morning Jack.'

Jack swung around to see Rosie standing in the doorway. As always, the sight of her made his heart race. He smiled.

'Morning Rosie. You all set?'

'Sure.' She looked uncertain and wasn't smiling.

'Everything ok?'

'Yes, of course. Let's get going, shall we.' She seemed to be avoiding eye contact. That anxious feeling settled in the pit of Jack's stomach again.

The horses walked at a steady pace on the edge of the road heading east out of town. It was only a few miles to travel, and although the conversation was sparse, the views of the valleys, hills and even mountains in the distance kept their attention.

'It's beautiful here, isn't it?' It had been a couple of miles since Rosie had spoken.

'It is. It's not only just amazing scenery, but it's damn good farmland.'

'Yes. I can see that.'

They walked along for a few more minutes in silence.

'Why did you come here Jack?'

'Why did I come here. You mean why did I move to Snowy Ridge?'

'Yes, Snowy Ridge. Why did you move here

when you had everything up north on the Sutherland Station?'

'Sutherland Downs, yes, I guess I did. But I wanted something of my own. I wanted to prove I could make it on my own. I wanted to be able to show I was the real deal, self-made, I guess. I've always thought to be genuinely successful, you had to make it on your own. So here I am.'

'You wanted to show you were the real deal?'

'Yes.'

'Who to?'

'Everyone and anyone, I guess.'

'Surely not your family and friends. Surely not. You've just come back from travelling halfway around the world to fight for your king and country. Surely that makes you the real deal. It does to me.'

'Thank you.'

They rode on in silence until Jack announced they were close to the picnic area. They turned off the road and followed a rough bush track for about half a mile. In contrast to the undulating country they'd been riding through, the picnic area was a couple of acres of river flats. Early pioneers had planted oaks and elms, and they stood in full leaf, providing shelter for the visitors. The road in was lined with poplars, and the riverbank was flanked by willows. It was quite an oasis out there in the middle of the Australian bush. There was even a small rotunda that had been recently painted, perched right in the middle of the area.

'This is pretty Jack.'

'Yes, it's nice down here. It's a bit of a change from the gum trees, much as I love them.'

'Yes. It just feels cooler here, amongst these English trees.' Rosie looked around her.

They sat and ate their sandwiches and talked about the week they'd each had. They spent some time each expressing their fondness for Tommy, and Rosie indicated how much she'd enjoyed Ed's and especially Elise's company.

'Elise was lovely.'

'I'm glad you liked her.' Jack smiled at Rosie. He poured them each a glass of wine.

'Sorry about the tin mugs. That's about the best you can expect on horseback.'

'Fine with me, I'm not precious, I can assure you.'

'Good. That's good.'

Jack took a sip of his wine, looked around the picnic area, then settled his gaze on Rosie. She sure was beautiful. Her red hair shone brightly where the dappled sunlight broke through the trees. Her blue eyes were bright, and she had a wise look to her. An old soul, he thought wistfully.

Rosie turned her eyes first to look at Jack, then her face. She held his gaze in silence for some time. He looked down at her hand and gathered it up in his before looking back at her. If he didn't know better, he'd have sworn there was tears in her eyes. Tears of happiness, he hoped, with all of his heart.

'Jack.' Her voice was almost a whisper.

'Yes?'

'I . . . I wondered why you are by yourself?'

'What do you mean?'

'Why are you by yourself? Why aren't you married? Why don't you have a girl?'

'Why?' Jack looked uncertain and wondered where this was headed.

'Look at you Jack. You are handsome, you're a good person, you're from a good family, you have property. Hell, anyone could see you're a catch. So why are you by yourself?'

'You've seen my house.' Jack tried to make light of the questions.

'Come on, you know what I mean.'

'Well, I could ask you the same question. Look at you, you are . . . you're beautiful, you're fun, you're smart, you are strong, need I go on?'

Rosie smile at him.

'You can if you like.' She gave a half-hearted laugh.

They sat again for a moment. His flurry of complements didn't seem to have the impact he'd hoped they would.

'Rosie.' He spoke slowly and carefully. 'I know this is all very quick. Very sudden, but you must know how I feel about you. I'm sure you do and, and unless I am mistaken,' he hesitated, 'you feel something too. Don't you?'

'I do Jack. Of course I do, but . . .'

'But what?'

Rosie was silent, and Jack just sat, holding her hand, giving her all the time she needed to form the words she was trying to say. Eventually, she seemed to steel herself and began.

'I came to Australia for a reason Jack.'

He sat silently, watching and wondering where this was headed. Rosie spoke slowly and with a look of reflection in her eyes.

'I came to find someone. A man.' She looked at him with a deep sadness that made him want to hold her and protect her from whatever it was. 'I looked and looked, but it was hopeless, I couldn't find him. I gave up a long time ago and accepted I would never find him.'

Jack was relieved.

'But now I think I may have found him.' She smiled sadly.

'Me?' Jack smiled and felt a warm flush of emotion flood through him. I'm her dream man, he thought. Is that what she's telling me? Regardless, something still gnawed away at his core like a termite deep in the frame of a building, rendering it fragile against the rigours of a storm. There was no happiness in her expression. On the surface, everything seemed ok, but he was blanketed by an overwhelming feeling that everything was going to come unexpectedly crashing down.

'Maybe. Maybe it is you Jack. I'm not sure.'

'Let's walk Jack.' Rosie stood and waited for Jack. He stood, and she studied him closely. She could be in no doubt how he felt about her. Not only did he tell her openly, but his eyes spoke volumes. They walked down toward the edge of the creek that wound its way along the edge of the picnic area. The current was strong as it flowed around stone worn over centuries and pebbles that had only recently rattled into position, shortly before tumbling on again.

'Look. A fish!' Rosie followed Jack's gaze and could just make out the small trout, sheltering near a rock, nose pointing upstream, tail waving like a flag gently blowing in a breeze. Rosie smiled and thought how perfect the day could have been. But would it be perfect much longer? She would know soon enough.

'Jack, when I said I came to Australia looking for a man, I didn't mean I was looking for a man for me.' He looked disappointed, and her heart sank. 'Wait, just hear me out.'

'Okay.' He reached for her hand to hold it as they walked, but she pulled away.

'I came to try and find a man for someone else, for my sister.'

'That's kind of you.' Jack smiled.

'Please, Jack, this is hard enough as it is.'

'Right, yes, sorry, go on.'

Rosie stopped walking and turned to face Jack. She offered both her hands, and he took them, looking deep into her tormented eyes.

'My sister Maeve, or Mary as we . . .' Rosie paused and gathered her emotions before they spiralled out of control. 'She was married toward the end of the war to an Australian, a soldier, I believe, in secret. She didn't tell anyone, not Mum and Dad, not even me. I don't really understand why.'

Jack shivered, and his breathing began to hasten. He was staring into her eyes with such intensity she was frightened, not of him, but for him.

'Jack . . .' Rosie felt the tears stream down her face, and her voice cracked. Jack's eyes were filled with tears. 'Jack, my sister Mary was a nurse in London.' Jacks breathing was shallow and quick. She could see he was desperately trying to keep control in the way men always do until they can no longer. There was no response from Jack. She supposed he couldn't form words. 'Jack . . ., my sister Mary was sick, terribly sick. She passed away.'

'No.' Jack just managed to force the word out. 'No, she's not my Mary. You don't understand. My Mary, my wife, was Mary Kelly, not Mary O'Reilly. You see? It's not her.'

It was too much for Rosie, and she let go of Jack's hands and covered her face and wept. She'd found him. She had found Mary's JS. It was a moment before she was able to look at Jack. He stood deathly still, his lips pursed, tears streaking his face.

'I'm so sorry Jack.'

'I don't understand. Your sister was not my wife, not my Mary. I don't understand why you are saying this.' Jack was starting to sound angry and frustrated.

'Jack, please.' Rosie placed her hands gently on his arms.

'No!' He shrugged her hands away, and she dropped them to her sides in a gesture of helplessness.

'Jack. One of the last things my sister said to me was to find Jack. She told me she called you "My man Jack from the Aussie Outback".' Rosie tried to smile through her tears, but Jack's grief-stricken groan shocked her.

'No, please no. Rosie no.' Jack crouched down, trying to bundle his grief into a ball. 'But her name was Mary Kelly.'

'Mary's dad passed away when she was just tiny, and my dad married her mum, and then I was born. Mum insisted Mary keep her father's name. She had loved Mary's father dearly. Jack, I'm so sorry.'

'I wrote to her. I wrote to her every month.'

'I know you did Jack, and she loved you more than life. She told me.'

'I never loved anything or wanted anything more than Mary. She was perfect. Perfect in every way, god how I loved her.' Jack was weeping through the words. Rosie knelt down beside him.

'She asked me to find you Jack. She asked me to come here, to Australia, to the sunshine and warmth and safety, and find you. And I have.'

'I wished I never came home to this place. I

should have stayed and been there with her. I should never have come home. I wish I was dead.'

'Jack no, no, never say that.' Rosie wrapped her arms around his shoulders. 'Mary would be so angry with you if she ever heard you say that.'

'She'll never hear me say that or anything else ever again will she?' Jack was angry and distraught.

They sat together in silence for some time before Rosie finally stood.

'Jack, I'm going to pack everything up, and we can head back to town. Okay?' He didn't reply.

Forty-five minutes later, they were almost back to Mrs Bourke's. Hardly a word had been exchanged on the whole trip. Rosie felt terrible, and Jack looked so distraught she wasn't sure what to do or say to help him. She had known he would be distressed. She had read the letters, and she knew how much love there was between her sister and her man Jack. She ached for him and for her sister, and part of her ached for herself and the loss of Jack. Her loss of Jack. She felt terrible even thinking of herself, and she pushed her feelings away, refusing to give them the air to breathe.

'Are you ok to get yourself home from here?' When Jack finally spoke, they were almost back in town.

'Sure, I guess. Where are you going?'

'Home.'

'I thought you were staying at the pub tonight?'

'I'm going home. I'll see you later.'

With that, Jack turned his horse away from Rosie and didn't look back. She sat and watched as he rode slowly away, shoulders slumped, head down, heart shattered in a thousand tiny pieces.

Rosie loved her sister with all of her heart, and so did Jack. They were tied together forever on that point, but now, only on that point.

CHAPTER TWENTY-ONE

Jack had spent the last few days trying to come to terms with the news he'd had from Rosie. He hadn't been able to talk to Rosie on the day of the picnic, he was far too distressed, but he had questions, lots of questions. His mind wouldn't slow down and give him a minute's rest. He'd spent a long time coming to terms with Mary's rejection. He had created a story, no detail, no facts, a shifting story designed to suit his mood, whatever that was when he thought of her. She'd had to stay with her family, she'd met another man, she'd simply fallen out of love with Jack and their dreams. In his lowest moments, he'd allowed himself to consider it was something far worse, she was unwell, she was . . . no, he never allowed himself to imagine she may have . . . no. And now, he was rewriting his understanding of the last couple of years. He was rewriting his reality. She was gone. It wasn't him, it wasn't their dreams, it wasn't her family, it was nothing either of them could have controlled. She loved him. She had always loved him, every bit as much as he still loved her, right up until when she . . . He had mourned her loss, and after a long time and with the arrival of Rosie, yes, Rosie, he thought he'd begun to feel okay. He'd begun to imagine her safe and happy, not with him, but still, safe and happy. Now, the grieving had begun all over again, this time, with no glimmer of hope to hang on to. And what of Rosie, had he imagined he was falling in love with her, with his sister-in-law? For some reason, that he couldn't really fathom, he felt ashamed of himself on top of everything else he was feeling.

The shearing shed was largely complete except for the cladding on the walls and the absence of any significant yards, other than a couple of pens constructed with timber posts and netting. Jack and a team of local lads had made considerable progress in the previous week. The yards would have to be built after shearing. The shearing plant had been installed and tested. There were three stands, but the upcoming shearing would only require two shearers. It had been weeks of hard work, and Jack needed to get the wool off these sheep before the grass began to turn, and the grass seeds littered the fleeces, reducing their value. There were the three hundred First-cross ewes and five hundred Merino wethers. It would be a comfortable four-day shearing. The ewes would be easy-going and the wethers far slower with their large, heavy frames and masses of wrinkles, slowing the shearers down. He needed to go ahead regardless of the state of the shed. If only he'd had a good relationship with Syd Fredericks. In that case, he might have considered asking if he could use his shed, but Jack was in no mood to pander to Syd or anyone else.

As a vehicle approached, Jack looked up from where he was working. He was instantly irritated by the distraction given the looming deadline and his desire to keep his mind busy and as far away from his heartache as he possibly could. He didn't need to talk to anyone. The team working on the shed had been left in no uncertain terms about his mood and had thankfully kept as clear of him as they could. He stood up, stretched his back and wiped the sweat from his brow.

'Get yourselves a cuppa if you want to.' Jack called out, and the men threw down their tools and gratefully headed for the shade. It was only 10:30am, but it was already hot, and they'd been hard at work for a few hours.

'How are you Jack?' Dr Hadley stepped out of his Land Rover and walked toward Jack.

'Not too bad, yerself?' Jack's reply held a tone of suspicion. A visit from Dr Hadley at your property was unheard of unless you'd done yourself some serious damage.

'Good. How's the shed going? Looks like you almost there?'

'Nearly. It won't be completely finished for shearing, but it'll be good enough for this year. As long as we don't get too much rain, we'll get through. A few walls missing, so there'll be a good breeze for the shearers.'

'They'll appreciate that.'

'I reckon.' They stood for a moment before Jack spoke. 'What brings you out here? I wasn't expecting you.'

'I've been in to see Syd and checked up on the little ones while I was there.'

'Are the twins alright?' Jack was immediately worried that something was wrong and couldn't help but picture Bonnie asking him to 'Put my children first'. He remembered how she'd initially expressed herself, put 'our' children first and how uneasy it had made him before she had corrected herself.

'The twins are fine. I was just doing some routine checks, that's all. It's Syd. He's a bit crook, that's all.'

I hope the bastard's in pain, Jack thought to himself, then felt a little guilty. There'd been more gossip about Syd looking for a buyer after Jack had made his offer. Even the men working on Jack's shearing shed had mentioned it. Jack had fobbed it off, feigning disinterest. Got more than I can cope with here, he'd replied when one of them had said it was a pity Jack wasn't buying the property. It'd be a bloody good property joined up with Snowy Ridge, the bloke had said. Like I don't know that Jack had thought.

'What's wrong with Fredericks?' Jack asked, not hiding his distaste for his neighbour.

'I'm not supposed to share patient information Jack, but it's nothing serious. Got a nagging gut ache. Not sure exactly what's wrong. Can't get him to come into town to check it out properly. Probably just an ulcer or something. I think he gives the grog a nudge in the evenings. Could be that.'

'How's Bonnie?'

'She seems ok. Not a very happy woman that one, not that I can blame her. Pretty tough for a young woman like that stuck out there with that cantankerous old bugger. But, she married him, so there must have been something there, at some stage. Not a lot of love lost between them now, I wouldn't think. But I've said way too much. You forget I ever said any of that, will you?'

'Mum's the word mate. Got enough to think about without worrying about Fredericks. Guess you'll want a cuppa, will you? I'm about to have one. Can't offer you much other than a couple of stale biscuits.'

'Good on yer. Just a cuppa for me. Stale biscuits sound good, but Bonnie already filled me up with a couple of slices of fresh cake.'

For a moment, Jack thought about the cake that Bonnie had bought him the afternoon they had slept together. Slept together, they'd hardly slept, he thought. The guilt made his stomach turn.

Jack and Hadley sat under the shade of a tree out of earshot of the men working on the shed. Jack poured two cups of tea from a billy that was slowly simmering over a fire not far from the worksite. Hadley began.

'How are you really Jack?'

'What's that supposed to mean?' Jack responded defensively.

'I know it's none of my business.'

'No, it's not. Don't mean to sound rude. But . . .'

'Well, I think we both know what we're talking about.'

'No doubt we do.'

'I thought you might want to know how Rosie is.'

Jack sat in silence for a moment. He did want to know. Although, if things had been normal, he wouldn't have expected to see her after the picnic for a few days anyway. But there was no denying he was missing her. It was made far worse by knowing there were no plans to catch up.

'How is she?'

'Upset.'

Jack looked up from his tin mug where he'd been swirling the contents and watching the floating tea leaves spin in a whirlpool.

'It was a shock. A huge bloody shock. Do you know what this means? Rosie's my sister-in-law. We're family. One minute I am a bloke whose wife dumped him, and I've finally turned a corner, feeling ok. I meet this woman, and obviously, you know, she's a bit of alright, more than a bit. Then, the next minute I'm a widower with a sister-in-law.' Jack pressed his thumb and forefinger into his eyes to stem the flow of tears. 'I don't know if I'm coming or going Doc. Really I don't.'

'I can't even begin to imagine what it must be like to have been through everything you've been through over the last couple of years.' Hadley rested a hand on Jack's shoulder.

'Is she ok?'

'She will be Jack. She's tough. But like you.' He paused, looking at Jack. 'She could do with someone to talk to. And like you said mate, you're family now.'

'I can't come in there at the moment Doc. I'm flat out here, and I can't afford to lose a day, let alone two. The shearers cut out early Friday at the Jenkins shed, and they'll be here Monday. We have to get a lot more done here before they arrive.'

'Fair enough. I understand. Other than the shed, are you all set for shearing?'

'Yeah, I've got Lenny Henderson coming over. He's a good young fella. I'll put him on a broom and penning up. I'll be roustabouting and pressing, and Kurt Schultz is classing. We'll keep up, just. Stuck for a bloody cook. Need someone to do smoko and lunch. I need to chase around and find someone. Hope like hell I haven't left it too late, or I'll be up the bloody creek.'

'Hah!' Hadley laughed.

'What?'

'Don't shout me down, ok? But why don't you ask Rosie? Kill two crows with the one stone.'

'You've lost yer marbles Doc. Not only does she have a job, which you know full well, but I can't ask her to come out here and cook for the boys and me.'

'Why not? I'm not suggesting she works for free. You could pay her. Barring any surprise births, I'm not expecting any babies for a couple of weeks, and if I get desperate, I could just fetch her, and you'd have to make do for a few hours. After all, like you said Jack, she's family now, and family sticks together. Someone's got to check in on Syd on Wednesday and bring out some extra medication. She could do that and then ride over and see you and work out a plan. What do you say?'

'I say, it's not just up to me. She has to be happy with it as well, and things are pretty bloody strange and awkward between us at the moment.' Jack rubbed his face in his hands. He stood up and paced back and forward for a moment 'Argh!' He punched his fist into his open hand in frustration. 'It would be good to see her, to be honest, and we have a lot to talk about.' He paused a moment, then. 'Okay.'

'Righto mate.' Hadley stood up and flung the contents of his mug across the ground to his side. 'I better get going and leave you to it. I'll have a chat with Rosie. I'm happy to give her the time off on the proviso if I need her, I can call on her. I won't push her, I'll just give her the idea to think about, and we'll see what happens. You good with that?'

‘Yeah, righto, let’s see what she says.’

‘If you don’t hear from me in the next day or two, you know she’s said yes.’

Hadley handed his mug to Jack and bid him farewell before walking off to his vehicle and leaving a moment later. Jack stood for a moment, watching the dust of the departing Land Rover and wondering whether he had been foolish in agreeing to the Doctor’s idea. Anyway, he thought, Rosie probably won’t want to come out here and spend a week cooking. Why would she?

CHAPTER TWENTY-TWO

It had taken quite some persuasion on Doctor Hadley's part to convince Rosie that she should take some time off and spend it with Jack. Not only would she be helping with the shearing, but also with his general well-being. After all, 'he is family,' Hadley had said, almost one too many times, and family is everything.

'I'll go out Wednesday morning and check in on Bonnie and the twins and leave the medicine for Syd. Then . . . I'll go over and see Jack and see whether he really needs me and wants me there. He and I just need to work out where we stand with each other now. It's all going to be very awkward. But, he was Mary's husband, and she loved him dearly, and in the end, she would be pretty disappointed with me if I didn't make sure he was ok. He'll be fine eventually. He just needs time.'

Hadley smiled to himself and closed the subject while he was still ahead.

Rosie arrived at the Fredericks property just before lunch. Her horse was loaded up like a packhorse, carrying enough clothing for a couple of days in case she decided she would just stay on and help with the shearing. She really wasn't sure how Jack would be and whether she trusted that Hadley had provided an honest and accurate account of what Jack needed and really wanted. She had been aware of the slight glint in his eye as he debated with her and couldn't help but think he was meddling in her relationship with Jack when he shouldn't be.

It was a warm day, and Bonnie was in the garden, sitting with the twins. Bonnie was pleased to see Rosie and smiled broadly. This must be tough, Rosie thought as she rode up.

'Hello Bonnie, how are you?'

'I'm good, thanks Rosie. You?'

'Fighting fit.'

Bonnie laughed as she walked over to the gate to greet Rosie, leaving the twins lying peacefully on a rug. She welcomed Rosie into the yard, and Rosie sat down on the edge of the rug and said hello to the twins while Bonnie fetched a cup of tea and some cake. The refreshments served, Bonnie joined Rosie sitting cross-legged on the ground.

'I have the medicine for Syd. I hope he is feeling better, is he?'

'His belly still aches most of the time. But he's ok I guess. He's out working.'

'Thank goodness for that. I guess a farmer can't afford too many days off to be laid up in bed.'

'No, that's true.'

'I hear on the grapevine your thinking about selling up?'

'Who told you that?' Bonnie looked angry.

'Oh, I'm sorry, I just heard it in town. I don't remember where. I think I overheard it at Bailey's.' Bailey's was the local general store and a great source of information about the goings-on in Granite Gully.

'Well, not if I have my way, we're not. He might be ready to pack up and live in town and sit in the pub every afternoon while I look after the kids, but I'm not. This place belongs to these two.' She reached down and gently squeezed little Charlie's foot, then tickled it, and he smiled at her. 'It'll be yours one day, won't it? 'She addressed the little boy. 'And you'll take care of your sister, no matter what. You hear me?' She tickled his stomach, and he rocked back and forth, smiling and gurgling.

'He's a handsome little boy Bonnie.'

'He is.' Bonnie replied, 'Just like his father.' She added in a whisper, but Rosie heard her. Handsome, Syd, Rosie wouldn't have put those two words in a sentence together, but he was her husband, after all. 'Where are you off to next, Rosie?'

'I'm heading to Snowy Ridge to see Jack.'

'I hope he's not unwell?' Bonnie looked up to check Rosie's expression.

'No, he's fine, as far as I know.'

'A social visit then?'

‘Kind of.’ Rosie liked Bonnie, but this was a small country town, and she wasn’t sure she should share too much with Bonnie. She was worried her business would travel around town faster than a bout of the Spanish Influenza.

‘He’s a good man Jack.’

‘He is.’ Rosie replied.

‘I wish I’d been lucky enough to marry a man like Jack.’

This was an odd twist in the conversation that unsettled Rosie. Rosie looked at Bonnie, trying to read her expression, but from what she could see, it was neutral, although she hadn’t taken her eyes off little Charlie the whole time they’d been speaking.

‘Are you and Jack stepping out? Do you mind me asking?’ Bonnie asked quite directly.

‘No, I don’t mind.’ She did, but Rosie disguised her disquiet with a smile and an indifferent tone. She paused as long as she could without it becoming obvious she was reluctant to answer. ‘Jack and I are just friends. Good friends, I would say, but no, we are not stepping out.’

‘Do you like him? I mean, really like him.’ Now Bonnie turned and looked directly at Rosie, and her eyes searched Rosie’s. She knew it would be difficult to completely disguise her feelings when caught by surprise as she was.

‘Yes, of course, I like him. As I said, I think you would say we are good friends. But it isn’t that simple.’

'Really, why not? He's a good man, a handsome man, and you're a fine looking woman and a good person.'

Rosie blushed. She was so taken aback by this conversation she wasn't sure how to respond.

'I'm not sure what to say Bonnie.'

'I understand, you don't need to answer.' She smiled at Rosie. 'It's written all over your face. Men are simple, they wouldn't see it, but I do.'

Rosie blushed again and turned her attention to baby Mary who was starting to look a little unsettled. She picked her up and held her close. She glanced back at Bonnie, who was watching her.

'You're good with her. You know that? She settles quickly for you.'

'I should be. It's my job.'

'It's more than that. You're a natural.'

They sat in silence for a little while.

'I baked a cake for you to take with you. I don't know how you're going to get it on that donkey you've got there. You'll break the poor thing's back if you put much more on it.'

'That's so kind.'

'I've wrapped it up in a cloth then newspaper and tied it with a string. As long as you don't drop it, it'll make the distance to Snowy Ridge, mostly in one piece, I hope.'

'Thank you Bonnie.' Rosie reached down and squeezed Bonnie's hand.

'There's something I want to tell you Rosie.

Something I know, but you have to promise you'll never tell anyone I told you, ok?'

'Ok, sure.'

'I think you should know this.'

'OK, I promise.' Rosie was intrigued.

'It's about Jack.' Rosie was immediately nervous as Bonnie looked at her with a sympathetic expression. 'He's . . . he's married.' Bonnie was watching Rosie for her reaction. 'Don't ask me how I know. I just do.'

Rosie looked at Bonnie and couldn't help but wonder exactly how she did know. As far as she knew, only Jack and Doctor Hadley knew that, but it was a small town, and perhaps Jack had confided with someone who broke his confidence.

'It's ok Bonnie. I know that.' Rosie gave a resigned smile.

'You do? And you don't mind.' Bonnie was surprised.

'No, I don't.' Rosie sighed. 'Like I said, it's complicated.' She thought for a moment as she held Bonnie's eyes. 'Can I trust you?' Rosie fixed Bonnie in a firm gaze. 'Can I really trust you?'

'Yes, of course you can. You don't need to worry. I hardly leave this place, and I don't have any real friends.'

Rosie felt terribly sorry for Bonnie, expressing her loneliness in such a matter of fact manner, but she knew it was true.

'Jack is . . .' She hesitated. 'Jack is my brother-in-law.' Rosie looked down at baby Mary. 'My sister Mary, was Jack's wife.' Saying the words out loud felt very strange and almost as though she was also hearing them for the first time.

'But . . . you said she'd passed away.'

'She did.'

'So, he's a widower?'

'Yes. Yes, I guess he is. That makes him sound terribly old and sad, doesn't it?' Rosie looked up at Bonnie with a threatening tear.

'It is sad.' Bonnie shook her head in disbelief.

'So you see, we are good friends, we're family.'

'And family is the most important thing, isn't it?' Bonnie added quickly.

'It is.' Rosie smiled at Bonnie.

They sat in silence for several minutes whilst they each came to terms with what they'd just shared and what it meant to each of them personally.

'Rosie.'

'Yes?'

'I have a favour to ask of you. Something very important.'

The day couldn't have gotten more strange and stressful if it tried, and Rosie hadn't even made it to Snowy Ridge.

'Okay.'

'Can you look after the babies for a minute while I get something from inside? I want to hurry in case Syd comes back.'

'Sure.'

Bonnie disappeared and returned a few minutes later. She sat down again next to Rosie.

'Syd's not back, is he?'

'No, I haven't heard him.'

'Good.' Bonnie reached into the pocket of her apron and took out two envelopes. 'I want you to do me a favour, something really important to me. Will you do that for me?'

'Yes, I can do that, I think, depending on what it is, of course.'

Bonnie turned the envelopes over so Rosie could see the writing on the front of the first envelope. It was marked 'Private – Doctor Hadley'.

'I want you to promise that if anything ever happens to me, you'll pass these envelopes on for me. This one is for Doctor Hadley, as you can see.' She handed it to Rosie. 'And this one is for Jack.' She looked warily at Rosie, and Rosie was careful not to react, although she felt an immediate note of concern laced with jealousy, an emotion she quickly tried to push away. Bonnie handed Rosie the envelope with the words 'Private – Jack Sutherland' very neatly penned on the front.

'What's this all about Bonnie? It's all very intriguing. Are you alright?' Rosie tried smiling and not overplaying her interest.

'It's private Rosie. Yes, I'm fine. They are a bit like a will, I guess, that's all. As I said, I need you to promise me, if anything, anything at all, happens to me, I want you to give these letters to Doctor Hadley and Jack. Only if something happens, and never to anyone else.'

'I will, I promise, but you're worrying me. Are you really ok? Are you safe? What is it that might happen?' Rosie couldn't hide her concern.

'I'm safe. I am Rosie. Don't worry about me.' Bonnie began to gather baby Charlie into her arms. 'Now, if you'll bring little Mary inside for me, that would be great. Then I best let you get on your way.'

Rosie gathered Mary up into her arms, kissed her chubby cheek, and followed Bonnie inside. It had been a strange visit, and it had momentarily taken her mind off seeing Jack, which was a relief. However, it also left her concerned for Bonnie's welfare and pondering what connection Jack had to Bonnie to warrant such a private letter.

CHAPTER TWENTY-THREE

It was a warm and very still day, and Rosie could hear the sound of hammers nailing and timber being sawn as she approached the Snowy Ridge house paddock. She looked toward the new shearing shed and could see a buzz of activity. There were four men all hard at work and, there, amongst them, was Jack carrying a long piece of timber over his shoulder. She was conscious of her heart racing, and she took a deep breath to calm herself.

Knowing her way around, she rode first to the horse yard, removed the bag she'd strapped to the saddle, then unsaddled her horse, removed its bridle and made sure it had hay and water. She picked up her bag and the cake she'd been given by Bonnie and walked towards Jack's house, looking at the building site as she went. She hadn't realised just how awkward this would feel and how uncomfortable she'd be. But heck, he was her brother-in-law, they were family, there was nothing strange about being here. As she walked, she watched as Jack picked up another piece of timber, balancing it on his shoulder again. He walked it over to where one of the workers took it from him and carried it into the shed. He looked sideways at her but hardly reacted, which made her all the more uncomfortable.

Rosie took her bag inside the cottage, then steeled herself to walk over to the building site. Jack was on another run with a piece of timber. Once he handed it over, he turned and saw her approaching. Momentarily hesitating he walked over to her.

'Hello Jack.'

'How yer going?' He asked, without the usual happy and excited tone.

'I'm ok. How are you?'

'Been better, but I don't 'spose that's a surprise.'

'No . . . no it's not.'

'How's the building going? You've got shearing next week, haven't you?'

'Yep, I do, and we're behind.'

'Oh, that's no good.'

Jack's tone wasn't particularly friendly. In fact, it was bordering on short.

'I've got a lot to do.'

One of the workers behind them, on the floor of the shearing shed, called out.

'Sorry Jack, can you turf up the tin o' bolts mate? We've run out up here.'

'Yeah, hang on.' Jack called back.

'Go. It's ok. I don't want to hold you up.' Rosie wasn't surprised to see the life had disappeared from Jack's eyes, and he looked exhausted. She followed him over to the shed, where he hoisted up an old oil tin with the lid cut off and a wire handle. It was half full of long bolts which were being used to secure the wall frame to the upright posts.

'How yer goin'?' One of the workers called out to Rosie.

'Hello.' she replied, waving to him.

Jack introduced the men.

'That's Barney, that's Roger, and over there, that's Stewie.'

Barney and Roger said hello, and Stewie nodded.

'This is Rosie O'Reilly. She's the local midwife.'

'Midwife? What do you need a midwife for Jack? You havin' a baby?' Barnie said in a stirring tone.

'Not that I know of.' Jack replied and tried to smile, although the midwife jokes were wearing thin.

'Well, you never know, I guess. They reckon one day man will walk on the bloody moon, so why not have a baby. Be a damn sight easier I reckon.' The three men all laughed, and Rosie pulled a face at them.

'How about you shut up and get back to work?' Jack replied in a good-humoured fashion. It was the first time he'd come close to joining in any banter in days, and the men looked pleased.

'How about we have some bloody lunch. It's near one o'clock, and I'm starved. He's a hard boss Rosie.' Barney was definitely the spokesman.

'No worries. Knock off and take a spell. I'll go get some food. I won't be long.' Jack looked frustrated.

'I'll help.' Rosie directed her comment to Jack then turned to the others. 'I have a cake if you men would like a piece?'

'Cake, yeah good on yer Luv. Things are finally looking up out here.' Barney turned to the other two. 'Come on, let's keep going until the grub's up.'

'Come on then.' Jack spoke to Rosie.

Jack and Rosie walked together in silence to the house. Jack stopped at the tank stand, off to the side of the house, filled an old gold mining pan with water and washed his hands. He walked inside, and Rosie was already standing in the kitchen with an apron on and arranging food on the table in order to make sandwiches.

'You don't have to do that.' Jack tried to smile.

'It's no problem. I want to help.'

Jack looked down at Rosie's bag in the corner of the room then looked back to find she'd followed his gaze.

'Doctor Hadley said you need a cook.' Rosie broke the silence.

'You've got a job already Rosie.'

'I've got time off as long as no one springs a new baby on us. We don't expect any.'

'I don't need you until next week. Shearing doesn't start until Monday.'

'It's after one, you haven't had lunch, and the

workers are complaining. I think you need me. Now, I assume it's sandwiches.' Rosie's tone was firm but friendly.

Jack didn't reply. He just nodded. He felt better at this moment than he had in days. He looked at Rosie, and she smiled at him. He felt his face flush, but couldn't help but smile back.

'Bonnie sent me off with this cake.' Rosie spoke as she untied the string and then unwrapped the cake. 'She's a nice woman.'

'Yeah, she seems alright.' Jack replied without much genuine interest. He had two other women who were occupying his mind.

'Had a strange conversation with her today. Left me a bit worried, actually. How well do you know her?'

'Not much at all really. I've just spoken to her when I've needed to visit her deadbeat husband. I feel sorry for her, stuck there with him.' Jack replied, sounding and feeling disinterested.

'Yes, I agree.' Rosie replied.

'I don't think she's that keen on him.' Jack added. 'She just doesn't have much choice. Sounds like he's no better than her father.' Jack threw in without particularly thinking about what he was saying.

'No better than her father? How do you know about her father? You must have had a bit of a conversation with her at some stage, have you?' Rosie's tone suggested her interest was piqued.

Hell, Jack thought to himself. He didn't want to

be trying to deal with everything that was going on in his life right now and adding in the complication of Bonnie and a past he just wanted to erase.

'Ah, dunno, I think she told me one day when I was waiting for Syd to come down after milking. Anyway, we better get this out to the boys, or they'll go on strike, and I'm far enough behind already.' Jack spoke quickly, effectively dismissing any further conversation.

'Well, I'm here to help Jack. If you'll have me.'

Jack looked at Rosie, and his throat ached. If you'll have me, he played the words over in his mind. If only you knew. She was beautiful, but she was Mary's sister, and he hadn't reconciled any of that yet.

'Ok, let's talk about it later. It's a paid job, though, and I don't want any argument.'

Rosie joined the men as they sat around in a circle under the shade of a big old Apple Box tree and ate their lunch. They all enjoyed the cake and washed it down with mugs of black tea. Barney led a chorus of complaints when Jack insisted they got back to work.

Late in the afternoon, the men finally decided it was time to finish up for the day. All the tools were put undercover and out of any unexpected weather. The good news was it looked like they were set for a run of warm and dry days. They would need to work right through until

Saturday evening to get the shed ready for Monday. Jack would need all of Sunday to muster and make the final preparations for shearing.

When Jack finally finished at the shed, it was nearly dark. He checked the horses for food and water and threw a few handfuls of grain to the chooks. They'd already roosted, so he locked the door to their pen, then fed the dogs. He was exhausted when he opened the door to his house, where he found Rosie sitting at the dining table.

'You're still here?' He asked in a serious tone.

'Yes, of course I am. You knew I was still here. Unless my horse has escaped.' She looked a little hurt by his comment. 'Would you like me to go?'

'You know that's not what I want. I'm sorry. I'm not really thinking straight at the moment.'

'I understand, and I don't blame you. This . . . this news . . . of Mary is all brand new for you. I am not saying it's easy for me, not one bit, but I've had a couple of years to come to terms with it.'

'And you had a chance to say goodbye.' Jack put his hand to his forehead, dragging his hair back in anguish.

'I know Jack.' This wasn't starting well, and Rosie was beginning to think she'd made a mistake coming out to see Jack and possibly staying on and working for him. Maybe it was all just too soon. She decided to change the subject and brighten the mood if she could. 'What are we having for dinner? Are you cooking?' Rosie smiled at Jack and was pleased when the corners of his mouth turned up ever so slightly.

'I'm not paying you to cook, then doing the cooking myself. I need to have a wash, but first, I need a beer. Would you like one?'

'Where are they?'

'In the water tank. I'll go get us one.'

Jack opened the door, and Rosie followed him out and around the corner of the house to the water tank. He stepped up on a stump especially positioned for the purpose, then onto the tank stand. From there, he climbed up a wooden ladder he'd constructed specifically for the purpose. He peered through an opening in the top of the tank. Rosie watched all this with interest. She watched as he pulled up a rope that had a hessian sack attached to it. She heard the clink of the bottles in the sack. He untied the rope holding the sack, reached inside and pulled out a bottle of beer, then tied up the sack again and carefully lowered it back down into the tank. He climbed down off the ladder and passed the bottle to Rosie as he did. She was surprised at how cold it was.

They walked back inside, where Jack took the top of the beer.

'I suppose I better get a couple of glasses.' Jack looked about, suggesting he wasn't sure where he kept the glasses, certainly not any that were appropriate for a female guest. 'Sorry, just trying to think where they are. I usually don't use one.'

'That's ok. I don't need a drink.'

‘You sure?’

‘Sure.’

Rosie watched as Jack upended the bottle and took a long and obviously very satisfying swig. He wiped his mouth with the back of his hand and looked at Rosie. Finally, he smiled. She held out her hand.

‘Maybe I will have a swig after all.’ That really made him smile, and he handed her the bottle. She upended it carefully, taking a more ladylike volume before handing it back, covering her mouth and trying not to burp.

Rosie watched as Jack moved the kettle onto the hot plate, and it began to simmer.

‘I have to have a wash. You help yourself to some more beer if you want. I’ll get us something for dinner from the meat safe after I’ve cleaned up.’

‘I can do that.’ Rosie replied.

Jack disappeared into his room, only half pushing the door shut. He returned just moments later, a towel wrapped around his waist and otherwise naked. Rosie was surprised and a little embarrassed and found herself unsure where to look. Unable to disguise her discomfort, she stood up to cross to the stove to take the boiling kettle off the hot plate.

‘What’s this for?’ Rosie said without looking up from the kettle, but Jack was suddenly by her side. Her heart raced as his hand brushed against hers as he grasped the kettle handle.

‘It’s the water for my wash.’

'Oh, of course.' Rosie turned away from him and moved quickly back to the dining room table. The last thing she wanted was for him to see the colour of her face. She could only imagine how red it would have been, given how hot her cheeks felt.

'Hey Rosie.'

'Yes? Rosie turned shyly to see Jack standing in the doorway.

'You better get used to this if you're staying for a few days. I'm afraid I don't have separate guest quarters.' He smiled. 'Anyway, we're family and hell, you're a nurse anyway.'

'Just go Jack.' She waved a dismissive hand at him, pulling a face in frustration, then called after him with an afterthought. 'I'm a midwife, babies Jack, not grown men.'

Rosie put her face in her hands and smiled, almost laughing in relief. Although this was extraordinarily awkward, she was relieved he seemed to be getting his sense of humour back and quickly. She hoped it might last a little while.

I better get that meat, Rosie thought, and she rummaged around in the cutlery draw for a sharp knife. She lit a kerosene lantern, just as she'd seen Jack do when she stayed that first night of the storm and headed out for the meat safe with an enamel plate and the knife. She was amazed at how quickly she had adapted to living in the country, although Mrs Bourke's establishment was far more civilised than Jack's. She was heading back to the kitchen with the meat she'd sliced from a mutton forequarter when she heard a noise and stopped in her tracks. She had turned off the kerosene lamp once she'd cut the meat and was able to see her way back, heading for the light coming from the little cottage windows.

Though the light was dim, she could see Jack standing a little away from the cottage. He was drying himself with a towel. Squinting to get a better focus, she suddenly realised he was completely naked. She was shocked, and she turned away but didn't move. Biting her lip, she had almost stopped breathing. Try as she might, she couldn't move off the spot. Fighting against a weakened will, she eventually turned back and stole another glance. His body was little more than a dark silhouette, with the first glimpses of moonlight reflecting off his bare and wet skin. A shiver ran down her spine from the nape of her neck almost to the base of her back, and she shook on the spot. She couldn't stop the shudder, and with fright, she took off for the house, worrying Jack would catch her watching him.

Once in the house, she put the meat in a pan and searched around for some vegetables. Eying the beer on the table, she grabbed the bottle, took a long swig, and then realised she needed to wash her hands. She made for the back door, but it opened as she crossed the room, and Jack strode in smiling. She backed away quickly. This time she couldn't tear her eyes away from his bare chest, muscular arms, and flat stomach. She finally caught herself and looked up to see a quirky smile on his tanned face. She thought about the first time she'd seen Woolly Jack, his long unkempt hair and bushranger beard. It was almost impossible to reconcile that person with this handsome man who stood in front of her.

'You ok?' He asked with a knowing smile.

'Yes, why wouldn't I be?' She couldn't help but sound defensive.

'Ok, don't snap at me.' He held his hands in the air in a gesture of surrender, and it didn't help one little bit. She hoped like hell the towel wouldn't drop to the ground. His biceps were flexed, his stomach was even flatter, and with his wet messy hair, she had never felt less in control of her emotions. But, even more terrifying was her physical reaction seemed very likely to undermine her.

'I didn't snap.' She tried to smile, but her voice was a little deeper than expected, and she choked on the snap.

'Okay, well I better get dressed for dinner.'

'Yes. Please.'

Jack began to walk away, much to Rosie's relief, and she watched as he walked toward his bedroom, trying not to imagine what the vision would be like on the other side of that wall in just a moment. She ran her eyes over his back and settled her gaze on his lower back, just above his hip.

‘What’s that?’ The words were out before she could catch herself.

Jack stopped in the doorway and turned around to see what Rosie was looking at.

‘Sorry, that was rude.’ Rosie apologised.

Jack looked down and ran his hand down his back to where a shape like a map of New Zealand just a couple of inches long covered his skin.

‘A birthmark.’ Jack chuckled. ‘Did you think I forgot to wash properly?’

‘No. Sorry.’

‘Don’t be. It’s a family thing. Ed has one just like mine, but higher on his back and mum has one on her shoulder. I guess if Mary and I had had children, they might have had them as well. Seems to be passed down.’

It was a sobering comment that quickly shifted Rosie’s mood, and she was actually thankful for that. She was struggling with her feelings for Jack, both emotional and physical and in this little cottage, she needed enormous control.

Jack disappeared into his room and called out. ‘Help yourself to a bottle of wine. I’ll finish the beer, what you didn’t drink of course, and then I’ll join you.’

Later after Jack and Rosie had eaten, they sat at the table, finishing the last of the bottle of wine.

‘I better not have anymore, but you’re welcome of course.’ Jack looked at his empty glass as he spoke. ‘I have an early start and still a hell of a lot of work to get done over the next few days. The boys will be back first thing in the morning.'

'Of course.' Rosie replied. 'I should get out of your way.'

'You're leaving?' Jack tried not to sound too surprised and disappointed.

'Well, not now.' Rosie replied with a smile, 'It's a bit late at night, don't you think?'

'Yeah, I figured you were going to spend the night with me.' Jack was trying to recover his position, but then realised how that had sounded and looking at Rosie, he could see she was embarrassed. 'I mean sleep with me, I mean, geez, you know what I am trying to say.'

Finally, Rosie smiled and showed she was enjoying Jack getting himself tangled in an uncomfortable knot.

'I know what you were trying to say, Jack, and yes, I am going to stay the night here tonight. I hadn't worked out what to do tomorrow. There's not much point in me staying here if I am going to get in the way. I could go back to town and come back Sunday if that would be easier for you?'

'No!' As soon as he'd spoken, Jack realised how forceful his tone had been, and he took a breath before continuing. 'I mean, no, there is no need for you to leave. You wouldn't be in the way at all. And it's good to have the company after work. If you wanted to stay, you'd be very welcome.'

'I really don't want to be in the way Jack.'

'Then don't be, get in and give me a hand. There's a lot to do, and I could do with the extra help. There are all the things I normally do when I'm not on the building team. There are animals to feed. The stock to ride around and check. There's plenty to do, I can assure you, and I'd really appreciate the help. All those things don't stop just because we're building a shearing shed.'

There was a long pause as Jack waited for Rosie's reply, so he tried again.

'I know . . . I know it's become awkward between us because of Mary and everything, but you just need to give me a little time. It's all been a huge shock. I'd known she wasn't coming to Australia for a long time, but I was so sure she was ok. Now, I find myself grieving, grieving for someone I loved so much. At the same time, I am so grateful that she always loved me, and then sad because she loved me and I lost her. It's such a god awful mess. And then . . . and then, there's you.'

'Me?'

'Yes, you. You can't believe how guilty I feel about my feelings for you. I feel terrible.'

Although he meant well, Jack could see the disappointment in Rosie's eyes, and he wished he could take his last comment back.

'There's no need to feel guilty about me Jack. I think we were only ever brought together so I could tell you about Mary, nothing more. No guilt Jack, I'm your sister-in-law.'

Now Jack couldn't hide his disappointment. He was sure there were the beginnings of tears in Rosie's eyes as she stood up abruptly.

'Now,' Rosie announced in an officious fashion. 'It's time you got some sleep, and me too. It's been a long and challenging day, and I'm exhausted. I'll sleep out here tonight Jack, do you have your swag? Roll it out, big brother, and I can get some sleep.'

'Ha ha, little sister. You're in the comfy bed, and don't get me angry by arguing. I changed the sheets for you when I got changed before dinner. And, I have this.' Jack pointed to a bundle leaning against the wall in the corner of the room.

'What's that.' Rosie inquired, looking intrigued.

'A stretcher. I'll bunk down on that. I'm that tired. I could sleep on an ants' nest.'

Rosie gathered her bag from where she'd left it earlier in the afternoon and went to walk into the bedroom. As she passed Jack, she placed her hand on his arm. She smiled, but her eyes betrayed the sadness she felt. She walked on and into the bedroom. Jack called after her.

'I want you to stay Rosie. Stay with me.'

CHAPTER TWENTY-FOUR

Sunday morning Rosie and Jack rose early and completed the morning chores in order to allow plenty of time for the final preparations for shearing.

The first task was to bring in the sheep for the first day of shearing. Two mobs of wethers were 'out back' as Jack had said, describing their location. 'Out back' meant they were in the furthest paddocks that were at the foot of Jake's Mountain. The country up there was hilly, dry and rocky. Jack explained he kept the wethers up there because they were Merinos, and they were prone to foot problems like rot and abscess. The dryer country kept their feet out of the damp, and the rocks helped to wear down their hooves, reducing the issues.

Jack and Rosie rode side by side with Jack's two dogs strolling along behind them. It took nearly an hour to ride out to the paddock where the sheep were.

'I should have bought them in a bit closer a week ago, but I was too busy. This'll take a couple of hours.'

'No problems, I'm happy to be here.'

'I'm happy you're here.' Jack smiled at Rosie, and she felt a warm glow.

'Ok, this is the paddock. Look, you can see a few up there under the tree.' Jack pointed to a peak covered in scrub and rocks, and Rosie could see the grey sheep lying about in the shade. They were almost camouflaged and would have been easily missed by the inexperienced eye.

'They're a different colour to the sheep that came from Sutherland Downs.'

'They'll all be the same colour after shearing, bright white. The ewes are probably still carrying a bit of red dust from up north, and the merinos are a greasier wool. They always have a bit of a grey tinge.'

They rode on until Jack stopped his horse and began to spell out the plan to Rosie.

'Ok, I'll go out this way.' Jack pointed out to his right and toward some rough looking country. 'And you can head down that way and around the edge of the slope there. If you head through those trees, you'll come out the other side to a bit of a clearing. You can mostly follow the fence until you get right to the back, where a gate leads up into the bush on the hill. Don't go through the gate. Just head up the hill there to the right, and by then, I should be coming over the top. When you see the first of the mob, just try and steer them down the gully and pretty much back the way you came. I'll put the dogs around them and work through all the trees and shady spots up on the hill. I've got to make sure we don't leave any behind.'

Rosie headed off, occasionally looking back at Jack as he disappeared up the hill and into the scrub with his dogs. She hadn't realised how much she would enjoy working on the farm. So far, her attraction to Snowy Ridge had simply been its owner, but the lifestyle was growing on her rapidly and not just for a quick change of scenery. She loved being a midwife and the sacred privilege of welcoming a new life into the world as often as she did. Still, she allowed herself just a moment to imagine what it might be like to live out here with a farmer, with Jack. What would it be like to build a house and share his dreams of growing a vast and successful property? What would it be like to have his children, her own little Jack, or perhaps a headstrong redheaded little Rosie? She smiled to herself, then quickly scolded herself for getting so far ahead. There was so much to work through, and for now, she needed just to be grateful for the fact they were friends again. Good friends.

She rode on through the trees, scanning about her, looking for any sheep resting in the shade, but there were none she could see. In the thick of the bush, as she walked her horse, she heard a scratching sound, and she reigned her horse into a halt to see what the noise was. She urged her on slowly, listening for the sound again. Suddenly, in front of her, a wombat scurried across her path on its stubby little legs. Both Rosie and the horse got a fright, but the wombat showed little if any interest in the horse. Rosie smiled as it disappeared between some rocks. She patted the horse on its sweaty neck.'

'Good girl Nell.'

Rosie rode on. It was nearly lunchtime, and she was a little hungry but knew she could do little but wait until the sheep were well on their way back to the house paddock. She became aware of the sound of a vehicle and stopped her horse again. She turned her head about, looking for the source of the sound. Finally, she spotted it in the distance, on Fredericks property, down on the flats. She continued on, occasionally glancing toward where she'd seen the vehicle when the view became clear of trees and small hills.

In the distance, Rosie could see the gate that Jack had mentioned., There was still no sign of Jack and the mob when she looked up the hill to her right, and she couldn't hear them either, although she fancied she'd heard the occasional bark. But a sound, carried on the still air, did grab her attention. It was the sound of a voice, actually voices, not just one. Rosie couldn't make out what was being said, but the sound was carrying well enough to know it was an argument of sorts. As she got closer to the gate and prepared to head up the hill as per Jack's instructions, she heard the vehicle again. This time it was much closer. When the vehicle appeared, she squinted and tried to see who was in it. It seemed to be travelling very fast across the paddock, given the rough conditions. Although it was just a couple of flashes between the trees, she was almost positive it was Bonnie. She tried to wave but knew that was a waste of time, so she continued on up the hill to meet up with Jack.

The next few hours were spent getting the sheep back to the makeshift yard at the shearing shed where they were left for several hours to empty out, as Jack had called it. They had water but no feed. As late as they possibly could, Jack and Rosie pushed as many wethers as possible under the shed to keep them dry for the next day's shearing. After finishing work very late, then cleaning up and eating, they were quickly into bed, anticipating a hard day's work the next day, the first day of shearing.

Jack had been up and about for quite a while. He left Rosie at the dining room table, finishing her breakfast, and went outside. He hadn't woken her, and she was a little annoyed at him. When he walked back through the door, it was 6:50am.

'What did you have to get done so early?' Rosie asked.

'I just let the wethers out into the yard. That way, we can get a bit of air under the shed and get rid of the stink and let them spread out a bit as well. You finished your breakfast?'

'I have.'

'Ok, let's go and fill the catching pens with enough for the first run, then I'm going to have a quick cup of tea before they all arrive.' Jack pushed the kettle over the hot plate on the wood stove, and it immediately began to simmer. 'Come on.'

Rosie leapt up from the table, and by the time she got to the back door, she almost had to jog to keep up with Jack. She glanced sideways at him with a look of what's the hurry. He was aware of her look.

'You can't hold these fella's up. They'll get started at 7:30 on the dot, and it won't be a good start if they're waiting for a sheep.'

'I can't wait to see the shearing.' Rosie sounded excited.

'You?' Jack looked at her with a bemused expression.

'Yeah.'

'You can't come in the shed.' He replied bluntly.

'What? What do you mean I can't come in?' Rosie looked astounded at the suggestion.

'Just what I said. You're a sheila.'

'I beg your pardon?'

'Not my rules.' Jack held out his hands in a gesture of surrender. It was a gesture he was using too often, and it was starting to annoy Rosie.

'If they want their lunch, they'll let me in, thanks very much.'

Jack burst out laughing.

'Good luck. I tell you what, I'll ask if you can

come in, but no promises. I've never been in a shed where a woman was allowed in, and I can't see how this one'll be any different. But I guess there's always a first time.' Without thinking, Jack swung his arm around Rosie's shoulder and pulled her toward him as they walked. She elbowed him in the ribs.

CHAPTER TWENTY-FIVE

It was lunchtime on Monday, the first day of shearing, and Rosie had prepared a cooked meal for the shearers and everyone else working in the shed. Jack had made a makeshift table and set it up in a small machinery shed a short distance from the shearing shed. The house paddock was beginning to resemble a shanty town with its array of buildings springing up everywhere. They looked like the sort of shacks that preceded the establishment of a new town, no doubt like Granite Gully had looked when the gold miners first arrived.

'Yer gonna join us for a feed?' The older shearer asked Rosie as she bustled about the table organising food for the workman as they returned from washing up at the tank. He was known only as Bluey, even on his Talley sheet.

Rosie looked up at Jack, who looked up from his Talley book where he was pencilling in the results of the last run. He gave her the slightest nod, and she could just see the corners of his mouth turned up ever so slightly.

‘If that’s okay Bluey, that’d be good.’ Rosie replied with a smile.

‘Course it’s ok, you done all the work dintcha?’

‘I think you fellas have been doing all the hard work.’ She knew how hard the shearers and the rest of the team had been working, but she’d been surprised what a hectic morning she’d had herself. She’d been warned by Jack a dozen times she had to be on time. As a result, she was anxious right up until the moment she started spooning the lamb stew onto the tin plates, alongside the mashed potato and boiled peas. Looking back at Jack, she could see that things must have been going well because he looked considerably more relaxed than earlier in the morning.

‘Is it all going according to plan?’ Rosie asked Bluey as the other, younger shearer, Ross, sat next to Bluey and started eating his stew like it was the first feed he’d had in days.

‘Dunno, is it Jack? What’re the numbers?’

‘Sixty-three for you Blue and fifty-nine for Ross. Sound right?’ Jack asked.

‘Yep.’ Bluey shovelled the peas on his plate onto the mashed potato, pushed them in, then covered the lot with stew and loaded his fork.

‘Mmm.’ Ross mumbled his reply with a nod. He had too much in his mouth to speak and didn’t look like slowing down. He kept his head down and was looking up with his eyes only. He resembled a dog protecting its dinner, Rosie mused.

The other men, Kurt and Lenny, joined soon after and once they were all seated, had a cool drink and a plate full of food, Rosie sat down next to Jack.

'What's with you two then?' Bluey looked at Jack and Rosie.

'What do you mean?' Jack replied, and Rosie could sense his irritation at the question.

'You an item?' Bluey persisted.

'No.' Jack replied. His tone was sharp and short, and Rosie felt a pang of disappointment.

'You look pretty cosy.'

Jack didn't bother replying, he just filled his mouth with stew. Everyone else at the table kept their heads down and tried not to look interested in the conversation.

'Hear you wanna come take a look at the shearing?' Bluey spoke directly to Rosie.

'Only if that's ok.' Jack chimed in quickly.

'Fine with me.' Bluey smiled at Rosie. 'How 'bout you Rosco?'

'Mmm.' Ross nodded, looking up for just a moment at Rosie, and then Jack, before returning to shovelling his stew in like he was stoking a steam train firebox.

Rosie found herself eating quickly, so that she could organise tea and biscuits for everyone. On reflection, she decided it would have been easier just to eat by herself once the men had all gone back into the shed. She'd probably do that the next day. It was a hard day's work keeping up with them.

Once the meal was finished, the shearers returned to the shed. With a couple of walls still missing, which, with good weather, wasn't a problem at all, Rosie could see them laying back against soft half-filled wool packs and getting a little shuteye. She was envious.

'Don't know how they do it.' Jack said to her as he followed her gaze. If I was to lay down now, I wouldn't be able to get back up again.' He turned to Lenny, who was enjoying seconds and wiping the last of the stew from his plate with a slice of bread. 'Come on Lenny, knock the rest of that off, and we better go pen up inside, then let the shorn wethers out into the paddock.' He turned to Rosie. 'You'll be right?'

'Yes.' Rosie looked at the table full of dishes and wrinkled her nose up. 'I'll get these done, sort out the afternoon tea and bring it up to the shed early so I can see a few sheep getting shorn.'

It was an hour and a half later when Rosie had washed up all the plates in a large galvanized tin tub and set them to dry. She loaded another batch of biscuits into a basket and walked up to the shed, exhausted but still with hours of work to do preparing stew for the next day's lunch.

She walked into the shed with the basket and smiled at Jack, who walked quickly over to her.

'Here, come and stand over here where you can

see what's going on.' He ushered her over to the edge of the catching pens but well away from the swinging gates.

Bluey's sheep was almost shorn. He ran the shears over its rump and down its back leg. The handpiece seemed to glide effortlessly through the wool. He ran the shears over the rump again and carefully around its backside, then over the rump one last time. With the sheep cleanly shorn, he pulled the cord that hung down from the shearing plant. His handpiece stopped immediately, and he dropped it almost as quickly to the floor and into position for the next sheep. He tipped the wether over toward the hole in the wall, and it stood up from where it had been balanced on its backside. As it stood, he gave it a good shove, and it took off down the shoot and out into the blinding sunlight outside with a pen full of other bright white, freshly shorn sheep.

Bluey stood up and stretched his back. His singlet was wet with sweat. He winked and grinned at Rosie as he walked briskly toward the catching pen on the opposite side of the board. He was a showman. At the catching pen, he picked up a dirty old towel that was hanging over the swinging door, wiped his face, then walked into the pen and upended his next sheep.

Rosie watched as he dragged the sheep out across the board by its front legs, balancing it on its backside. Once in position near his handpiece, he gripped the sheep between his thighs. He pushed its right front foot back and hooked it at his waist about where his singlet met his belt. Then he moved its head backward so that it was not far from his armpit, and next to that, its left leg was hooked behind his arm. Rosie could see that the sheep was stretched taut as he began to shear its belly. In what seemed like just a few strokes of the handpiece, the belly was shorn. The wool, which looked like a very small fleece, was thrown across the board and out of the way of the shearer. Lenny appeared, picked up the belly wool, and threw it into a hessian wool pack that was hooked open against a wall.

Rosie stood, transfixed, as Bluey continued to shear the merino wether. The handpiece glided across the sheep quickly and gracefully. Bluey moved the sheep between positions skilfully, with little struggle from either the shearer or the sheep. Within a few minutes, the process was over. The sheep was spirited through the hole in the wall, and Bluey was crossing the board, preparing to drag another sheep from the catching pen.

Rosie watched, fascinated, until the end of the run at 3 o'clock. Then, the shearers disappeared to wash up for afternoon tea. At the same time, Lenny and Jack skirted the last of the fleeces, tearing away wool contaminated by burs and sweat dags. They swept the board clean and refilled the catching pen. They tallied the sheep that had been shorn during the after-lunch run and let them out into the paddock. By the time they had completed all of this, most of the half-hour afternoon tea break was over, and they quickly gulped down a mug of hot black tea and ate some biscuits. As they did, the shearers began shearing the first of the sheep in the last run of the day. Just a few minutes later, it was time to lift and throw the first of the fleeces. Rosie strolled over to speak with Jack.

'Well, I better get back down to the house and start preparing tomorrow's stew. It'll be pretty similar to today. I hope that'll be okay.'

'That'll be absolutely fine. I reckon you could feed these blokes the same thing for three weeks running, and they wouldn't really care. Anyway, it was a good stew, so they wouldn't want to be complaining too much.'

'Well, I'm glad you enjoyed it because that's what you're having for dinner tonight.' Rosie smiled at Jack.

'Suits me, as long as there's a beer.'

'What time do they finish shearing?'

'5:30 on the bell. They'll be gone fifteen minutes later.'

'Okay, well, I'll have a beer on the table and ready for you by 5:45.'

'Hah!' Jack gave a snort. 'I won't be back at the house for a fair while after that. They might finish work, but Lenny and I will keep going for a while. We've gotta do the final count out, let the sheep out into the paddock and make sure they get a feed into them before it starts to cool down tonight. Then we have to shed tomorrow's sheep. All going well, I should be back at the house by about 6:30. I'll definitely be keen for a beer and a wash before dinner if that's okay?'

'That's more than okay. You're not sitting at the table until you've had a good wash. I'll heat up some water for you. I might have one first before you get back. What about Lenny? Do we have to feed him dinner?'

'No, he'll get going as soon as he possibly can. As soon as we have the sheep under the shed and make sure they're out of the weather, he can head home. He'll need a rest. He's been working his backside off all day. He's a good young fella.'

'Okay, I'll see you soon.'

'Yep, see you then.'

Jack had been right. Although things had run very smoothly, it was nearly 6:30 before he found himself strolling across the paddock from the shearing shed to the house, completely exhausted. House, he thought to himself, he still felt it was generous giving the old tin shack such a title. He and Lenny had managed to force one hundred and eighty wethers under the shearing shed floor in preparation for the next day's shearing. There were enough sheep to get them through to afternoon tea, which meant, even if the weather broke and the sheep left outside got wet, it would still be a worthwhile day of shearing for the team.

Jack walked under the veranda and collapsed in

a chair. For a moment, he was too exhausted to even think about taking his boots off. Things had changed around the house in the last few days, and walking into the house in dirty work clothes was one thing, but strolling in, in boots covered in sheep shit and dust, was something else, and he wasn't prepared to risk a tongue lashing from Rosie.

As he sat, he heard Rosie singing in that wonderful accent he loved so much.

'As she wheeled her wheelbarrow,
  through streets broad and narrow,
  Crying, "Cockles and mussels, alive, alive, oh!'

It was one of the most beautiful sounds he'd ever heard. He sat in silence and listened. The Irish lilt in her gentle voice brought tears to his eyes. His fatigue made his emotions surface far more quickly than they normally would have. Her voice made him think of Mary. He'd heard her singing in the same beautiful voice, just the once. He'd been equally enchanted at the time. He let his head fall back and shut his eyes.

'She died of the fever, and nothing could save her,
  And that was the end of sweet Molly Malone;
  But her ghost drives a barrow thro' streets
  broad and narrow.'

Jack could hear the sadness in Rosie's voice as she sang that last line before stopping. He couldn't help but wonder if she was also thinking of Mary. He remained in his seat with his eyes closed.

A moment later, Rosie's voice pierced the silence. There was a small shriek before she cried 'Jack'. He opened his eyes with fright as she did her best to duck past him, wrapped only in a towel. He couldn't drag his eyes away from her. Her shoulders and arms were completely bare, and that was one thing, but nothing to compare with her bare legs as she ran past him. Suddenly, the fatigue from the hard day's work disappeared, and he felt full of energy and anxious. He'd seen Rosie come in from a wash on several occasions in the last few days, but each time, she had been either fully dressed or wearing a cotton dressing gown and had been completely covered up. He laughed to himself, conscious that his heart was beating quickly. He took a little time to take off his boots before knocking on the door.

'Is it okay if I come in?' Jack called out

'Yes.' Rosie replied in a clipped voice.

He walked into the kitchen and was surprised when she came out of the bedroom just a moment later, her hair dishevelled but otherwise dressed and looking presentable.

'I'm sorry.' He said when he noticed the colour of her cheeks, 'but I did say I'd be back about 6:30.'

'I know, it's my fault, I lost track of time doing the cooking. I thought I had plenty of time before you returned. I'll know better next time.'

'That's a shame.' Jack grinned.

'Behave yourself. Don't forget you're my bother-in-law.'

'Argh, I haven't forgotten.' Jack struggled to hide the disappointment in his voice.

'Here's your beer.' Rosie placed a glass of beer on the table for Jack, alongside the open bottle. 'Have that and then you should hurry up and wash up for dinner. It won't be long, and you smell.'

'I smell. That's nice.'

'Yes, you smell like a sheep. It's not such a bad smell, but I prefer soap. Leave your clothes on the chair outside, and I'll wash them in the morning.'

'You don't have to do that.'

'I know, but I'm happy to. I have to wash mine. I've almost run out of clean clothes.'

'You could just wear that towel around here. I don't mind, and I promise not to look.'

Rosie pulled a mock angry face at Jack, but it was obvious she was enjoying the banter.

'Drink up your beer and go have a wash. Do as you're told before I slap you.'

'You're a very bossy sister-in-law.' Jack watched Rosie as she fussed about the kitchen preparing dinner. 'You have a sweet voice.' He added quietly.

'Pardon?'

'I said you have a sweet voice. I enjoyed listening to you sing. The song was a little sad, but I could listen to you for hours.'

'Thank you.' Rosie's cheeks had coloured again. Her complexion always made it hard to hide how she was feeling. 'I didn't know you were listening.'

'You know your sister loved that song.'

Rosie froze on the spot. It took a moment before she could look at Jack.

'I do know that.' She spoke quietly with more than a touch of melancholy. 'We used to sing it together when we were children. Occasionally Ma and Da would take us to the beach, and we would sing together as we strolled along in the sand. We'd search for hours for magical seashells to take home for our collections.'

'I know that too.' Jack answered, seeing the love in Rosie's eyes for her sister. 'After Mary and I got married, we were able to take two nights by the sea down south at Brighton. One night we went for a walk along the beach. As you know, it was wartime, and we were all permanently on edge. We were always wondering what was about to sail into port, emerge from the ocean, or fly overhead. But we managed to try and live normally for odd moments between the madness. We had some of those moments in Brighton. Walking along the beach was one. Mary spotted a rare colourful shell. It really did stand out from the rest. I remember this like it was yesterday. She said, look at this one, as she picked it up. It's beautiful. It makes me think of my sister. I didn't realise how much I missed her. You wait until you meet her. You will love her, she said, smiling at me.'

Jack stopped speaking and watched Rosie, who was staring back at him, her eyes glistening with tears. He reflected for a moment on what he'd just said. You will love her. How right she'd been. He continued his story.

'Anyway, she also said, that she and her little sister, Roisin, loved to sing while they . . ., while you, collected shells. I asked her to sing for me. It took a little persuasion, but as reluctant as she was, I think she really wanted to, and she enjoyed it. She sang just what you did before.'

Rosie's cheeks were wet with tears when he crossed the room and took her in his arms, pulling her in tight against him. She leant her cheek against his chest and wrapped her arms around his waist. Jack rested his chin on the top of her head, squeezed her tight again, then couldn't stop himself kissing the top of her head.

'You ok?' He whispered in a gentle voice.

'I am, thank you.' She squeezed him back then pushed away to look up at him while he kept hold of her shoulders. She smiled through tears. They held each other's gaze a long while before Rosie finally broke the moment, putting her hands flat on his chest and pushing him away. 'Now go. You still smell like a sheep.'

'Okay, okay, I'm going.'

CHAPTER TWENTY-SIX

Syd walked toward the door that led out of the kitchen and into the backyard. Sitting down on the doorstep, he struggled to pull his boots on. His bulging belly was getting in the way of a lot of things now. He huffed and puffed uncomfortably.

'Ey.' He called back over his shoulder to Bonnie, who was cleaning up the breakfast dishes in the kitchen.

'What?' She replied in a frustrated tone.

'Come 'ere.'

She walked over and stood behind him, looking down. Her dislike of Syd had taken on new proportions since the babies had been born, and she was always relieved when he finally left the house to go and work. Today would be a good day. He was heading out the back of the property to do some fencing, and he would be gone for most of the day, except lunch.

'What?' She asked again.

'You'll have to bring me lunch out to the paddock today.'

'Why?' Bonnie couldn't hide the anger in her voice.

'Alright, don't get yer bloody knickers in a twist, girlie. I'm replacing that gate in the gully, and I got to pull it down and put it back in one day, so the stock don't get through. Besides, I've got other things to do tomorrow, and I don't want to be going back out there to finish it off in the morning. I won't have time.'

'What are you doing tomorrow that's so important?'

'Well, it's none of your business actually, but I am going into town for a meeting.'

'A meeting about what? Who with?'

'What are you, a bloody policeman? Never you mind what the meeting's about. It's business and not yours. Okay?'

'This is my place too, you know.' Years of frustration at being treated like the hired help were starting to take their toll. That, coupled with Syd slowing down and looking less threatening than he had when they first married, was buoying Bonnie's confidence.

'Give it a break, will yer? Just bring me bloody lunch out and leave it at that.' Syd stood up slowly and stretched his back.

'You been talking to that Taylor bloke again.' Bonnie pushed.

'What?'

'Taylor. I hear things you know.' She snapped back at him.

'Like what?'

'You been talking to Taylor about buying our property, haven't yer?'

'My property, remember that. You're only here by invitation. And so what if I have, anyway?'

'What about our kids? You gonna just sell it out from under them, are you?'

Syd didn't respond, just stood looking at Bonnie through his dirty spectacles and scowling.

'Well, are you?' She screamed. She completely lost her temper with Syd for the first time ever. 'Are you? Answer me.' She screamed again.

'You'll watch how you speak to me girl, if you know what's good for you.' Syd's eyes narrowed like a snake about to strike.

Inside, both the children had started to cry. Bonnie hung on as long as she could before tears began streaming down her face.

'You're a pig.' She managed to blurt out between sobs. 'You don't care about anyone. No one but yourself. You don't care about your children.'

'And you've forgotten your place round here.' Syd shouted back at her. Pulling himself slowly to his feet, he leaned in toward her, jaw jutting out and spoke in a low and menacing growl. 'You need to shut your mouth before you talk yourself into a whole lot of trouble. Get yourself inside and look after those bloody screaming brats, and don't forget my lunch, or you'll be sorry. You hear me?'

Bonnie slammed the door shut in his face. There

was a massive crash, and the twins screamed. She walked into their room.

'There there, it's ok. Mummy's just a little cranky with Syd. That's all.' She settled the children as the tears spilt from her eyes. She gathered them up one at a time and took them into the kitchen. She never referred to Syd as Dad or your father. She put the kids down on a rug on the floor in the kitchen and went back to the dishes.

An hour and a half later, Bonnie had cleaned up in the kitchen, tidied the twins' room and put them back to sleep. She'd made she and Syd's bed, although she rarely slept in it and made the bed in the spare room where she mostly spent her nights. It had been easy to persuade Syd that she would be up and down all night long with the twins, and it would be better that she slept in the spare room rather than continually disturb him. He was happy with that. There'd been a few occasions since the birth when he'd told her he wanted her in their bed after dinner, at least for a short while, he'd said. She'd managed to find an excuse each time, fill him with more food and pour an extra whiskey, and he hadn't put up much of a fight.

Bonnie tidied up the lounge room, waiting for the first inevitable squawk. She picked up a bottle of whiskey that Syd had been drinking from the night before and placed it back on the cabinet where it lived. Looking at the bottle for a moment, she was reminded of that wonderful afternoon with Jack. Jack was a kind man, a good man. That had been the only time she had ever enjoyed laying with a man, but it had left her wracked with guilt and the fear of being found out. As it was, that wasn't the only thing it had left her with.

She was still bitterly angry with Syd when she looked through the curtains, making sure he'd gone and, oddly, wanting to make sure no one else could see her. As if they ever could, she realised, no one came near this place. Syd's demeanour made sure of that. She took a glass from the old timber cabinet and poured herself a whiskey. She remembered how good it had made her feel when she was with Jack. All her problems had seemed to disappear. Jack had been the first man to see her for who she was, an attractive, smart, desirable woman. She upended the glass swallowing its contents in one gulp before coughing several times while she waited for the burning in her throat to subside. She poured herself another glass and did the same. Disappointed when she didn't get the warm fuzzy feeling she'd had last time, she poured another and was well into the third glass when it finally hit her. The room began to spin. She looked at her glass, and it was empty, so she filled it yet again, spilling a little on the cabinet. This time she slowed down and sipped the drink, but it was too late. She was well and truly tipsy, and the impact of the strong liquor was bearing down on her like a tidal wave.

With the bottle in one hand and the glass in the

other, Bonnie crept over to the twin's bedroom door and put her ear against it. It was all quiet, and she smiled as she staggered off toward the kitchen, sipping the whiskey as she went.

She stood at the kitchen sink, still frequently sipping on the whiskey, as though there was a destination to be reached quickly, not a journey to be savoured. She stood looking out the window toward the paddocks.

'This is my property. And this is Charlie's and Mary's property, you old baassaard.' Her words were slurred. 'You're not gunna steal it off us, not now, not never.'

Bonnie looked around the kitchen, blinking her eyes, trying to focus and wondering what to do next. Lunch, she thought. Make the old bassard's lunch. She took a loaf of bread from the bread tin, fetched a knife from the cutlery draw, cut four misshapen slices, and laughed aloud when she looked at them. Then she sliced some lamb and put it on the bread.

'Was zat?' She spoke to herself as she noticed something red on one of the slices of bread. 'Sauce?' She looked down and could see blood coming from her finger. 'Oh shit.' She laughed. 'Here you go, darling Syd, have some sauce. She wiped the blood off her finger onto the bread and turned the slice over to hide it. She hadn't even felt the cut.

An hour later and another half glass of whiskey was when Bonnie had finally loaded the twins into the Land Rover and had them secured precariously on the back seat. Even in her drunken state, she knew she was taking a considerable risk with the twins, but she didn't stop. Her anger was still simmering, and she was finding it difficult to form sensible and rational thoughts. She'd had the good sense to top up Syd's whiskey bottle with water, but not the mind to realise both the colour and taste would be a dead giveaway.

As she rattled along the track toward the gully paddock, she occasionally turned around to check on the kids in the back seat. On one occasion, she turned back to the front to find she'd driven right off the track and was heading for a rock. She just managed to swerve and maneuver the vehicle back onto the track, which was really just a couple of wheel ruts. Thankfully the kids hadn't been flung off their seats.

Up ahead, she could see the tractor and trailer and then Syd, wrapping wire around a freshly placed gate post. She pulled the vehicle up, but Syd didn't look up from the knot he tied in the wire. She got out of the vehicle.

'Here's your lunch.' She did her best to hide the slur in her words.

He turned around and looked at her. She held out a small bundle, the sandwiches wrapped in newspaper.

'Stick it on the trailer.' He turned back to what he was doing. 'Yer bring tea?'

'Nah.' She announced defiantly, swaying on the spot.

He turned around and looked at her, squinting his eyes, assessing her.

'You can boil a bloody billy. You're not a bloody cripple.' Bonnie returned his gaze and felt good. With her hands on her hips, her head tilted back, and her chin pushed forward, she was focussing on not swaying too much.

He just stared at her, not speaking, before walking slowly toward her. She watched him as though he was a wild dog stalking her, preparing to flee if she had to. He was only a couple of feet away from her when he spoke.

'You've been drinking. I can smell it from 'ere.'

'So what if I have? You can hardly talk, can yer?'

'You've got them brats to look after.'

'They're fine.'

'You call yourself a mother?'

'You call yourself a father, do you? You're no bloody father.' Bonnie's tone was venomous. Syd grabbed her wrist and shook her arm.

'Take a look at yourself. Is this what you do every day when I go out and work? I should have bloody well known. Well, you're gonna cop it later on, I'm telling you now.'

'Get your hands off me.' Bonnie pulled her arm back, but she couldn't break his grip.

'You don't deserve to be a mother. You're no good for nuffin. I work my arse off every day to provide for you and them kids, and look how you repay me. Sitting at home drinking me grog and abusing me.'

'You don't deserve to be a father.' Bonnie spat back at him. In her rage, she couldn't think of anything more clever to say. 'You get drunk every night, and you're trying to sell the farm out from under us so you can sit in the pub and drink away their future.' Bonnie pointed back toward the Land Rover where the babies were starting to cry. 'Oh, I know men like you. I had that done to me, and I'm not gonna let you do it to my children.'

'I'll do what I bloody well like. Young Charlie'll be looked after. You don't have to worry about him.' Syd shouted in reply.

'And what about Mary?'

'What about her? She's no bloody use to me. If you'd been smart, you'd a stopped at one. One boy. That's all I wanted.'

Bonnie's temper burst, bubbling up from her stomach, through her chest, out her mouth and along her arms. She swung her arm and a closed fist at Syd's head.

'You Bastard.' She spat the words at him.

Syd caught her arm by the wrist again, and he viciously pulled it back down to her side. With his face just inches from hers, he spoke in an unnervingly steady voice through clenched teeth.

'You get your arse back in that vehicle now and get back to the house where you belong. I'll deal with you later, and I can tell you,' he spoke the last words slowly and with a pause between each of them, 'I will deal with you.' He shoved Bonnie hard in the direction of the Land Rover, and she fell to the ground and began to cry. 'Go on, bugger off.' He yelled down at her.

With that, Syd picked the sandwiches up off the trailer and walked back to the post he'd been working on.

Bonnie slowly lifted herself up off the ground. The cut on her finger was bleeding again, and she'd hit her elbow on a flat rock. Pain seared up her arm. Her rage was boiling over. She looked back at Syd, who was back wrapping another wire around the gate post as though nothing had happened. The babies were crying relentlessly now, and her nerves were shredded. Later, she wouldn't remember the moment she picked the hammer up off the trailer.

The first blow cracked Syd's skull on the back of his head. He dropped to his knees where he'd stood. His eyes were wide, and there was a look of terror and helplessness on his face as Bonnie moved around and stood in front of him, hatred burnt deep into the weary lines etched in her young face. He clutched the gate post, holding himself up as he knelt.

'They're not your children, and they will . . . have . . . this . . . farm.' She spoke calmly and clearly. He didn't respond. He closed his eyes as the hammer came down upon his forehead. Blood sprayed out across the fence post and Bonnie's dress.

There was complete silence, nothing more than a distant and quiet birdsong, the buzz of insects and the slightest rustling of leaves high in the treetops. Even the children were silent. It was as though everything, all of nature, stood still in shock and wonder at what had just been done.

Bonnie dropped the hammer. For a moment, she stood staring down at Syd's body. She felt strangely peaceful. Then the children began screaming again, and she was brought back to the present and the enormity of what she'd done hit her like a freight train. She ran back to her vehicle, started it, jammed it in gear and took off for home as quickly as she could.

Bonnie didn't notice the woman on horseback up the hill in the neighbour's property watching her vehicle race across the paddock.

CHAPTER TWENTY-SEVEN

Tuesday and Wednesday were punctuated by the same strict and time-sensitive shearing routine, and they flew past in what seemed like a flash. There wasn't a moment to relax. Every waking moment was allocated to moving sheep, feeding shearers and shed hands, preparing for the next day and wrapping up the last.

'Well, we are almost there. Just one day to go.' Jack spoke as he walked through the door after having washed up. He wore nothing but a towel wrapped around his midsection, and Rosie couldn't help but run her eyes over his chest and arms. Having seen him like this nearly every night since she'd been staying with him hadn't helped to cool her desire one bit. She turned back to the stove to hide from what she knew she desperately wanted.

'What's the program for tomorrow?' Rosie asked as she took a pie out of the oven and dropped it quickly on the stovetop, pulling a face as the heat seeped through the tea towel and into her fingers. It was a welcome distraction from the heat pooling elsewhere in her body.

Rosie was surprised by how quickly she'd settled

into a routine around the farm with Jack. It was hard work, but she'd enjoyed every minute of it. She'd loved working with him, talking with him, teasing him, having dinner with him, listening to his stories from the shed, and his complaints about the workers. And then she'd loved hearing the shift in his breathing each night as he collapsed into a deep sleep. She'd even enjoyed cooking his meals and watching him eat as though he hadn't for days. She was going to miss all this. She would miss it a lot.

'We've got about half a day's shearing. We'll cut out just before lunch. Bluey and Ross will want to sharpen their combs and cutters. They've got a shed Friday. Then they'll be keen to have a few beers. A few sandwiches will be good if you don't mind, but they won't eat much. They'll be more interested in the grog.'

Rosie looked back at Jack, who was still standing just inside the door wrapped in the towel.

'I don't mind at all. You're paying me, don't forget.' She kept her eyes firmly fixed on his, not trusting herself to let them wander.

'Am I? I don't remember that.' Jack laughed.

'You are. Maybe I should go on a stop-work until I see the cash.'

'There won't be much. After I take out all of your board and keep and the wine you've drunk, feed for your horse, getting the comfy bed.' Jack raised a finger with each item he listed. 'I reckon after all that, you'll be paying me.'

Jack went to walk past Rosie to go to the bedroom to change for dinner. He bumped her playfully with his hip, and not expecting it, she fell toward the stove. He reached out quickly, wrapping an arm around her and pulling her toward him and to safety. She found herself, hands on his bare chest, and looking up into his dark eyes, full of desire. They stood for a moment, with not a sound but their breathing.

Rosie felt Jack pull her closer, and she knew instinctively he wasn't going to let her go this time. Regardless being released from his strong arms was the last thing she wanted. She closed her eyes as his lips brushed hers. Their mouths fell open with desire, and he kissed her passionately. Rosie couldn't help but moan quietly with pleasure as she wrapped he arms around his neck, pulling him as close as she could, but it was still not enough. She took a handful of his hair and pulled him into a deep and desperate kiss, and he responded in kind.

Jack picked Rosie up, swinging her into his arms as though she were weightless and carried her into the bedroom. He lay her on the bed. She felt like she would melt right into the blankets as she watched him standing there. She caught her breath sharply as he began to unhook his towel, and she gasped as he let it fall to the floor, standing completely naked in front of her. He lay down on the bed beside her, then covered her body with his kissing her neck, her chin and then her lips with increasing urgency. His hands explored every inch of her until she could stand it no longer. She pushed him over and onto his back then stood up from the bed. She slipped her dress off, all the time watching him, with her heart bursting from the desire in his eyes. She slowly took off her underwear, and he looked starved of love and desperate for her. His face looked as though he'd witnessed a miracle as he gazed upon her naked body, and she smiled. He reached out and put his hands on her hips, pulling her toward where he sat on the edge of the bed. He kissed her breasts gently as she cupped the back of his head in her hands and kissed his damp ruffled hair. He could wait no longer, and he swung her around gracefully and onto her back on the bed.

Rosie felt the warmth and weight of his muscular body, soft and hard, against hers. She'd never felt anything like the emotions she was feeling in that moment. Looking down at her, their lips so close she could feel his warm breath, he whispered. 'Rosie, beautiful Rosie.'

'Jack.' She whispered back.

'I love you Rosie. With all my heart.'

Rosie smiled and felt tears escape and caress her temples.

'I love you Jack.'

Jack moved back slightly, then looking deep into Rosie's eyes, he moved forward, and she gasped, cried out in pleasure, and reached up to kiss him passionately, clawing at his back.

CHAPTER TWENTY-EIGHT

The next day, just on lunchtime, the shearers had cut out, and they were all enjoying a cold beer. The dogs stood up from where they'd been lying flat in the dust not far from Jack's feet. As one, they both looked in the direction of the track that led in from the road. One growled quietly before they both took off, running toward the gate. Everyone in the group turned to watch the dogs.

'Got a visitor.' Bluey announced.

Dust billowed up from a vehicle travelling unusually fast along the track.

'Who's that? Rosie asked Jack, who'd begun to stand up.

'Dunno.' Jack replied as he put his beer down on the stump he'd been sitting on. He stood with his hands on his hips, watching along with Rosie and the shearing team as a vehicle pulled up at the gate.

Rosie and Jack had agreed to be careful not to bring attention to themselves in front of the others. It had been torturous trying not to steal a glance or share a knowing look while their thoughts returned to moments of the night before, over and over. Although they were both exhausted, having had little sleep, they were both so happy they didn't care. All they wanted was for shearing to be over and for everyone to go, to leave them, just to each other.

'It's Artie. Arthur Braxton. The neighbour from the other side of Glencoe.'

'Hah!' Bluey announced. 'We start there tomorrow. I told him I'd drop in this arvo and say G'day. Must have decided to come and see us here instead.'

'I'll bring him up for a beer.' Jack said as he strolled over to Artie, quickly getting out of his vehicle and striding toward the gate.

'How yer going Artie?' Jack called out as he approached the neighbour.

'Yeah, alright Jack.'

Artie was a tall and wiry gentleman who looked like he could do with a good feed. His skin was stained copper by the sun, and his face was weathered beyond his years.

'Time for a beer?'

'No. Thomo sent me.' Artie's tone was direct and to the point.

Jack knew Sergeant Will Thompson, not well, but well enough to address him as Thomo, the same as everyone else in town did, well, those over sixteen years of age that was. Any younger than that, and you'd have got a friendly but firm clip under the ear for being cheeky.

'Thomo, what's up?'

'There's a problem at Glencoe. He's there now.'

'What sort of problem?'

'Syd's gone missing. Apparently, young Bonnie called the station this morning when he didn't return home from out in the paddock somewhere.'

Everyone seemed to refer to Bonnie as young Bonnie, seemingly because her age contrasted so much with old Syd's.

'Surely he's just out the back or on the hill or something?'

'Yeah, that's what I'd a thought, but the thing is, he didn't come in last night. He's been gone since breakfast yesterday. Apparently, she couldn't go looking for too long with the twins and all.'

'What? Why didn't she call someone or come get me yesterday arvo?'

'I dunno. I don't know the answer to that one. She reckons she took a look around herself last night but couldn't stay out too long because of the twins, and when she got back and sorted them out, it was too late to call Thomo.'

'That's bloody ridiculous. She could have just called the pub and got Archie to send someone to fetch him.'

'I know mate. Doesn't make any sense, but I gotta say, she's not in a good way.'

'What do yer mean?'

'She's been on the bottle. I've just come from there, and she sounded like she'd had a skinful. Kids are screaming in the background. The place is a bloody pigsty, husband's missing. All a bit bloody odd.'

'Shit. Okay, what does he want me to do?'

'Bring the boys and come and help us find him. We've gotta find him this afternoon. If he's crook out there in the bush somewhere, and he's been out a night already, he may not make another night.'

'He hasn't just gone to town or something and not told her?'

'No, Thomo's checked in town, and no one's seen him.'

'Okay, I'll round these fellas up. They've had a couple themselves, but they'll soon sober up.'

'He told me to tell you to bring the girlie with you. He's rung Doc Hadley, and he's on his way. Someone's gonna have to look after the kids until she sobers up and Syd's found. I'll see you over there, ok?

'Yep, right behind yer.'

It took less than ten minutes for the entire crew to get into their vehicles and hit the road to the Fredericks's property. A short time later, the convoy led by Jack and Rosie arrived at the house. Artie was standing in the garden talking to Sergeant Thompson. Everyone exchanged greetings as they got out of their vehicles. Everyone knew everyone on a first name or nickname basis, and no time was lost on pleasantries.

'You best go in and check on the kids and

Bonnie, please Rosie. I did my best with them, but I'm not a dad, just an uncle. Try and get a strong cup of tea into Bonnie if you can. She'll probably need to get some sleep. Looks like she hasn't slept all night.'

Rosie disappeared inside quickly.

Thomo took Artie and Jack aside.

'I'll be with you fellas in a moment.' He called to Bluey and the boys who were gathered over by the garden gate, talking quietly.

'Listen, Artie, Jack, I don't know this young sheila in there,' he glanced toward the house, 'but there's something fishy about all this. Do you blokes know her?'

'Not much mate.' Artie replied. 'The wife chats to her on occasions. Drops in for a cup of tea from time to time just to make sure she's ok with the youngins and all. Bit of company too. It can't be easy for her, living with Syd.'

'Why's that Artie?' Thomo asked.

'Ah, he's just a cranky old bastard, that's all. A little bit of Syd goes a long way, wouldn't you say Jack?' Artie looked to Jack for support.

'Too right. He's a right pain in the arse and pretty bloody rough on her too.' Jack couldn't hide his distaste for Syd.

'So, do you know her much, Jack?' Thomo asked, still trying to get an understanding of what was going on here at Glencoe.

'Nah, not really. I've seen her a few times when I've been over here to see Syd, but that's about it. Syd usually dominates the conversation.' Jack did his best to speak with confidence.

'It's all a bit strange. According to the girl, I don't know if Artie told you Jack, but Syd's been gone since yesterday morning. If I didn't know better, I'd guess she's been on the grog for most of that time, at least. If not, she's come out of the gates early this morning.'

Jack was worried and wished he could go inside with Rosie and see what was happening with Bonnie.

'Alright you lot,' Thomo called out to the shearing crew, 'come over here, will yer?'

The shearer's wandered over, and the group formed a half-circle around Thomo.

'Righto, we got a bloke who's been missing for more than twenty-four hours. We've got a lot of ground to cover. I can get more neighbours over if we need them and a few blokes from town, including the Doctor, but I'm hoping we'll find him quickly and with a minimum of fuss. You'd have to reckon he's done himself some damage, and that's why he hasn't made it home. His missus is upset and a bit crook, so the nurse is looking after her and the kids. They'll be alright. We're going to break into three groups. Jack and I will head out toward the back on the track along the boundary. Jack's seen some of that ground, so he knows the lay of the land. The only thing I got out of the girl was he'd been out fencing earlier in the week. Now, it might seem silly, but we need to search these near paddocks first in case he's wandered back, injured and collapsed. Artie will split you up in pairs, and you'll need to drive where you can, but get out on foot amongst the scrub and rocks. You could miss him pretty easy out there.'

A short while later, Thomo and Jack were driving slowly along the track that led out toward the hills at the rear of both Glencoe and Snowy Ridge. The properties bordered Jake's Mountain.

'I don't reckon he'd be out here.' Jack said.

'Why's that then?'

'Well, I looked across at his machinery shed. The Land Rover and the tractor were both parked in their bays. He'd a brought a vehicle if he was working out here. Surely?'

Jack was as perplexed as Thomo was.

'I know.' Thomo replied. 'But he could have walked, couldn't he? If he was walking the boundary, checking the fence. He might have just come out with the strainers and some pliers.'

'He might have, but it seems a bit unlikely. You know Syd. With that gut, I don't reckon he walks too far.'

'The girl, Bonnie, the only thing she said between the blubbering and carry on was that he'd been doing some fencing in the gully out back. Artie reckons this is the track.'

'Yeah, it is.' Jack confirmed.

They drove on for a while longer, scanning the

paddocks about them and wondering if they really had any chance of finding Syd amongst the stands of trees and rocky outcrops.

'If he'd sort shelter overnight, then passed out or worse, you could drive right past him, and you wouldn't see him, and he wouldn't see us.' Jack commented.

'Over there!' Thomo pointed through the windscreen.

Jack followed where Thomo was looking and could see he was pointing at two gate posts. The bark had only recently been stripped off them, and the timber looked fresh and hadn't weathered into the grey that coloured the bush, the rocks, the fallen trees and even the sheep.

'They're new posts. He hasn't even swung the gate yet.'

They motored slowly over toward the posts. Jack pulled the vehicle up, and they hopped out.

'Shit, what's that stink?' Jack scrunched up his face and looked at Thomo, who was doing likewise.

'Not good,' was all Thomo said in reply.

Rosie pushed open the front door nervously, wondering what to expect. She walked along the hall that led to the kitchen at the rear of the house. She knew the layout, having been to visit Bonnie on occasions. She passed the main bedroom on her right and peered in through the open door. The bed was unmade and empty. She moved on, stopping at the children's bedroom where the door was only slightly ajar. She pushed it open as slowly and as quietly as she could, assuming they were inside and possibly sleeping. When she had the door open enough to crane her head around its edge, she could see the children in their beds. Charlie was asleep and still. Mary was awake, staring at the ceiling, her legs and arms waving about happily. Rosie pulled the door shut and ventured on along the hall.

Just before the hall opened into the bright kitchen, an open double doorway led to the lounge. The curtains were drawn, and the room was quite dark. Looking away from the light streaming into the hall from the kitchen, it took Rosie's eyes a moment to adjust to the dim interior of the lounge. Finally, her gaze settled on the forlorn figure slumped in an armchair.

'Bonnie.' Rosie spoke quietly. There was no movement. 'Bonnie, you okay?'

Bonnie raised her chin from her chest slowly. Her face was wet with tears, her eyes were ringed grey and blue, her hair was hanging loose and looked like it hadn't been brushed in days, and she was wearing a nightdress.

Rosie crossed the room and knelt beside the armchair. She could smell whiskey and unwashed skin.

'Bonnie, darling, are you okay?' She took Bonnie's hand in hers.

'No.' Bonnie replied in a pitiful, barely audible reply.

'It's okay, sweetheart. The babies are okay. The men are out looking for Syd. They'll find him soon enough, and everything will be ok.'

'It won't. It won't be ok.'

Rosie watched Bonnie as she spoke and wondered what she could do. She was surprised by her condition. She'd expected her to be up and about and anxious, but she looked more like a grieving widow.

'Come on Bon, let's get you cleaned up and a good strong cup of tea.' As she spoke, Rosie took in the chaotic scene that included a mostly empty bottle of Scotch and a glass, on its side, on a small table on the other side of the armchair. 'You've had a bit to drink then.' It was more a comment than a question.

'Mmm.'

Rosie stood in front of Bonnie, and taking both of her hands, began to pull her to her feet.

'Come on, up you get. Let's get you to the bathroom for a wash, and I'll get you some fresh clothes.'

It took a good twenty minutes to get Bonnie into some sort of presentable condition. Rosie had her washed, dressed, her hair brushed and sitting at the kitchen table when she put the kettle on. She found some bread. Although it was stale, it was edible, and she made toast.

'He's been gone for days.' Bonnie was mumbling.

'What do you mean he's been gone for days?'

'He's been gone since Sunday. Since Sunday lunchtime.'

'But it's Thursday. Bonnie, it's Thursday, that's four days ago. If he's been gone since Sunday, why didn't you report it on Sunday, or at least on Monday?'

'I didn't know what to do.'

'What do you mean you didn't know what to do?'

'Just that, I didn't know what to do. I panicked. And then, by the time I realised I just had to do something, it was too late.'

'I don't understand.' Rosie tilted her head slightly sideways, squinting at Bonnie and focussing on her words.

Suddenly, the conversation was interrupted by a squawk from down the hallway.

'That's Mary.' Bonnie rubbed her face in her hands. 'She'll be hungry, and she'll need changing.' She looked up at Rosie with a pitiful face. 'I've been looking after them you know. I know I'm a terrible mess, but I've been looking after my babies. They are the only thing that matters now.'

'It's okay.' Rosie replied. 'I'll go get her and bring her out here, and we can sort her out. Are there clean nappies in their room?'

'In the laundry.'

'Okay, I'll get her, and I'll take her to the laundry, clean her up, and get her dressed. I guess she'll wake Charlie up?'

'Yes, he'll wake up soon enough. He's always hungry. But he sleeps very well.' Bonnie smiled through her tears as she talked about her babies.

Rosie pushed the bedroom door open slowly and quietly crossed the room to where Mary lay in her crib. The sight of Rosie seemed to settle the little girl, and she lay quietly waiting to be picked up. By the time Rosie got to the laundry, Bonnie had found a nappy and folded it ready for Mary. She was running a little water into the sink and preparing a cloth to wipe the child down. Rosie put Mary down on her back on the laundry bench and removed her nightdress and nappy. Bonnie handed her the cloth that she had soaked in warm water and rung out. Rosie carefully wiped Mary down, cleaning her up.

'There you go bubba, you're all fresh now.' She leaned down and kissed Mary on the forehead. 'Okay, over you go.' She turned Mary over to repeat the process and stopped deathly still at the sight of her bare leg.

Bonnie looked at Rosie, concerned and wondering why she'd stopped and had such a shocked look on her face.

'What is it? Is everything okay?' She asked urgently.

Rosie hesitated before she spoke, then having collected herself, cleared her throat and went on.

'Yes, yes, everything is okay.' She began to wipe Mary over with the cloth. 'I hadn't noticed this before.' Rosie ran her fingers over the birthmark at the top of Rosie's leg, just below her hip.

'It's a birthmark.'

'Yes, I know what it is.' Rosie hesitated for a

moment, trying to control the shake in her voice. 'It's quite an unusual shape, isn't it?'

'I think it looks a little like a map of New Zealand. I don't know where she got that from. No one in my family has a birthmark like that as far as I know.'

'What about in Syd's family?'

Bonnie looked up at Rosie, and Rosie could feel her eyes watching her.

'I . . . I have no idea.' Bonnie replied apprehensively.

'Does baby Charlie have the same mark?'

'No, he doesn't. Just Mary. So maybe it's just a one-off.'

'Hah.' Rosie's voice croaked again, and she found herself clearing her throat again. She could still feel Bonnie's eyes upon her. She turned and smiled at her. 'Maybe it is.'

Jack knew the smell of dead animals only too well. Thomo knew the smell of death, but not just animals.

'What the hell is that? Whatever it is, it's been dead a few days.'

'You're right there.' Thomo replied. 'I'm starting to worry now.'

'About Syd?'

'Yes, about Syd. I'm starting to think we're not gonna find this fella alive. We better take a look around and find out where that bloody smell's coming from. It shouldn't be too hard to find, just follow your nose, if you can do that without losing your lunch. Better prepare yourself mate.'

Thomo wandered off in one direction, toward a stand of trees in amongst some rocks, and not too far from the gate where they could see Syd had been working. Jack headed off in the opposite direction, down toward a Gully and in the direction of the boundary of his property. The further Jack walked, the stronger the smell became. His stomach tightened with nervous tension, and the stench made him gag. He walked to a group of rocks, climbed on top of them, then leapt from one to another, searching for the source of the terrible smell. There was no sign of whatever it was that was so horribly dead. Casting his eyes back in the direction of where Thomo was searching, Jack could see a patch of bracken fern that had been disturbed. It was about thirty yards down the slope from the gate, in the direction of the gully. He leapt off the rock that he was standing on and walked quickly toward the bracken. The stench got stronger, and he buried his nose in the crook of his elbow.

Jack could see something had crushed the foliage. He stepped carefully and tentatively into the thick bracken, hoping that it wasn't a wild pig that had done the damage. There weren't many in the area, but they were starting to come down off the mountain and beginning to cause problems with the fences and pastures, and they were dangerous. He walked in nervously. It was nearly waist high in parts as he followed the crushed pathway. And then . . . there it was, a body.

'Thomo, over here.' Jack yelled and waved his arm, then doubled over and coughed furiously, trying not to throw up.

Thomo ran over to Jack, from where he'd been searching.

'Don't run mate, he's not going anywhere.' Jack staggered out of the bracken, not looking back.

Jack stood well back from the bracken patch while Thomo surveyed the scene. It was quite some time before Thomo came back out.

'Christ mate, your guts must be made of steel.' Jack said, looking in wonder at Thomo.

'Not really mate, but it's only gonna get worse, so I'm trying to see as much as I can now.'

'Fair point. What do you make of it? What do yer reckon happened to the poor bastard?'

'Well, between you and me, it's no accident. You've only got a look at the bracken to be able to see he was dragged in here. If he'd staggered in here by himself, it wouldn't be nearly as much of a mess. And there are no animals in these parts that would've dragged him in. They would've just chewed on him where he dropped.'

'So you think someone did it to him?'

'That's what I'm thinking at the moment, but you better keep that under your hat. I'm gonna poke my nose around here for a while and see what I can work out. I'll need you to go back to the house, pick up Doc Hadley, and bring him out here. Hopefully, he's arrived by now. And you'll have to break the news to the other fellas and tell them to get on home. There's nothing they can do to help here. In fact, they'll just be in the way. But tell them they need to keep their mouths shut, and if they don't, they'll have me to answer to.'

'Sure thing mate. Geezus, what a bloody mess. Poor Bonnie, and those kids. What a terrible mess.' Jack stood, hands on hips, shoulders slumped.

'Jack, this bloke's been dead for days, several, I reckon, not just twenty-four hours like Bonnie said. There's something really fishy going on, and I have little doubt she's got something to do with it.'

Jack was more than pleased to be back in the vehicle and travelling away from the horrible scene as quickly as he could. His mind was awash with concern about what had actually happened. He couldn't imagine for a moment that Bonnie was actually responsible for Syd's death, but there was no doubt that bloke could make your temper boil over and who knows what could have happened. But, the more he thought about it, she just might have had made a mistake, a really terrible mistake.

Fifteen minutes later, he pulled up at the house. The shearing team were still walking the paddocks close to the house. Jack drove about, catching their attention and waving them back to the house yard.

Rosie and Bonnie both looked up from the kitchen table where they'd been sitting having a cup of tea with Doctor Hadley when they heard the sound of an approaching vehicle.

'Listen. That sounds like a vehicle. It might be Jack. Hopefully, this is a good sign.' Rosie tried to sound positive. 'Come on Bonnie, let's go and see what the news is.'

'You go. I'll just wait here.'

'You sure?'

'Yes.'

Rosie got up from the table, squeezed Bonnie's arm as she passed her and headed toward the front door. Hadley had already gone outside, leaving the front door open. Rosie could see through the screen door that Hadley was talking to Jack, and by the look of the faces and body language, it wasn't good news. Rosie pushed open the screen door and walked toward Jack, just as Hadley strode off toward his vehicle.

'Well?' Rosie said. Her hands were on her hips and looking up into Jack's eyes.

'Not good news, I'm afraid. We found him. He's . . . he's dead.'

'Oh, my God. How? What happened?'

Jack took Rosie by the arm and led her further away from the house. With their backs turned away from the house, he asked.

'How's Bonnie?'

'Not good. She's been drinking, and things are a mess in there.'

'Are the kids ok?'

Rosie looked deep into Jack's eyes for a moment before answering.

'They're fine. I've cleaned them up, and her too. I've given her a strong cup of tea. She's tired and needs rest, but other than that, she's fine, physically fine, that is.'

'Something really bad's happened here Rosie. Thomo's hinting at a murder. He says Syd's been dead for days.'

'Yes, Bonnie just told me he's been missing since Sunday. Where was he?'

'He was out in the gully paddock, not that far really and not far from our boundary.'

The use of the word 'our' was not lost on Rosie. Jack continued.

'You know where we were mustering on Sunday, the paddock where we picked up the wethers?'

Rosie nodded.

'Not far from there.'

Rosie was taken back to Sunday when Jack had sent her out around the paddock, close to the boundary fence, searching for the wethers. They'd split up at one point, and he'd headed in the opposite direction on his horse. She recalled hearing the sound of angry voices and then seeing the Fredericks vehicle travelling fast, too fast, across the paddock a short time later.

'You know,' she started, 'when we were mustering on Sunday, I thought I heard two people arguing. It could only have been Bonnie and Syd. Who else would've been right out there? And then, a couple of minutes later, I saw the Land Rover flying through the paddock really fast. I didn't really think much of it at the time. Why would I? Now, I'm starting to wonder if something happened then?'

Jack watched Rosie as she spoke. She looked calm, almost detached from the situation, and he wondered how she was coping. He'd been exposed to so much tragedy, death, horrible injuries, and amongst them all, many were his friends. He was shocked by what they'd found out in the paddock, lying in the bracken fern, but he was, to some extent, still desensitized. As callous as it seemed, it helped that it was Syd.

'Are you okay?' He placed a hand on Rosie's shoulder, but she pulled away and turned from him. He thought little of it. 'Thomo asked me to take Doc Hadley back out the paddock. He's gonna want to put Syd in the vehicle and bring him back. I think he probably wants Hadley to have a look around, and have a look at the body, and see if there's an obvious cause of death. I'm just gonna talk to the boys first.'

Rosie turned around and followed Jack's gaze. The shearing team and Artie, who'd had been out searching, were now all walking back towards the house.

* * *

Rosie walked into the kitchen and sat down at the table next to Bonnie. Bonnie had hardly moved in all the time Rosie had been outside talking to Jack.

'Bonnie, I have some bad news.'

'I know.'

'They've found Syd. I'm very sorry,' she hesitated for quite some time, steeling herself, 'I'm very sorry, but he was dead. There's been some sort of horrible accident.'

Bonnie looked up from where she'd been staring at the table and looked directly at Rosie.

'It was no accident.' She said with a note of resignation. 'It was no accident Rosie. I did this.'

Although Rosie suspected Bonnie had something to do with what had happened, she was still shocked at the revelation. There'd been the lies about how long Syd had been missing, the argument she'd heard, and the state of both the house and Bonnie when she'd arrived. They were all parts of the jumbled jigsaw that would form a more precise picture over the coming hours and days.

'Bonnie, what do you mean?'

'I mean just what I said. I did it, and there's no hiding it.'

'Oh, Bonnie.' Rosie grasped Bonnie's hands in hers. 'Why?'

'Because . . ., he was going to do it.'

'He was going to do what?'

'It's just history repeating itself all over again.

He was going to sell this farm. He was going to take away any future my children have. He didn't care about Mary, just like my father didn't care about me. He only cared about little Charlie. I had to protect them. I had to protect her. I had to protect myself.'

Rosie squeezed Bonnie's hands tighter.

'But Bonnie . . . I don't know what to say.'

'There is nothing to say. I shouldn't have done what I did. I went too far, way too far. But what is done is done now.'

The two women sat in silence for some time.

'It's up to you now Rosie.'

'What's up to me?'

'I gave you the letters. You promised me you would pass them on. You have to pass them on to Dr Hadley and Jack. You have to, please Rosie.'

'I will. I will Bonnie. But I have to ask you one thing.'

'What?'

'The babies, Bonnie, is Jack their father?'

An hour and a half later, Jack's vehicle ambled into the house paddock and pulled up near the gate to the garden. Rosie walked out of the house and along the garden path. She took a handkerchief from her pocket and covered her face. Jack got out of the vehicle and stepped away from it taking long deep breaths. The second vehicle pulled up just back from the first, and Dr Hadley and Sergeant Thompson got out and joined Jack.

Sergeant Thompson left the others and walked into the house to speak with Bonnie by himself. Hadley ushered Jack and Rosie together to speak.

'This is a terrible mess.' Hadley started. 'Someone, and that someone is you Rosie, is going to have to look after these children until we find out if they have some relations who can care for them.'

'Me?' Rosie sounded reluctant, to say the least. So much so that both Jack and Hadley looked at her in surprise.

'Well, yes, you.' Hadley responded. 'Unless you have a major objection.'

'How, where?' This wasn't part of Rosie's job, and that, along with other recent revelations, wasn't endearing her to the prospect.

'I guess you could look after them here. It's just for a couple of days. They need care, and we need to manage that. Bonnie didn't have friends in town who knew her and the children. However, if you're not keen . . . then I will ask around in town and see if we can find them a temporary home.'

Rosie thought about Bonnie and what had driven her to do what she had done to Syd, and she knew she couldn't let her down. Bonnie would be distraught if she was told her children were being farmed off to a complete stranger. She couldn't be absolutely sure what was in the letters to Jack and Doctor Hadley, but she had a good idea. She would have liked to have known and now, more than ever.

'No, don't do that. We'll look after them.' Jack interjected urgently.

'No, I'll look after them.' Rosie said firmly, looking directly at Hadley, dismissing Jack.

She turned her eyes only, looking sideways at Jack for just a moment. The look in her eyes was enough to stop Jack in his tracks, and she was thankful he didn't argue with her.

'Okay then, that's sorted, I guess.' It was clear Hadley could sense the tension. 'So I guess the easiest thing would be if you just stayed here for a couple of days in this house if you're comfortable with that Rosie. Will you stay as well Jack? Just for a couple of days until we get this all sorted out.'

'Yes, of course. If that's the easiest thing to do.' Jack replied.

'I think it is, everything the babies need is right here, and they'll be most settled in their own home. Even though they're only little, no doubt everything that is going on will upset them at some level, even if they are blissfully unaware.'

'No.' Rosie broke in again in a determined tone, and both men looked at her, surprised again. 'I'll take them with me into town to Mrs Bourke's. I'm sure she won't mind, in fact, I think she'll be very happy to have all the activity in her house. Something to focus on. And that way, if I need to go to work, I'll have a babysitter.'

'You know I could babysit.' Jack said, sounding a little irritated. 'I do come from a big family with lots of babies. I've had plenty of experience.'

'It's up to you Rosie,' Hadley said, 'you decide what works best for you.'

'I've made up my mind. I was heading back to town today anyway. The shearing is over, and I've finished my contract. I'm ready to go back home.'

Jack was shocked, and his mouth fell open. She was heading back to town today. Where had this come from?

'It is getting late.' Hadley said. 'Can I suggest that you at least consider spending one night here, or if you really don't want to, then over at Snowy Ridge, then bring the babies in tomorrow. You'll have quite a bit of packing up to do before you can head off into town. And we don't know how much longer Sergeant Thompson will be with Bonnie tonight. Until he tells us what's going on, we can't put any plans into action. I'm going to head inside now and see how things are going. Can I suggest you two take a few moments to sort out whatever it is that's causing this . . .' Hadley spoke in a parental tone while looking at each of them in turn, waving his hand back and forth between them. They both looked down at the ground and then away from each other before Jack spoke.

'There's no problem here Doc, I'm not sure what you're talking about. Do you have a problem Rosie?' Jack looked at Rosie, daring her to speak.

Rosie was silent, but her face spoke volumes.

'Right,' Hadley said, 'I think I'll leave you to it.'

* * *

'What the hell is wrong with you?' Jack made no attempt to hide his irritation.

'Don't you speak to me like that.' Rosie replied, matching his anger.

'I have no idea what's got into you. Isn't there enough going on right now without you and I having some argument over God knows what?'

'Sure.' Rosie replied in an overly sarcastic tone. 'Once we find out what's going on, we'll pack up the babies with enough stuff to get us through tonight over at Snowy Ridge, and we can be one little happy family in your shack. And while we're there, I'll explain to you what the problem is.'

'Fair enough.' Jack stood, arms crossed over his chest, exasperated, staring at Rosie.

They stood in silence for quite some time before Dr Hadley came back out of the house.

'Right, I'm off. Jack, you'll need to help me get Syd into my vehicle, and I'll take him to town. I'll have to do an autopsy.'

'Just take mine Doc, it'll save us a lot of unpleasant work moving him around. If you're okay with that, we'll just take your vehicle back to Snowy Ridge tonight and bring it into town for you in the morning. I can bring my vehicle home then.'

A few moments later, Hadley drove off. And a few minutes after that, Sergeant Thompson came out of the house, walking alongside Bonnie, each of them carrying a baby. Bonnie was in tears, and the babies were unsettled. Rosie rushed to Bonnie.

'It's okay Bonnie, I'll take care of them until you get this sorted out.'

'Do you remember what you promised Rosie? You remember . . .'

'I do, it's okay, Bonnie it's okay.' Rosie did her best to reassure the distraught woman.

Bonnie looked from Rosie to Jack.

'Rosie has something for you Jack, from me.'

Thomo handed Charlie to Rosie.

'Come on Bonnie. I'm sorry, but we need to get going.' Sergeant Thompson said, turning to her. Jack stepped forward to Bonnie and, her face flooded with tears, she handed little Mary to Jack.

'You look after her Jack. Remember, family is the most important thing, the most important thing in the world.' Bonnie could hardly get the words out, and as she did, she buckled at the knees, and Sergeant Thompson had to grab her and support her. He helped Bonnie to his vehicle, and they left very soon after.

CHAPTER TWENTY-NINE

Rosie and Jack got out of Hadley's vehicle with their instant family back at Snowy Ridge. Jack parked close to the house to easily transfer the babies, their clothing, food, blankets, and much more inside.

'The babies can sleep in your bedroom, in the bed with me.' Rosie commented as they stepped inside. 'Here, hold Charlie while I put a blanket down. They can lay on the floor while we get set up. You better light a fire and warm this place up. It's too cold. Then, when you're done with that, go out and get something for our dinner from the meat safe, and I'll cook.' Rosie handed the little boy to Jack, who held a child in each arm. She paused for just a moment looking at him and could see the likeness in Charlie's eyes. There was no mistaking now, he was Jack's son, and Mary, named for her sister, was his daughter. The anger bubbled up again, and she swallowed it down as best she could, but there were tears in her eyes. She turned away quickly, hoping Jack hadn't noticed.

'Rosie, what's the matter? Talk to me.' Jack tried in a soft and conciliatory voice.

'Later Jack, later.' Rosie walked off into the bedroom to set everything up for the night.

Jack and Rosie ate dinner almost entirely in silence. Only the most necessary of words were exchanged, pass the salt, have you finished, pass me your plate, I'll do the dishes. It was the most awkward meal Jack could ever remember having, and yet he was sitting with a woman he loved so much it hurt. She was a woman who, only twenty-four hours before, had lain in his bed. He'd held her in his arms with her head on his chest as he drifted in and out of sleep brought on by pure love.

'I'm going to have a drink.' Jack said as he stood up from the table. 'Can I get you one?'

'No, thank you. I have two babies in the other room who need me. They've had days of a poor drunk mother looking after them, or maybe not. They don't need any more of that.' Rosie replied in a sharp tone.

'Yeah, right.' Jack sat back down and dismissed the idea of a drink. 'They seem okay, are they? They've not been harmed in any way?' Jack was concerned and not just in a way that any reasonable person would be for two vulnerable children. This was different. After what had happened between he and Bonnie, although it was just physical, he had felt a sense of responsibility to her.

'They're perfectly fine.' Rosie's words were clipped, and it was clear she was still upset.

Although Jack had no idea why Rosie was so angry with him, he had a feeling of indefinable apprehension and, strangely, a sense of impending loss.

'They seemed settled now, so perhaps we can talk?' Jack assessed Rosie's expression while waiting and hoping she would respond. 'Come on Rosie, what's going on? One minute I am the happiest man on earth, and I thought you were happy too, and now, you'll hardly talk to me, and you're so angry. I have no idea why. I know it's been a terrible, terrible day but . . .'

Rosie cut Jack off mid-sentence.

'Stop Jack. Just stop.' She fixed him with a look that made him shiver. 'Is there anything you want to tell me about Bonnie?'

Jack looked at Rosie, holding his expression as neutral as he could, but his stomach tightened.

'What do you mean?' he spoke slowly.

'Is there anything you want to tell me about those two babies in your bedroom?' Rosie pointed past Jack to the bedroom door.

Jack could feel the room closing in around him. This morning he'd woken to find the night before wasn't a dream, and he'd wrapped his arm around Rosie. She'd shuffled her bare body up against his, and he'd dozed with his face buried in her beautiful hair. The years of pain and heartache had finally gone. But now, they were coming back with all the force of a spring thunderstorm.

'What do you mean?' He tried again, in an even more deliberate fashion.

Rosie stood up from the table without speaking and, opening the door to the bedroom quietly, disappeared for a moment before returning. She stood opposite Jack looking down at him. Finally, once Jack thought the tension would crack him, she threw an envelope on the table in front of him.

'What's that?' Jack asked.

'It's a letter, I presume. For you. From Bonnie.'

'What's in it?' Jack asked, looking at the envelope on the table suspiciously but not touching it. The weight of the world seemed to have landed on his shoulders, and part of him just wanted to stand up, throw the letter in the fire and walk outside and get some air. It was suffocating in this tiny house, and he wished he was anywhere but here right now.

'I have no idea. It's a letter to you. Bonnie asked me to give it to you if anything ever happened to her. She gave it to me last week on the day I arrived. She gave me one for Doctor Hadley as well. I'll give him his tomorrow.'

Jack just sat with his arms folded, looking at the letter.

'Well, are you going to open it? Do you want me to leave?'

'No,' Jack whispered, 'stay right there.'

Jack picked up the envelope slowly and peeled it open. He could see it hadn't been opened, so he assumed Rosie really did have no idea what was inside it. He pulled out a single sheet of folded paper, opened it out, scared of what it might say.

Dear Jack,

If you are reading this letter, then something bad has happened to me. I don't know what that might be, but I know it won't be good. I have something I must tell you if your instinct hasn't already told you first. I know we laid together only once, but I will always remember it as the only time a man cared for me and maybe even loved me, if only for a moment in time. I will hold that memory dear to me for as long as I live.

Jack, they are yours. You are a father. They are not just mine. They are our little boy and girl. Just look at them, and you will see. You can never be in any doubt.

You must take care of them. You must love them. You must give them everything you ever had, please. Don't let them, your babies, end up like me, especially sweet little Mary. Give her the love of a devoted father, please.

Remember Jack, family is everything. It is the most important thing in the whole world.

I entrust their care only to you Jack, just you.

Be happy Jack,
Bonnie.

Jack didn't look up from the letter for minutes. Before he did, he folded the letter carefully and put it back into the envelope. He put it on the table. It took all his courage to look up at Rosie, who hadn't moved an inch the whole time. He wiped the tears from his eyes with his thumb and forefinger. Looking at Rosie, he could see she was also in tears and was making no attempt to hide her emotions.

'You're a father Jack.' She said quietly. He didn't reply, just looked at her. She walked away.

The following day, Jack walked into the kitchen wiping his face with a towel, then running his fingers through his hair. There'd been no more conversation the previous evening, with Rosie disappearing into the bedroom early and closing the door behind her. During the night, he heard the babies stir and Rosie moving about soon after. She came out into the main room, where he was lying awake on his stretcher. He'd hardly slept a wink.

'What can I do?' He'd asked, sitting up.

'Nothing. Just go back to sleep.' Rosie's words were short and sharp, and against his better judgment, Jack lay back down and just listened as she moved about tending to the children, his children.

Jack put the kettle on the stove, checked the firebox and added some wood. As he shut the door to the firebox, he heard the door to the bedroom open and the sound of the children. Rosie walked into the room. She was dressed and looked as though she had been up for some time.

'Good morning.' He said cautiously.

'Good morning.' Rosie replied.

'How are the kids?' He asked with a smile that wasn't returned.

'Go and say hello. You're their father. You don't have to ask.'

Jack walked past Rosie, and she deliberately stepped well out of his way as though the thought of him brushing against her was abhorrent. He looked at her as he passed, and she met his eyes for a moment before turning away.

In the bedroom, the babies were lying side by side. Rosie had placed pillows down either side of the bed so they couldn't roll themselves off the edge of the bed. Jack walked over and looked at them, properly, for the first time as their father. It had taken hours of lying awake to begin to digest and accept the news.

'Hello, little man.' He said to Charlie as he tickled his stomach. Charlie gurgled and smiled at him. Thoughts of Bonnie's letter and her words came to him as he looked at Mary. He picked her up and held her face close to his, and, at that moment, he was lost in the love of this little person. 'You are beautiful, aren't you. I'm going to take care of you, I promise.' He whispered, then kissed her cheek before cuddling her. He sat down on the bed, next to Charlie with Mary in his arms and looking up, he found Rosie in the doorway watching him, tears in her eyes.

'Rosie.' He tried, but she just looked at him with his children. 'Come here, please.'

Rosie turned and walked away. He heard her in the kitchen, and he guessed she was making breakfast.

When Jack returned to the kitchen a little while later, Rosie was sitting at the table eating.

'There's porridge on the stove. You should eat up so we can get going. I want to get the babies into town and settled into Mrs Bourke's. There's a lot to organise.'

'Rosie. It's only seven-thirty. What's the hurry?'

'What's the hurry?' Rosie snapped. 'The hurry is two children that need looking after, that's what the hurry is. They're in charge now Jack, not you, so you better start thinking about what you're going to do if they don't let Bonnie out.'

'What are you talking about?' Jack was doing his best to be calm and not show his frustration, but the last forty-eight hours had turned his life upside down more than once, and he was struggling.

'I'm talking about if they lock her up for murder. That's what I'm talking about.' Rosie was little short of shouting, and Jack moved to shut the bedroom door. 'Then you'll have two children to look after, and how the hell are you going to manage that? And . . . if they don't lock her up, what will you do then? Are you going to move in with Bonnie and set up a happy little family?' If

Rosie could look daggers, then Jack would be a bloodied mess lying on the floor, taking his last breath.

'For god's sake Rosie, how about you let me explain.' Jack tried to push back against the torrent of anger.

'Go ahead Jack. It's pretty simple. Either you slept with her, your neighbour, your married neighbour that is, or you didn't, and be very careful how you answer that.' Rosie pointed at Jack in a warning.

'I'm not going to deny we slept together . . . once. Just once, but that doesn't mean they're my children.'

'Oh, come on, now you are just being a bloody fool. Have a look at them. They're as much Sutherlands as you are Jack, and no one is ever going to think otherwise. You come with me.'

Rosie stormed past Jack and into the bedroom, where the children were beginning to grizzle, responding to the loud voices. She picked up Mary, and immediately Rosie's tone of voice softened.

'Come here buba.' Rosie gathered Mary into a cuddle and kissed her cheeks, then held her face against hers. 'I just want to show Daddy something quickly.' Rosie's tone was a little sarcastic at the word Daddy. She placed Mary back on the bed and lifted her nightdress until she'd uncovered the birthmark. 'Recognise that, Jack?' She turned and looked at Jack, who'd moved up next to her.

'You know what that is, don't you. It's the Sutherland brand. Charlie doesn't have it, but I can tell you, he is definitely her brother and, therefore, your son.'

Jack stood staring at the birthmark, shocked. There was absolutely no doubt now. He was a father, he was their father.

'Rosie.' He put a hand on her shoulder, and she shrugged it off immediately.

'Don't Jack. Don't you touch me. You can't be telling me you're mourning my sister, then how much you love me, while all the time your sleeping with your neighbour's wife and god knows who else. How many other children do you have in the district?' She shouted the last words at him, and both the babies began to cry.

Jack picked up Mary as Rosie was picking up Charlie. He walked into the main room, then opened the door and stepped outside. He needed to get some air and to get away from Rosie's rage.

After a few minutes, he walked back inside.

'Right. I'll bring the Land Rover over. Then I'll come and help carry everything outside. Put your bag out, and I'll load it all in.' There was an air of finality in the words 'your bag'.

Jack lay Mary back on the bed. And stormed past Rosie, who looked to have finally calmed just a little, having had an opportunity to vent the tip of her anger.

'Jack.' She said as he barged past, but he ignored

her and headed outside. When he returned with the vehicle parked just outside, she was making no attempt to hide the fact she'd been crying. Regardless, all of the children's belongings and her bag were ready in the kitchen, and he loaded them into the Land Rover. Ten minutes later, they were on the road.

As they were driving, Jack laid out his plans in a business-like fashion.

'I am going to meet with everyone I can today. I'll have to speak with Bonnie. I have some ideas to discuss with her. I'll talk to Sergeant Thompson and Doctor Hadley, so I can understand what rights I have with the children. I can only assume that Syd had family who may try and claim the children. I don't know what my rights will be. This could take weeks to sort out.'

'So you're going to try and keep them?' Rosie asked quietly.

'Of course I am.' Jack replied angrily. 'They're my children, and they're my responsibility. I'll stop at nothing to take care of them.'

'How do you propose to look after two babies by yourself out there on the farm? Really, you have no idea what you are getting yourself into.'

'What would you have me do? Just give them up for adoption?

'No, I am not saying that. I am just saying you have to think this through carefully.'

'And I will. I have a big family, and they care

about me. And they will care about my children. I'll work this out with my family.'

Rosie felt the pain of rejection and the heartache of missing her family. But she was still angry with Jack and felt betrayed, although she was unsure if that was about Mary or herself.

'It will take time Jack.'

'I know that Rosie. Give me some credit. I know it'll take time, and I know they'll need to be taken care of until I can sort this out. So, in the meantime, I will have to make arrangements for them to be looked after.'

'Well, I'll look after them at Mrs Bourke's until you can sort yourself out.'

'If that works and Hadley and Thompson agree to it, then that'll be a good outcome. I'll pay you and Mrs Bourke, of course, for your time and to cover the cost of any food and clothing.'

The words stung, and Rosie looked out the window. Yet again, the tears snaked down the soft skin of her cheeks, and she hoped Jack didn't hear her sniff.

CHAPTER THIRTY

Jack parked Hadley's vehicle outside Mrs Bourke's house, and she appeared on the veranda just moments later.

'Hello there, you two. Have you got the children? Let me see them. Bring them in, come on.' Mrs Bourke was excited, and her face was alight with a huge smile.

Hadley pulled up behind them in Jack's vehicle whilst Jack was unloading the children's belongings. He got out and strolled over to Jack.

'Need a hand?'

'Yeah, good on yer.' Jack replied as Hadley bent over to pick up a basket off the ground.

'How's it all going?'

'Okay.' Jack looked at Hadley warily, wondering just how much he knew.

'Were the kids okay last night? Did they settle?'

'Yep. Rosie's a natural.'

'How about you and Rosie? Did you two settle whatever your issue was?' Hadley asked with caution.

'Ah, no, if I'm honest. Rosie's Irish temper is still on fire, and I'm well and truly the target. And to be honest, I've had just about enough for the moment. There's enough to sort out without Rosie making it ten times worse.'

'Can I ask what's going on?'

'You'll find out soon enough. Too soon for my liking. I believe she has something for you from Bonnie, a letter.'

'About?'

'The kid's, I'm guessing, but I don't know for sure. As soon as you're able, I'd like to speak with you and Thomo. Do you have time this morning?'

'I do, just come by the surgery and pick me up, and we'll go up to the police station.'

'Come in and take a seat.' Sergeant Thompson directed Jack and Hadley into a room where they sat around a table. 'What can I do for you, gentlemen?'

'You better take a look at this.' Hadley pulled the envelope that Rosie had given him out of his pocket, taking the letter out and handing it to the Sergeant.

> Dear Doctor Hadley,
>
> I write to you to inform you that Mr Jack Sutherland is the father of my twins Charlie and Mary. Mr Sutherland and I lay together, but once and as nature would have it, I fell pregnant. At that time, my marriage was not a happy one. My husband, Sydney Fredericks

and I, had not slept together as man and wife for some time. This is how I know they are Mr Sutherland's children. They can be no one else's. On this, you have my word.

In the event that anything ever happens to me such that I am unable to take care of my children, then Mr Sutherland must take them into his care. He is their lawful father and has a right to have them and to give them the best life he can. This is what I want for my children.

As a Doctor, I trust that you will act in their best interests and do everything possible in your power to see my wish is met. I am entrusting this duty to you, and I thank you.

Yours Faithfully,
Bonnie Fredericks.

The Sergeant drew in a long breath through his nostrils and exhaled slowly through his mouth, rubbing his chin furiously before speaking.

'Well. I'll be buggered Jack. This is an interesting twist.' He looked across the table at Jack with a grave expression. 'This true?'

'It is.' Jack answered with as much confidence as he could muster. Thomo shook his head.

'You're lucky all you got was a couple of kids Jack, and not an arse full of buckshot, or maybe a damn sight worse. It might have been your body we were pulling out of the bracken. What the hell were you thinking?' Sergeant Thompson eyed Jack for a moment before continuing. 'Don't bother answering that. I know the answer already.'

'It wasn't like that. It's not that simple.' Jack rubbed his face in his hands.

'Well, what do you want from me?' Thomo asked.

'It's simple, and it's not simple. They are my children, I know they are. Hell, one of them even has an identical birthmark to me and others in my family. It's the Sutherland family mark. It's there clear as day on the little girl Mary. I want these children. That's what this is all about. If they can't be with their mother, then they need to be with me. I need to know what the likely outcome for Bonnie is going to be.'

'Not good Jack, not good. There are two ways this can go. She's already pleaded guilty, so now it's just a matter of how her case is presented. If she pleads guilty and they base her case on being a wife that'd been knocked about by her husband, then she might get a bit of time off her sentence. I'm thinking she'll probably still get fifteen years. The trouble is, I'd never heard anything about Syd knocking her about and the Doc here, and I haven't had a chance to discuss this. That's a private conversation we'll be having later today.'

Jack looked at Hadley but could tell by the

slightest nod and his expression that he had nothing to offer to help Bonnie's case. Thomo continued.

'The other option is she pleads temporary insanity, says she was driven to kill him by the fear of what he was going to do to her, or to the children. Effectively, that would be a bit like self-defence, but it's a long shot, I gotta say.'

'Why is that?' Jack asked, holding on to the only glimmer of hope he could see.

'As I said, if there's no recorded history, no complaints, no bruises. It's going to be hard to convince a jury he was a credible threat. Certainly not one that warranted killing the poor bastard with a hammer, that's for sure.'

'But what if they do accept it? What would the outcome be?'

'Possibly not good anyway. The last thing you want is for her to end up in an asylum.'

'But it's temporary insanity. Surely an asylum's not necessary.'

'I don't disagree Jack. But if they do say she needs treatment and a doctor labels her insane, temporarily or not, she might end up in an asylum. If they put her in there, she might never get out. If she's not round the bend before she goes in, it won't take long before she is. I honestly think she'd be better off in the Goulburn gaol. It's a bloody hard place, but if she keeps her head down and minds her own business, one day she'll get out and be able to see her kids again.' Thomo looked at Jack and Hadley, then said to Jack. 'She's going to need a lawyer.'

'I've been in touch with the family lawyer, and he's organizing a good criminal barrister. I'll cover that.' Jack replied, feeling defeated before this had even begun. 'There's something else.'

'What's that Jack?' The Sergeant replied.

'I want to buy the Fredericks farm.'

'Shit Jack. Now's not the time to be thinking about expanding your bloody empire. Syd Fredericks is only just cold. For god's sake, haven't you got enough on your plate with those kids?'

'It's not that at all Thomo. That farm belongs to those kids. I know that's what Bonnie wants. I, or we, the Sutherland Family, can buy the farm and keep it in trust for the children. At least that might give Bonnie some peace of mind. So I need to know if she is willing to sell it to me. I need to know if I can buy it?'

'The magistrate's going to have to decide that Jack. I can't be sure about that one. Bonnie's up on a murder charge. I don't know how they'll feel about her selling a farm and setting up trusts while she's on trial or in the lock-up waiting for one.'

'Everything will go to the kids. The money we buy the farm with will be theirs, and the farm will eventually be theirs also. It will all be in the contracts of sale. Bonnie doesn't stand to make a cent out of this. Only the kids.'

'And what about when she gets out of gaol.'

'I'll see she's looked after. I'll promise her that, and I believe she'll trust me.'

'How are you going to look after these kids Jack? What's going on with you and that Rosie? Plenty of talk around town about her staying out there with you. You going to make an honest woman of her? Those kids need a mother. You can't look after them by yourself.'

'I know that Thomo, and no, there's no Rosie and me. It's not common knowledge, but she is actually my sister-in-law.'

The Sergeant's eyes widened in astonishment. He looked toward Hadley for confirmation, and Hadley nodded.

'Geezus Jack, where does this all end. I didn't know you were married.'

'I'm widowed.' The words still felt strange and difficult to say.

'I'm sorry mate. I really didn't know.'

'No one does.'

'So what are you going to do if Rosie, your sister-in-law, isn't willing to help?'

'I have a big family Thomo. I might need to go home to the family property for a while. Home to Sutherland Downs.'

'Take your time,' the Sergeant said as he closed the door to the room where Jack sat at a table opposite Bonnie.

'How are you coping.' Jack asked, wondering

what to expect. Bonnie looked exhausted and like she hadn't slept for days.

'I'm fine. How are my babies?'

'They're fine too. They're with Rosie. She's back at Mrs Bourke's with the kids. Mrs Bourke's the old School Principal's widow. She's a good woman.'

'Yes, I know of her. When can I see them?' Bonnie sounded a little frantic, and Jack couldn't imagine what she was going through. Even he was wondering how long she'd be held in custody in Granite Gully before she was sent off for trial. Sergeant Thompson had hinted she might have to wait up to two weeks for the magistrate to arrive, to review the evidence, and decide if it was sufficient for her to stand trial in a court in Goulburn.

'Doctor Hadley is organising for Rosie to bring them in later today to see you.'

'Thank you, I need to see them. I'm desperate to see them.' Bonnie wiped the tears from her puffy eyes.

'Bonnie, we need to talk, we need to sort things out. We don't have much time.'

'Today?'

'No, not today, we can wait a while, but we might only have a week or two to get everything sorted out to make sure the children are safe . . .' Jack hesitated then added, 'with me.'

'You will take them Jack, won't you? You will look after them, please promise me. You're their father.'

'I know Bonnie. I know I'm their father, and you have my word. I will do whatever it takes. I am organising a lawyer for you. I will do everything I can to help you, and I can assure you, I will take care of my children, of . . . our children.'

Jack spent the next half an hour explaining his plans, what he thought was involved in securing his rights over the children, and his plan to buy the property.

'If . . . if you go to prison, when you come home, you will have a house on the property at Snowy Ridge, I promise you that. I will have my lawyer write that into the contract of sale.'

'And what about Rosie?' Bonnie asked.

'What about her?' Jack replied, trying to hide his irritation that Rosie always came up in every conversation. Deep down, if he was honest, his exasperation was that he couldn't give the answer he desperately wanted to.

'You two are a couple. I've seen you. She'll be a mother to my children while I'm gone. She's a good person. They'll be safe and well cared for with Rosie and with you Jack. Whatever happens to me, if I know they are safe and happy, I can survive, however long it takes.'

Jack didn't have the heart to tell her that he and Rosie were now anything but a couple and all because of the children and Bonnie herself. He wanted her to have any peace of mind she possibly could, and if he and Rosie being a couple brought her some comfort, then he'd live that lie.

'Bonnie, I know the children are mine. I've seen the birthmark on the top of little Mary's leg. It's the mark of the Sutherlands. I have the same mark. But how did you know for sure? Surely you must have wondered whether they were Syd's children?'

'Jack, when I came to see you that day, I never meant for what happened to happen. I won't lie, you're a handsome man and, . . . well, Rosie is very lucky and so are you. Syd and I hadn't shared our marriage bed in months. I couldn't have cared less if we never did again. I hoped we wouldn't. When I realised I might have been pregnant, I panicked at first. But then, I realised I had to somehow cover my tracks, our tracks. That's when I really began to drink. I'd never had a drink before that afternoon I spent with you. That afternoon will be the only time in my life that I ever enjoyed being with a man.' She paused for a moment, collecting her thoughts and looking wistfully at Jack, obviously remembering that afternoon. 'I drank to give myself courage. The courage to sleep with Syd again. At least for a short while, long enough that I could claim he was the father. That's what I did. He believed it. You heard him, he thought he was wonderful, he'd performed a miracle on his barren wife, when all along he was the barren one. It was all far too easy in the end.'

'But how did it all go so horribly wrong?'

'He was selling the farm out from under us. We were headed to town to live in a house while he drank away their future. He didn't love them, and God knows I was never anything other than a housekeeper and a breeder, or so he hoped'.

When we argued that last day, and he admitted he was going to sell the farm, I asked about the children, how they'd be looked after. He said Charlie would be fine and not to worry about him. I said, what about Mary, and he said, what about her? She's no bloody use to me. If you'd been smart, you'd a stopped at one.'

'That was it. I snapped. I'd been drinking, I wasn't thinking straight. I just . . . I just hit him.'

Jack sat watching Bonnie. He was exhausted just listening. He put his face in his hands.

'I'm so sorry Bonnie.'

'It's okay Jack, I did this. Like I said. As long as my children are ok, I'll get through this.'

'But this is my fault.'

'How!' Bonnie sounded startled. 'How Jack?'

'I tried to buy your farm. I slept with you. God, what have I done?'

'This all started long before I ever met you Jack, long before. This all started when I was born, born a girl, not a boy. And later, when my father sold me to Syd. Sold me, can you even believe what I'm saying? I should have killed that pathetic old man years ago.'

'Don't ever say that again Bonnie, never, promise me. Don't let the judge or anyone else ever hear you say that.'

'I won't, I promise.'

'I better go. I have phone calls to make. I'll see the children later today before I go back out to the farm. I'll be back to see you again in the next day or two as soon as I have some answers. If there is anything you need, just let Sergeant Thompson know, and I'll sort it out.'

'Thank you Jack.'

Bonnie stood up, and Jack moved around the table and held her in his arms for a long time before giving her a kiss on the cheek then leaving.

Rosie and Mrs Bourke made their way across the road, carrying the children in the direction of the police station. Rosie was exhausted. It had been an emotional couple of days in so many ways, both good and very bad. Her anger with Jack had subsided somewhat, particularly when she'd finally had an hour or two to examine her feelings and see them for what they really were, terrible jealousy. She'd sat on her bed when they'd finally gotten the children settled for their morning nap and just stared at the wall in front of her. Up until that moment, she hadn't had the space to be anything other than reactive. She hadn't had five minutes just to think, to think how all of this really made her feel. Twenty four hours earlier, she had never been happier, and her life was near perfect. Hours later, everything was unravelling like a ball of string falling from a building, and soon there would be nothing left of what it had been for that wonderful fleeting moment.

Jealousy, was that all this was? She loved Jack. She wanted Jack, and she knew he felt everything that she did. But how could she live with this man? How could she plan a life with him, with his children? Could she ever treat them as though they were her own? Knowing how they came to be, the product of an affair, two married people, two drunk and foolish people. Could she ever love them as though they were her own? The thoughts made her angry, sad, jealous and all at the same time. It was simply overwhelming. But, underlying all this turmoil, she kept coming back to Jack, a man she loved, a man she believed was a good man. Deep down, a good man. He'd made mistakes, but he was a good man. A man who'd loved her sister, a man who loved her.

Rosie made up her mind she needed to hear him out. If he still wanted her, she would hear him out, and they could work this out with time. Given enough time, it would all work out.

Rosie climbed the stairs to the veranda that extended along the front of the police station just as the door opened, and Jack burst out. He looked as exhausted as she felt, and he looked even more upset than he had earlier in the morning.

'Hello.' He said curtly.

'Hello, Jack.' Rosie said in a deliberately friendly tone.

'The kids okay?' Jack squeezed Charlie's hand and then did the same to Mary. 'I need to talk to you.'

'The kids are fine.' Rosie turned to Mrs Bourke.

'Can you please take Mary inside, and I'll be in, in just a moment. Thanks.' Rosie was pleased she'd have a chance to talk to him. It was a start. Perhaps they could organise a cup of tea when the kids were asleep, and they could talk about this whole awful mess and try and clear the air a little. She'd invite him over later this afternoon, or maybe even for dinner. She knew she'd reacted strongly when she'd heard the news, but it was a shock, a huge shock. Surely he'd understand that, he had to. In truth, she was still in shock, but she didn't want to do any lasting damage to their relationship. If they still had a relationship? She wished for a moment her mind would just slow down.

Jack ushered Rosie to one end of the veranda, for privacy, she assumed.

'I'm glad we're talking.' Rosie said nervously, watching Jack fidget.

'Yes.' He said abruptly. 'Listen. Bonnie thinks we're a couple.'

Rosie's stomach fluttered just a little at the thought. She held his gaze.

'She thinks we are a couple and that together we'll be looking after the children.' Jack paused for just a moment.

'Okay.' Rosie said carefully. She was leaving the door open as much as she could for Jack to say what he was thinking and what he was feeling.

'Whatever the hell you do, please don't say we're not.' He said in a terse tone, almost suggesting she would expose the ruse at the first opportunity she had.

For a moment, Rosie was dumbfounded. When she finally found her voice, Jack spoke over the top of her.

'It would bloody well break her if she knew. I don't want her to know. Okay?'

'Okay.' Rosie replied quietly.

'We can't keep this pretence up for long, I know, but I need a while to get things sorted out. Then, I can put her mind at ease. I just need to get my plan together.'

'Okay.' Rosie replied again. Looking at him, she could see nothing in his eyes. Nothing at all to make her feel they had any connection left. Nothing other than the time, however long it would take, for him to implement his plan. His plan, that didn't include her. Then, he looked like he'd be happily rid of her. Her heart cracked, a hairline fracture waiting for the slightest pressure that would break it completely and cleanly.

'Jack, can we at least talk?' Rosie tried looking at him, unsure he had even registered she was talking to him. 'Jack?'

'What? Sorry.' He rubbed his face.

'I said, can we talk about what's happened? What we're going to do?'

'I have to go. I have phone calls to make. There are some people to see, and I need to get home and check on the stock and feed the dogs and horses. Thanks for looking after the children. I'll take them off your hands just as soon as I possibly can. I may not be in for a couple of days, so here's some money to tide you over until I can come back.' He pulled out his wallet and handed over some cash. 'If it's not enough, just let me know, and I'll make up the difference.'

'Right.' Rosie replied, taking the money, feeling and looking stunned.

'I better go.' He reached for little Charlie's hand and squeezed it again.

She watched as Jack disappeared down the stairs and crossed the road disappearing along the footpath and toward the pub. She stood, shell shocked again.

The next few days went by quickly. Rosie had the very busy routine of not one but two babies. As much as she was exhausted, she was enjoying having the children. It was made somewhat easier by having Mrs Bourke, who'd been an enormous help. Rosie had been called out only once to assist in a birth at the bush hospital, but it had been straightforward, and she'd only been gone for half a day. In a quiet moment, sitting on the veranda having a cup of tea, she had had to admit to herself that she was becoming attached to the children. She knew she would miss them if they weren't around. It hadn't taken long to grow her affection for them, and she supposed it was partly because they were Jack's children. She hadn't heard from Jack since she'd seen him outside the police station. She'd been told by Dr Hadley that the Magistrate would arrive in town earlier than originally thought, in just a couple of days' time. She'd asked Hadley if he knew what Jack had planned, and Hadley had seemed reluctant to share whatever it was he knew, and so she hadn't pressed him. All he gave her was an assurance that Jack seemed to have a sensible plan. When Hadley had asked her about her relationship with Jack, she'd had no choice but to confirm that it appeared that it was over.

Rosie and Mrs Bourke had the children on a rug on the front lawn of Mrs Bourke's house when Jack arrived unexpectedly. He pulled up, got out of the vehicle and came into the garden.

'Hello everyone.' Jack addressed the group. Charlie looked anything but interested, Mary seemed to smile, and Rosie and Mrs Bourke chorused, 'Hello Jack.'

'Can I get you a cup of tea Jack?'

'Yes please, Mrs Bourke.'

The older lady disappeared inside, and Jack positioned himself on the rug near Rosie and the children.

'How's it all going?' He asked.

'Good, they are well behaved little mites. We love having them, really.'

'That's good.' Jack's tone was serious and business-like. 'It won't be much longer, I promise. I'm making arrangements as quickly as I can.'

'It's no trouble Jack. Really.'

Rosie looked at Jack, but he didn't reply. Time, she thought, he just needed time, that's all. It had been quite a shock, and she needed to give him time. She'd quickly come to terms with what had happened and now better understood her own reaction. As much as she wasn't entirely over it, she didn't want to be so stubborn as to lose Jack just to make a point. She was about to ask Jack about his plans when Mrs Bourke arrived with tea and biscuits on a tray.

'Here you go,' she said, handing the tray to Jack. 'I'll leave you two to it, shall I.' She went to move off when Jack stopped her.

'No, don't go away, let me get you a chair. I wanted to tell you my plans now that I have some clarity and certainty over what I can do. It concerns both of you, so please stay.'

'Well, I'll just fetch my tea Jack, and I'll be right back.'

Once Mrs Bourke was gone again and out of earshot, Rosie thought she might broach the subject of their argument and their relationship.

'Jack . . . I just wanted to say . . .' Rosie couldn't complete her sentence before she heard the screen door squeak open again and Mrs Bourke's footsteps on the timber veranda floor. She sighed loudly and smiled at Jack, but he didn't appear to be in tune with her frustration.

'Right.' Mrs Bourke sat down. 'Go ahead Jack, you were saying?' The old lady asked with enthusiasm.

'I've been organising a lot of things over the last couple of days. I've been making some arrangements, but some of my plans still can't be confirmed until after I have spoken to the magistrate in a couple of days. The main thing I want, and I am confident I will get, is immediate legal custody of the children. They're mine, after all.'

Mrs Bourke looked very uncomfortable with this comment, and Rosie hoped Jack would leave out any unnecessary details. She had had an awkward conversation with Mrs Bourke, where she'd found herself defending Jack and embellishing the story to make it more palatable to the old lady. It had taken her quite some time to assure Mrs Bourke that Jack was a good man and that there had been some extenuating circumstances that had led to the procreation of these two lovely babies. She wasn't sure she believed that herself, but Mrs Bourke had seemed to buy it.

'I hope to be able to take the children as soon as Monday next week, all going well.'

Rosie looked at Jack and wondered where he would take them but assumed he was about to ask her to join him, paid or otherwise. He couldn't possibly manage them by himself. He'd need help, hired or otherwise.

'Oh, you're taking them back out to the farm?' Mrs Bourke asked with a smile, being ignorant to Jack's living conditions on Snowy Ridge.

'To a farm, yes, but not mine.'

Rosie watched Jack closely, wondering what was coming. She'd heard he wanted to buy Glencoe. She realised it would make sense to take them there, with the room and appropriate conditions for young children.

'I'm taking them home to my family property, Sutherland Downs, up near Bourke.'

'What!?' Rosie couldn't contain her surprise. Jack looked at her, almost equally surprised by her outburst.

'I'm going home to Sutherland Downs.'

'But what about Snowy Ridge?' Rosie tried not to sound frantic. Her throat began to close, and her chest tightened. She tried to slow her breathing.

'I've made arrangements for a caretaker. A local bloke will look after things until we employ someone permanently, or we send one of our stockmen down from up north. That's one of the things I've been organising over the last couple of days.'

'What about Bonnie? You can't just take the kids away from her.' Rosie countered.

'Bonnie will be gone all too soon.' Jack spoke quietly now. 'They are saying she'll almost certainly be sent to trial in Goulburn, and they'll move her as soon as the weekend.'

Rosie was speechless.

'So, how long will you be gone for?' She asked with trepidation.

'I'm not exactly sure. A while, I guess. A while for sure.'

'How long is a while?' Now Rosie's tone had a tinge of anger. Her voice was shaky, and Mrs Bourke put a hand on Rosie's shoulder, trying to calm her.

'Like I said, I don't know. Maybe four or five years, maybe longer. I want them to come back here, back to their farm eventually. I'm going to buy it. I'm making arrangements with Bonnie and our lawyer, but the magistrate will also have to approve that. Not sure if she can sell a property while she's standing trial. We'll see.'

'Four or five years?' Rosie cried out.

Finally, she seemed to have caught Jack's attention, and he was watching her, surprised.

'Yes, four or five years. Not until they can go to school at least.'

'That's fine then.' Rosie stood up and stormed off before Jack could see how upset she was.

Jack sat with Mrs Bourke in quiet for a few minutes before leaving to attend to more business in town.

'Have you spoken to Rosie?' Hadley asked Jack as they went over the details of what they would need to present to the Magistrate on Jack's behalf.

'Yes, I saw her this morning.'

'How'd that go then?'

'I went through the plan with them both, she and Mrs Bourke. And in the end, Rosie stormed off again. She's been angry with me, actually mad as hell, ever since she found out about the kids. So it's not surprising she stormed off again. I guess I can't blame her. There's nothing much I can do. I've got to focus on these kids and all the things I have to organise. Everything else has to take a back seat for now, and that's just the way it is.'

'I see.' Hadley looked at Jack over the top of his glasses, assessing him.

'My brother and sister-in-law will be down on the weekend, and all going well, we'll leave for Sutherland Downs on Monday.'

'I see.' Hadley said again, still watching Jack.

'What does that mean? You see.' Jack couldn't hide his irritation.

'Nothing, I am just wondering if you have thought this all through carefully. You're in a heck of a rush. Have you covered everything you should have in your plans?'

'I believe I have. It's all I have been able to think about since we found Syd and I found out about the kids.'

'Ok then, if you say so.'

CHAPTER THIRTY-ONE

Ed and Elise arrived late Saturday night at Snowy Ridge. They spent the night on Jack's farm, and not for the first time recently, Jack wished he'd had the foresight to build a larger home as he lay on the stretcher in the kitchen trying to get to sleep.

His mind was racing. He kept coming back to Hadley's words. Had he thought everything through? He believed he had. He'd successfully started the process of buying Glencoe. He'd been granted custody of the children pending any unforeseen objection in the next six months, which he took to be a reference to a possible objection from the Fredericks family. He was confident that wouldn't happen. He'd engaged a well regarded local stockman on an above award salary. Then, he'd given him the authority to employ two other stockmen as required to help manage Snowy Ridge and Glencoe in his absence. He was disappointed that the family would have to fund this, at least for a while. One of the most important aspects of moving to Snowy Ridge was proving to himself and his family that he could be successfully independent. Of course, he had hadn't foreseen this major hiccup in that plan. The only thing that was unresolved was the situation with Rosie. He'd had to push his feelings for Rosie aside whilst he got all of this organised. That was just how he worked. But the moment the plans had been settled and he had a semblance of control, his thoughts returned quickly to Rosie. He was still shocked by the intensity of her reaction and unsure what he could do to resolve the trouble between them. Earlier at dinner, Elise had had a bit to say to him, including some guidance.

'What's going on with you and Rosie?' She'd said.

'I'd have thought that was pretty obvious. She's as mad as hell with me and doesn't seem to want anything to do with me anymore.'

'I thought you two were a good match.' Elise had persisted.

'Me too. But that's not enough to get past what happened. The thing with Bonnie and me, that was a few hours, just once, that's all. Just once.'

'A few hours! You've got stamina.' Ed chimed in with a chuckle. Elise slapped him without a smile.

'Shut up, you bloody drongo.' Jack wasn't at all amused with his brother. 'You know what I'm talking about. I was drunk, so was she, I . . . we, made a terrible mistake.'

'Mmm.' Elise sat with her elbows on the table, head in hands, watching her brother-in-law. She turned to look at her husband. 'Haven't you got something to do outside, a chore or something?' she asked Ed.

'Me, no, why would I? I'm a visitor.'

'Go. Go find a chore to do, and take your time. Take your beer with you. Talk to the dogs or something. Anything.' She shooed him away like an annoying hound.

Ed got up from the table like a scolded child and went outside. He raised his eyebrows at Jack as he passed. 'Good luck.' He whispered as quietly as he could, and the corners of Jack's lips turned up ever so slightly.

'Right. Now we've gotten rid of him, let's talk properly.' Elise took a firm tone with Jack.

'Okay then, what? What do you want to know?' Jack asked, resigned to the grilling coming his way.

'I want to know if you love her?'

'Geez Eli, give me a break, will yer? I've only known her a while.'

'Come on, I've seen you two together. I'll be blowed if you two aren't head over heels for each other.' Elise sat quietly, obviously giving Jack time to relax with the question. 'Come on Jack. You're talking to me, not that big donkey out there.' She pointed at the door.

'Ok, yeah, I guess I am pretty keen on her.'

'You guess you're pretty keen? You're such a romantic.'

'Okay, what do you want me to say? I love her,

alright? I love her, but she doesn't seem to feel the same way anymore.'

'How do you know she ever did?'

'Because she told me. Alright?'

'Alright. Now we are getting somewhere. When did she tell you?'

'The night before we got called over to search for Bonnie's husband.'

'I see.' Elise raised her eyebrows. 'So you told her you loved her too?'

'I did.'

'And now you're just going to throw it all away?'

'It's not just up to me, you know.'

'You need to speak to her Jack. We're going Monday. If I didn't have Tommy to get back to, we could wait around a few days while you sort this mess out, but we do have to get back. Your nephew's a handful, and I promised Grandma Sutherland we'd be back as soon as we could.'

'Don't remind me. I'm going to cop it from the old man, aren't I? Turning up with two new grandchildren.'

'I reckon your ear will get a good old bashing from your Dad. Your mum was shocked for sure, but, as soon as she sees the babies, and because they're yours, she'll love 'em to bits. I know it's horrible circumstances, but it's good they're so little in some ways. They'll suffer less, and your whole family will get to see them grow up, as they should.'

'I guess so.'

'So. What are you going to do about Rosie?'

'I'll go see her tomorrow and make her talk to me, and I'll listen. I'll cop it on the chin, both barrels, and then hope like hell she'll begin to forgive me and take me back.'

'Good boy. That's better. You have to appreciate what a shock she's had. I couldn't imagine telling Ed I loved him, then finding out the very next day he had a couple of kids with the neighbour's wife. I'm sorry, but that's not something a woman can just dismiss without having doubts. Just give her a chance.' Elise reached across the table, and squeezed Jack's hand, then stood and walked to the door, turning the handle and shouting out. 'OK, you can come in now.'

Ed nearly fell through and onto the floor, having had his ear pressed against the door.

The following day, Jack was up early and ready to head into town to see Rosie and sort this whole mess out.

'Good luck.' Elise called as Jack drove off smiling, finally relieved he knew what he wanted and how to fix everything. He bounced about on the seat of his Land Rover as he travelled faster than he'd ever done, desperate to get to town and see Rosie and put things right. He couldn't help but smile at the thought of putting an end to at least this part of the turmoil. And, he was especially looking forward to taking her in his arms again and feeling those soft lips.

He roared along the main street of Granite Gully, attracting more than a bit of attention from some of the locals who were out and about. He was tempted to wave and smile, but he contained his enthusiasm. It was Sunday, so most people were home and would be heading off to church or catching up with the chores that fell behind during the week, like gathering and chopping firewood, tending to flower and vegetable gardens and gossiping with the neighbour over the fence.

Jack pulled up outside Mrs Bourke's and leapt out of his vehicle. For a brief moment, as his stomach fluttered nervously, he wished he'd brought flowers. Apart from the excitement of seeing Rosie, he was very excited to see his children. Being a father was a feeling that was quickly growing on him. He'd become aware of how often he thought about the children and began to imagine them growing up and their future. He pushed the front gate open and strode down the path in a determined and confident fashion. He took the veranda steps, two at a time, and knocked on the front door louder than necessary. From inside, he heard footsteps, and he couldn't help but begin to smile in anticipation.

The main door opened slowly. In what seemed to be a cautious manner, a young woman remained behind the screen door looking at Jack.

'Yes?' The young woman said. Jack didn't recognise her, but he knew nothing of Mrs Bourke's friends and relatives, so he wasn't overly surprised to be confronted by someone new. There was a quiet laughing and cooing sound from inside that Jack recognised as the children.

'G'day.' Jack said with a smile. 'I'm Jack Sutherland. And I think that's my children I can hear inside.' Jack said proudly.

'Jack?' Mrs Bourke's familiar voice came from inside. A moment later, she appeared next to the girl and quickly pushed the door open. 'Jack, come in, come in, I wasn't expecting you.'

'I'm sorry, it wasn't really a planned visit. A bit last minute, actually.' Jack followed the women inside.

'This is Cathy Martin.' Mrs Bourke introduced the young girl to Jack as they walked into the lounge room, where the children were sitting on the floor on a rug with toys and looking happy and content. Jack sat down immediately, picked up Mary, and gave her a hug and a kiss on the cheek before gathering up Charlie and hugging him to his chest. 'They're quite the handful.' Mrs Bourke commented as she looked down at Jack, smiling. 'I'm going to miss them, truly I am, but I am probably getting a bit old for all of this. I think I'll be exhausted when they go.'

'Not long now then.' Jack replied, looking down affectionately at his children. 'Where's Rosie?' he asked without looking up.

'She's gone.' Mrs Bourke sounded surprised by Jack's question.

'Gone, gone where?' Jack asked matter of factly.

'I thought you knew Jack.'

'Knew what?' He was watching Mrs Bourke now and couldn't hide the concern he felt immediately.

'I thought you knew she was leaving. Leaving Granite Gully.'

'I don't know what you mean. I had no idea she was going somewhere, anywhere. When is she coming back?'

Mrs Bourke turned to the young girl.

'Cathy, you look after the kid's, please. Mr Sutherland and I are just going to sit out on the veranda and have a chat for a few minutes.'

The old woman led Jack back out through the front door, directed him to a chair, and then sat down beside him.

'I'm afraid Rosie left this morning Jack. She caught a ride with Gordon Palmer in his truck to Albury. From there, she's getting on a train and heading to Sydney.'

'Sydney. Why?' Jack was shocked.

'To nurse. She's going to take up a position in a hospital in Sydney. She said she'd done that when she first arrived from Ireland, and she didn't think she'd have any trouble finding work. She just said it was time. She even spoke once or twice about maybe going back to her family in Ireland.'

'Which hospital?' Jack couldn't hide the anguish in his voice.

'I'm not sure Jack. I'm sorry. She wasn't in a mood to talk when she was leaving. It was all very sad. She was upset, distraught, actually. She and Doctor Hadley had a long chat yesterday. As I understand, she resigned on the spot, then made a phone call to a friend in Sydney and was gone very early this morning with Gordon. The Doctor did his best to persuade her to stay. He argued the point over and over. She'd be close to boarding a train by now.'

'So you have her contact details?'

'No, not yet. She said she'd be in touch as soon as she got to Sydney and had settled with a job and a place to live.'

Jack slumped in his chair and looked up to the roof of the veranda overhead. What had he done? Why had he been so slow? Why had he been so stupid?

'I will leave you all of my contact details Mrs Bourke. I want you to give these to Rosie. I am sure she could find me if she wanted to, but I will write everything down for you. Please pass it on when she calls you.'

'Of course, I'll do that Jack. But Jack . . ., can I ask you something?'

'Sure.'

'What happened between you two? You seemed to be a perfect match for each other. I'm old, I've been around a long time, and I had a long and happy marriage. I think I have a good idea when I see two people in love and two people made for each other. I don't understand what went wrong.'

'I know. I agree with you, Mrs Bourke, but I

have made some stupid mistakes along the way, and this one might just turn out to be the worst of all.'

Mrs Bourke patted his arm.

'You find her Jack. And when you do, I think you'll find she'll forgive you. Don't give up.'

Jack left a little while later after spending some more time with the children. He farewelled Mrs Bourke and told her he'd see her early in the morning. He visited Dr Hadley before heading back out to Snowy Ridge. He'd had nothing more to add to the story he'd had from Mrs Bourke. Rosie had swept over her tracks well, and she wouldn't be found until, and if, she decided she wanted to be.

CHAPTER THIRTY-TWO

It was a bittersweet return. It was Tuesday lunchtime when Jack, Ed, Elise and the two babies arrived home. His mother Claire was first to come through the grand old door of the two-story homestead that had been in the family for generations. She beamed with happiness as she welcomed her children home. She was down the stairs and along the garden path in a matter of moments and was taking little Mary out of Jack's arms and smothering her with kisses before even saying hello to Jack. Eventually, she drew her eyes away from the little girl's face and looked at Jack.

'Hello darling.' She said and kissed his cheek. 'And where's my little boy.'

'Me?' Ed asked, standing with little Charlie in his arms.

'Don't be stupid.' His mother said dismissively as she gently pinched Charlie's cheek and then smothered him as well.

Jack's father, Edward Senior, had followed his wife reluctantly along the path and was far more reserved. Standing back a little as though a guest at this party.

'Jack.' He said formally.

'Dad.'

'Ed.'

'Dad.'

Claire looked at the three of them and huffed.

'Come on, let's get these two inside and out of the sun before they fry.'

There was a squeal, and Jack looked up and smiled as his nephew Tommy ran along the path towards his mother, who was lifting bags out of the vehicle. Claire looked toward Edward as Elise took up Tommy into her arms and gave him a big hug.

'Look at this Grandpa. What a family.' Jack looked at his mother, her arms stretched out, gesturing toward the group, thinking he'd never seen her look happier. His father, however, remained on the spot, with a sour look on his face. Jack could only imagine what was coming when his father got him alone.

Later the family were outside in the garden having drinks in the cooler evening air. The Sutherlands would often bring family and friends into the expansive garden that surrounded the big two-story building that looked out across the paddocks in every direction. It was an oasis in a harsh landscape, a landscape so different to Snowy Ridge, where Jack had spent the last couple of years. The environment was equally as unforgiving but in different ways. The extreme weather and temperatures of the snowy mountains could transition from freezing winters blanketed in snow to drought-stricken summers. Life in either landscape, the northwest of New South Wales or the Snowy Mountains, was equally as threatening to the uninitiated and equally as isolating for the uncertain.

The children had finally been settled and put to sleep. Meeting his cousins for the first time had sent Tommy into a fit of excitement. The excitement had inevitably ended in utterly silly behaviour, an angry father and Grandfather, and finally, in tears. Jack hadn't won votes from any of the adults as he spurred Tommy on until the final meltdown.

The men, Jack, Ed and Edward Senior, had gathered near a fire in the garden not far from the huge dam that held water storage for the garden and the house during prolonged dry spells. The cicadas buzzed like hundreds of small machines, and the men had to raise their voices to be heard over the din. Jack looked at this father, who'd hardly acknowledged him since he'd arrived earlier in the day. Finally, his father spoke in a gruff voice.

'What are your plans for Snowy Ridge then? How are you going to manage that from up here? You can't be traipsing up and down the road every five minutes to check the bloody stock. Did you think that through before you up and left?'

'I didn't just up and leave. I put a hell of a lot of thought into what I should do. I didn't have much time to sort things out, but I think I've done the right thing.' Jack couldn't control how defensive he sounded. His father squinted his eyes at him and looked a little like a snake about to strike.

'So did you put much thought into getting into bed with your bloody neighbour's wife, or didn't you have much time to think that one through either?'

'Dad, go easy.' Ed stepped in. 'I think Jack's had a hard enough time lately. Another tongue lashing isn't going to help anyone.'

'Might help me.' His father barked back. 'What about your mother? How do you think she's going to feel telling her friends that her son brought a couple of kids home that he sired with the neighbour's wife, a woman, who on top of everything else, is a bloody murderer?'

Jack stepped forward, his fists clenched, his chest tightened, and rage threatening to burst. He pointed at his father.

'You . . .' Jack started, but Ed got between his father and Jack.

'Enough, both of you.' Ed snapped.

It was too late. Claire and Elise, who'd been standing aside in the garden talking about the children, had been alerted by the body language at first, then had been alarmed as the voices rose. They quickly made their way across the garden.

'What on earth is going on?' Claire asked sharply.

'It's ok mum, it's ok.' Ed did his best to calm the situation. 'Just a little difference of opinion. All sorted now.'

'Hah.' Edward scoffed. 'You know Jack, you're the first Sutherland to bring home children out of wedlock like this. I'm disappointed and ashamed of you.'

'Edward!' Claire was horrified. 'That's enough. That's enough, everyone. It's time everyone was in bed. Go, go now. Go on!' Her last command was aimed directly at her angry husband.

The next morning Jack was introduced to a young teenage girl named Ruth who's father was a stockman on Sutherland Downs. Ruth would be working at the homestead as a nanny, now that Jack's children had arrived and arrived without a mother. Ruth was glad of the opportunity. Her parents were grateful to the Sutherlands for providing an extra wage for their family. Everyone seemed happy with the arrangement. It was important to get Ruth settled with the children quickly so that Jack could take up responsibilities back in the paddocks as a head stockman alongside Ed. Although, in truth, Jack's mother and Elise had already taken charge of the children from the moment they arrived at Sutherland Downs. Their father ruled the workforce with an iron fist and only answered to one person, his wife, Claire. Claire was the kindest and most gentle person any of them had ever known. Still, she would not be crossed by any of them and particularly when it came to family. Jack took some pleasure in knowing just what an ear-bashing his father would have gotten for what he'd said to him last night, but still, it didn't help soothe the wounds the words had inflicted on him.

After breakfast, the men were heading out to do some fencing that had been planned for several weeks. Jack sat on the back of the old Bedford truck on a toolbox amongst coils of wire and a pile of timber posts. Three dogs raced back and forward across the tray, looking ahead, oblivious to the red dust that billowed up from the tyres, completely clouding the track behind them. Jack's father was driving, and Ed sat in the cabin with him. Once or twice Jack looked through the window and could see they were deep in conversation, and he wondered what they were talking about. Was it him? Was this how it was going to be? An outsider in his family's home. His thoughts turned to Rosie, and the happy days they'd had together on Snowy Ridge, his home, their home. He knew, in his heart, whatever happened, he would always think of Snowy Ridge as Rosie's home.

CHAPTER THIRTY-THREE

The days turned quickly into weeks and then months on Sutherland Downs, and Jack had returned from a short trip back to Granite Gully. He'd spent just four days back on Snowy Ridge and Glencoe. The title of Glencoe had been transferred to Jack and the proceeds of the sale deposited in a trust fund for the children. Although their future was never in any doubt, this transaction had definitely secured it as far as he was concerned. They would have access to the funds as soon as they turned twenty-one, and if it was shrewdly invested, it would be a tidy sum by that time.

Bonnie had been tried in the Goulburn Gaol. With the support of Doctor Hadley, and the testimony of locals who knew Syd's character, the Sutherland legal team had been pleased with the result. Ten years' imprisonment. The children would be almost teenagers by the time their mother returned home.

Jack climbed out of his ute and stretched his legs. He was hot, tired and sweaty. He was looking forward to seeing the children, but he'd been sorry to leave Snowy Ridge, where he felt more at peace than he ever did on Sutherland Downs. The relationship between he and his father had improved considerably, but it was still more business-like than personal. His father had quickly softened when it came to the grandchildren and was proud as punch, although he was careful not to show it too openly.

Jack walked from the machinery shed where he'd parked his ute, through the back gate and wound his way through the garden heading toward the house. His mother looked up from where she'd been weeding a rose bed, brushed the dirt from her hands on her apron and walked over to him.

'Jack. Darling, how are you?' As always, his mother greeted him as though she hadn't seen him for months, although it had only been days. She came to his side and kissed his cheek. 'The kids will be pleased to see you. How was your trip?'

'It was good, thanks. Things seem to be under control down there. The boys are doing a good job. I really need to get down there soon for a longer trip though. The place is getting looked after, but it's only being maintained. We're not really improving the property. Well, not as quickly as I'd like, that's for sure.'

'Come in and see the kids and then we'll sit down and have a cup of tea, and you can tell me all about it.' Claire ran her hand across Jack's face. 'And do me a favour Jack. Have a shave. You know how your father is. I'll give you a haircut tonight. You need to look after yourself.'

'I am mum, I am.' Jack replied wearily.

An hour later, Jack was seated in the garden with his mother and a cup of tea and sliced fruit cake, talking about the children and Snowy Ridge.

'I'm glad to see you and your father are getting along a little better.' Claire commented, watching Jack closely. 'I know he is a cranky old thing, but he is very proud of you. He's just too stubborn to tell you himself. And I know he's a bit old fashioned, but even you must be able to see how much he loves the little ones.'

'I know. And I don't blame him. I buggered up really bad, but in the end, if I hadn't, I wouldn't have those two inside, so something pretty good came of it.'

'What about you Jack? Are you really ok? I was told not to bring up the girl, but Elise did tell me you were very keen on a young lady. Rosie, wasn't it?'

'Yep, Rosie. And yeah, she was alright, a real good sort, the best actually.'

'And . . .' Jack could see his mother was treading very carefully. 'Elise also told me that she was Mary's sister.'

Jack looked at his mother, feeling suddenly so sad his chest ached.

'Yes, Mary's sister. What a mess ey? Can you believe it? Have you ever known anyone who could make more of a mess of things than I've done?'

'Come on darling, granted, it's a lot of bad luck, very bad luck, but it's not your doing.'

Jack and his mother sat in silence for a few minutes, looking into the garden. The other men were out working and wouldn't be back until dark. Elise was inside with Tommy, and Ruth had the twins in bed having a nap.

'A lot of bad luck 'ey?' Jack finally commented. 'I met the most beautiful and wonderful woman in the world in England. I married her in secret. How stupid was that? Then, I left her behind when I came home. If I'd have brought her out here, you know she never would have gotten sick.'

'You don't know that Jack. She might have been sick a long time before it actually got on top of her.'

'You're right, I don't know it, and I never will, just like I will never know if she would have lived if I'd have brought her home straight away. You know, I wanted everything to be perfect. You should have seen her face when I told her I planned to buy a property just for her and me, more than a thousand acres. A place where we could bring up all of our children, a million miles away from all the horror of the war, the constant bombing of London, the terror of wondering every time I got into the cockpit if I'd ever get out alive again.'

Claire reached across and covered her son's hand

with hers, but didn't speak, just allowing him to continue.

'You know I thought she'd fallen out of love with me, or she'd fallen in love with someone else. I thought maybe she couldn't leave her family. Family was important to her. I just had no idea she was sick. I never thought for a moment . . . If I'd known, I'd have gone to her straight away. I'd have been there holding her hand to that very last moment, I would have been there. But I wasn't, and I will never forgive myself.' Jack wiped the tears from his eyes, and his mother lent her head against his shoulder.

'And then, there's Rosie. I feel terrible, but I think I loved Rosie every bit as much as I loved Mary. It was like Mary sent her. How the hell can you explain us both ending up in the same place like we did, the same small town in the middle of nowhere.'

'Loved her? That sounds like you don't love her anymore. Do you think you're really over her Jack?'

Jack looked at this mother, but he knew there was no use lying to her.

'No. Of course not. I'm not over Mary, and I'll never be over Rosie.' Jacked rubbed his face. 'You do know that what happened with Bonnie was before I ever met Rosie, don't you? Long before. It would never have happened if I'd known Rosie. I was happy with Rosie. She was all I could think about. You should see her Mum. You'd love her.' Jack smiled at last.

'Tell me about her, darling.'

'She's beautiful. Flaming red hair and eyes as blue as the water around a tropical island. She's kind and caring, but what a temper and headstrong.' Jack chuckled. 'Just like you.' His mother gave him an affectionate slap on the arm. He continued.

'She's smart and practical. She was taking to life on the farm like a duck to water.'

'Life on the farm, ey?'

'Yes, well, she came out to cook for shearing. It was during cut-out we found out Bonnie's husband Syd was missing, and that's when everything went from good to bad, from happy to downright sad.'

'I see.' His mother raised an eyebrow. 'So where did she stay during shearing, dare I ask?'

Jack was relieved that not all of his secrets had been shared by Ed and Elise.

'She stayed in my house. In my bedroom, but not with me. I bunked down on the stretcher in the kitchen.' Looking at his mother, Jack could see she wasn't entirely convinced.

'She sounds like a good woman Jack. How hard have you really tried to find her?'

'I've tried. Believe me, I have. Every time I go to Granite Gully, I ask Doctor Hadley, who she worked for, if he's heard from her. I even go round and see her old landlady, Mrs Bourke. She rang Mrs Bourke, not long after she left and let her know she was safe and sound, living with a friend. She said she had a couple of irons in the fire in regards to a job. Mrs Bourke said she passed on all my details to Rosie, just like I asked her to. But that seemed to be enough for Mrs Bourke because, although Rosie's never rung her back, she's not in the least bit worried. It just makes me wonder if she knows more than she is letting on. And Doctor Hadley's no wiser than Mrs Bourke. So, it's done and dusted Mum. She's gone. Somewhere in Sydney is all I can guess, and I'll never see her again.'

'Why don't you go to Sydney and look for her? It's not like you to throw the towel in so easily. The last thing you want is more regrets, like those you have about Mary.'

'It'd be like trying to find a needle in a haystack down there. You know there's something like one and a half million people jammed in that city. I don't think she wants to be found, and that's the sad truth. Sydney, hah.' Jack sighed. 'Why would anyone want to live in that place?'

'Beats me darling.'

'What beats you?' A gruff voice came from behind Jack and his mother, and they both turned around to see Jack's father and Ed approaching.

'I didn't hear you get back.' Claire said, looking at the two men, their clothes dirty and wet with sweat.

'We parked around the front. Got to offload some dung for the garden. We brought back a small load from the horse yards. Thought you'd like it for the roses.'

'Phew, you smell like it too.' Claire scrunched up her nose at them as they came to stand next to her.

'How's the farm?' Jack's father asked him.

'Good. All in order.'

'Good.' His father replied, and the conversation seemed over. 'They don't sell razor blades at Granite Gully then?' There wasn't the slightest hint of humour in his father's tone. Jack rubbed his face, and his mother looked sympathetically at him. 'Do yourself a favour and have a shave mate.' His father continued. 'We might be way to buggery out here, but that's no excuse to let the standards drop.' His father turned and walked away.

'How yer going mate?' Ed asked with a smile, and Jack was pleased to see his brother's friendly face.

CHAPTER THIRTY-FOUR

Claire was on the first story veranda that overlooked the front garden and the long driveway that led to the homestead. She was enjoying a cup of tea and a few moments reading a book. The grandchildren had been particularly noisy and needy this morning, and it was all Elise and Ruth could do to keep up with them, so Claire had joined in to help. She found herself hiding where she hoped she wouldn't be found, at least for a little while. Her few short moments of peace were interrupted when she glanced up from turning a page in her book to see a pall of dust in the distance, indicating a vehicle approaching along the driveway. Claire put her book down and stood up to watch.

The vehicle approached slowly, and Claire could see it was a truck. She wondered who it was, there was no one expected, and there was virtually no such thing as a drop-in at Sutherland Downs, so she was intrigued. Her interest faded into frustration quickly when she realised it was Kenny Burton in the transport truck from the hardware in town.

'Damn.' Claire cursed out loud. 'What's he doing here?'

She dropped her book on the table next to her cup of tea, then headed inside and downstairs to the back of the house. Kenny was a regular visitor and knew his way around. He'd taken the truck round to the rear of the house yard where there was a collection of sheds, including the machinery shed and the store. The brakes squeaked as he pulled the truck up. It was laden with fencing materials, coils of wire, steel posts, and hessian sacks of grain to supplement the feed for the horses and stud bulls. There was even a small, corrugated iron water tank to replace a rusted out tank at the milking shed.

Claire strode toward the truck in a business-like fashion while shielding her eyes from the sun with a hand as Kenny got out and swung his door shut behind him with a bang.

'How yer goin', Mrs Sutherland?'

'Kenny, how are you?' Claire did her best to smile but couldn't hide her frustration. 'You're two days early!'

'Yeah, I know, sorry about that.' Kenny replied.

'Well, there's no one here except for all the girls. Old Sonny's here, but I'm not gonna let him lift any of this stuff. He'll drop dead from a heart attack.'

'That's ok, I can unload it all. If you just point me in the direction of where you want it.'

'That's a lot of work Kenny.'

'No worries. I'll take me time, no rush. I've got all afternoon.'

'Well, you make a start, and I'll have a cup of tea and some sandwiches for your lunch in a half hour. Does that suit you?'

'Yeah, good on yer Mrs Sutherland. That'll be real good.'

'Ok then. Head on over to the machine shed. You can drop off the fencing materials first. You'll see where they go if you back into the far bay. They go up on the landing at the back. Be sure and put them in neatly and in the right spot, or Mr Sutherland will do his block. He's very particular.' Claire rolled her eyes, and Kenny smiled.

'Gotcha, no worries.'

'Ok then, I'll go and organise some lunch for you.' Claire turned away and began to walk back toward the house when Kenny called after her.

'Mrs Sutherland.'

Claire turned back.

'What is it?' Claire stopped dead in her tracks.

'You've got a visitor.' Kenny announced as a young lady appeared, walking around the front of the truck and towards Claire. Claire stood still staring and found herself lost for words for a moment.

'Hello, Mrs Sutherland.' The young lady stepped tentatively toward Claire and smiled shyly.

'Hello.' Claire responded quietly.

'This is . . .' Kenny went to introduce the young lady, but Claire cut him off mid-sentence.

'I know who this is.' Claire announced, with a stunned look on her face and holding the young lady's gaze.

Kenny reached up onto the back of the truck, quickly unhooking a small tarp that had been covering a suitcase and lifted the case down and sat it on the ground next to the young lady.

'I'd carry it in for you luv, but I better get started with this lot.' He motioned to the stores on the back of the truck. 'I'll just go over and take a look where it's all going Mrs Sutherland and then I'll come back and get the truck if that's okay?'

The young lady turned to Kenny and smiled. 'Thanks Kenny.'

'No worries, have a good visit.'

Claire looked down at the suitcase and then back at the young lady in front of her. Finally, she smiled a warm smile, then walked toward the young woman.

'You know who I am?' The young woman looked surprised.

'Of course I do.' Claire responded, looking her over, then fixing on her eyes again. 'Flaming red hair and eyes as blue as tropical island water. You can only be one person, you're Jack's Rosie.'

The young woman's face coloured. She let out a huge sigh of relief, and her eyes glistened with tears.

'I am. I'm Rosie.'

'You're every bit as beautiful as Jack said you were.'

Rosie smiled through her tears.

'I am sorry to turn up unannounced. I . . . I just wasn't sure if Jack would be happy to see me or not, and I wanted to see him more than anything, and I wasn't going to give him the chance to say no without hearing me out.' The words spilled from Rosie's mouth in a rush.

'Hah!' Claire announced loudly, clapping her hands together excitedly, then chuckling. 'I think you're safe there Rosie. Come here.' Claire grabbed Rosie, pulled her in and hugged her tight. 'You are a sight for sore eyes.' She whispered in Rosie's ear.

The hug was broken by a shriek from behind Claire.

'Rosie, is that you? It is.' Elise ran to Rosie and took her in her arms, and hugged her as well. 'Good god. You're here, thank goodness. Jack is going to die when he sees you. He's been moping about for months pining after you.'

'Hello.' A little voice came from behind Elise, and the women all looked down.

'Hello Tommy.' Rosie said and extended her hand to shake his.

Tommy went to Rosie's suitcase and did his best to lift it, without a hope in hell. The women all smiled at him.

'Come on. Let's get you inside. I'm afraid the boys are away for another two nights out mustering. You're going to have to wait a bit longer to see Jack, but that will give me a chance to get to know you first.' Claire wrapped an arm around Rosie's shoulders. 'I can't tell you how pleased I am you've come to Sutherland Downs.'

CHAPTER THIRTY-FIVE

The muster was almost over, and the Sutherland men were heading home. They were only a few miles away from the homestead and moving one last mob into a new paddock. The day was already hot as hell, and they'd all had more than enough. Tempers were frayed, and no one could think of anything other than a cool shower and a colder beer.

The stockmen who'd been on the muster had been given leave to head home early. There was only enough work for a few men now, and the Sutherland men figured they could handle the rest by themselves. They pushed their workers hard, but they were always fair and, as a result, well respected by everyone who worked for them.

'Go ahead and open the gate, will yer?' Edward directed Jack, who nodded and kicked his horse into a trot. He rode up to the gate, and leaning down from his horse, unlatched it and shoved it forward. The gate started to open, then seemed to twist on its hinges and dropped enough to stop, caught in the red dust. Jack had to lean down, lift the gate, and gently kick his horse on while carrying the gate into the open position. He turned the horse around to quickly duck back through the gate ahead of the sheep moving toward him at pace. As he rode back through the gate, Jack was caught unaware as the horse shied, leaping suddenly to its left. He looked down to see a huge King Brown Snake more than six feet long, slithering quickly along the ground in the direction of his horse and through the gate. The snake was equally as scared of the horse and reared up defensively. Jack felt the horse lower its rump and leap into flight. It brushed tight against the fence post as it charged through the gate, and Jack's left leg caught the post, and he was pulled backward. The stirrup let go of its hook, and Jack's leg was pulled right back, twisting, over the horse's rump until he lost balance and fell off its right-hand side. Even in the chaos of what was happening, he wondered where the snake was as he fell to the ground. He needn't have worried, it was long gone. He landed with a jarring thud and scrambled to suck in air as pain seared through his ribs and lower back. His right leg was still caught in the stirrup. The horse, who had stopped, momentarily stunned by Jack's fall, took off again, Jack in tow. His body, sliding along the ground, seemingly chasing the horse, only served to frighten it even more. There was no chance it would stop on its own. They crashed through small knee height thorny shrubs and over rocks ripping at the skin on Jack's back. Red dust billowed up from the body behind the horse. He'd travelled more than fifty yards when the back of his head bounced on a rock, and everything went black. He wasn't conscious as Ed caught his horse by the reins and finally stopped its flight.

Jack's father was by his side in a flash, kneeling next to his injured son. Jack was out cold. When Ed lifted Jack's head to lay a jumper under it to make him more comfortable, his hand came away covered in blood. He looked at his father and could see he was equally as worried.

'One of us better get home, get a vehicle and call town for the Doctor. You better go. You'll be faster than me.' Jack's father barked the instructions at Ed.

'You sure?' Ed asked, looking at his father and how uncertain he looked. The normally unflappable, hard as steel old man was rattled, squatting down by his younger son. His eyes were wide, full of fear, and his lips were pursed.

'Just go, for god's sake, go. I'm not leaving him.' Ed Senior barked. 'Never.' He added quietly. 'Never, Boy.' He directed to Jack as he picked up Jack's hand, holding it in his, for the first time in twenty years.

Ed leapt up into the saddle and turned his horse for home. He looked back once over his shoulder then kicked his horse into a canter. There was no use starting at a gallop. It was damn hot, and there were a few miles to go. If he flogged the gelding straight up, the horse would break down by the time he was halfway home.

More than a mile into the journey, Ed looked down and could see the white sweat foam where the reins rubbed against the horse's neck. He was worried he was pushing the horse too hard but more worried about Jack. He had to push on as hard as he possibly could, whatever the outcome. He'd run the last half mile on foot if he had to. He hoped Jack had regained consciousness and that his father was okay. A head injury out here could be a life sentence, a very short one. He just couldn't believe his little brother had been all the way overseas, for two years, risking his life continually, only to return home and to be facing death out here on Sutherland Downs just months later.

Ed leaned forward and patted the horse's wet neck, and did his best to encourage him.

'Come on boy, a couple of miles, and I'll give you a big feed, a drink and a day off.'

He looked up from the horse and into the distance, looking for the first signs of the buildings. He could make out a small shape against the mottled backdrop of trees and the heat haze. As he continued on, the shape became more visible, and he was able to see it was two horses, side by side. He breathed a sigh of relief. Help was close. He kicked his horse on again, moving quickly toward the oncoming riders.

As he got closer, he could see they were strolling

along at a slow walk, and he quickly recognised that one was Elise. He was always pleased to see her, but not often as much as he was right now. He could send her back for a vehicle. She knew her way around, and he'd have no trouble describing Jack's location, which was only a few miles from the homestead. As he closed in, he could see she had another woman with her, but he didn't recognise her.

He kicked his horse on and was at the other two women quickly. They were both smiling as he approached, but the look on his face left no uncertainty that something was wrong, very wrong. Elise pushed forward.

'Ed, what is it, what's wrong?' He saw her look down at the horse that had been worked hard. He was a good horseman, and he would never have pushed a horse like that without it being an emergency.

'It's . . .' He stopped. Finally, recognising the other rider amidst the confusion of horses, people and panic. 'Rosie!' he was startled and took a moment to reset.

'Hello Ed.' Rosie replied with a cautious smile, clearly wondering what was going on.

'What is it Ed?' Elise pushed him.

'Don't panic . . . either of you, okay?'

'Okay,' Elise asked anxiously, having precisely the opposite reaction that Ed had intended.

'It's Jack.'

'What is it?' Rosie cut over Ed, sounding frantic.

‘He’s come off his horse.’

‘Is he okay?’ Rosie asked urgently.

‘I’m not sure. Dad is with him. He got dragged along behind the horse, then belted his head, and it’s cut pretty badly. There’s a lot of blood.’

‘Where is he?’ Elise asked.

‘He’s not far from the gate to the East River paddock. You know it?’

‘Yes.’ Elise answered

‘Thing is. He was out cold when I left him with Dad. Elise, you need to go home and get a vehicle and get mum to ring town and a doctor. Rosie, it’s good you’re here. You’re a nurse. You’ll have a better idea of what to do than we will. You can come back with me.’

‘Your horse Ed. He looks spent.’ Elise said.

‘Yeah, he’s buggered, the poor bastard. Let’s swap. It’s further back to Dad and Jack than home now, and your horses are fresh. Rosie and I can ride hard.’

Ed was off his horse, making the necessary adjustments to stirrups and ready to go in a matter of moments. He and Rosie left, with the horses kicked into a canter, again.

CHAPTER THIRTY-SIX

Jack's head throbbed with pain. He knew he was moving, and he could hear an engine. The bloody spitfire. He was in the spitfire. How the hell . . .? He needed to open his eyes, but he just couldn't. He tried once, but the light was blinding.

'I thought I crashed you already, you bastard.' He mumbled.

'It's okay, Jack, it's okay.'

A woman's voice, it's a woman's voice, it's Mary he thought. I'm dying.

Flashes of Sutherland Downs, hot sun, red dust came to him. Then Snowy Ridge, his children, little Charlie and Mary. Then Rosie. The image of Rosie's face was so vivid he could swear she was with him.

'Rosie.' He murmured, then winced at the pain in the back of his head.

'I'm here Jack. I'm here. Hold on. Please hold on.'

Even in the fear of darkness and pain, he couldn't help but smile as he dreamed of his beautiful Rosie.

The old truck rattled along slowly in the hot sun, through the red dust, and finally into the shade of a big tree near the homestead. Jack didn't register the flurry of movement and emotion about him as he lay unconscious.

The local Doctor arrived a good hour after they'd made Jack as comfortable as they could in bed in his room.

'He's really knocked himself about.' The Doctor had addressed all of the adults over a cup of tea before he left. 'I could take him back into town, but frankly, that might be just as dangerous as leaving him here. You have to understand, he's not out of the woods by any means. He's lost a lot of blood, but that's not the issue. We've stopped the bleeding, on the outside, that is, but it's what's going on on the inside that I'm worried about. If he's still bleeding internally, then he's in real trouble. I'm sorry, but I have to say, you need to pray for the best and prepare yourselves for the worst. I have made him as comfortable as I can, and I'll try and get back out again tomorrow if I can.'

Rosie was taken right back to the horrible final moments when Mary had passed away. She was overwhelmed by the sense that another person she loved was about to be torn out of her life. She wandered out into the garden by herself as the family saw the Doctor off, and Claire had returned to Jack's bedside.

All around Rosie, everything was quiet, as though holding its breath along with her. She made the sign of the cross on her chest and began to pray, but found herself talking to Mary, begging for her help and guidance, and begging for Jack's life.

'Are you okay?'

Rosie turned around to find Jack's father had walked quietly up behind her.

'I am, thanks.' Rosie replied, then thought better of it. 'No, I'm not actually.' And hot tears streamed down her cheeks.

'He'll be ok, you know. He's a Sutherland.' Edward's tone was proud. 'He's as strong as an ox. And as silly as one at times.'

Edward didn't smile, and Rosie saw the sadness and fear glistening in his eyes. She mustered the most cheerful smile she could. Edward continued. 'You should go back in, I think. And talk to him. I think, more than anything, if he knows you're here, he'll come back to us. He'll have everything he ever wanted. Everything to live for.'

Rosie looked at Edward and could see so much of Jack. She stepped forward and wrapped her arms around him, as much for herself as for him. He hugged her back for a moment before pushing her away.

'Ok. That's enough. In you go and see my boy.' He spoke gruffly. She thought of her own father.

As Rosie walked back toward the house, she looked back, and Edward hadn't moved. He just stood still, hands by his sides, looking out into the garden.

Jack woke but kept his eyes closed tight. He'd woken a few times since the fall and tried to open his eyes, but the bright light had only served to sharpen the throbbing headache that started right behind his eyes and spread all around his head. Pressure. It felt like his head might burst.

He could hear voices. He must be dreaming again. Was he dead? He asked himself, matter of factly. I must be close to dying, he thought, and he felt a wave of sadness overcome him as he thought about Rosie, and Mary and little Mary and Charlie and all of his family.

'Would you like a cup of tea?' A woman's voice. It sounded like his mum.

'Thank you, I would.' It sounded like Mary. No, not Mary, Rosie. They sounded so alike. Both of them were so close he could hear them but not see them, not touch them. Was this heaven or hell?

He drifted off into the darkness again.

He wasn't sure how long he'd been out to it again when he woke. In fact, he didn't know what he was, dead, alive, asleep, unconscious.

The pain in Jack's head had subsided significantly. He felt relatively comfortable. He was aware now he was lying in a bed. It took him some time to pluck up the courage to open his eyes, and when he did, he only inched them open a sliver. Darkness. It wasn't as dark as when he had his eyes completely closed, but regardless, all was black. He let them open completely and was relieved as his eyes became slowly accustomed to the light, and he realised it was night. The darkness was night.

Lying still and staring at the ceiling that was slowly forming barely distinguishable shapes as his eyes adjusted to the light, he became aware of a feeling on his arm. Soft hair. Then the sound of breathing. The slow and steady rhythm of sleep.

Jack turned his head slightly, managing the pain as he did. A mop of hair covered the edge of the bed, his arm and even spilled onto his chest.

'Rosie?' He whispered to himself in disbelief.

'Mmm.' There was the slightest sound from the woman seated at his bedside, but she didn't wake. It was as though she acknowledged him in her sleep, perhaps her dreams.

Jack looked toward the window and could see by the curtains that the very first rays of morning sunlight were waking the world outside. He was happy to lie still and watch the woman by his bed as the darkness faded and the colour of her hair brightened like a sunrise. As the room lit, so did his heart.

Rosie stirred in her sleep at the bedside and slid her hand up onto Jack's chest without lifting her face. Jack wasn't sure if she was awake as he slid his hand over hers. She lifted her head from the bed and looked at him, and smiled through tears. He smiled back.

'Jack.' She whispered.

'Rosie.' He replied. 'I missed you.'

'You scared me.'

'I'm good. Just a bump.'

'Just a bump? You could have . . .' She was fighting her emotions. 'I'm just so relieved you're back.'

'You're staying?' He looked serious.

'Forever.'

'Good.' He smiled again.

'I love you Jack. More than anything.'

'I love you too, Rosie O'Reilly.'

The End